I0601923

REBIRTH

RAVIN TIJA MAURICE

Rebirth

Copyright 2017 by Ravin Tija Maurice

Second Edition

All rights reserved. This book or any portion thereof may not be reproduced or used in any manner whatsoever without the express written permission of the Author except for the use of brief quotations in a book review.

Cover Art & Interior by RMGraphX

ALSO BY RAVIN TIJA MAURICE

THE AFFLICTED SERIES

REBIRTH

IKON

PROPHECY GIRL

BELIEVER

For Janet Ravin, may she rest in peace.
For Khaleesi, my legacy.

THE QUESTION ISN'T WHO'S GOING TO LET ME; IT'S WHO IS GOING TO STOP ME.
~AYN RAND.

People are like stained-glass windows.
They sparkle and shine when the sun is out,
but when the darkness sets in,
their true beauty is revealed only if
there is a light from within.
Elizabeth Kübler-Ross.

PROLOGUE

A Castle in the Outer White Western Carpathians
Kingdom of Hungary – Winter 1574.

SCREAMS RIPPED THROUGH THE CASTLE LIKE A BLADE splitting open flesh. The sound seemed to bounce off the cold stone walls and linger in the air, causing everyone inside to pause.

For only a moment, Kristina stopped scrubbing the floor of the banquet hall. The scream was familiar, a sound she knew like her own heartbeat.

A baby was coming. The words spoken about the young mistress must be true, and now the time had come. She paused only briefly then returned to her duty, the raspy sound of the brush scraping on stone masking the coming footsteps.

"Kristina!" the harsh voice snapped, causing her to jump up in surprise. The brush clattered to the floor beside her.

Kristina dutifully bowed her head. "Have I done something wrong, Madam?"

"You are a midwife, yes?" the woman who stood in front of her asked. They knew each other well. The woman was the Vezető Komorna, the head of the servants in the castle. She had given Kristina her job.

"Yes, Madam, but I…."

"Come quickly! Your expertise is needed," she said, seizing Kristina's arm and pulling her away.

"But, Madam, I have very little experience. I am not sure I can do this alone," Kristina said as they continued into the depths of the castle.

Kristina had never been in this part of the building. Lower servants were forbidden to enter where the family resided.

Voices grew louder, and another scream startled them as they walked.

"Kristina, listen to me very closely," the Komorna said as she stopped, grabbing her by the face. "If you value your life, you will not look directly at any of the people in this room! Do you understand what I am saying? Promise me you will not look!" she cried. Panic made her eyes glow.

"My word, Madam, I will not," Kristina replied. They continued up a flight of stairs that wound upwards. Kristina kept her eyes lowered so she would not be tempted.

The rustling of silk along the floor was almost as loud as the moaning from the bed. They entered the room but did not dare step past the doorway. Kristina bowed as low as she could, her nose nearly touching the floor.

"I've brought the midwife, Madam," the Komorna said. A beautiful pair of soft leather shoes came into Kristina's view.

"My people will assist you," the owner of the shoes said, "should you be in need."

Kristina could tell by the way she spoke that this was a well-bred, educated woman. She wondered if this was the young mistress' mother. She had only caught a glimpse of the young lady's dress, and her beauty had been the talk of the castle since they arrived.

"You may approach," the Komorna assured. Kristina kept her head down and slowly moved forward; a curtain had been put up to hide the identity of whoever the mother of this baby was. She suddenly felt for the child she was about to help bring into this strange world. The labour was quick, and the loss of blood minimal. The only person that Kristina made eye contact with throughout the ordeal was the new infant. She wrapped the baby as best she could, cleaning the child off in the way she learned from her mother. With the swaddled infant in her outstretched arms, she lowered her head and offered the child out into the darkness.

Before she could give it another thought, the baby was gone. Kristina suddenly found herself being pulled back through the castle, the Komorna returning her to her original duties.

"Tell no one what you saw," she said, and then left as quickly as she had come.

Dumbfounded, Kristina watched the empty doorway the other woman had passed through. Everything happened so quickly; she wondered for a moment if it had all been a daydream. Her mother had warned her that such things might happen. The highborn had illegitimate children all the time and went to great lengths to conceal the event. It was a midwife's duty to aid the delivery, not make judgments.

"If the baby is healthy and you have done your best, that is what is important," her mother would say. "Put the rest from your mind."

So Kristina did exactly that, and soon the rhythmic sound of the brush on the stone was all that consumed her thoughts.

The next day, Kristina was taken from her regular cleaning duties to assist in the kitchen. A large meal was being prepared for the visiting family, and all the hands that could be spared to peel, chop, stir or clean dishes were taken into the kitchen.

Kristina's first job was to tend to the goulash, a delicacy of the cook. She was given a spoon and told to stir.

She turned the wooden spoon slowly through the large pot that hung in the hearth. The thickening stew smelt fragrant of pork and dried herbs that Kristina tried her best to recognise.

"You stir slow and even," the cook uttered. She lumbered over to Kristina and dropped some more meat into the pot. She was a big, solid woman, who smelt mostly of pork and her own filth. She had a heavy Hungarian accent and an excess of hair on her face.

Kristina nodded and continued to concentrate on the pot. The cook went back to the cutting table and returned with a variety of vegetables in her hands. As she dropped the pieces of carrots and potatoes into the pot, she said a few words that caught Kristina's attention. Her mother had spoken similar words when she cooked.

The cook smacked Kristina's arm, startling her. "You stir slow and even! Most important for the goulash!"

"I'm sorry," Kristina replied, quickly turning her eyes back to the stew.

The translation was rough, but she believed the cook had asked The Fates for help with the preparation and consumption of this meal. How strange, Kristina thought to herself. Improperly cooked meat could cause illness, but not enough to necessitate a discussion with the powers that be.

She continued to stir at a steady pace with the steam rising from the pot close to scalding her hand. The cook had her own magic, and Kristina knew enough not to disrupt it.

The food was carefully placed onto elaborate silver platters and bowls. Upper house servants came into the kitchen and took forth the meals to be served. Kristina thought of the baby and her mother, wondering if either would be present. A dinner of such proportions could be a celebration of the birth.

Kristina stayed behind to help clean up when the other servants who were brought in returned to their duties. Soon it was only the cook, Kristina, and a young man who could have been the cook's son. She swept the floor in silence, observing as the cook bundled and hung dried herbs above her workbench. Softly humming to herself, the plump woman took the ends of a few branches and crumpled then into her palm. When she thought Kristina wasn't watching, she approached the soaking pot that had held her prized goulash. Palm up, she held her hand over the mouth of the pot and muttered some words that Kristina couldn't understand. A puff of pale smoke rose from her palm and into the air; she then turned her hand over and dropped its contents into the water.

Kristina stared at the floor. She concentrated on the movement of the broom and the sound it made. She recalled how the old woman had done something similar many times before, concocting a mixture of herbs to purify water, believing it to clean the grime from the cooking pots. It was an old trick that wise women used to make sure their tools were cleansed of previously rendered ailments. Cook wiped her palm on her apron, leaving a dark smear down the already filthy fabric. The large woman lumbered along, cleaning up her kitchen at a steady pace. Kristina finished sweeping the floor, then left to return to her other duties within the castle.

The servants' quarters were modest, but very clean. Lower servants and kitchen maids all lived together in two small rooms on the lower levels of the castle, next to the kitchen. Because of their close proximity to the kitchen fires that seemed to burn endlessly, the rooms were always warm.

Kristina lay on one of the hay beds on the floor in the larger of the two rooms. She and two of the other maids were finished with their duties and were trying to have some peace before the rest of the girls came down for the night.

"Did you hear that screaming two days past?" the younger maid asked, her eyes wide with suspicion. "It sounded as if someone was being tortured."

"Perhaps they were being forced to sit through the Catholic Mass," her companion replied smugly.

"Natasha!" The younger girl gasped, "I hope you don't say such things in public! Maids cannot say such things without consequences."

Kristina tucked the small gold cross she wore around her neck into her dress. The Eastern Orthodox Church was the religion in which she was raised, and it was the most persecuted during these tumultuous times. She had learned long ago not to speak of such things. They should know better, she thought to herself.

"I think another unwanted child tore its way into this world," the other maid said.

"How do you know?"

"A girl so young? Hiding away in this place? You're a fool if you believe otherwise," the older girl retorted.

"I wonder who it could be?" the younger one asked. Kristina closed her eyes as the girls continued to gossip, trying only to think of sleep.

"Kristina! Kristina!"

Jerked out of sleep by the Komorna who stood beside her bed, she jumped up and stood wearily.

"Kristina, gather your things. I need to speak to you privately," the Komorna said sharply.

Kristina picked up the small bundle of items at the end of her bed and followed her out the door. She was suddenly afraid: a midwife asked to return so soon after a birth was a bad sign.

"Is more required of me?" Kristina asked.

"No," she replied. "The party left a few hours ago. I shall explain, but we must go somewhere more private."

Out of one of the rear exits, they left the castle in silence. Snow was knee high around a small path that led out into the garden; Kristina tried her best to shield herself from the bitter east wind. She held her small bundle of belongings to her chest as she followed along behind the Komorna, the cold wet snow slowly starting to soak through the bottoms of her shoes.

The sun was getting low in the sky, and she knew that once the sun had set, the cold would be unbearable. She hoped that they would not be going far.

The gardens broke off into a thick forest. As they reached the edge, a small cottage appeared in a clearing not far in the distance. They continued on, their way mostly cleared by the trees protecting the forest floor from the snow. Kristina could smell wood burning and a pungent mixture of sage and another herb she couldn't quite place.

The Komorna went towards the large wooden front door and went inside, Kristina following closely at her heels.

She closed the door behind them, and Kristina was thankful for the blanket of warmth that followed. The Komorna shook herself to clear the snow off the bottom of her dress, seemingly unaffected by the cold. Kristina thought the Komorna seemed on edge, as she had been the last time they saw each other. A short time had passed but it had seemed like an eternity.

"Please sit, Kristina," the Komorna said, motioning to a large chair by the fire. "Would you like some ale?"

"No, thank you, Madam," Kristina replied. She watched her as she filled a large tin cup to the brim. She seemed older now than she had before. Her blonde hair shimmered with a hint of silver and she appeared pained when she moved. Kristina sat down, finding the soft feather cushion on the chair to be extremely comfortable.

"You know, Kristina, I see much of myself in you," she began. "Except you are much more talented than I… too much for this sort of work."

Kristina took a shallow breath. "Am I being dismissed, Madam?"

"Oh Heaven's no! I trust you, and I think you are better suited for something more than this life. I have a job for you, and I believe it will help you on a better path," she said. She settled back in the chair across from Kristina and took a sip from her mug.

"I am honoured that you think so highly of me, Madam," Kristina said. She bowed her head in respect and tried to show her how grateful she was with her eyes.

"Kristina, the job I have for you is very important and depends on your total discretion. It could bring you great wealth and prosperity, but comes with a price. If I were younger, I would do it myself."

"May I ask what this price is, Madam?"

The old woman leaned forward to make an urgent request. "You must give me your solemn vow that if you take this position that you shall leave Hungary immediately and never return for the rest of your days."

She paused for a moment. "Do you want to know what I'm requesting, Kristina?"

Kristina hesitated for a moment, and then nodded in agreement.

"Well," she began, inhaling deeply, "in addition to leaving Hungary, there will be a large purse. You and the baby will be well taken care of."

"Baby, Madam?"

"Yes. The baby you helped bring into this world. I want you to take the baby, leave Hungary and raise her as your own."

Kristina watched the woman sip her ale. What was being offered, this proposal, seemed too good to be true. She pinched the inside of her wrist to make sure that she hadn't, in fact, fallen asleep on her hay bed in the servants' quarters at the castle. Thoughts swam through her head about whether she was willing to sacrifice her life to find out.

"The baby is unwanted? The little girl is unwanted, Madam?" Kristina asked. The maids' gossip had been true. She felt badly for the young mistress, having to part from her baby in such a way.

"If you will take her, then she is not unwanted. What do you think?" she said as she finished her ale and set the mug on the table beside her chair.

"May I ask you some questions, Madam?"

"Of course, of course…please do. I would be very upset if you had none."

"First, I must ask, how would I leave Hungary? My family is poor, and I have no means to do so on my own. Where would I go?"

"I have made some arrangements for you. A carriage to take you out of Hungary, a house for you to stay in until you can find your own."

"Madam, I—"

"Yes, Kristina?"

For a moment Kristina hesitated, her face flushing nervously until she felt the courage return to her voice. "Madam, this may seem like an unusual request, but I have nothing and I…the snow is very bad…and you see I can't travel the way that I am. Surely I would be no good to anyone especially a child, if I was to catch my death in the cold?"

"What are you getting at? I told you a carriage would be provided."

"Begging your pardon, Madam, I am not used to making any such requests for myself. However, to be able to travel, don't you think I should be properly outfitted? For you see, Madam, I have no winter cloak or shoes."

The Komorna laughed loudly at the absurdity of Kristina's request, as if she seemed to have no idea of what she was being asked.

After catching her breath, she leaned back, thinking she had underestimated the young woman who sat before her. A girl who thinks of such practical things in a situation like this is indeed the right girl for the job!

For what seemed to be an eternity, the two women watched each other, awaiting some sort of response. One did not know what to make of the other: the old and tired woman who presented the offer, and the young, innocent woman whose life would be forever changed because of it.

Kristina weighed the possibility of what the offer entailed: a new life, a fresh start. I could give her a life I never had, she thought to herself, and any other children I bore afterwards.

Kristina inhaled deeply, and then said with as much confidence as she could muster, "When would I leave?"

"Tonight, under the cover of darkness." the Komorna replied. "The child was christened this morning. Her name is Anastasia."

How odd to name a baby you do not intend to keep, Kristina thought. She did not speak her mind, however, because it seemed unnecessary, and she did not want to jeopardise her position.

"The family left you 50 gold pieces."

"I am sorry, Madam, they...what?" Kristina gasped in disbelief.

"I know it seems like a large amount, but spread through a lifetime it is not so, considering the expense of rebuilding. The state of affairs in Transylvania is volatile at best."

"Transylvania?"

"The home I have arranged for you to stay at is in Transylvania. You don't have to remain there, but they are a good Protestant family and will help you on your way. The house is a stable working farm with five children and a new babe to come any time, if it hasn't already. The wife has agreed to nurse Anastasia. I have also secured a wet nurse to travel with you. She has been well paid, but you can dismiss her if you feel it necessary when you arrive. I told her the baby is yours and, for some reason, you are unable to feed her. Do not be concerned, this sort of thing is not uncommon, I can assure you," she explained.

"What is the nurse's name?"

"Magdalena. She is a Slovak peasant girl, like you."

Kristina did not correct her. Her mother was, in fact, from Transylvania. Kristina did not know her father, though her mother claimed he was some kind of gypsy prince. He was long dead, so she thought little of it.

The Komorna stood and motioned to leave the room.

"I will send someone to fetch you a cloak and some shoes," she assured. "I will also prepare some other things for you to travel with. I won't be a moment."

The Komorna clapped her hands, as if to signal the time had arrived, and swept from the room in the flourish normally used by women of much higher standing.

Kristina valued these last few moments alone and used them as a time to reflect. She was about to become embroiled in a very great secret, something she would have to maintain for her lifetime. Of course, she wanted children, but never anticipated to have to embark on such a journey alone.

Her mother had raised all of her children alone, and did not have the financial support that Kristina was about to receive. She would be able to give little Anastasia the entire world—perhaps not the sort that her birth mother would have, but that would not be an issue.

Anastasia was her baby now.

The heavy falling snow sounded like raindrops against the window. Travelling would be rough, but if the weather was all they had to deal with, they would be lucky. Even though the countryside was littered with thieves, they surely would seek shelter from the bitter cold rather than wait outside for a carriage to come along.

Kristina looked at her shoes. They were slowly beginning to dry, but the short walk in the snow had done its damage. She thought of her modest shoes, unable to stand anything outside the castle walls. She wondered if it was an omen, a sign from God. Once exposed to the outside world, would she crumble just like her shoes?

A pair of dark leather boots appeared on the floor beside her feet. They stretched up all the way to the knee. A baby cried in another part of the house, the soft whimper of hunger. A warmth swelled inside Kristina, filling her whole body and emanating to its edges.

"Try these boots," the Komorna said, her voice centering Kristina back into the room. "If they do not fit, I shall have to find another pair."

Kristina slid off her shoes; they tore like paper from the moisture. It was as if she was peeling away a layer of her old life to cover with a new one. She pulled the boots onto her feet. The thick supple leather was smooth and soft and felt like nothing she had ever touched before.

"Are they suitable?"

"They're exquisite." Kristina's breath caught in her throat.

"Good, good!" The Komorna nodded. She seemed pleased. "I shall see to the other items and a meal before you go." She left the room again, leaving Kristina staring at her feet.

As preparations were being made, the two women enjoyed a large sumptuous meal.

"This should fill you for some time, I hope," the Komorna declared.

Even though her tiny cries could be heard from wherever she was in the house, the baby was still not brought to Kristina. If she was being hidden till the last possible moment, Kristina considered, it could mean that something was amiss. She was the first to view the child, so she knew it was not malformed. Perhaps the child would only be handed over when there was no possible chance to return her?

After the meal was finished, the Komorna left the house without saying a word. Kristina assumed it was to ensure the two were not missed at the main house. The maids who had been in the room with her when she was called had probably spread a rumour of some kind about where Kristina had gone. No matter, it would only be of significance to the Komorna, since she would be the one to have to see them again.

In the silence, Kristina closed her eyes and uttered a silent prayer; it was not a prayer typically said in these situations.

She first said the words of her church, asking Jesus for help to complete the work she was about to begin in His name. She then said the words her mother had taught her; she believed in asking the earth and the other elements for their blessing, since if they were working against you, success would never be possible. Some had called her mother a wise woman; others, a witch. She spoke the words in her mother's Transylvanian tongue as quickly as she could before the head of the servants returned.

"Mother earth, guide my journey," she began, "take me safely. Give me strength to help this child, fire to keep me going, breath to help me speak, and the nourishment of your soil to help build our life. We cherish your gifts and beauty. So let it be."

With a sudden blast of frozen air, the door flew open. Great swirls of large, white snowflakes blew in and fell to the floor. The Komorna had left without a cloak; she began stomping her feet in an attempt to rid herself of the specks of white still stuck to her. Kristina could not help but look at her with surprise.

"What's the matter child? I do this all the time! A cloak is too much trouble for such a short trip. Besides, it is not so cold when the snow falls."

She progressed farther into the room, dropping a bundle in an empty chair by the window.

"Get all the warmth you can from the fire now, Kristina," she advised. "The sun is going down, and we must make ready."

The large black carriage looked like a spot of dirt on the white landscape. Snow was still falling, only not as much and the cold was beginning to set in. Four monstrous, ebony chargers stomped about, impatient, puffs coming fast from their nostrils. The driver and another man were wrapped heavily in fur. Resembling animals themselves, they attempted to give the horses some food so they would not disturb their mounts. A series of servants quietly loaded the carriage, strapping luggage to the roof and putting blankets and pelts along with heated rocks inside the compartment for warmth. There were also small containers of food, bread, some cheese, and preserves that would travel well and could last several days so the carriage would have no need to stop.

From the side, with a heavy wool cloak pulled tightly around her, Kristina watched the process. The reality of the situation was beginning to set in.

The carriage windows were drawn, causing them to look black, sealing its contents from the outside world. Or rather, Kristina wondered, was the world being kept from its contents?

The Komorna suddenly appeared, stray pieces from her tightly bound hair sticking to the side of her face. She looked tired, more so than she had earlier. A dull and darkening shadow fell across her face, but it was most noticeable in her eyes. She was carrying a large basket that appeared to be piled high with blankets. She wove effortlessly through the group of people and headed towards Kristina. It was not until she cleared away from the path that Kristina noticed the plump, fair-haired girl who trailed behind her.

She handed off the basket to Kristina with a stiff nod. "This is Magdalena, the wet nurse. Magdalena, this is Kristina."

Kristina took the basket and felt something move inside of it. It occurred to her in that moment that the basket contained the child that was supposed to be hers.

She smiled at the Komorna and bowed slightly; she wanted more than anything to express her deepest thanks and gratitude…to tell the woman who had given her a life that it had meant the world and more to her, but there was no time now.

"You best be on your way now," the Komorna said. Kristina tried to convey the well of emotions in her eyes; she hoped desperately that the old woman understood her.

The three walked to the carriage, and Magdalena ascended first. Kristina passed the basket to the girl, then turned back to the other woman.

"Thank you," Kristina whispered, biting back tears. "And God bless you, Madam."

"And you as well, Kristina," the Komorna said, fighting tears of her own. She helped the girl get her footing onto the carriage rail, then disappeared.

Kristina turned around to take one last look at her surroundings; somehow she knew she would never again stand on the soil of Hungary. Because of that, the castle now seemed far less frightening than the day she had arrived.

She entered into the carriage, the door swiftly closing behind her. Magdalena was sitting across from her, bundled under a pile of furs in the already warm carriage. The girl had placed the basket on the seat beside Kristina.

A gentle coo came from the basket. Kristina leaned over to see small dark eyes staring up at her. Bundled tightly in a series of blankets and swaddling cloth, only the baby's perfectly oval-shaped face was visible. Her milky white skin seemed to glow; her mouth a lovely bow shape.

Kristina touched the tip of her finger to the baby's cheek, and she cooed again happily as the carriage lurched forward. Warmth flowed through her finger and onto the baby's skin, covering her in an iridescent glow that made her shimmer like a pearl. It radiated off the child's skin and out into the carriage, bathing the passengers in an otherworldly light.

Kristina kept her hand in the basket as she eased back into her seat, pulling a pelt up over her legs. She closed her eyes and knew that when she opened them again, it would be the beginning of a new life.

Arefu, Wallachia – Fall 1610

There is something I must tell you

ANASTASIA DID NOT FALTER AS SHE CONTINUED TO crush herbs. Her mother had been badgering her to make tea since the moment she'd arrived, and she resolved that she would not be distracted.

Her mother, frail and dying, tried to pull herself up but was too weak. The coughing was so loud it rattled through her body and into the small palette which she laid upon by the fire. The house was agonisingly hot. Anastasia had hoped her mother would sweat the sickness out, but instead, the stifling heat only heightened the putrid smells of a woman caught in the grasp of the illness that would kill her.

"Stasia, please come here." Her mother's voice was hoarse and ravaged. "I must tell you something, and I fear if I do not do it now I shall lose my nerve."

Her violent fit of coughing finally subsided. Anastasia gathered hot water from the pot by the fire, poured it into a small pot with the herbs, then returned to her mother's side.

Her mother pulled in a laboured breath, then began, "When I was a young woman, I worked as a maid in a castle in the Carpathians, in Hungary. A friend of my mother's gave me the job; she was head of the household. I had many skills. My mother taught me everything she knew, including how to be a midwife. As fate would have it, that skill put me in a position I still do not quite understand."

Anastasia poured some tea, and then helped her mother sit up so she could try to drink it on her own.

"The castle was owned by a very rich family and not used often," she said, struggling for breath. She slowly turned her head towards her daughter to ask, "Do you know of the Báthory, my darling?"

"Yes, of course," Anastasia replied.

"It was winter, and the family unexpectedly arrived unannounced. We servants did not really see them much because we were mere house servants, and not their personal attendants. Especially elusive was the young mistress, who was kept in seclusion. One afternoon I was called from my duties."

She paused, once again struggling to breathe clearly as she tried to sip her tea. She carefully studied Anastasia's face, almost as if she was awaiting an intense reaction.

"I was called from my duties to deliver a child. I was not to look at anyone, and a partition was set up so that I could only see the lower half of the girl's body. When the job was done I was sent back to work and sworn to secrecy."

"Mother, I do not understand. What makes this so important?" Anastasia wiped a damp cloth across her mother's brow.

"Soon after, I was called to the cottage where the Komorna, the head of the servants, lived. It was a good trudge through the deep snow. I remember it so well because my shoes fell apart. Needless to say, that was the least of my concerns, as something bizarre happened. The head of the servants asked me to take this baby I had just delivered and leave Hungary, never to return."

Anastasia was shocked. "What did you do?"

"I took the baby and I left. They gave me enough money so that I would never have to work another day in my life, and the baby and I would live very well."

"What happened to the child?"

The old woman steadied herself, holding onto Anastasia's arm. She fixed her sharp gray eyes onto her daughter and affirmed, "You are that child, Stasia."

Anastasia abruptly stood up, knocking over the stool she sat upon. She stumbled as she tried to gather her wits about her, and crossed the room to tend to the fire.

"I am sorry I waited so long to tell you, child, but I did not have the heart," Kristina pleaded. "You are the child of a Báthory. Perhaps that would explain your...compulsion...?" her mother began, a coughing fit interrupting her.

Anastasia looked at the feeble body of the woman who raised her. Suddenly, she could no longer think of her as mother, but as simply, Kristina.

"I am sorry, Stasia. I could not carry such a secret to my grave," she stressed.

"And what am I supposed to do with such information?" Anastasia exclaimed.

"Nothing. I raised you. I brought you into this world. No, I did not carry you in my womb but that does not make me any less your mother," Kristina shouted. She started coughing again; the potent stench permeated the house making Anastasia nauseous.

"Why are you so sure you will die?" Anastasia asked. This question had been plaguing her thoughts for many days.

"Stasia, please. You are not blind," Kristina replied.

Anastasia's face hardened. "What if I don't believe you? I know my husband will never believe I am—"

"My apologies, my dearest child, but I did not choose well for you. Your husband is a fool. If you choose not to believe me, make it your own choice, not his. But you and I both know I speak the truth."

Anastasia's eyes began to well up with tears. "How can this be? Could this explain my affliction? How could you not mention it then?"

"Stasia, you were ill. It would have only made the situation worse. I am the one who raised you! Do not forget that!" Kristina's voice rose as she became more agitated. "Whose seed you were is irrelevant. I am your mother! Do you hear me? You are shedding tears over something that will never affect you! This changes nothing!"

Kristina's coughing worsened leaving the old woman breathless. Anastasia remained silent in spite of the fact it took everything she had not to scream in Kristina's face that this had indeed changed everything! Clenching her fists, Anastasia turned away and closed her eyes. Still reeling from the shocking revelation, she took a deep, steady breath to center herself. Once again, she resolved not to become distracted. She returned to her tasks and began making a light broth to try to get something into the sick woman's stomach.

I.

THIS STORY BEGINS, AS MANY OTHERS HAVE, WITH A
mother. Mother, being the giver of life, the nurturer, the provider, the
first teacher...the first object of worship.

My mother's name was Anastasia. My name is Katrine. I was of
the age where my relationship with my mother was the center of my
universe. She was teaching me to be a woman, to be a wife and a mother
myself someday. She told me to treat the earth as you wish to be treated,
for the key to life is woven deep into the soil with roots like stitches in
a piece of needlework. It is the place where all things come from and
should always be respected.

As far back as I could remember, it seemed since the moment I first
opened my eyes, my mother had been my idol. I admired her as the
center of the universe long before I knew anything of Our Lord. She
cherished me even though I was not the son my father had wanted;
though he got his wish a few years later.

From the moment I was brought into this world we were inseparable.

One morning, in the autumn of my 16th year, she left our cottage as the sun was rising. She took a horse and rode alone. When I awoke and found her gone, I was alarmed. Father would not explain; he busied himself and asked me to hold off my questions, not answering the few I was able to ask.

That alone gave me cause for concern.

She returned as the sun was getting low behind the trees. The setting sun was still bright; it had been a warm autumn. I wanted to go out and greet her, but Father would not allow it.

She came inside. Her eyes were cold and dark, with a certain emptiness to them that I had never seen before. She removed her cloak in silence and hung it next to my father's on one of the pegs beside the front door. Their cloaks were made of the same wool and blended seamlessly into the dark wood of the walls.

Father watched her carefully, studying her movements for any sign of her mood. There was no evidence of sadness or tears on her face. She had not lost her beauty because of such sorrow; her demeanour only added to her features. However, her beautiful face was blank.

Being a daughter, I was expected to keep close to my mother until I found a husband, and when I was told not to be near her, I always took it as a form of rejection.

I could sense by her behaviour that something very serious had happened, and that made me afraid.

She approached my father and quietly whispered a few things before going into the kitchen. She said nothing to me as she passed where I sat by the fire working on my embroidery. I pulled the stitch I was working on through the fabric, put it down and went over to my father.

"Father, will you tell me now what has happened?"

"Your grandmother is dying," he replied quite curtly. Stunned, I walked away from him and into the kitchen.

"Mother, are you alright?" I asked. She wiped her hands on her apron, and half-heartedly smiled, never directly looking at me.

"I'm fine, Katrine. But there are some rough times ahead," she said as she returned to removing the skin from the potatoes.

"May I come with you to Grandmother's?"

"No," she replied sternly. "I must face this alone."

I did not argue, and began to help her prepare dinner. Until she had married, she had remained close to her mother, just the two of them for most of her life, and now it would be the two of them at the point of her death.

I thought she would be grieving, or perhaps seem to have some sort of relief over the matter. Her mother had been ill for what seemed like my entire life, which was why I barely knew her. Mother spoke very little about her or her childhood, telling me only things that had happened after she was married. I had a deeper feeling that there were elements of this situation I did not understand.

My parents said very little to each other while we ate supper. Mother put my brother Bodi and me to bed, and once again, I was not given the chance to ask questions. Seemingly, I thought that was the end of it.

I awoke in the night to find my parents arguing. Father's voice was thunderous among the cool calmness of the dark and sleeping house.

"How could you believe anything that old witch says?" he said angrily.

"That old witch is my mother, Nikoli," she replied. "You did not say such things when you were asking to marry me, or during the birth of either of our children."

"But, Stasia, the idea that such blasphemy could be true..."

"But nothing! Royalty hide illegitimate children all the time."

"The Báthory, Stasia? Those people should not be referred to as royalty," he said, exasperated.

"They are, regardless of your opinions, Nikoli. And I am one of their daughters."

"So you believe Kristina's death bed ramblings?"

She sighed. "I can't escape the truth."

Mother was gone when I woke the next day.

"You will mind your brother today, Katrine," Father declared. "And bring my meal to the workshop."

Before I could speak a word, he left out the back door. Bodi came out of his bedroom and looked around; I could tell he was confused.

"Where's Mother?" he asked.

I walked over to the fireplace and picked up my sewing. "She's gone out."

"Why didn't you go?"

"I don't know," I replied. "Go eat some breakfast. There is some bread on the table."

Bodi shrugged his shoulders and went about eating. He was younger than I was by three summers and did not like to accept when I was in charge. I was uncertain if it was because I was a girl or that someone other than our parents was appointing the rules.

"May we go outside and play a game, Katrine?" Bodi asked me as he ate.

"No. There are many things to be done around the house before Mother gets back," I asserted.

"You cannot do them yourself?" he retorted.

I spread my work out before me and found a warm spot by the fire, preparing myself for the day.

"Not all of them," I said. "But I am sure you would much rather clean up with me than go sit in the workshop with Father."

He rolled his eyes and continued to eat while I went to work. The piece of embroidery I was working on was the largest and most detailed piece I had ever attempted, a task that had kept me busy for most of the summer. It was a talent my parents had assured would make me appealing to a good husband. I trusted what they said, since their job was to guide me.

Bodi cleaned the floor while I prepared lunch. I made us something, and then took another plate and mug of ale out to the workshop.

It was a small building, sitting a ways from the house; Mother said that if it caught fire at that distance it would not carry to the main house. The farm where we lived had belonged to my father's father and had remained prosperous since his death. Grandfather had always been very wise to have more than one way to make money in case there was an accident.

My father's family, by trade, made enamel. Mostly my father made things for the church and rich people, but lately he had been trying different things. He had begun to teach Bodi, but since the boy was struggling, he stopped for a while.

I quietly went inside, where Father was busy working on something. I did not want to disturb him.

"Lunchtime already?" he asked. He didn't raise his eyes from what he was doing.

"I'm sorry if I bothered you. I'll leave the food over here," I said as I motioned toward the bench and put the plate down.

As I turned to walk away, he asked, "Would you like to see what I'm doing?"

I approached him slowly and leaned over his shoulder. In front of him was a round piece of metal about the size of my palm. It held the beginnings of an elaborate pattern with a variety of colours beginning to work their way out from the middle.

"It's beautiful," I said. "It reminds me of a tiny piece of embroidery."

He sighed. "That is what I was hoping for. Thank you, Katrine."

"Of course, Father," I said.

I began to walk away when my foot scuffed along something on the floor. I bent down and pulled something blue and dull off the dirt floor.

"Father, I found this blue piece on the ground. May I keep it?"

"Take it. It's scrap," he waved. "Oh, and if your mother returns before I come inside, come and get me."

I put the piece of scrap in my pocket and headed back to the house. It was time I returned to Bodi and my chores.

Almost a fortnight passed, and my parents' late night argument became a memory. Mother came and went and, though I carefully observed, there was no sign of what she was going through. For the days she was gone, I was given more duties around the house, and it seemed to keep my wandering mind occupied. Lately, I did not feel the same when I looked at my parents, or anything else for that matter.

One late afternoon, I was bringing vegetables in from the garden when Mother stopped me.

"Please go into town and get me some flour, Katrine," she said, handing me a small purse.

"Should I take the wagon?" I asked.

"No, the bag is not that large, you will manage."

I set out alone on the walk into town, trying to be aware of all that was going on around me. Darkness was beginning to fall.

Our village was entirely surrounded by trees that stretched almost twice the size of the cottages, even taller than the church tower. They felt more like massive structures than living things.

It had been a hot summer but a prosperous one. My father's farm was not the only one that did well at harvest time, and I was not alone as I walked. People paid me no mind and went about their business. I arrived at the baker's cart rather quickly, got the flour, and started for home. I tried to hurry: Father would be angry if I was out alone when it got dark. He believed it was improper for a girl of 16 to be unaccompanied at night.

I cradled the bag of flour in my arms as if it were a child, but I stumbled several times on the edge of my skirt. My attempts to move quickly were proving unsuccessful. As I tried to smooth out my slow and awkward movements, something deep inside me said I should run away and hide somewhere until the morning. My legs began to grow shaky, as if they were trying to warn me about what lay ahead.

As I neared home, I noticed a large, decorated carriage parked out front; a small coachman was dozing in his seat. Two of the largest black stallions I had ever seen were at its head. Looking at them sent a cold chill deep in my bones. I was quite sure there were the four horsemen in the stories I had heard about the Apocalypse.

I stopped to examine the carriage on my way into the house. I had not seen something so magnificent in all my life and could not imagine why such a thing would come to our farm. Father made enamel for all sorts of people, including members of the church, but none that travelled in ways such as this.

I was suddenly overcome with a feeling that something was amiss and quickly headed into the house.

Along with my parents, I could hear voices I did not recognise. There was yelling, and my father was angry. I placed the bag on the floor beside the wood stove and walked quietly into the main room, all eyes turning on me as I entered.

We had three visitors, all old women. The most senior of the three stood with an air of authority. Although worn and frayed, I could see her dark blue dress was made of thick silk, the kind rich women would wear. But it had a layer of dirt on it, that made me wonder if it was passed on to her. In the dim light, her golden hair shone with an unusually youthful luster, but the harsh lines in her face betrayed her age. On her hand, she wore a ring cast in gold and set with a stone that resembled the eye of a cat. My gaze fixed upon it, and I began to feel light headed.

"Stasia, who is this?" she inquired as she glided toward me. She placed a bony hand on my shoulder.

"The resemblance is uncanny," she continued, eying me up and down

Confused, I turned to my mother, demanding an answer. But Mother remained silent.

"Why yes, she does!" another of them sneered. Her round, bulging eyes made her leathery face appear even more frightening. She had a necklace made of teeth round her neck that forced me to look away.

"She's quite beautiful. I'm sure Her Ladyship would approve."

The third remained silent, meanwhile. She was plump and looked like the baker's wife from the village. Her discomfort was obvious as she cast her eyes to the floor. Her face appeared drained of colour.

"What is your name, child?" the eldest woman demanded of me. A cold shiver ran down my spine, as if the devil was breathing on my neck.

"Katrine," I proclaimed. "Why are you here?"

"We are here for your mother," she said. "We're here to take her home."

"She is in her home! And you will do no such thing!" Father shouted.

"She is needed elsewhere, sir. We have come to take her to her family," the younger woman replied calmly. "And we are not asking your permission."

"Do I not have a say as to what happens to my own person?" Mother exclaimed.

"You will come with us now," one of the women ordered my mother. The two others watched me carefully.

"No!" Father said angrily before I could reply.

"Fine. If you will not deliver her willingly we will take her by force," the one with the necklace of teeth announced. I screamed as they began to advance upon my mother. Clearly, these three were witches, and I immediately crossed myself.

"Will you promise not to hurt them?" Mother demanded. The women stopped. "Darvulia, if I do as you ask, if I go with you now, will you promise not to hurt them?" she urged.

I started to cry.

"You will do no such thing!" Father yelled.

"Do you promise?" she again cried out. The woman approached her carefully.

"You will not go with these witches, Anastasia!" Father roared.

She turned to him. "I will not have it on my conscience if they hurt you!"

"If you come with us, they will not be harmed," Darvulia replied evenly. My sobs continued as Father's expression turned to stone.

Suddenly, she grabbed me by the wrist. "The girl comes, too."

"Let go of me!" I said angrily. The woman removed a knife from within her skirts and pulled me close to her body.

"The girl comes too," she continued, "for insurance."

"I will go without the bullying," I insisted. "I need to be with my mother!"

"Fine," she scoffed, letting me go.

Mother tried to gather herself, holding back her tears. She put her hand to Father's cheek.

She took a few calming breaths, then whispered to him, "Know that I have done this to save you, and I hope that you will not think you should have done something in return. Pray for me, and the Lord will keep me safe."

I turned away, as my mother put her arms around my shoulders. I could not bear to look at their faces. I wanted to run to my father and cling to him for dear life, but I knew better. As a female child, I was a burden, and with my mother gone, he would need me to work and could not pay my dowry. My place was with my mother now, and I could not let her face whatever this was alone.

I took my warm cloak from the hook beside the door, wrapping it around my neck. Mother did the same and clutched my hand tightly in hers. Her face was empty, her dark eyes cold, but she stayed focused on me. I tried my best to comfort her.

The woman named Darvulia swung the door open, and I hung tightly to my mother's hand. I would be nothing without her. Going with her seemed natural, even if we were walking to our deaths.

I glanced briefly back at my father and my brother; one last look was all I could manage. I then pulled my hood over my head, and we stepped out into the night.

II.

Birthright

WE SPED OUT INTO THE NIGHT IN THE BACK OF THE carriage, a canopy of darkness surrounding us from the height of the trees in the forest.

"Are you taking me to see my father?" Mother asked Darvulia.

"Your father?" she laughed. "No, no, Stasia! Your father was a nameless peasant. The one who employs us now is your mother."

"My mother?" she replied, her voice full of contempt. "My mother is dying."

"We are not speaking of Kristina, dear," the woman with the necklace smiled, and her face had a frightening glow. "We mean your *birth* mother. Your mother, the greatest woman in all the land.…The Countess Erzsébet Báthory."

Stunned, the breath caught in my throat. Was she serious? What did she mean by this?

"My…my…," Mother began, trying to form words but she could not manage to do so. I stared at the roof of the carriage and silently prayed for God to save us or strike us dead so we would not have to endure what these witches had planned for us.

Darvulia cackled, "What do you suppose the girl is doing, Erza?"

"She is praying to her God, Darvulia," the woman with the necklace mocked, leaning over and touching my knee. "Don't waste your time, my dear."

Confusion clouded my thoughts, leaving a heavy weight of anxiety in my stomach. All members of the Báthory family were rumoured to be cruel and insane, and the women were no exception. I put my hands in my pockets and found a small piece of metal. I pulled it out into the open and found a shiny blue cross. It was the piece that my father had called 'scrap'. I had forgotten about it. I examined it more closely, and the dark blue background of the cross was highlighted by small pieces of light blue and red, which were used as accents in the elaborately twisting filigree that dominated the cross face. Looking at it gave me some hope. If I could receive something of such beauty without even trying, maybe God was watching over us after all...or it could be my last link to life the way it used to be.

Darvulia leaned in closer to my mother. "Your birth mother is in grave danger, Stasia. Forces conspire against her at this very minute to imprison her and to steal her lands—and your birthright!"

"We are taking you back to her," Erza affirmed. "Together, our magic is strong. We shall avenge her and your family's name!"

We rode on into the night, while my mother sat in stoic silence. I sat quietly and prayed to God without moving my lips, my silence not absolute. From listening to their conversation, I knew these women to be witches, or necromancers, or handmaidens of the devil; whatever name a person chose, it did not matter. They were all of those things and more.

"Don't you care to know what we shall do with you, Anastasia?" the woman called Erza asked. As she stared into my mother's eyes, I could see the devil reflected back through her gaze.

"We're going to give you the life you were destined to lead as the first born daughter," she continued. "But we will perform the ritual before we take you to the Countess."

I had no idea what they meant, but my mother seemed to understand.

"And if I refuse?" Mother managed to say.

"Then we shall bring her your blood," she replied. "We will need it for the spell. The forces conspiring against her are strong. You have agreed to this much, so why would you refuse your Birthright?"

"Because then we may shake hands with the devil," I uttered. I started my silent vigil again. Only God could save us now.

After some time the witches began to doze off. Out of fear, I could not sleep. Suddenly, I saw the situation as a chance to escape.

But we would have to jump from the moving carriage.

The thought frightened me. Considering the consequences, however, I finally decided that either we take the chance of dying in the forest, or we accept the fate these witches intended for us. I watched the three of them as I reached for the door handle.

It didn't move in my hand. It was locked, and Mother and I were trapped.

I started to pray again. I continued to ask God, why? What have we done to warrant this? I was a good, virtuous girl; why would He not save us? Was mother destined to suffer for the sins of her kin? Were their crimes against humanity so evil that anyone who carried the Báthory blood must suffer?

"Don't be afraid, child," the other witch, the one who looked like the baker's wife and who had not spoken until this point, suddenly said. I had not noticed that she was watching me.

"The things you have been told, what you have been conditioned to believe is not always the reality of the world," she began. "You are praying for God to save you because you have been 'good'. But what you may not know is that the only way humans learn is through suffering."

I said nothing. I was not educated enough to argue with her, but I did not believe that God as I knew Him would wish for such a thing.

"Of course, you would have better luck praying to the forest for help, since it is in closer contact with the governing powers of the universe," she added.

I still said nothing, but I made brief eye contact. She was less frightening than the one called Erza, and especially less frightening than the old Darvulia.

"No need to speak, my dear. I do not blame you for being frightened, and I will not hold it against you. But I hope you will open your mind and your heart to the possibility that the world is not so black and white, but rather, lovely shades of gray," she said.

Thoughts began to swim wildly in my head. After some time in silence, I asked her, "What is 'shades of gray'?"

"Oh child," she explained, "gray is what happens when you mix black and white together. The saying means 'the spaces in between'."

"Oh," I replied. I did not quite understand what she meant, but I was impressed by the depth of her answer. Rather surprisingly, she smiled kindly, and I almost felt comfortable with her.

"May I ask you something?" I said after another silence.

"Of course, child. I will try my best to answer, but I must admit I am not the brightest woman."

"Do you think I could learn to read?" I blurted before I could stop myself.

"I do not understand," she said.

"You said my mother is of noble blood and you are taking us to claim her Birthright. If I am to be part of this...this situation, do you think I could be educated? One of my greatest dreams is to learn to read. I have always been fascinated by books but was taught very little. I always hoped that one day I would be able to tap into their knowledge," I explained. I had to force my hand to move quickly toward my mother to help stop myself from saying any more. My honesty with this other witch unnerved me, as I had never been that open with another person.

Perhaps she had enchanted me somehow.

In any event, she grabbed my hand with both of hers.

"My dear, I promise I will make sure of it. Even if I have to teach you myself. You have my word."

"Thank you," I said shyly.

"I must say, child, you look so much like the Countess, she will be happy for such a grandchild. Your beauty is inherited."

She let go of my hand, and when she touched her fingers to my cheek, it took all my strength not to pull away out of fear.

"Do not be afraid, child. You will not be harmed," she said and smiled again.

"How can I be sure?" I demanded.

"We have no intention of harming you or your mother, and I am sure the Countess will be most pleased to finally meet you both."

"I don't understand any of this."

"Countess Báthory bore your mother out of wedlock. The woman who raised her, your grandmother, was actually the midwife who delivered her."

I was stunned. "Does the Countess ever speak of her?" I nodded towards my mother, who was sitting in silence.

"No. Countess Báthory's husband and his family were not to know she existed, but they are dead or far away now. I am sure she will be pleased to see your mother. But before we can go to her, we have to perform a special ritual to quicken the magic."

Again, my breath caught in my throat. "Do you mean witchcraft?"

"Not exactly. It is more of a natural magic, to connect her with the forest and help encourage her powers. I am not sure if you have been gifted as well, child, but we shall see."

"What is your name?" I finally asked her.

"Kardoska," she replied. "Roza, for short."

"May I call you Roza?"

She smiled, and bowed her head slightly. "I would like that very much. What is your name again, child?"

"Katrine," I replied.

"Well, Katrine, you should try to sleep now. We have a long journey ahead," Roza said.

I leaned my head on my mother's shoulder; her body was rigid. I sat as still as I could so I could listen to her breathing. I was afraid, even more so because she sat as if she was already dead. My mother had not spoken in what seemed like an eternity. I wanted to know the thoughts in her head, and if she had a plan that she might share with me.

But soon, the long hours of the day caught up with me. With the rocking of the carriage and the rhythmic sound of the others finally sleeping, I finally drifted off myself. For how long, I did not know. It might have been minutes or it might have been hours.

"What do you suppose she is doing?" Erza's voice suddenly woke me, but I kept my eyes closed.

"Maybe she's in shock that something such as this could happen," Roza murmured, and I knew then that they were speaking about my mother.

"Quiet, you old drunk!" Darvulia snapped. "What do you know!"

I wanted to say something in her defense, but continued to feign sleep. My mother's welfare had to take priority, even though she had not moved or spoken.

It all fell on me now.

I opened my eyes, blinking and trying to adjust to the light. It was morning now. The witches all stared at me; apparently, they had been waiting for me to wake up.

"Good morning, child," Darvulia said. "Are you going to remain silent like your mother?"

"No," I replied. "But I would be more inclined to speak if I might have something to drink."

Roza handed me a tankard. I took it warily, but my thirst finally overcame my mistrust, and I drank heartily. The water tasted cleaner than any I had ever had. Being careful not to empty it, I gave it back to Roza.

"Thank you," I said. "Will we be stopping and leaving the carriage any time soon?"

"We will stop on All Hollow's Eve, in time to perform the ritual," Darvulia answered. "And not before."

"What if I have to...relieve myself?" I asked. A chance to run could save us.

"We will not stop before it is time, so you best get comfortable," Darvulia snapped, "and be careful how much liquid you consume."

"What do you know of the woman who raised your mother?"

Erza suddenly demanded.

"Very little," I replied, thinking of my grandmother. "I hardly ever saw her."

"So the midwife did her job well," Erza said, nodding to Darvulia. "We should tell the Countess to have her rewarded. Do you believe she taught the girl anything?"

"I do not know. Her magic was very old and different than what I know," Darvulia snapped.

"Send the reward to my father and brother," I interrupted them.

"Why?" Erza asked.

"Because I believe the woman who raised my mother will likely be dead soon, if she is not already."

Erza almost smiled. "Is that so? That may explain your mother's state, if all of these events led up to where you currently sit. Perhaps the midwife told her on her deathbed. Oh, how dramatic!"

"Only she can answer that," I replied. It seemed now that I was on my own in regards to the events that would alter my life. It was I who would have to take on the motherly role to protect us both.

I wished I knew something of the only grandmother I had ever known. It seemed she had been a very interesting and unusual lady.

The witches talked amongst themselves all throughout the course of the day, while I remained silent, listening intently. The more they spoke, the more I realized that every part of my mother's early life I had known to be true was a lie. Her birthplace, the 'father' my mother had never known, the money my 'grandmother' claimed came from her dead husband, the amount of travel she had done after being banished from Hungary with the illegitimate daughter of Countess Erzsébet Báthory... so many things beyond who her real parents were, and the endless talk of witchcraft. Mother did not move or say a word throughout all of this, and I wished more than anything she would, even if only something trivial.

Then, all of a sudden, after what seemed like an eternity, the carriage came to a stop. There was no warning or obvious purpose; it simply slowed to an eventual halt.

"What's happened?" I asked.

"It appears you may have gotten your wish, child," Darvulia said.

She unlocked the carriage door without another word, stepping out into the night.

III.

The Beast Within

I DID NOT KNOW HOW LONG WE HAD BEEN IN THE carriage, or how far we had travelled. It was difficult to focus my senses; the darkness of the forest was all I could see. In the distance, I heard the faint sound of a river as it broke the silence of our surroundings.

Darvulia and Erza had exited the carriage before us, each walking out into the woods alone to look for something. Mother had come out with me, and I could see that she had become more alert as we stood and waited. She hung tightly to my hand while her eyes surveyed the woods, cold black emptiness in her gaze. I wanted her to hold me but looking into her eyes made me fear it would bring no comfort.

"What are they doing?" I asked Roza when the other women were out of hearing range.

"They are looking for a spot to perform the ritual, Katrine." She appeared nervous, uncomfortable…almost frightened.

"Does that mean it is All Hollow's Eve?" I asked, and Roza nodded.

"How long have we been travelling?"

"Today is the third day," Mother finally spoke, her voice sounding quite unnatural. Roza and I looked at her in surprise.

"Say no more, Anastasia," Roza said sharply. "I think this may be simpler if you do not speak."

They briefly made eye contact then said nothing further.

Darvulia came out of the trees then, Erza close behind her. Both women appeared satisfied.

"Come now!" Darvulia called. "We will make ready."

Her words seemed like a foreign language. I watched and waited for her to say something I understood.

"Have you gone stupid, girl?" Erza grumbled. She grabbed my upper arm and pulled me forward, while my mother kept her hand in mine.

Darvulia laughed insultingly. "Maybe she's finally beginning to understand! The girl obviously got none of the Countess' intelligence. She is as dumb as the old drunk!"

Erza sneered and continued to pull me along; Roza had fallen behind us. We kept walking deeper into the woods until I could see a clearing through the trees. Erza pulled my mother and me apart, shoving me hard into Roza's arms.

"Hold the child back, if it is not too difficult for you!" she ordered Roza.

"Mother!" I cried as they pulled her away. I continued to call her name as the witches tied her to a tree and made their preparations; not once did Mother look at me.

"She will be alright, Katrine," Roza quietly assured. "Please stay calm, or I may have to tie you up, as well."

"Why does she not look at me? Why does she say nothing to comfort me?" I whimpered. My eyes grew hot, welling with tears that fell onto my cheeks.

"It is hard to offer comfort at a time when you are deathly afraid," Roza mused.

"You said she would not be harmed!" I tried hard to breathe normally, beginning to feel dizzy.

After my mother was tightly bound, Darvulia and Erza gathered items from around the clearing. They put little bits of herbs and leaves in a circle around my mother and made a small fire. When they completed it, they gathered a few things in their hands. From what I could see, they held various twigs and leaves as they stood on opposite sides of the fire.

Each woman then threw something into the flames and chanted words I could not hear.

It was beginning.

The witches circled the fire, tossing more things into it. They continued to chant in unison, their skin bathed in moonlight. I watched the two pearlescent creatures as they moved wildly, their bodies twirling, faces contorted. They approached my mother and all sound seemed to be gone except for my screams.

I could see that my mother's lips were moving as if in silent prayer; it was so fast I could not begin to understand. The flames then turned a bright blue. The witches did not falter as they began to rub their sticks and leaves forcefully across my mother's skin.

A loud thunderclap made me jump, and heavy drops of rain came rushing down moments later. Roza pulled me closer to her; she was beginning to shake violently. Mother continued her own sort of chanting, as if she was trying to counteract their spell. Darvulia suddenly grabbed my mother and pulled out some of her hair. She stared as she threw it into the fire, only now noticing the ethereal blue colour of the flames. She turned to move back towards Mother, and that is when the ferocious ripping began.

Mother's face was twisting in agony. The terrifying sound of bones cracking and flesh pulling apart echoed in my ears. It was as if she was still there... but yet, she was not, her body violently morphing, face and body mutating into a thing that could only be described as a nightmare. The torsion of her face was horrifying as it stretched and snapped her bones, pushing forward a monsterous jaw filled with razor sharp fangs. Her eyes rolled back into their sockets, only to emerge the colour of blood, emanating an eerie glow, with pupils black as night. Her ears were growing, long and pointed like those of a wolf, coarse tufts of fur sprouting from where her once smooth skin was. The flames, too, were growing, enhancing in their flicker the frightening form that was appearing before us, bathing everything in a strange blue light.

I screamed for my mother. I screamed with every ounce of strength I had left, not allowing desperation or fear to grip me anymore in their clutches.

"Mother! Mother! Please Momma, please don't leave me...please! Momma!" I screamed, struggling to break free from Roza's arms. If only I could get to her, she would recognise me and she would stop....this nightmare would finally stop.

"God, please help us!" I cried into the darkness. "Please save us!"

But my mother could no longer hear me...she was not even there. In her place was a massive, terrifying beast breaking free of its binds of both human skin and rope.

The witches began to recoil in terror, although still chanting. Darvulia pointed at the beast and shouted something in a strange tongue, a beam of white light firing out of her fingers. The beast suddenly lunged at her, its teeth sinking deep into her throat. With an effortless tug of its massive jaw, the beast tore Darvulia's throat to shreds, her head dropping to the ground. It tossed her body aside, smashing it into a tree, discarded.

Horrified, Erza tried to escape. As she ran in our direction, Roza pulled me away to hide behind a tree. The beast caught Erza's arm. It pulled her apart limb by limb before it sprung towards us.

I tried to pull away from Roza but she kept me close. I could feel her laboured breath and heart pounding in her chest. The beast stopped, then approached me slowly. I looked into its eyes, and I thought I saw my mother.

I stood perfectly still as the beast came closer. I wanted it to kill me, to tear me limb from limb as it did to Erza. I was certain that death would be my only release from this surreal nightmare.

"I will not let you die, Katrine!" Roza cried. "I made a promise and I intend to keep it!"

It seemed like the beast understood Roza; it reached its paw out to me as a person would a hand. My mother—now this beast—beckoned to me. Before I knew what was happening, my arm was in agonising pain as the beast raked its claws across it. Roza threw me to the ground.

I shut my eyes, squeezing them tightly, trying to block out the world. The pain in my arm was hot as if on fire. I focused all my strength on moving my fingers, trying to make sure my hand was still attached. As I did so, the heat shot up my arm and through to the edges of my body, making bright, white stars dance behind my closed eyelids. The pain was so severe I thought I might vomit. The world behind my eyelids swirled and I became light headed, the heat now turning into excruciating pain that throbbed throughout my entire body. Roza climbed over me in an attempt to shield me from any further assault.

"I will keep you safe," she repeated over and over, the thump of her heart falling in tune with the rolling thunder. As I prayed for all of this to end, another great clap of thunder shook the ground along with a flash of lightening that illuminated the beast. I could not reconcile how this terrifying creature was once my mother; it held me in its gaze, as if it were trying to read my mind, trying to hypnotise me. Panic welled up inside of me, and as I cursed the monstrous creature that had possessed by mother, the beast let out a blood-curdling roar and bolted into the night.

The rain continued to pour and, finally, there was no more thunder, no more noise except the falling rain and the beating of my own heart. We lay perfectly still, Roza and I. I wondered now if Roza was dead and I was being sheltered by a corpse. I wanted to move but could not bring myself to try, let alone look to see if the beast was truly gone. I could not let the thoughts of what had transpired sink any further into my being.

The blackness began to consume me, my body going limp just before I passed out.

I did not want to open my eyes. My face felt warm and dry. I was hopeful that upon awakening, I would have found myself to be sleeping beside the gates of heaven. I slowly opened my eyes; the forest floor lay in front of me. There were no signs of the rainfall, only the dry earth and leaves.

Roza was sitting in my line of sight, her arms wrapped tightly about her body and knees pulled up to her chin. Her eyes were still wide. She looked as if she had been awake for some time. I was secretly relieved I was not alone, as fear still lingered within the pit of my stomach.

Then the terrible memories rushed through my head again like running water. The witches, the moonlight, the ritual, the violence, pieces of their bodies being flung all around. The image of my mother's transformation, her flesh ripping, as the beast that took her place cleaved its way out of her body. All of this was now forever seared into my mind.

I sat up quickly, hoping the motion would shake the thoughts away.

"Heavens above!" Roza cried. She crawled over to me and pulled me into her arms.

She stroked my hair and held me close to her chest. "Praise be to the gods you are alive! Are you hurt badly, Katrine?"

I could not bring myself to speak yet.

"It's alright, child. You do not have to speak. I shall protect you and take care of you as if you were my own," she continued and began to rock me back and forth. "We shall go on without them. We shall continue to Csejthe, to the Countess, your grandmother. She will know what to do to protect you."

I kept my head to her chest as I held out my aching arm for her to see. The fabric had stuck to my arm with a mix of blood, dirt and rainwater holding it into place. She gently peeled it back and said, "Oh, it's just a scratch. We shall find a stream in which to clean it up and you will be good as new."

Roza pulled me up. "Come, Katrine. We should leave this place. Animals will surely come to feast soon. Let us make our way towards the carriage and continue on to Csejthe."

My mind began to wander; I wanted to be with my father very badly. I would even find comfort in the constant chatter of nonsense from Bodi, any reminder of my stolen life. I thought of asking her to take me home. Nevertheless, I could not. Father would never take me back. It was a sad but unfortunate truth. Without my mother, I was nothing more than an expense he did not need.

Roza brushed the hair off my face and smiled at me, trying to offer some comfort. As a result of these bizarre events, we were now bonded in a way that most people could not understand. Only the other could soothe the pain and offer comfort when the nightmares took hold. I could not leave her now. In a sense, Roza had become my new mother.

Roza placed her hand on my shoulder. "The carriage awaits, dear. I said I will protect you, and I intend to keep that promise. I believe the Countess is the one who can help us."

I followed her out of the clearing, holding her hand. She stopped suddenly and pulled me away from something; it was a severed hand that lay discarded on the ground. Small black lumps scurried over the white skin. I wanted to scream but had no voice or sound in me to do so. Looking at it reminded me of my own injured arm, the long gashes nothing akin to what Roza called a 'scratch'. I had no memory of what caused the injury; the last thing I remembered was the beast trying to reach out to me.

The carriage was exactly the way we had left it; however, its driver was nowhere to be found.

"Boy!" Roza yelled loudly. "Boy? Where are you, it's time to go!"

There was a rustling from behind some trees and the carriage driver came running towards us from his hiding place. He looked not much older than Bodi.

"Yes, Mum!" he scurried into his seat, clearly frightened by the events of the night before. "But, where is the mistress and her aide?"

"They are gone. I am the mistress now," Roza said firmly, "and we must hurry."

She opened the carriage door and ushered me inside. In the daylight, I could see that the carriage was, in fact, rather beautiful. I was glad to behold its lush red velvet seats and piles of soft pelts. I did not have a chance to examine them or to see what other treasures the carriage might hold, for Roza came in behind me and quickly closed the door. She opened the small window, and in an instant we were moving. I was quite relieved to be leaving that place.

Roza began to rummage around on the floor, eventually leaning over to pull some things out from under the seat across from us.

"Please give me your arm, Katrine," she said. I held out my injured arm to her. She unscrewed the lid from the tankard and poured some water on it. She used a soft cloth to clean the grime from my skin.

"I must be honest, child, I have no clear memory of how you received this gash. The last thing I remember was the beast trying to...," she began, and then catching her breath, declared, "Oh dear! That beast tried to kill you!"

I thought I might remind her that the beast was my mother and that if it had truly intended to kill me, I would not be here, but I did not speak.

"No need to say anything. I am sure there was no part of your mother left in that abhorrent creature! No matter," she said shaking her head in disbelief. After she felt she had done what she could, she gave me back my arm. I tried my best to get comfortable, removing my wet cloak and setting it on the floor. The ache in my arm had dulled to a slight throb now.

"What do you know of magic, Katrine?" Roza suddenly asked. I stared blankly at her. I did not feel like speaking, especially if it had to do with talk of magic or my mother. The mother I knew, knew nothing of magic.

"I was asking because I saw what your mother was doing and I wonder if that's how she...," she turned to face me, "I swear to you, Katrine, the ritual alone would not have created that beast. It would not have turned her!" She sighed loudly. "None of that was supposed to happen, but no matter now, my dear. You and I will continue on as planned without Darvulia and Erza."

I wondered if my mother had intended it, to kill us both so we would not have to suffer whatever fate the witches had planned.

After we spent considerable time riding in silence, Roza finally offered, "Shall I tell you a story, Katrine?"

I turned my body so my eyes were focused on her. Roza was going to tell this story whether I wanted to hear it or not.

"I met the Countess, your grandmother, almost one year ago," she began. I was living in a rundown shack in Csejthe. My husband had been dead for some time, praise the Lord his soul, and my children had no interest in me. I had succumbed to the drink, you see, and I was just wasting away. I heard that the Countess was in need of servants, not just young maids. I am trained as a bread maker, so I went to the center of town where all applicants were to meet and took my chances.

"I stood in the square with the other women; there were so many young girls I thought I would never have a chance. A carriage sat parked there. In fact, it is the same one we are sitting in now, and two older women were standing outside its doors examining the girls. They were Jo Ilona and Dorka, the women who run the Countess' household. They came to me; Jo Ilona asked what I could do and why should they take me. I told her of my bread making skills. They already knew of me, for they had once taken some loaves to the castle. I was proud that they brought me over to the carriage."

As Roza rambled on, I said nothing, only brushing the hair off my face. I was beginning to dry off and feel a slight bit better. I was almost warm.

"A woman's head leaned out of the window," Roza went, on, "and my goodness, I had never seen a woman of such beauty! There were many stories, legends of how exquisite the Countess' looks are, but they are only words until you see her face. Clear, milky white skin, and the most beautiful shiny black eyes that can enchant you. Shiny dark hair and slim elegant hands; a goddess in human form she is! She only smiled slightly at me, but I felt I should weep from joy. She asked me if I would come with her to work and live at the castle, and of course I accepted! That very day I closed up my shack, and I have been at the castle ever since."

I sighed and smiled slightly at her. It was a nice story. Probably the nicest one I had heard about Countess Báthory. The rumours of her using sorcery to preserve her beauty were only quiet whispers and by far not the worst of the tales about the Báthory family.

"Do you not wish to speak, Katrine? Are you angry with me?" Roza asked, suddenly hurt.

I tried to tell her with the solemn look in my eyes that I was not angry, only that I was tired. Tears began to well up in my eyes, however. Too many things had happened.

"Oh please, don't cry!" she said, and she pulled me close. "You don't have to speak until you are ready."

I smiled and bowed my head, a silent thank you. I leaned into Roza's body and closed my eyes, her heartbeat soothing to my ears.

When sleep came I didn't fight it. I was safe.

I stayed somewhere between sleep and consciousness for some time, but visions of the beast would not allow me to totally give over. Roza had left the window open, and the sounds of the forest crept into the carriage sending my thoughts in a million different directions. I had to be slightly awake in case the patter of what I thought were paws came too near.

A soft snoring arose from Roza, her body emanating comforting warmth as she slept beside me. I wondered about her children, why they had no contact with her. I thought she would have been a good mother.

The carriage kept moving. The night grew so dark I could no longer see the bench in front of me. I wondered how long we would go on like this, silently praying to God that Countess Erzsébet Báthory, my grandmother, would be our saviour.

IV.

Aftermath

I OPENED MY EYES AND WAS BACK ON THE FOREST
floor. I sat up and looked around, the scene almost the same as the first time.

*"Are you alright, Katrine? I didn't want to wake you," my mother's voice came
from behind me. I turned and she was sitting crouched behind me, her knees pulled
tight to her chest. Her eyes were wide, dark and shiny like black diamonds.*

"I'm fine, I think, Mother," I said. "Are you hurt at all?"

*She smiled. "No, no, my dearest child. I am quite well. We are safe now. We may
have to walk for some time, but that is a better predicament than our previous one,
don't you think?"*

*"What happened to the...the witches? Where are they?" I asked. "I cannot
imagine they will leave us alone if—"*

*She grabbed me and pulled me close to her body. I could feel her heartbeat thudding
against my ears.*

*"We will be fine because they are dead. There will be nothing more to worry about
because I have taken them from this earth. My own mother taught me well. My magic
is strong, and now I know I can protect us both," she assured. "We will never have
to be afraid again."*

"What are you saying? I don't understand."

"I am saying that you have the same power inside of you, Katrine. Do not be

afraid to use it."

Roza was stroking my hair as she rocked me back and forth. I opened my eyes but remained still.

"You were crying for your mother," she said. "You must have been having a nightmare. I have decided that we should stop in the next town. Sleep in a real bed may do you some good."

I sat up and looked out the window. I could smell the brackish air of a river or lake. I had no idea how much time had passed or how far we had travelled.

Roza stuck her head out the window and hollered up to the boy in a language I couldn't understand.

"Good heart in that boy," she mused sitting back down, "but not very much of a brain it seems."

The wound on my arm was itching now, the skin around it red and raised. I held it to my face to sniff it—my mother always said an infected wound smelt sour—but it seemed fine. Roza quickly grabbed my arm and examined it herself.

"Looks like it is beginning to heal," she said, satisfied. "When we stop, I will make something to help quell the redness. We have made some progress in our travels, and we'll be coming into town soon."

I nodded and tried my best to stay calm. I really did not want to leave the carriage, spend a night in a town I did not know, or sleep in someone else's bed. Unfortunately, I was in no position to complain or argue.

"Do you want to talk about the nightmare?" Roza prodded. I shook my head no. I felt a small twinge of guilt but still could not bring myself to speak.

"Let me tell you another story then," she began, "but I'm not sure which one! Ah, there are so many."

I touched my hands to my mouth, trying to show her I was thirsty. She handed me the tankard. I drank only a little, as we did not have much left.

Something suddenly caught my attention out the window. I leaned over and stuck my head out: all and I could see was water, a vast and mighty river.

"It's the Danube, Katrine. Have you never seen it before?"

I shook my head no. I could not hide my excitement. I had heard tales of the great river since childhood, but I never thought I'd see it with my own eyes. That excitement was short lived, however.

The carriage started to slow, and the scene outside became more strange as we eased our pace. Roza took my hand.

"Prepare yourself, child, for what you are about to see. We shall be stopping shortly."

This town on the Danube was very different from the one in which I grew up. The destruction from war was everywhere: buildings lay in ruins, and similarly destroyed expressions haunted the townspeople's faces. Even the children were left with eyes cold and empty, aged beyond their years by the horrors they had seen.

Roza had given me a cloak that she pulled from the compartment underneath the seat. Eyes turned as we both exited the carriage, yielding expressions I could not understand. People strained to see my face under the hood. I had not noticed the crest on the door of our carriage, the wyvern with its three talons, signage of the identity of its passengers and crest of the Báthory family.

These people thought I was a Báthory.

My stomach turned and I became very nervous. Being mistaken for another could be a dangerous thing. Roza, meanwhile, did not seem to be concerned as she motioned to the boy to take the carriage behind an inn. She then pulled me to the front door.

Inside, the main room was in a flutter over our arrival. Despite the possible dangers, the reality was that the Báthory were upper nobility, royalty, and a certain level of respect was required.

A man with mottled skin that looked like rotten fruit, similar in age to my father, approached us, wiping the palms of his hands on his pant legs.

"Good evening, My Ladies," he said, bowing slightly. "I am the owner of this establishment. How may I be of service to you?"

"We'd like a room for the night," Roza said.

He smiled. "Of course! I shall have our finest room made ready. Would you care to have some of our cook's goulash? A fresh pot has just been made."

I smiled and nodded to Roza. The innkeeper escorted us to a small table in the back.

"Please send food to our carriage driver," Roza told him. "He should be back in the stables with our horses."

She gave him some money, although I didn't see how much. I had none, and I was glad to see she did. I then wondered what sorts of supplies had been left in the carriage by Darvulia and Erza.

I took the hood of the cloak down, but kept the cowl wrapped around me. I was cold and wanted to keep my wounded arm covered. Now that my face was visible, the staring became more obvious.

"I told you that you're beautiful, my dear, and it seems that your resemblance to the Countess is so incredible that others can see it as well," Roza whispered to me. I smiled and nodded, trying my best to show her I was listening and that I understood.

"I always wondered if I had a granddaughter by either of my children," she continued. "I was so looking forward to being a grandmother but, sadly, it will never be. My children will not speak to me, they hate me. Their father did that to them before he died."

I reached across the table and took her hand to quiet her. I was lucky that my parents got along even though their marriage was actually arranged by their parents. I had known that since I was quite young.

"Hey, girl, you are Báthory, yes?," a man sitting a few feet away from us asked. Before I could answer, he continued, "Your family have been very brave against the infidel, you should be proud! We lost a great defender when Black Bey died. He was the greatest warrior Hungary has ever known! Was he your father?"

I looked at Roza, who signaled me to say yes. When I nodded at the man and smiled, his expression turned to a glow.

"It's a shame," he said. "The world lost a true hero with the death of Ferenc Nádasdy." He then returned to his conversation with his companions.

I did not know the name 'Black Bey,' but I knew Count Ferenc Nádasdy. Count Nádasdy was Countess Báthory's dead husband. He was a major factor in why my mother was given away as a baby—because she was not his daughter. In fact, my poor mother's life would have been very different had that brave hero been her father.

All at once, two heaping bowls were placed in front of us, full of steaming brown liquid, the aroma of the goulash filling the room like clouds of steam. It smelled comforting, almost like home.

I ate heartily, and still hungry enough to have Roza ask for seconds. The next bowl came with a small loaf of fresh bread that crumbled in my hand. When Roza ate a mouthful of bread, her eyes closed and a smile slowly started forming on her face.

"Beautiful," she said happily. "The mark of a good baker is when the bread makes you feel pleased after you eat it. This meal will do you good, Katrine. After this you shall sleep well, I guarantee it."

I cleaned my plate and ate all the bread, as if I might never eat again. The bowls were removed and mugs of warm liquid put in their place.

"Wonderful meal!" Roza said to the innkeeper. I smiled at him, trying my best to express my gratitude through my facial expressions.

"Oh, I am so glad you enjoyed it," he replied. "I have come to tell you that the room is ready whenever you would like it."

I lowered my eyes in thanks. Despite the ordeal I had been through, I had never been treated so well. I would remember this place forever.

He and Roza spoke while I took a sip from my mug; it was warm ale that smelt of herbs. It felt soothing as it went down my throat and into my stomach.

"Drink up," Roza said as she swigged from her own mug after the innkeeper had walked away. "Drink, then off to bed with you."

The best room in the inn, I believed, also happened to belong to the innkeeper and his wife. I had had my suspicions, and they were confirmed by the angry, hairy woman who glared at us from the kitchen doorway. Led by the innkeeper with a glowing taper in his hand, we walked past her to a small stairway close to the kitchen.

"Up these stairs, first on the left," he said, pointing up into the darkness. He handed Roza the candle, his smile so wide I thought it might cause him pain the next day.

"Thank you, Sir. Good night and God bless you," Roza said. She took my hand and led me away; I smiled at them both as we passed.

The room was modest. In the corner was a wooden table with a jug and bowl for washing, along with a mirror hanging on the wall behind it. A fire burned steadily in the hearth.

"Not a bug in sight," Roza said as she pulled the bed apart and remade it. "You will have a good sleep tonight, my dear. I will make myself a bed by the hearth."

I pulled on her arm and shook my head furiously; I was too scared to sleep alone.

"Alright, it's alright! Please stay calm! We will share the bed, if you like," she said, smoothing her hands over my hair. "Now, let me fix you up before we get some sleep."

She pulled me toward the mirror and the washbasin. I finally got a look at myself. We only had one mirror at home and it was in my parents' room. I did not get much opportunity to see my own reflection, and I was surprised by what I saw.

I looked like my mother, the way I remembered her when I was small, before Bodi came along. I saw a stunning vision… creamy white skin, clean and bright with a curtain of long dark hair falling to my elbows.

And the eyes. They seemed new, as if my own childish ones were replaced with something dark and deeper. They were her eyes now…her stunning black eyes.

Roza poured some water from the jug into the bowl, dipped a cloth, and gently wiped my face. I smiled at my reflection and at her.

"We shall have to get you a gown before you meet the Countess," she said. "We can't have you looking like anything less than a princess."

We both cleaned up. Roza plaited my hair before we went to bed and explained how it would help stop the tangles. I put another log on the fire before I crawled into bed, with Roza beside me. I silently thanked the Lord for the food and the bed, and for not leaving me alone.

I stared at the wall until I heard Roza's breathing slow its pace and her soft snores gently taking over. My eyelids were now growing heavy. I could finally allow myself to fall asleep.

A strange sound made me stir, but I did not open my eyes. I listened quietly. It sounded like a dog scratching at the door, wanting to be let in. The sound grew louder, and I moved closer to Roza in an attempt to feel safer.

"Katrine! Katrine! Wake up!" my mother's voice declared from beside me. I felt her place her hand on me and shake me slightly. As I opened my eyes, Roza was gone but I was still in the bed in the innkeeper's room.

"Mother?" I asked warily, sitting up now.

"Didn't you hear me at the door?" she demanded.

"No," I replied. "I only heard scratching. I must have been dreaming."

"You heard me, and you didn't come?" she said mournfully, her eyes wide with sorrow.

"I...I'm sorry, Mother," I mumbled, "I had only heard the animal scratching."

"No matter. Come now, we must be going," she said, as she started towards the door.

"Yes, Mother, but we have to find Roza."

She turned quickly to me. "Pardon?"

"Roza. She brought me here, she helped me after—"

"Katrine, what are you babbling about? Who is this woman?"

"She was one of the—"

"The witches? Are you talking about one of the witches, my dear? I think you must be feeling ill. They're dead, I killed them all."

She said this with so much determination I could not question it.

"Now, are you coming or not?" she pronounced as she made her way towards the door.

Suddenly I opened my eyes and stared out into the dark room. The fire had died down but the room was still warm. Roza's body heat made me feel as if the warmth was right in my bones. It was calm here and I felt safe. This visit with my mother had only been another dream.

The rest of the night was long, and I tried my best to sleep. It felt as if it took an eternity, for each time sleep would almost be upon me, I thought I heard those scratches at the door—the ones my mother claimed were hers. There were only a couple of hours left until sunrise, and I desperately needed to return to sleep, to have some sense of peace. Finally, I was able to slip into silent slumber.

Not long after, Roza stirred, quickly getting out of bed before I opened my eyes. I stayed in the warm little nest I had made for myself with the heavy covers, not wanting to leave the safety of the bed, willing sleep to return.

I listened to her rustling around the room, tidying up and possibly waiting for me to wake. After several moments, she went towards the door. Stricken with panic, I quickly sat up, fearing what might be on the other side. Fortunately, it was nothing. Seeing me awake, Roza hastened over to me, leaning down beside the bed.

"Katrine," she smiled.

As I looked up at her, she whispered reassuringly, "You shall sleep some more. You are safe here. I am going to go find you a dress and bring you some nice warm food for breakfast." She brushed the hair off my face. "We can't have you going to Csejthe looking like you were attacked by a wild animal." She suddenly caught her breath, mortified by the blunder. "Oh, darling, I am so sorry! Please forgive me! I meant nothing by it."

I smiled at her and nodded; she sighed deeply in relief.

"I will be back soon," she said, as she headed out the door.

I looked around the room. Bathed in the morning light that streamed from the window, it appeared slightly more modest than the night before. Nevertheless, the accommodations were still so much more luxurious than any I had ever been in. I moved to the middle of the bed and spread out; I had never slept in a bed so large! For a moment, I found myself giggling, my smile wide with excitement that added to my warmth.

I wondered if this was what life would be like if I were to be accepted as a Báthory.

Roza returned sooner than I expected; she carried a plate in her hands.

She laughed when she saw me in my current state of elation.

"I think you shall do well as a lady of means," she commented. "But it seems that for you to look the part, is more difficult than I had originally anticipated."

She sat on the bed with me, a full plate of bread and cheese between us. I broke off a piece of each and began to eat. How it reminded me of home. I wondered if that feeling of missing home would ever pass, or would it always linger when I ate.

"We do not have the time to stay here while a dress is made," Roza continued. "Perhaps I shall attempt to sew something while we ride, but I am not very skilled."

Just at that moment, there was a knock at the door. Roza glanced at me briefly before going to answer.

"Pardon me, Madam," the innkeeper said nervously when she opened it, "but I may have solved your dress issue for the young lady. When you are ready, may I take you to my sister's home? She has daughters who are similar in age and may have something suitable."

"Thank you, Sir," Roza said cheerfully. "Please tell your kin we will pay handsomely. I will prepare My Lady and shall come to you when we are ready. Is it far?"

"No, no, Madam. We can walk. I shall be downstairs awaiting your arrival," he said, bowing slightly and quickly leaving.

"The Fates appear to be smiling on us," she said happily, returning so that we could finish our meal.

We washed up, and I looked at myself in the mirror again; my skin looked creamy and warm after the rest and food. Roza pulled my hair back, combing it through with her fingers. I looked well, thanks to her help but, unfortunately, not well enough to pass for royalty.

She wrapped my cloak around me, grabbing it from a hook on the back of the door. I had forgotten all about it; I must have discarded it on the floor on the way to the bed. She put the hood down so my face was visible but kept it wrapped around my body. The cloak did help with my appearance. It was soft, warm, and regal.

"At least you have a lovely cloak," she stated triumphantly.

I nodded in agreement and smiled.

"You see? I knew sleep would do you good. We'll be alright, you and I," Roza said happily, "whether you decide to speak again or not."

The innkeeper was in the kitchen when we came down; Roza went to retrieve him while I waited in the main room. At first, I moved to follow her, but a smell coming out of the kitchen made me hesitate and then hold back. I could not tell what it was, but it sank into my body and brought out something from deep inside me. I had the most powerful yearning; the sensation overwhelmed me, and it felt as if my blood was stirring. I desperately wanted to know what that smell was because, in that moment, I needed whatever it was.

Roza and the innkeeper finally came out of the kitchen. He was covered in that potent smell.

"I apologise for keeping you waiting, My Lady," he said humbly, "but we were just getting meat prepared for the goulash. Now, if you're ready, we shall be off."

I nodded my head rapidly, and we headed out. Was that smell swine, or was it chicken? God, I hated chickens, such vile dirty creatures. I could not figure out why the smell of a dead animal would make me feel this way.

We walked out into the town square and headed down a short road. People again stopped what they were doing to look at us, and their nods and bows along the way made me feel rather good and important. Nonetheless, despite all of the distractions, I could not get that smell out of my mind.

The innkeeper took us to a modest house just outside the main part of town. I held tightly onto Roza's hand as we approached the door. He knocked, and a woman who had an uncanny resemblance to him answered. She glared at us; it appeared that she had heard nothing of our arrival.

"Sister, I have come to ask if you have any dresses you could spare for the young lady who is in need," the innkeeper asked hopefully.

She snorted loudly. "I cannot imagine why you would think—"

"Excuse me, Madam," Roza interrupted, "but the young Mistress

Báthory is in a desperate bind," she continued as she pulled money out, "and we will pay you well for your trouble."

I wasn't sure if the woman's eyes began to sparkle at the name Báthory or at the sight of the money, but her expression quickly changed and she welcomed us inside.

She brought us upstairs and into a bedroom with two large beds. All the children must have slept in this room. I wondered how many daughters this woman had and if she had sons who also shared this space.

She opened a large chest at the end of one of the beds, similar to one my mother had, and began to pull dresses that she laid out for us to view.

"These are the ones I think may fit," she said, sizing me up quickly. "You are about fifteen or sixteen years, My Lady?"

I nodded, while Roza began to examine the dresses. I was surprised at the variety of colours she had available: dark blue, green, brown—all a refreshing change from the gray dress I had always worn.

Roza decided on the blue and the green before taking a moment to examine closely the brown. Two were quite enough, in my opinion; I felt a small twinge of guilt that we were taking her daughters' church clothes, but in exchange, Roza began paying her enough so that she could have very grand clothes made for her entire family. Nice things were expensive, especially when children were constantly growing.

The lady of the house pulled one last dress from the chest. I must have gasped loudly, because the three turned around to look at me. I had never seen a dress in such a stunning crimson colour! I remembered when my father used the pigment in his enameling; the effect was always beautiful. My thoughts turned to the cross he made. I checked my pockets to make sure it was still there.

"And the red as well," Roza declared. She handed the women some more money and scooped the dresses up in her arms. We exchanged pleasantries then left the house, along with the innkeeper.

As we made our way back through town, the powerful smell from the inn hit me again. A grizzly looking woman was pulling a cart covered by a blood stained sheet through the town square. I could feel myself breathing deeply, hungrily gulping in the surrounding air and the heady smell. Whatever it was, my body wanted it. Badly.

During all of this, Roza had been watching me carefully. Disturbed by my reaction, she immediately pushed me on towards the inn, but I could not take my eyes off the cart. I kept turning around to catch a glimpse of it and draw in the intoxicating odour. As we neared the inn, Roza said something to the innkeeper then quickly pulled me inside and led me back up to the room.

"What's wrong with you, Katrine?" she demanded as she closed the door behind us. "You were staring at that cart like a rabid dog! Are you hungry or just feeling ill?"

I shook my head no, and then plugged my nose with my two fingers to try to indicate that it was the smell.

"What? It smelt bad?" she asked. I shook my head no. In my mind, it actually smelt quite good.

"You liked it?" She was shocked now. "Why? It reeked of gore and... and blood..."

I sat on the bed and stared at the floor. I felt sick to my stomach; the idea was indeed disturbing, but I could not escape how I'd felt about that smell.

A look of sheer panic washed over Roza now, and for the first time during this whole ordeal, she looked truly disturbed. I looked up to her helplessly, and her face suddenly filled with pity for me.

"It's alright," she quickly said. "It's alright, everything will be alright. No one saw anything, and all you did was look. Nothing happened," she added, trying to convince herself. "Now, we will get you washed and dressed and leave immediately. There is no time to waste."

I took the cross from my pocket and sighed deeply. I was not sure that where we were, or where we would go, could change anything— especially the smell of death.

V.

Awakening

WE WENT ON FOR SOME TIME WITHOUT STOPPING, sleeping in the carriage and occasionally getting out to relieve ourselves. The level of urgency in our mission seemed to rise with this new issue; we never spoke of it after we left that first village.

I am not sure what our driver did for sleep, or anything else for that matter, since I never saw him when we stopped. Perhaps this may have been common, but never having travelled a great distance before, I had no way to judge. It was getting colder by the day, and snow was starting to fall regularly. Thank the Lord we had the pelts to keep us warm; otherwise, we may have frozen to death.

"We shall stop again for the night this time, instead of just for food," Roza announced. I smiled contentedly. Throughout all of this, I had still not spoken and it felt to me as if we had been travelling for a fortnight. She opened the carriage window and stuck out her head. A blast of cold air hit me quite hard.

"The temperature seems to have dropped since yesterday," Roza commented. "No matter, we have crossed into Hungary now, and it won't be much longer to Csejthe."

I smiled, hoping the fear wasn't so obvious on my face.

"Would you like to hear more about Csejthe?" Roza asked, and I nodded eagerly. Roza's willingness to speak had eased the pressure and anxiety of me not wanting to do so.

"When I was not baking," she began, "I was ordered to collect more girls from the village to work in the castle. It was a difficult job, you see, because the Countess is very strict and has very high expectations of the people she keeps in her household. Most of the time, I would go with Jo Ilona, who was one of the Countess' most trusted attendants—she had been in her service for many years—and Dorka, another servant. Other times, the Countess' dwarf, Ficzko, would come. He was an odd young man." She paused, her eyes squinting with concern. "He was filled with such anger, the likes of which I had never seen before." She shook her head in disbelief. "Nevertheless, we would go and get girls from all over the county, and oh, how they would run to our carriage!

"In the beginning, we had to turn girls away! Then, it all started to change...," she murmured, tilting her head to the side. "Something was happening. Girls would come to the castle, and then they would disappear mysteriously." Roza leaned in for emphasis. "—Or be found dead! People thought the Countess was harming them. There was a wretched priest in town who was saying horrible things about her, accusing her of having tortured them to death, but I never saw anything! The girls were reluctant to come with us after a while. Some came anyway, crying like they were being sent to execution! How ungrateful they were. Being a servant in a noble household is good, honest work! I always wanted to ask them what they thought their life would be if they did not have this job, if they knew how lucky they were."

I forced a smile again, trying to look more positive than I felt. My fear was getting worse, though. I was already worried about what to expect when we arrived at the castle.

"We tried to tell them, Katrine," she said, taking my hand and patting it gently, "that the rumours were untrue, that they were headed for a good life. But, the fact was, even I started to wonder, even though I knew enough that sometimes a servant could be there one day and gone the next, with no explanation."

She looked to me as if she wanted some sort of assurance, but even if I were to speak, I would not know what to say. I knew nothing of a household servant's life.

She sighed loudly. "In any case, you have nothing to worry about, my dear. I'm sure you will be given a place of honour."

A myriad of thoughts spun through my mind now. I wondered what would happen if I was not accepted. God forbid, if the Countess didn't believe me.

Meanwhile, Roza stuck her head out the window and yelled something to the carriage driver. We started to slow our pace and turned off the road that we had been travelling on since we left the first village.

"I know this town," Roza said as she watched the scenery through the still open window. "We stopped here on our way to collect your mother."

She had spoken very little of the journey and the events before she and the witches had arrived at my father's house, and now she began to recount the tale. I listened eagerly.

"Darvulia spoke of the midwife who raised your mother. She believed the woman could cause us some problems if she was around," Roza said. "I had never heard Darvulia say such things about anyone, almost as if she was intimidated by the midwife's powers. Could you imagine? I wonder what your mother learned from her....and you say you know nothing of magic?"

I shook my head no, but I was starting to wish that I did.

A fresh layer of snow was starting to fall when we stopped, the temperature rapidly beginning to drop as the sun set. Stepping out of the carriage was a relief, regardless of the cold. My legs had begun to grow stiff and full of aches from lack of use.

I tried to appear as regal and dignified as I could while I waited for Roza outside the carriage. The blue dress and cloak helped my appearance; however, my demeanour, in my opinion, was surely a dead giveaway. I was unsure of how to carry myself as a woman, let alone a member of the nobility. I felt strange and awkward as we walked from the stables to the connecting inn.

This town was quite different from the last; the ravages of war were more evident at every turn, the situation much more desperate. It was as if it had been destroyed so many times that the townspeople stopped trying to put it back together.

Inside the inn, no one paid us any mind. The innkeeper treated us as upper class with money, and our room was more of what I'd expected our lodgings to look like.

Roza inspected the bed again, but this time there wasn't a good result.

"How on earth can someone sleep in a bed full of fleas?" she hollered. "I'll have to spend some hours trying to clean it, hours that should have been spent sleeping!"

She sighed deeply, and got down on her knees to look under the bed.

"We'll use the chamber pot, then I'll go for a quick walk and try to find some herbs for the bed. Would you care to join me?"

I nodded weakly and shrugged.

"—Or you could sit downstairs and eat," she suggested, "I won't be long. It will be good for you to be on your own for a while. Maybe you'll finally decide to speak. Come. I'll get you set up at a table before I leave."

We found a table in the back corner of the main floor of the inn. Very few people were there, and none of them looked up as I sat down. Roza ordered us both some food.

"I'll be quick as I can," she said, putting a hand on my shoulder before setting out. I was completely alone in a strange place and hadn't spoken in days but, oddly, I was not frightened. A tiny bit nervous perhaps, but not frightened.

A man with a heavy limp brought the food. His left eye was missing; he had a large scar running through the tightly shut lid. He reeked heavily of smoke and that special smell which I had begun to recognise as blood.

He brought two bowls of stew and some bread. The stew had a thick, clear layer of liquid on the top. I tasted it, and realised it was grease that the cook hadn't bothered to skim off. I would have to point that out to Roza before she ate. I dug my spoon down to the bottom and stirred the stew as best I could. Doing so helped enormously with the taste. I slowly ate small spoonfuls while I waited for her to return.

Meanwhile, I noticed a man watching me from across the room and tried very hard not to meet his gaze. He was big, and it appeared that he might have been a soldier at one time. It hadn't been that many years since the fighting had lessened, but the few years of present calm had certainly put weight on him.

He smiled at me, using one hand to scratch under his belly. I was a bit worried, being alone and a young woman, that he might do something. I tried to ease my mind with the thought that Roza would be back soon.

He said something I didn't understand, and seemed offended when I didn't reply. Roza would have to teach me this language, as it sounded like the same she spoke to the carriage driver.

"The man wants to know where your husband is, My Lady," the innkeeper said to me as he suddenly appeared beside my table.

"I am travelling to meet him now," I replied. I surprised myself that I had actually spoken those words aloud. The man said something else to the innkeeper, who chuckled.

"He says it's dangerous for a young woman like you to travel alone, and that he would gladly be your escort," he winked at me.

I smiled, feigning confidence. "Thank him for his generosity, but since I'm not travelling alone, he has no need to worry."

The innkeeper said something to the man, and I suddenly detected the one word I understood quite clearly.

"When you say 'witch,' are you referring to me or my companion, Sir?" I demanded. Both men stopped and turned to me. "Because you should be careful where you direct such accusations."

I stopped myself before I said more. I couldn't believe that the first thing I'd spoken in days was a threat, particularly one I had no ability to carry out. Fortunately, the two men pretended to ignore me and continued their conversation. Although I couldn't understand the words, I knew they were at my expense. I determined then and there that, when I became a more learned woman, I would avoid these sorts of situations.

So confused now by my own reaction to the man and the exchange that just took place, I tried to occupy myself with eating until Roza came back. She arrived a short time later after I had finished my food.

The innkeeper came over with two mugs of ale.

"I want to apologise for earlier, My Lady," he said to me. "Too much ale seems to lend itself to bad behaviour. No one believes either of you are witches."

"Thank you," Roza replied before I could. When he walked away, she turned her attention back to her food.

"S....st....st....," I tried to say 'stir' but all at once I couldn't. I had no idea why my power of speech suddenly left as soon as Roza appeared. I helplessly made the motion in the bowl.

"Oh! Yes, of course," she said, stirring the goulash for me. She leaned forward. "Did that man say something to you while I was gone?"

I nodded and tried to signal with my hands, like a puppet show, that we had argued.

"I'm not sure I understand, but it appears you defended yourself quite well," she mused. "I am also pleased to find you can speak when necessary."

I watched her eat; she said nothing more about the matter. There was no anger on her part. I simply sat and drank while she ate, like we had done so many times before, and then we retired to our room in silence.

Roza ground the herbs she had gathered and scattered the dust on the mattress after she had peeled back the covers.

She remade the bed and smiled at me, content with her work. "Perhaps now we may not get eaten alive in our sleep!"

As we had done in our first room, we shared the bed. I would not have had it any other way. She added logs to the fire so the room was quite warm when we got into bed.

"Goodnight, my dear," Roza said, finally settling in. "Soon enough, we shall be in Csejthe, where we can begin our new life."

The window slid open quite easily and it took little effort to lower myself down and onto the street. I did not realise I was awake and outside until my feet touched the ground, but I still felt as if I had no control of my own body and its movements.

I began to walk around the town; it was dark and very late and appeared to be deserted. I didn't know what I was looking for or if I would even find it, but I felt compelled to keep moving.

A large dark figure was lumbering towards me. I could tell it was a man and could smell the drink on him quite clearly.

"Unseemly for a young woman of your stature to be wandering the streets alone," he called out, "especially at night."

I recognised the voice: it was the man from the inn. It now seemed my body had found whatever it was looking for. He smiled at me, and I could see the desire swelling in his eyes. He grabbed me by the upper arm.

"I had a feeling you would come looking for me."

He pulled me closer to him; his breath was hot on my neck. I could smell that intoxicating scent under his skin, the one that had haunted me so, the one that I believed was blood. I wanted it, but it was so much more than that. I *needed* it.

He went to kiss my neck, and in the space of a blink, I had him by the head, biting down hard on his throat.

The blood exploded into my mouth and I drank with a fury I didn't know I possessed. His body lurched and heaved with what seemed to be both pleasure and pain, but he did not fight me. My hold on him was strong and steady—my one hand holding him by the neck, squeezing the blood from his jugular, my other hand now over his heart, feeling its rapid beat, gauging what life he had left in him. I could not stop myself, nor did I want to. This was a hunger that was more powerful than anything I had ever felt. As the blood poured down my throat, my body sprang to life with waves and waves of energy, so much so that I thought I might explode. I continued to swallow the thick, metallic fluid until there was no more, his body going limp and cold. Still in my grip, I lowered him to the ground. It was hard to separate myself from him; I could feel the warm blood trickle down from my mouth. Licking my lips, I finally took my mouth away from his neck and breathed deeply. It felt like I was taking my first breath. I felt like I had a new body.

I used the man's cloak to wipe the blood from my face. Thankfully, my dress wasn't dirty.

I knew I was supposed to be repulsed by what I had just done, and on one level I was, but for the most part I wasn't. It all seemed so natural, like breathing.

I stood up and began to head back to the inn. I didn't check to see if he was dead, for it seemed almost silly.

I climbed back in through the window and found all as it should be there. Roza's light snore was comforting. I put another log on the fire then returned to my place in the bed. She had not even noticed that I had moved.

I awoke the next morning to find Roza pacing in front of the fireplace. I thought I was surely found out and that we were in trouble.

"It's a bloody blizzard!" Roza exclaimed after she realised I was awake. "You can't see past the tip of your nose! We're stuck here until the snow clears."

That caused me some alarm, but I tried to appear calm.

"And why on earth did you leave the window open?" she demanded. "Do you want to catch your death?"

I opened my mouth to try to say something but again couldn't find the words. I wasn't sure how to explain that I drank a man's blood and did not know whether or not he was still alive.

"I have a horrible feeling about this place, Katrine," Roza continued warily, "like some evil is brewing. I may keep you in this room until it's time to go."

She began pacing again. I really wanted to say something now and was determined to try.

Suddenly, there was a sharp, quick knock; Roza whirled around as if to demand an answer from me, then threw open the door.

"I am sorry to disturb you, Madam," the innkeeper said, almost shaking in the doorway. "But there has been a tragedy in the town square. One of our regular patrons was attacked by some sort of animal last night. They found his body in the snow. You ladies should not go outside."

"Have they found the beast? Do they have any clue what it may be?" Roza asked cautiously.

"No one is sure. A wolf likely. It left a great hole in the man's neck, so please be careful."

"Thank you, sir. We appreciate the warning. I will be down to the kitchen for some food shortly," Roza said as she closed the door slowly.

She shot me a glare now, her eyes examining my face as if it was some sort of map. I tried to remain blank. She looked at the window, then back at me.

"Should I ask?"

I shook my head no, then suddenly smiled mischievously.

"Oh dear," she said, sighing. She returned to her pacing.

Deep in thought, she suddenly stopped, then turned and asked, "Was it the first?"

I slowly nodded, and she went back to pacing.

"S...S...Sit down, Roza. You're making me nervous," I forced the words out. Surprised, she stopped instantly and sat on the edge of the bed. "Everything is fine. I promise."

"It is not fine," she retorted. "This is all because of the scratch you received. It is changing you. We must get to Csejthe, for I am not strong enough to fix this on my own," Roza said worriedly. "The magic is too strong."

I sighed. "I told you I am fine. Truthfully, I have never felt better."

"You killed a man last night and drank his blood, Katrine. You are far from fine. But I cannot help you on my own."

"I don't need help!" my voice suddenly rang out clearly. "I feel wonderful and, besides, I think after what happened to my mother, this is what the Lord wanted."

Stunned at my response, Roza snapped,. "I hate to upset you, my dear, but the reality of this is that you are closer to Hades than anywhere the Lord may be. I hope you can hold off for a while now because, frankly, we may have some problems if bodies start to accumulate in this small town."

I didn't reply, just watched her and waited for her to say something else.

"Why did this happen?" Roza asked. "No, wait. What I meant was, did something compel you to do this? What on earth...."

"I don't know." I shook my head. "I got up, went out the window, and it just happened. It came over me. When we left the last town, something had changed inside me. When I smelt the blood, my body reacted before my mind could."

Her eyes grew wide with horror. "Do you not understand what you are? What you have become? And what you have done?"

Her words suddenly infuriated me.

"And did *you* not understand what could happen when you and those witches came for my mother and me?" I snapped.

Roza would not be blamed, however. "Whatever has happened is because of what your mother herself did during the ritual," she retorted.

"Don't you dare blame her!" I yelled. I started to rise from the bed, and Roza immediately shrank back in fear. I stopped myself when I realised what I was doing.

"I'm sorry, Roza. I'm not going to hurt you. None of those things matter now. What's important is that we go someplace where we are safe. We will then deal with this and whatever else is thrown at us."

"Yes. Yes, of course," she said, still watching me cautiously.

"Are you afraid of me, Roza?"

She hesitated for a moment before saying, "Should I be?"

"No, of course not. You are all I have. We're family now, and I would never hurt you."

I took her hand and held it in between both of mine, trying to comfort her.

"Thank you, child," she replied with tears in her eyes. "That means more to me than you will ever know."

We sat in silence for a while, until I finally asked, "Roza, what if they don't believe me?"

"What do you mean, child?"

"When we finally get to Csejthe…to the Countess, what if she doesn't believe me? What if she doesn't believe that I am her granddaughter and that my mother was her illegitimate child?"

Roza paused and then said, "I don't know, dear. I had not thought of that. However, I don't believe when they look at you there will be any question. The resemblance is uncanny."

We spent the remainder of the day in familiar silence.

VI.

Release

SNOW FELL ON AND OFF FOR A FORTNIGHT. ROZA KEPT
me in the room except for the occasional night down in the dining hall.
Fortunately, I did not have any more of what we had come to call an 'out
the window night'.

When the snow stopped for three straight days, we began to make
ready to leave. As we were gathering our things, there was a knock at the
door.

"Hello, Madam," the innkeeper said, wringing his hands. "I'm sorry
to disturb you. I was wondering if you and the young mistress would be
willing to attend a service in the town square. I am requesting this of all
my patrons."

"What sort of service?" I asked. I was not even aware of anyone else
staying at the inn.

"The local clergy have some concerns, and we would be honoured if
a member of the Báthory family was present," he explained.

"What sort of concerns?"

He sighed. "There is some worry that the attack some weeks ago was
a....I am a bit embarrassed to say it, but some think it was a *strigoi*. They
want to do something to help protect the town and its people."

"I could not participate in anything that could be considered witchcraft," I said firmly. I remembered our prior conversation about witches and tried not to smile.

"Oh no! It's nothing like that, I swear!" he declared. "The clergy are good Christian men and the service is all by the word of God. They will use the ancient rites to drive away the undead."

I smiled at that and said, "Then we would be honoured, good sir."

"Thank you, My Lady. We shall begin in one hour." He bowed and quickly took his leave.

"Are you sure that is wise?" Roza questioned me as soon as she had closed the door.

"I see no problem. Why would there be? I am no *strigoi*."

"We are not sure what you are, my dear, but I can't imagine this so-called service will do any good. I wonder if these God-fearing imbeciles will ever figure out that their prayers will not save them from a *strigoi*," Roza laughed to herself.

"I am alright, Roza. I have not had another 'out the window night', nor have I had the urge. We shall deal with the problems as they arise," I replied. "Now, I should wash my face before we go."

We headed into the town square with the other people coming out of the inn. Roza wrapped herself in a heavy shawl she had retrieved from the carriage.

"Roza, we shall get you a cloak," I said as we stepped outside. The sun was hurting my eyes.

"Ladies have cloaks. Their women have shawls," Roza said bluntly.

I turned to say something, but the sun was so irritating my thoughts were scattered. I used my hand to shield my eyes as we continued to the square, to the exact spot I had left the body. A wash of laughter passed so fervently through me that I had to bite my lip to conceal it.

A group gathered around three men who were standing higher than the rest; we stood near the back. The smallest of the three raised his hand to call attention. The prayers began, and I felt every muscle tense. The sun felt like searing heat, the kind one feels from standing too close to a fire. My body started to ache, my stomach twisted in knots.

I stood as still as I could manage even though I felt like screaming in agony. I was no *strigoi*, but my body was clearly not happy being outside.

"Katrine?" Roza whispered to me. I turned to look at her, gripping her upper arm for support. She pulled me closer.

"Lower your head so you appear devout. These people will have much to say if you appear ill."

"I think it's the sun," I managed to whisper through my gritted teeth.

"Are you sure?"

I sighed. "Roza, I know it's not the other..." I waved my hand in the direction of the priests.

"I think we should leave as soon as humanly possible," she murmured. "Weather be damned."

I took a few deep breaths to try to ease the tension, but it didn't help. The ache didn't lessen, and I felt like my body was becoming as solid as a rock.

After what seemed like an eternity the service ended; before anyone could stop us we were rushing back towards the inn. Strangely, my body began to relax once we were back inside.

Roza rushed quickly around our room now, gathering the few things we had brought inside while I stood in the doorway, breathing deeply.

As I braced myself on the side of the frame, I told her, "I think I'll be alright as long as I stay out of the sun. If it is too dangerous—"

"Then we shall face that danger, Katrine. Your condition is becoming too strange, and we need help," she said without looking at me. "Besides, we have lost too much time already."

After we settled our bills and headed towards the stables, Roza went ahead to find the boy. I could hear her yelling for him again; he came scurrying out and ran to beat us to the carriage.

"Nice to see you, Miss," he mumbled, opening the door for me. "Glad to be heading home."

I smiled and nodded. "Yes, dear boy. It's high time we left this place."

The carriage moved slowly and carefully through the mountains of snow. Any problems could halt us indefinitely, and we did not have time to waste. However, my concerns about what would happen when we arrived outweighed any I had about our journey.

"Only days now," Roza said after she wrapped us in the pelts found under the seat. "We may have to wait till we arrive to celebrate the Christmas holiday."

"Do you think we will get there in time?" I asked.

"I am not sure. The truth is that I am not even sure of today's date," she replied. "But the celebrations will last for some time at the castle. I'm sure they will even be extended when you are presented to the Countess."

"What will it be like?"

She smiled widely. "Better than you could possibly imagine. I am sure it will be one of the greatest experiences of your young life."

"I am looking forward to it," I said, closing my eyes until sleep took over.

I was jolted from my seat when the carriage came to an abrupt halt.

"What's happened, what's going on?" I demanded.

"I don't know," Roza answered worriedly. She was about to open the window when screams erupted.

"That's the boy!" she cried out. "Must be bandits."

"Well, we have to help him," I proclaimed. I tried to rise but she pulled me back down.

"Have you lost your mind? They could kill us both!"

"But are you going to drive if the boy is hurt?" I hissed back. "I will not stand by and do nothing while criminals hurt that poor boy!"

Before she could stop me, I was out the door and up to my knees in snow. All I could see was some shadowy figures on top and in front of the carriage, nothing clearly identifying what sort of people I was dealing with.

"Excuse me, kind sir," I shouted into the darkness, "but unless you have a explanation for stopping my carriage, we are in a hurry."

"Is that right?," a gruff, male voice called out from the darkness up ahead. "Well, I can't guarantee you will be reaching your destination, Missus. Especially with your carriage."

"If you plan to rob me, you could at least do me the honour of showing me your face," I called back. Meanwhile, Roza stared out at me in horror from the open doorway.

Two of the figures came towards me now, while one stayed back, holding tightly to something smaller and moving, which I assumed was the boy.

"Close the door, Roza," I said flatly.

"Not in this life!" she hissed.

I made eye contact with her and her eyes widened. Before she could say another word, I started towards the men, my body moving faster than my thoughts.

I didn't see their faces. I didn't need to. Instinctively, my body rose up out of the snow and landed on the one on the left, similar to the way an animal drops out of a tree to kill its prey. I bit down hard into his neck, harder than I had that first time. His blood gushed like a waterfall, blackening the snow beneath us. The bandit's body slackened before I let him drop, tearing a chunk out of his throat.

I spat the piece of flesh into the other man's horrified face before I reached over and grabbed him, as well. What good fortune, I thought to myself as I sated my sudden, bizarre thirst. I drank as much of his blood as I could manage before twisting his head until I heard his neck snap.

With relative ease, I tossed the limp body down beside his friend and turned in the direction where the boy was being held.

"Katrine!" Roza suddenly yelled from the carriage. "I have the boy here!"

I sighed in relief. While the third robber ran for his life, I cleaned myself off before climbing back inside the coach.

"Thank you for saving me, My Lady." Shaken but unharmed, the boy gratefully waved and called down to me as he took his seat.

"Of course, dear boy," I said. "Now, let's get moving!"

Inside, the cold was beginning to affect my legs, causing me some discomfort. Roza handed me a cloth when we were finally seated and on our way.

"I will do many things for you, Katrine," she said calmly, "but I will not clean your face after that. You will have to do that yourself."

I took the cloth from her, slightly irritated. "You make it sound as if I did something bad. Did I not just save us from disaster?"

"I am trying to pay no mind to the slaughter," she said with a shudder.

I leveled my gaze at her now. "Has your opinion of me changed, Roza? Have I frightened you?"

"No," she said quietly, "but I am a bit concerned about your situation."

I handed her back the blood-soaked rag, which she discarded out the window.

"Is my dress dirty?" I asked. She turned up the small lantern we had burning above us.

"Thankfully no," she replied. "But you should be more careful."

I could not help but laugh at this, and that was when she looked truly frightened.

"Oh, come now. You cannot tell me that it isn't a tiny bit funny," I said.

"It surely is not! I am being entirely practical, since you have so few... oh, dear," she said, covering her mouth in shame. She was now hiding a tiny smile.

"But you are correct, Roza. Making sure I keep my dress clean is practical, and I should be more careful.

***

"Katrine!," my mother's voice called as she shook me out of my sleep. I opened my eyes; we were seated inside the carriage. She was in the place where Roza had been sitting before I'd fallen asleep.

"What is it, Mother?" I asked.

"You have been sleeping for ages and I haven't been able to raise you," she said. "I was frightened."

"I am alright, Mother, just very tired. Where are we going?"

She smiled. "I have decided we shall go to see Countess Báthory."

"Why?" I asked. I sat up straighter, trying to focus on her and her excited face. She was so beautiful.

"Because if she is my mother then I think it's about time I introduced myself, and I hope we can give you a better life," she said proudly.

"What about Father? And Bodi?"

Her face hardened. "What about them? Your father let us go. No matter how hard he works he'll never be able to give you a decent dowry. He has his son, and now I have to do what is best for my daughter."

"But Bodi is your son, too, and I am also Father's daughter," I argued. "You should try to have the best for both of your children."

She turned away from me and said coldly, "Nikoli has his son. He will be happy."

She was hiding something from me, and I wasn't sure what. I knew my time with her was limited, and there was only one way I would figure it out.

"What are you hiding Mother?" I asked boldly.

"What do you mean?"

"You called me your daughter, and Bodi his son. But we are both your children," I replied. "I don't understand."

"You are my daughter, Katrine," she said evenly. "Do you understand that? You are my daughter."

"Are you saying father is not my father?" I questioned, panic now in my voice. "I don't understand. Am I illegitimate? Is Bodi my brother?"

She grabbed me forcefully and pulled me into her embrace, hugging me tight to her chest. I could hear her heart beating.

"Don't ever forget you are my daughter. Promise me, Katrine," she urged, and she sounded like she was crying. "Promise me that no matter what happens, you will never forget you are my daughter."

"I promise, Mother," I answered into her chest, not understanding. "I promise. I will never forget."

VII.

THE GREAT CHARGERS THAT PULLED OUR CARRIAGE had difficulty ploughing their way through the snow. We moved at a very slow pace so as not to stress them too much. Roza said we still had quite a way to go and the last thing we needed to happen was to lose the carriage.

After the incident with the bandits, we spoke nothing of my 'condition', and I felt no twinges or compulsions to act on my urges. I did not make any further mention of my fears about meeting the Countess or how her family might react to me. I began to lose track of time and the days going by.

The sunlight cast a glow off the snow-covered landscape, causing my eyes agonising pain. I remembered when I was a child, loving the blanket of warmth from the afternoon sun as it pushed its way through the trees. It had always been my favourite time of day, and the idea I might have to avoid it was unsettling.

Both windows were open, and I stayed out of the direct line of light. After some time staring blankly at the wall, Roza suddenly sat up and pointed out the window.

"Ah! Finally!" she called out happily, then called up something in a different language to the boy.

"We are here?" I asked hopefully.

"Yes, Katrine," she smiled happily. "We have finally arrived in Csejthe. We're going to take up residence at the inn, then prepare for your official entrance."

I was delighted. "I am so glad this journey is almost over," and sighed in relief.

"Almost over?" she declared, laughing. "My dear, this has been the easy part. We may be done with the physical travelling, but this is far from over. Only more complicated things are coming next."

Before I could ask what she meant by that, we began slowing our pace to almost a crawl before fully stopping. The boy hollered something, and Roza stuck her head out the window again to hear him. When she pulled her head back inside she looked panicked.

"Is something wrong?" I asked.

"It appears we have drawn a crowd," Roza murmured.

"What, in this weather?"

She gathered our things into a bundle. "You must remain composed, Katrine. You are a noble lady now."

All the people that circled around us surprised me. They were of all ages and classes, with a small group near the back that I recognised as gypsies. As we descended from the carriage, they watched me with suspicion, all of them, as I followed Roza through the flurried paths. I wondered what they were thinking, if they had lost a daughter, if one of their own had vanished while in the Countess' service. I wondered if they recognised the carriage, or Roza. These people were apprehensive. Something was wrong here.

I could see that some of the snow had been cleared from the streets; small paths from place to place connected the village. The two-story stone and wood buildings appeared weighed down by the snowfall which laid in masses on the rooftops. I could suddenly see in my mind where the girls had stood in the square, hoping for work at the Countess's castle.

As we approached the inn, I noticed a large, heavyset couple blocking the doorway.

"Do you have a vacancy?" Roza inquired of them.

"Yes, we do," the man replied finally. "Please come in."

We followed them inside, and the first thing I noticed was how clean the main floor of the inn was. The dark wood panelling gave it a luxurious feel, and I was drawn immediately to a portrait of a woman hanging over the immense fireplace.

Her dark eyes were haunting, penetrating, adding depth to her stoic expression. Her petite lips were perfectly formed with a small, polite nose. Her features were framed by her large white collar, a ruffled halo round her neck. The dark hair, the colour in stark contrast to her pale skin, was pulled away from her face in a style decorated with pearls. She was beautiful, adorned in a simple dress with white sleeves, skirt, and dark-coloured bodice that enhanced her appearance, highlighting certain features. She was slender, with exquisite, delicate hands.

My mother had once told me that attractive hands were a desirable trait in a woman, so they were often highlighted in portraits. This woman was so grand looking; I had never seen anyone quite like her. I couldn't take my eyes off her, no matter how hard I tried. The innkeeper noticed this and approached me.

"It is a good rendering of Countess Erzsébet Báthory, the Lady Nádasdy," he said heavily, "or the Widow Nádasdy, whichever you prefer."

It seemed fitting, as I looked into this woman's eyes, that she was the woman that brought my mother into this world—my own grandmother and the very woman we had come to see. The resemblance was indeed uncanny, as Roza had said.

"May I ask how old this portrait is?"

"I believe it is from when she was first married," he replied, and there was a definite edge in his voice now.

I said nothing. I simply stood there and admired her until I felt Roza's hand on my arm, guiding me to our room.

"Something doesn't seem right," Roza said when we were finally alone.

"What do you mean?"

"I don't think I can explain," she replied. "But the way the people looked at us, their faces. Something seems amiss."

"So what shall we do?"

She put the bundle of our things on the seat beside the window. "You shall stay here while I go out and ask some questions. Maybe I will try to find Jo Ilona. Get some rest or go down to the common room, but whatever you decide, please don't go out into the village until I return."

"Do you think something is seriously wrong?" I asked, sitting on the edge of the bed.

"I am not sure. Better that I find out than you. Promise me you will stay here."

"Of course," I nodded.

Roza pulled her shawl tightly around her body and left. I was alone again for the first time in weeks.

I sat by the window, out of direct sunlight, and watched the goings on in the town square. I watched a mother walking through the snow with her daughters, one about my age and the other older and frail looking, with an expression of pure sadness on her face that I could see even from my second story window. I was confused, sad for the daughters and their situation but also wishing I could have one more moment of that common life with my mother.

After some time, Roza finally returned looking flushed, with a deep scowl on her face.

"There appears to be something very troubling afoot."

"Such as?"

"Rumours," she replied angrily, "of horrible things. More viscous lies of things going on at the castle."

"Of what sort?"

"They claim the Countess is murdering her servants!" she yelled at me. "That all those times I was helping find girls for service, they were being taken in to be tortured and murdered!"

"But why? Why would she do something so horrible?"

Roza sat on the bed trying to catch her breath. I had heard stories of the cruelty of the Báthory, legends of demon possession amongst not just the men but the women as well, but torture and murder of servants?

"I'm sure I have told you that the Countess is very strict, but she would never torture or kill anyone!" Roza insisted.

I tried to calm her. "There is nothing we can do at this moment. We just have to wait until we can go to the castle and see for ourselves."

"Yes," she sighed, but she was still furious.

The rhythmic sound of scratching stirred me from my sleep. It reminded me of the sound of horse hooves on the ground as they walked.

I sat up in bed and looked around; my mother was sitting by the fire.

"What's the trouble?" I asked her.

She kept her eyes on the flames. "I don't feel right, Katrine."

"You never told me if Grandmother passed on," I said. She turned to me, and her eyes were red as if she had been crying.

"Yes, my dear," she nodded, turning back to the fire. "Kristina has passed. It seems strange to call her mother after all of this."

"But she sacrificed her life so you could have one. You should honour her memory, at least."

A smile crossed her face. "You are wise, child."

"Did Grandmother teach you magic?" I suddenly asked.

She said nothing and remained turned away from me.

"It seems strange that you would not tell me the truth after all of this," I went on, and it felt odd to be so direct with her. The small amount of time I had with her loosened my tongue, however.

She sighed loudly. "She taught me everything about life, but what aspects of it could be considered magic I am not sure. I was young and knew no different."

"Did you ever ask her?"

"Not directly," she began, "but when I had questions about church and the Lord that she could not answer, I became suspicious."

"So, she did not believe?"

"No! She did! But she believed in the old Christian ways, the orthodox ways

which are different than what we know now. There has been much change in the church since I was young."

"Do you miss her?"

"More now since I have so many questions," she mused. "But I had missed her since long before she died."

"I wish I had known her better," I muttered. "Why didn't I?"

The scratching got louder, like a knife dragging through wood.

"Do you hear that?" I asked.

"Hear what?" she replied. "I only hear the fire."

I got up and went to the door, pausing for a moment with my hand around the knob. Was I prepared for what lay on the other side? I tried to brace myself for a possible attack, as I turned the knob and flung open the door.

A monstrous beast stood in the hallway before me, parts of it illuminated by the glow of the fire. Immediately, I recognised it from that fateful night. It had the face and the muzzle of a wolf but was much larger. Standing on two feet, it was bigger than I was; it may even have been double my size. I could not see the whole length of the animal, but I could see its eerie red eyes, massive maw, glistening pointed teeth, and the most enormous paws I had ever seen. I was frozen as our eyes locked.

The beast lifted one paw as if it was reaching out to me. My heart suddenly ached, and I couldn't stop myself from crying. I stuck out my hand; I wanted to hold that paw as I would have held my mother's hand. The two couldn't possibly be one in the same! They were both in the same place at the same time, yet it just wasn't possible. I tried to pull my hand away but I couldn't. It was coming closer now....

I was startled out of sleep, covered in a cold sweat. The scratch on my arm was throbbing and itching. I went to the washbasin hoping the water would soothe it. It was sore to the touch, and the skin around it rose into a bump. The scratch itself seemed deeper than the last time I cleaned it. Somehow, it had become inflamed again.

I cleaned it the best I could with the little light left from the dying fire and went back to bed. There was no point in waking Roza. We could dress it properly in the morning.

VIII.

Grișa

THE DAY BEGAN LIKE ANY OTHER.

We rose early, a habit Roza and I had started so we could include as much in the day as possible. I had many things to learn before I made my entrance at the castle.

Rumours were already travelling around the village about the goings on behind the castle walls. Indeed, we did our best to keep to ourselves and not attract any further attention. We sent the carriage driver out to run our errands and mostly kept to the inn.

A few days prior, Roza had some fabric sent up from town. She had decided to try her hand at making me a dress. A new shift and petticoat accompanied the shiny blue fabric, which was thick enough for winter but would also do well in warmer weather. I wondered about where the money came from, but said nothing to her. She seemed so happy with the idea, and I didn't want to spoil it.

At night, when the inn was quiet, Roza had been teaching me simple magic—useful spells—things she said would be helpful in a time of need. I had also begun to learn new things about plants and herbs that had nothing to do with food. I prayed to God every night not to view this instruction as witchcraft..

After we rose that morning, Roza finished fitting the bodice on the dress so she could do the sewing work while we ate in the common room. We dressed and went downstairs. I sat in a place where I could look out the window and, if I turned my head, would have a good view of the Countess' portrait. I enjoyed the idea that she was with us while we dined.

"Roza," I began, "I was wondering if you remembered when I asked about learning to read?"

She paused, raising her eyes to me for a moment. "Yes, I do. And what of it?"

"Do you think you shall have time to teach me before we go to the castle?" I asked, lowering my voice. Even though we were alone in the common room, we could not take the chance of being overheard.

"We have more important things to deal with, Katrine," she shook her head. "When you are accepted, your education will become top priority, since it will help in finding you a good husband. For now, it is important that you learn some basic spells rather than letters."

"And what if I do not wish to be married?"

She laughed. "I'm not sure anyone wishes to be married, child."

"Yes, but considering my condition, I am not sure it would be wise."

"We will worry about that when it happens," she replied, focusing intently on her sewing. I stared out the window and my mind began to wander.

The innkeeper brought us a plate of bread and cheese. He caught my attention as I heard the plate touch the table. I tried to put what Roza had said out of my mind. She had promised that she would teach me to read, given me her word, and now she appeared to be breaking that promise as if it meant nothing. Learning to read was my dream, one of the few dreams I had left after everything that had happened. I tried to put the anxious thoughts out of my head.

"Do you think if I made sure my skin was covered I could go outside today?"

Roza sighed loudly. "You've asked me the same question every day,

Katrine. Unless you can find a Turkish parasol to hold over your head to block out the sun, you must stay inside."

The first tiny flecks of snow appeared past the window, barely visible but quite beautiful as they fell to the ground. Even though it was wet and cold, I actually liked snow. It had a way of making the world look like it was wiped clean with a pure, white blanket.

I turned my attention back to Roza, who was still deeply engrossed in her sewing. I thought of returning upstairs alone, my anger at her creeping back to the surface. She seemed to have a clear idea of the direction my life would take once the Countess accepted me, and I was unsure how I felt about it. After all that had happened, I could not stomach the idea that I did not get to decide what my own life would be like.

"Where are you going?" Roza asked as I stood up to leave.

"I don't feel much like sitting here. I'm going back upstairs," I said.

"Why on earth would you do that? There is less to do up there than down here."

"I will do as I please, thank you," I snapped, heading off towards the stairs.

"Maybe it will give you time to practice your curtsey," Roza retorted.

"I think I'd rather go for a walk," I shot back, heading boldly out into the sunshine.

I quickly went into the square, not bothered by the cold. I wanted to go someplace where I could see the castle, assume a vantage point from where I might be able to assess what was going on and think in silence. Roza's broken promise was burning me inside, and my body was beginning to feel as it had that night I jumped out the window and killed that man.

I needed some sort of a plan, something I could follow through on alone, if necessary. I could not rely on Roza forever, and I had to accept that. If the Countess accepted me, I would be taken from her, anyway.

I had been walking for quite a while, deep in thought, when I realized

I had already reached the outskirts of the castle. If I walked along the outskirts, I could approach the castle without attracting attention. Once moving, I forgot about the sun and the cold, my head clearing as I developed a steady pace.

I circled back behind, keeping my head low. As I got closer to the castle, I noticed a small patch of forest. I stepped into it and walked toward a small clearing. At its edge, I found an open view of the castle, along with a large rock for me to sit on. It seemed oddly perfect, as if someone had set it that way on purpose.

The castle was made of light coloured brick that blended into the snow. It sat on a hill; the surrounding wall was taller at the lower part of the hill and grew shorter as it circled the higher ground. A single main tower stretched into the foggy clouds; I wondered how far one could see from the top window. If I ever got into the castle, if it ever became my home, I would go stand at that spot as often as I could. The world would be a very different place from such a viewpoint.

The castle seemed quiet, as if empty now. I suddenly had a horrible feeling in the pit of my stomach, an overwhelming sense of fear.

This place was supposed to solve my problems, be the answer to all my prayers. Yet the idea that the Countess might not accept me continued to trouble me, that it was possible all of this had been for nothing.

Meanwhile, what had begun as a light sprinkle of snow earlier in the day was now beginning to pick up, which meant it was time to go back.

I grudgingly stood up, taking one last, hard look at the castle. I decided in that moment I would do everything possible to speak with the Countess and tell her my story. I had no other option.

Making my way out of the forest now, all at once I heard someone or something walking behind me in the snow. I stopped to listen: the heavy tread made me wonder if Roza had followed me. Turning around, I saw nothing; she would hide from me, I thought. As I strained to see, I could make out strange prints that quickly faded in the falling snow.

I picked up my pace. I could still hear what sounded like the trot of four paws keeping up with little effort. I stopped suddenly and turned again, catching a glimpse of the back end of some large animal.

Without a second thought, I hiked up my skirts and ran.

I didn't care who saw me. All that mattered in that instant was putting as much distance between the beast and myself as I could.

I had not done what I had set out to do. I had not thought of a plan, and if I got back to the inn and Roza was gone, I had no idea what I would do.

I ran as fast as I could. A plan would be of no help if I were dead.

I ran through the square, back into the inn and straight to our room, slamming the door behind me.

"Katrine?" Roza rushed over to me. I hunched over, trying to catch my breath. "Katrine? What's wrong? Where did you go?"

"I went for a walk," I gasped, "and something was chasing me."

Roza looked very afraid now. "Soldiers?"

I took a deep breath and shook my head. "No. An animal of some sort."

"Wolves?"

"I don't know. I didn't get a clear look. But it was rather large."

"Do you think it could be—" she began, and then waved her hand. "No, no. Never mind. It couldn't be."

"Couldn't be what? I don't understand."

"I was going to ask if you thought it might be *the* beast, if it could have followed us all the way here."

She paused, then picked up something off the bed and held it up, trying to distract me.

"Forget about it now. You are safe."

She then held up the dress triumphantly.

"You finished the dress already?" I asked.

"Yes," she replied. "Now, come try this on."

The thick blue fabric felt softer than I imagined as I slipped on the dress. I was truly impressed by how well it fit.

"Perfect!" Roza exclaimed, looking on admiringly.

The moment was suddenly broken by a high-pitched voice.

"Father! Father!" I heard a boy yell from below. I quickly slipped back into my gray dress, and we hurried downstairs. The innkeeper was rushing to the front door, where a boy stood who couldn't have been much older than Bodi. I had not known the proprietor had a son.

Darkness had fallen by now, and the boy stood amidst patrons who had gathered in the inn for dinner.

"What is it, boy?" the innkeeper demanded.

"The castle, the manor house," the boy cried out, trying to catch his breath. "The Palatine and his men have raided the castle!"

"What? Why? What about Countess Báthory?"

"She has been arrested along with three of her women and her man servant!"

I started toward the center of the room, Roza close at my heels.

"What's the charge?" I demanded.

He looked nervously at me. "Murder," he choked, "for torturing and killing her servant girls. It's being said that soldiers found a girl drained of blood in the great room, dead, and another still alive in the dungeon, pierced with holes!"

Roza and I exchanged a brief glance; I was feeling light headed.

"The Palatine took the servants away but the Countess is being held prisoner in her castle," the boy said to his father.

At this, Roza grabbed my arm and rushed me back up the stairs to our room.

"Why did they not take her?" I cried.

Roza tossed her sewing basket off the bed. "What are you rambling about, girl? Spit it out, for God's sake!"

"Why did they not take the Countess away with her servants when they were arrested?" I anxiously asked.

"To avoid a scandal," she said angrily. "But this is an outrage! These charges are disgusting and false!"

"The boy said they found a dead body in the great room, Roza."

"A venomous lie! The boy is just regurgitating rumours," she declared, pacing around the room. "I shall go to the castle and see for myself what has happened."

I grabbed her arm. "So they can arrest you, as well? Have you gone mad?"

She stopped and stared at me coldly, studying my face.

"Why would you say such a thing?" she wanted to know.

"It seems obvious to me. You are known to be one of the Countess' women; you arrive here with me in a Báthory carriage under a cloud of secrecy, then appear at the castle asking questions? It doesn't make sense. They would arrest us both simply because of who they think we might be. I may not understand the ways of the world or be very smart, but even I have enough common sense to know that!"

Roza's worried expression immediately shifted to anger. She slapped me hard across the face.

"How dare you! What would you know about the world, you stupid girl! Do you not understand we are lost now?" she hollered in my face.

Before I could think twice, an overwhelming instinct took hold of me: I struck her with a fierce blow, and she crumbled to the floor.

"Don't you ever hit me again!" My voice was like a low growl now. "Who are you to hit me!"

She remained on the floor clutching her cheek, as I circled her.

"Roza, if you want to put yourself at risk, that's your choice, but you will not make that decision for me! Do you understand? We will lay low and wait it out. If these charges are false, I am sure it will end soon."

I looked upon the crumpled figure. The woman who had once frightened me so, and for whom I felt such childish love, was now nothing more than a common servant.

"Go back to the main room and listen to the gossip if you feel so inclined," I sneered.

She got up and left without another word. In that instant, I knew I would survive, even if she never came back. I had become a monster. Just like my mother.

It seemed like Roza was gone for hours. I eventually started a new fire in our hearth and, by the time it was roaring, Roza returned, saying nothing to me. Out the window was pure blackness.

"Is there news?" I finally asked.

"No," she said, looking uncomfortable. "The Countess is being held at the castle, and Dorka, Jo Ilona, Katarina Benicka and Ficzko are in prison in the town of Bytca."

"So they have names now?"

"Excuse me?"

"The servants who were arrested: before, they didn't have names. Now they do. Were they your friends?"

"I don't know if friend is the proper word," Roza said thickly, "but I know them. I worked with them quite closely."

Her voice low and flat. I remembered in that moment that those were the same people she had spoken of when she'd told me stories about the Countess and her castle. Roza looked about to cry now, and my feelings for her suddenly softened. The rage had passed, and I was myself again.

"I am sorry, Roza," I said quietly, biting back my own tears now as I approached her. I understood loss. I still felt close to her and, at the moment, we had no one but each other.

"No need, my dear," she replied, and her voice sounded tired. "Your loss was just as great. We must cling to each other and hope to come through this unscathed."

"We shall, I am sure of it," I assured, holding her hand in both of mine.

She sighed. "Then your determination will be what sustains us, Katrine."

My vision was blurry at first, tired and overwhelmed by the strain. It took a moment for my eyes to re-adjust after being in the candlelight and smoke for so long. I had to stay within the confines of the church until darkness fell. No matter how much I tried to fight it, my difficulties with sunlight were only getting worse.

We went to the church along with the other townspeople every day since the arrest. Many were praying for the souls of the condemned, Countess Báthory's servants who had been taken to Bytca for trial. Meanwhile, Roza and I were listening for any hint of information.

We learned that Darvulia had been mentioned often during the interrogations and torture, the witnesses saying she had been dead for several years. A woman they called 'the forest witch', a certain Erza Majorova, the Mistress of Miava, was also in custody. Supposedly, she helped the Countess make cakes used to try to poison the King and the Palatine. And yet, these two were the very same witches, along with Roza, who had taken my mother and me. I continually pondered how this was even possible, how the witches could be in two places at once, let alone one of them dying more than once—unless the witnesses were lying about them.

Roza said very little through all of this and, luckily, she wasn't mentioned in the town gossip.

The Countess was quite notably absent. The talk going around was that she would be tried separately because of her status, but they all seemed to know that she would not receive the same fate as her accomplices. Her noble family would likely send her to a convent, possibly out of the country, to live out the rest of her days.

However, the people of Csejthe wanted blood. Her blood. It seemed they thought it was a divine right. Unfortunately, the world did not work that way. She would likely not bleed for those they had lost.

The stares at us had worsened these past few days; my resemblance to the Countess must have been stronger than even I had imagined. It connected me to her, even though the townspeople had no idea who I was, and it seemed like they hated her. Likely, they hated me, as well, as a result of that. I would have to accept this, since it seemed to be a consequence of my new fate.

As we were exiting the church, the priest informed all who were present that the executions would take place the next day by the river in Bytca. Roza's face went deathly pale, and a voice called out, wondering if the Countess would receive that fate also.

"No," the priest replied coldly, almost angry. "That is still undecided."

Outside of the church, a few of the men announced they would be taking carts to Bytca, for any who would like to attend the execution and in need of transportation. For a moment, I thought of taking our own carriage, but the Báthory seal on the door made that an impossibility now. I listened carefully to the time and the place to meet, then headed back to the inn with Roza on my arm. We would likely have to go in disguise.

As neither of us could eat, we retired to our room.

We moved around in silence that night, and I had no idea what to say to comfort her. I could not imagine what she must have been thinking.

Ironically, for the first time since that bizarre night in the forest, I was afraid. When we finally went to bed, I fell into a dreamless sleep.

IX.

I COULD SMELL FIRE AS WE RODE INTO BYTCA. WE SAT on the back of a hay cart, our faces covered, along with a small group of people who could not contain their excitement. My stomach was turning and Roza clung tightly to my hand.

"We do not have to go," I said quietly, for the fifth time since we'd left the inn.

"No, we must," she replied sharply.

The cart had come to a stop and she pulled me off in the direction of the crowd. A massive flaming pyre was erected by the river, the tips of the flames and black smoke stretching into the clouds.

Roza and I stood at the side of the gathering crowd, where we had a clear view of a hooded man sharpening an axe. My stomach ached. I was as horrified by the idea of this situation as I was by the size of the crowd gathered here to watch.

The prisoners were sitting, almost in a heap, shackled together: two older women and a small man.

"That's Ficzko," Roza told me, gesturing to the dwarf. "Dorko and Jo Ilona. Katarina is not there. Maybe she's already dead, or free. No, they would not have set her free."

I wasn't sure which woman was which, and I could not ask Roza. The prisoners' eyes were wide and empty; the fair-haired woman stared out into the distance. Ficzko appeared angry and defiant. Roza was clearly frightened by him, even though he was locked in chains. She clung so tightly to my hand I thought my fingers would break.

However, Roza had stayed with me when my mother turned into a monster; if she wanted to watch this happen, I would stay with her.

The priest from Csejthe appeared at the front of the crowd. The pain in my stomach got worse as the executioner walked over to the prisoners. My body stiffened and it hurt to breathe. The executioner then went over to the fire, while the fair-haired woman was pulled forward. I could not get a clear view of what he was doing, but the executioner pulled some sort of object from the flames with a gloved hand.

"The court has passed its judgment, but now it is in the hands of our Lord. Pray for the damned, good people, and may God have mercy on their souls," the priest called out to the crowd. I could not understand how these people could seem so excited by this spectacle of torture and death, but I knew nothing of what they had suffered. We had overheard that the Countess and her people were convicted of killing sixty or so young girls, the number rising each time the story was told. It was obvious that one dead child was far too many.

Roza's grip tightened as we watched the fair-haired woman, whose hands were stretched out. The executioner grabbed one of her fingers with what I now saw were heated tongs. The smell of burning flesh grew stronger as he pulled her finger out and tossed it into the flames. The noise of the cheering crowd drowned out the cries of the condemned woman. The smell of fresh blood started to overpower me, and it took everything I had not to lose control.

When the fourth finger was removed, the fair-haired woman fainted. The executioner struck her on the head with a sickening thunk, then threw her body into the fire.

"Why is she not screaming?" Roza asked me as we watched the body engulfed by the flames. The condemned woman did not move or fight, so the blow to the head had most likely killed her. Surely if it hadn't, the flames would have revived her. Perhaps God had intervened on her behalf at the last minute.

They had some difficulty rousing the other woman, who had fainted after watching what had previously happened. With much less pomp and circumstance, they pulled out her fingers, as well. Another blow to the head, and the second woman was cast into the fire. Roza's body jerked violently when the flames erupted anew.

Another cheer went up from the crowd, and Roza let out a sob. She began to shake violently. I wanted to hold and comfort her, but I was not sure I could. She dug into her apron and handed me a kerchief, putting one over her own face. At the pungent smell of burning flesh, I did the same, even though it didn't do much good.

Nothing could cover the smell of burning death.

The executioner grabbed Ficzko and yanked him forward. I was certain it broke some of his bones. He was pushed down and kicked in the ribs with an unnecessary amount of force. The executioner's large, gloved hand pulled the axe from the ground, and he clutched it by the heavy handle. As Ficzko's head went down on the block, his neck exposed, the axe rose up then struck down hard.

Blood squirted in the air as the axe rose and fell, again and again; it took four blows to take off Ficzko's head.

I could suddenly taste sulphur in my mouth, my stomach lurching wildly. The executioner lifted the head by the hair and showed it to the delighted crowd. Then he casually tossed it into the flames along with the small body.

"I am deeply sorry, Roza, but we must go now," I said urgently. She stared at the fire, as if she hadn't heard me.

"Roza, the blood," I said, coughing. "I have to go."

She didn't move, and did not even realise she was being spoken to. She was somewhere else entirely.

Desperate now, I dropped her hand and ran back to the cart. I sat in the back with some of the other people, covering my face. It had been too long since I'd had blood and another second could have caused a scene more horrific than any execution. I tried to focus on my breathing, keeping my face covered as the cart started to move.

Roza needed time alone, and I would give it to her. I was sure she could find her way back to the inn; also, this was my problem, and I needed to learn how to handle it by myself.

She did not return until much later. I assumed she had stayed until the great execution fire had burned to a pile of ash. Her face was pale, her eyes cold and empty. She looked as my mother had when she returned to my father's house after tending to her sick mother. It seemed somehow ironic that such faces surrounded both of my grandmothers.

"Are you alright, Roza?" .

"I am," she said. "Are you?"

"Yes, I suppose."

Roza tilted her head backward, as if she were trying to shake off the horror of the day. I approached her now.

"Roza, I have a plan."

"For what, my dear?"

I took a deep breath, and stated firmly, "I am going to the castle to speak to the Countess."

Exasperation immediately lined her face. "It's not as easy as it may sound, Katrine," she said tiredly. "The Countess has been confined to the castle and is awaiting her fate. She may not be able to receive visitors."

"This confinement business," I continued. "Do you think it involves a large number of guards?"

"I, I don't know," she replied. "I suppose. Why, what on earth are you planning?"

"A visit with her," I affirmed. "Getting in to see her will give me the opportunity to use the magic you taught me."

"I can do no more today, Katrine," Roza said, exhausted, sitting on the bed. "I barely have the strength to stand."

"I had planned to go alone," I said quickly.

"When?"

"I shall be at the castle by dawn."

She took a deep breath and stood up. "There is nothing more I can do, then. Very well, you will be washed and fed before you go, and we shall do one final test of etiquette. That much I can do."

Night came quickly and, by the time the sun was beginning to rise, I was ready to go. I left Roza sleeping as I put on the dress she had made for me, and I used a piece of string to hang my father's enamel cross from my neck. I opened our window which, thankfully, looked out onto the forest, and bundled myself in my cloak.

"Katrine."

Roza's voice startled me. "I'm sorry. I tried my best not to wake you—"

"I was not really sleeping. I just wanted to wish you good luck," she said. "You look beautiful."

I moved back towards her and hugged her tightly. "I will be fine. We will *both* be fine. Leave the window open for me."

I went back to the window and, without looking back, lowered myself out into the early morning sun.

X.

The Countess

I TRIED TO STAY CONSCIOUS OF MY SURROUNDINGS, moving quickly towards the road that led to the castle. I pulled up my skirts trying to keep the bottom of my dress dry; luckily, the snow was not too deep. A cold chill drew a line up my back, reminding me of the feeling I had when the witches first appeared, when my life changed. And when I thought more deeply, I realised it was the moment I had lost my mother.

The silence that I noticed that day in the woods was all consuming. The lack of activity in the castle was evident as I approached the gate. There wasn't even a watchman on the wall, and that made it easy for me to slip past and into the empty courtyard.

The first thing I noticed was the tower and, part of the way up, a dark window. I wondered if the Countess was being kept up there. My back and shoulders suddenly felt heavy, as if the world had just put all its weight upon me.

I headed for the only door I could find. I did not have time to waste.

I went through the ground level of the castle still without coming across anyone. I was overwhelmed by the smell of death, hanging like a heavy cloud of smoke in every room. The heady scent of blood took form as a presence in the room, as if it were another person standing beside me. Once grand rooms were stripped down, almost bare, the enormous stone fireplaces empty and cold. I could only imagine what had once been, but could not risk standing still to dwell on these thoughts.

As I ascended the stairs, I sensed four people close by. I stopped before I reached the top, preparing some of the herbs I had in a pouch attached to my waist. Creeping up the last few steps, I recited the incantation Roza had taught me and blew the contents of my palm out in front of me. The herbs turned into a fine mist that drifted out into the air. If the spell worked, in several minutes whoever was around me would be fast asleep for several hours.

I waited a few moments then crept through the hallway, until I found the corridor guarded by three armed men. Two were already snoozing on the floor and one was slouched over in a chair. Securing a large key from one of the sleeping guards, I tiptoed past them to the door at the end of the corridor. The spell had worked quite well; unfortunately, I had not thought what to do if the spell had put the Countess to sleep, as well.

Making my way to a large oak door, I could hear a rhythmic sound coming from inside, the tap of someone's shoes moving deliberately across the stone floor. It sounded as if someone was pacing.

Quietly unlocking the door, I stepped into the threshold of her chamber, my eyes focusing immediately upon the statuesque figure that had stopped in front of the room's only window. I could hardly believe that I was actually here, standing before the Countess herself. This now infamous woman was my noble grandmother, the woman who, at this very moment, had the power to either save my life or quite possibly end it.

She turned toward me and my heart jumped into my throat as I dropped into a low curtsey, the tip of my nose almost touching the floor. It was so quiet I could hear her startled breath from across the room.

With my head still bowed, I managed to raise my eyes slightly to catch a glimpse of her. She was beyond beautiful. Ageless.

"Who are you?" her strong and steady voice commanded.

"Your…Your Ladyship, if I may have the opportunity to explain…" I stuttered.

"What on earth could you have to explain to me?" she said, her voice full of contempt. I stayed perfectly still; I dared not move and risk angering her in some way.

"Well, spit it out, girl! Do not waste my time," she snapped. She did not ask, however, how I'd managed to gain access to her locked and guarded chambers.

"I believe I am your granddaughter, My Lady," I said with as much confidence as I could muster, still maintaining my respectful genuflection.

"The product of one of my husband's indiscretions!" she exclaimed. I could hear the swoop of her heavy silk skirts brush the floor as she turned away in disgust. "Well, I hate to disappoint you, but he is long dead and I cannot—I *will not*—help you."

"No! No! It's not what you think! Please, My Lady. Allow me to explain," I countered, surprised by my bold reply. She paused and turned back around, raising her hand in a curt gesture, signaling me to stand.

"Fine. I could use the amusement. Explain yourself."

I took a deep breath and slowly rose. I closed my eyes out of fear and respect, and began: "Before you were married, I believe you gave birth to a daughter in the year 1574, in a remote castle in the mountains. The baby was given to a midwife and they were banished from Hungary—"

"Oh, you believe that, do you? And did this baby have a name?" she demanded, her voice cold and approaching anger. I desperately hoped I had not gotten the information wrong; it was all Roza knew and I had been practicing it for weeks. I was so afraid, I was shaking; I prayed she did not notice.

"Anastasia," I replied solemnly. "My mother was christened Anastasia."

Silence. Deafening silence. With my eyes still closed, my mind was now racing, and the fear began to consume me. I was preparing not only for the pain of rejection, but also for the pain of her wrath.

"Why have you come?" Her strained voice cut through the silence.

Could she be crying? It took all I had not to run to her and finally look upon her face.

"I have nothing. I cannot help you, or her," the Countess finally said. "As you can plainly see, I have been reduced to nothing."

"My Lady, all I wanted was to meet you."

"What is your name, child?"

"Katrine, Your Ladyship."

"Katrine," she said, softly. "Katrine, please come closer so that I may see you."

I opened my eyes, tears welling within them, and eagerly obeyed. Our eyes met, and I had a flash of being a child and looking up into my mother's face. The family resemblance was uncanny, almost frightening. The Countess' dark gaze was so much like hers, so penetrating I felt like she could see inside my soul. I was mesmerised.

The Countess smiled. The expression lit up her porcelain skin, which was so perfect, one could never guess her age. Her elegantly shaped face was like a beautifully carved image, her dark eyes holding a gilt of something mysterious and forbidden.

"My, my. You are a beautiful young girl," the Countess mused, appraising me now.

She walked around me so she could examine me fully. The intense look on her face was unsettling, but I did not want to stop her from looking at me. Her gaze drew me in, her commanding presence was awe inspiring. She cupped my chin with her hand, her touch cold, the soft pad of her thumb running along my jawbone. It sent shivers through my body. Her touch activated something inside me, her underlying scent bringing forth the well of feelings I'd had when I'd taken fresh blood. Waves of warmth rose up from deep within me. My skin began to flush, my breath shortened, and my body overcome with strange feelings that I'd never had before. I desperately wanted her approval and felt a comfort with her that I did not understand. I wondered if this charm, this power she had when she simply looked at you was part of what made her infamous. Part of why she was so feared. I could not help but think of the girls she had apparently killed, wondering if they had succumb to the primal desire to give themselves to her, to be absolutely obedient, to hand themselves over, body and soul that radiated off her body like an otherworldly energy.

The new part of me that was awakening responded to her as an equal, the connection running deeper than simple familial relation. Were we so much the same? She took her hand away from my face, and suddenly I snapped out of my stupor and became very aware and ashamed of my thoughts. Dear God, what was I doing? How could I think such things or feel that way about her? What on earth was she?

"One of the prettiest girls I have ever seen," she remarked, and I saw something in her eyes as her mood quickly switched. "—And of Báthory blood, without a doubt. God sending you here shows that He does indeed still care and has not turned his back on me completely. Where is your mother?"

I stared at her, still somewhat entranced. I so wanted her to be pleased with me. I only ever wanted her to smile at me, and she had asked me the one question that could completely destroy this moment.

I said the only thing I could think to say: "She....she could not be here."

The Countess sighed, and my heart sank.

"Oh, precious child, I have so much to tell her," she said with sudden sorrow in her voice. "Foremost, please tell your mother that I love her and have thought of her often. Had it been up to me I would have kept her, but my own mother was a formidable woman."

She continued to look at me, her gaze steady and hypnotic. "Her father, your grandfather, was so captivating he was almost otherworldly. He gave me many gifts and, with your arrival, it seems he continues to do so. I would be pleased if you both called yourselves Báthory."

"Thank you, My Lady," I said, my cheeks still flushed. I was overflowing with happiness. "I hope this will not cause trouble with your family—your daughters—"

"Think nothing of it," she scoffed. "They are their father's children now, or involved in their married lives. I care not for what they think."

"Is there anything I can do for you, Your Ladyship? I cannot repay your kindness, but surely—"

"Please, Katrine. I insist you call me Grandmother."

I could feel my face burning a bright scarlet, and I could not stop myself from smiling. I would never forget this moment.

"Can I do something for you in this trying time, Grandmother?"

"I am unsure of anything at this point, my dear," she began, and her eyes were filled with anger. "I fear you may need an army. What I do know is that good people have died and I am imprisoned under false charges. You must swear to me you will do nothing in my defence. Enough blood has been shed because of this. I could not bear the thought of you being caught in this web, as well! Swear to me you will not!"

"I swear," I said, tears falling down my cheeks now.

The Countess watched me intently, as if she were deeply confused by my tears. I once again felt quite vulnerable, trapped in her gaze.

"Wait," she finally said, raising her small, delicate hand, "there is something you may be able to do for me."

"What? Anything," I said without thinking. In truth, I would have jumped from her window if that would please her or help her cause in any way.

"When I was taken prisoner, those bastards stole my diary. That foolish priest said it was taken as evidence of my crimes, which are entirely false! He is just trying to find something he can use to excommunicate me, in order to soothe his conscience! The idea that those vile men are reading it....well, I just cannot stand it!," she yelled, and I saw a flash of the fury she had inside her. I now understood how someone could be afraid of her; it was terrifying that someone so beautiful could have the potential to be so ruthless.

"Would you like it returned to you?"

"No, no," she replied. "I want it destroyed. That way my private thoughts will stay as they are. I will understand if you cannot do this for me, as it could be potentially very dangerous."

"Of course I will do it," I declared. "Where is it being kept?"

"Wonderful!" she exclaimed, as she turned away from me and walked over to a dresser.

Her skirt made a rustling sound like feathers as she moved. It was such a beautiful sound. I hoped that one day I would make that sound. She opened a drawer to retrieve something.

"They took my letter chest containing the diary off to the town church.

You will find the diary inside with my marital initials engraved on the front, E N."

She returned to me and held out her hand, placing a small key with a head that resembled a fan into my palm. It was so light it seemed as if it was not real. She smiled slightly.

"Fortunately, they did not take the second key."

"I will find it and destroy it, Grandmother," I promised confidently. "I will return tomorrow."

She closed my fingers around the key and held my hand in hers. Our eyes met once again, and I felt a part of me connect deeply with her, as if her gaze had continued to awaken the part of my being that was like her, the pieces that were Báthory.

"You are truly a gift, Katrine Báthory," the Countess said proudly. In that moment, I felt anew, that all would be right in this world, because she was now part of my life.

"Thank you, Grandmother. I will be back tomorrow, I promise you."

She wrapped her arms around me, and I once again felt the warm waves from within swirling through my body as she held me. I had never in my life felt such fulfillment, such love. She gently kissed my forehead and sent me off. I knew I did not have much time to waste and needed to leave the castle before the guards awoke.

A woman heavily wrapped in shawls was standing outside the gate when I stepped out. She was staring at some wood that had been erected as a place to hang the condemned. I quickly realised that it was Roza. She ran to me and covered my shoulders with one of the extra shawls she had around her body.

"Can you believe that thing is supposed to be a symbol of justice done," Roza jeered, motioning to the wood. "It's a bloody nightmare is what it is!"

I began to sob uncontrollably. She clutched me tightly to her as we walked in the direction of the town.

After leaving the Countess, I could no longer feel anything. My soul had separated from my body. I was watching from outside myself as Roza dragged me back to the inn and up to the room.

I fell onto the bed and sobbed, my heart aching so badly it radiated heat throughout my body.

"What happened, Katrine?" Roza asked quietly.

"She...she...she believed me," I said. "She told me to call myself Báthory. She said I was beautiful. She said I was a gift from God."

"Child, that's wonderful news!"

"But don't you see?" I said, as I began to cry harder. "She was so kind to me, more than anyone has ever been in my life, and I can never return that kindness! She is being held prisoner, perhaps with more awful things to come, and I cannot help her. She wants me in her family, but...I... seeing her that way is so heart-breaking!"

"Katrine, I understand."

I tried my best to breathe calmly. "She can't help me, though. I may now be a Báthory, but I am still alone in this world."

I sat up and wiped the tears from my face, while Roza remained standing close to the fire. Then I pulled the small key that the Countess had given me from my sleeve and proudly showed it to her.

"She asked me to find her diary," I explained.. "They took it as evidence. It's being kept at the church."

Roza nodded. "I hear that's where all the things they took are being kept. We will make a plan while we have our morning meal. It is disgusting that those horrible men would take her diary. Did they forget who she is?"

"Roza," I interrupted, "you can help with the plan, but I must carry it out alone."

"What? Why?"

"Because if I have to do anything horrible, I do not want you involved. I could not have that on my conscience," I explained.

She nodded solemnly, then left the room without saying anything more. I did not intend to hurt anyone, but realized then that I might have no other option.

XI.

The Mission

AS DUSK FELL, I BEGAN TO MAKE READY FOR PERHAPS the most important task I had ever undertaken. My grandmother's life might be at stake and, at that moment, I could have been the only one who could help her. I had never felt more determined about accomplishing anything as I had that night.

"I should not be long," I said, pulling my cloak on around me.

"What do you need me to do?" Roza asked.

"I don't know," I replied.

She shifted nervously on the bed; we had gone through every possible problem I could face, and I felt confident. Roza, on the other hand, was extremely nervous.

"Try not to pace," I finally advised. "Other people may hear you and get suspicious."

I opened the window, and a blast of cold air came into the room. The temperature had dropped significantly since the sun went down.

"I'll leave the window open," Roza muttered anxiously. "Please be careful, and let The Fates guide your way."

When I arrived at the church, I went around to the back seeking another entrance. I made my way toward the only door I could find. Even though it was bitterly cold and there seemed to be no one around, I could not take the chance of being seen at the front doors.

The Fates were indeed with me that night. The large wooden door was strangely unlocked. Stepping inside, I was consumed by heavy darkness. I gave my eyes a few minutes to adjust before I stepped inside and shut the door behind me. The smell of incense and candle wax guided me through the darkness into the main chapel.

In one of the far corners, close to the front where few common people would go, was a cluster of furniture that appeared too grand for this modest place. After moving some objects around, I found a cabinet with the initials EN printed elaborately in gold on the doors.

I pulled the key that the Countess gave me out of my sleeve, opened the lock and pulled out the only thing I could find: a book covered in the softest leather I had ever touched—a grand diary, befitting its owner.

Suddenly, candlelight illuminated the dark church, and a male voice called from somewhere behind me, "Excuse me, Madam?"

I calmly locked the cabinet and took the book in my hand. I turned slowly around to meet his face; it was the same priest from the execution site.

"Madam, you are stealing evidence!" he exclaimed. "You are risking very much for a matter that has already been resolved."

"Begging your pardon, Father, but if this matter is indeed resolved, then you have no need for such personal artifacts," I replied, taking one step closer to him. I could feel the rage welling up inside of me. Looking into his eyes, I could sense something dark and evil about him, a thing that made him unworthy of his religious station. He was no man of God, this man, this supposed holy man! Undoubtedly, he was the same wretched priest whom the Countess had mentioned.

"Madam, I cannot allow you to do that," he said again, this time lunging towards me and reaching for the diary. Faster than I could think, I grabbed him with my free hand and pulled him against me, the book falling to the floor.

"I believe you are not a good man, Father. You are closer in kin to the Devil than any God I know," I growled at him.

He called me *strigoi* then began to pray, his words getting faster as he stared into my eyes.

"Do you not know that He wants us to suffer, Father? You would have better luck praying to the forest, since it's closer to you than the Lord will ever be," I snarled.

I effortlessly spun the priest around so that I could cover his mouth with my hand, and twisted his scrawny neck backward. In the dim light, I could see the blue veins branching out through his pasty skin and feel his pulse racing when I bit into him as hard as I could.

The blood came so quickly it seemed like I couldn't swallow fast enough. My body began to react instantly, jumping to life with energy and strength I did not know I possessed. He jerked violently and foolishly tried to break free of my fatal embrace. I immediately seized his arms and snapped them like twigs. He jerked again in agony, his screams muffled by my hand. I must admit, there was something about his pain that imparted an additional level of pleasure to my experience; I lost track of everything except how much better I was feeling. His frightened squeaks, the strange half moans and half screams that came from him made me smile. I found them genuinely amusing.

My arms finally began to ache under the weight of the priest's body. The flow of blood began to lessen, and I grew tired of him. I pulled myself away, throwing him to the ground. His skin had turned an even starker white, the colour of fresh snow. Not a single drop of blood was left in him. Could I have drained him completely?

My head was spinning, my recharged body causing time itself to speed up around me. Roza and I had planned exactly what to do if this happened, but my thoughts were suddenly racing so fast now, I couldn't put it all together. Instead, I wiped my lips, breathed deeply and tried to steady myself.

The longer I stayed here, the higher the risk I took of getting caught. I picked up the body and headed towards a nearby door. I was unsure of where it led but recalled Roza saying something about a door inside the chapel that led to the bowels of the church and eventually the crypt.

Body rejuvenated, my senses were sharp and I had no trouble seeing in the heavy darkness. I made my way through the doorway and down the spiraling stairwell. I could hear the rats screech and scurry all around me. Even though it was bitterly cold, I could still smell the mould and stench of death as I proceeded deeper into the subterranean chamber.

I laid the body out upon a stone slab inside the crypt, placing the priest's hands one over the other, on top of his chest, as was customary.

I was surprised by the number of coffins that lined the walls, wooden boxes piled in stacks on top of each other like firewood. I did not have time to look around or think much about what I was seeing, though, as time was of the essence. I hurried back upstairs into the chapel, grabbed the diary, and left the way I came in. I tucked the book under my cloak as I stepped outside into the frigid night; the town was still dark and quiet.

I leapt up to the window, grabbing onto the ledge with my free hand. I tossed the book over and pulled myself up and inside. Roza was sitting on the edge of the bed like a cat ready to pounce.

I immediately went over to the fire to warm myself.

"You took too long, Katrine," she said, and I could hear the fear in her voice. "Did you have some difficulty?" Her face was full of panic.

"I have the diary, and no one is coming to arrest us," I reassured her. "So, the difficulty is not important enough to discuss."

"Did you kill anyone?"

I rubbed my hands together and stared into the fire.

"Katrine?" she said again.

"Is it important, Roza?"

She leveled her gaze at me. "If you tell me what the difficulty was, I can draw my own conclusions."

"The priest," I answered bluntly, my eyes still focused on the fire.

"You had difficulty with the priest," she repeated. "Did you do as we discussed?"

"Yes," I said, growing impatient. "Everything is fine. You have no need to worry. Now, if you don't mind, I would like to sleep for a few hours before we destroy the diary."

I put the book under my side of the mattress then got under the covers. After sitting in the same spot for some time, Roza slipped into the bed beside me. I assumed she was contemplating the fate of the priest. Her body seemed stiff and tense as she shifted around in bed trying to get comfortable. I thought about telling her that she should not worry herself about such a man: evil hidden beneath the robes of the so-called holy—that God did not choose this man, that he was not worthy of His blessing. Now that I had seen it for myself, I understood, but the very idea that a priest could be so despicable was still unsettling.

I closed my eyes and tried my best to think only of sleep. If I were to survive, I could not dwell upon what had happened tonight. In any case, I had the Countess' diary: only that was important.

We walked out into the woods at midday. I felt well rested and nourished. The sun was not even an irritant, and it was at its fullest. Hours had passed since I collected the diary and killed the priest and, at any moment, Roza and I expected to hear that the body had been found.

She was concerned about how we should react so as not to rouse suspicion. I told her I would think further about the subject once I had completed my primary task: first, the diary had to be destroyed.

We walked far enough into the forest that the village blended into the background. At the first clearing, Roza went quickly to gather firewood. I clutched the book tightly to my chest and stared at my surroundings, the landscape spinning around me. My body began to ache, and an overwhelming sense of loneliness spread throughout. I thought I might vomit. Roza's chatter finally caught my attention.

"Everything is damp," she complained. "We may have some difficulty starting a fire."

Snow had already begun to fall in large flakes, while Roza made a stack of all her gatherings. She came and stood beside me, while my nausea worsened.

"It is your turn, child," she said. I turned and looked at her, unsure of what she meant.

"It is a good time for you to practice," she continued. "Start the fire, Katrine."

She was right. We had no fear of the elements. That was why she suddenly appeared so calm. I pulled some herbs from the small pouch I had taken to carrying at my waist, reciting the short incantation Roza had taught me as I cast them onto the firewood. There was a small puff of smoke as the fire sparked then sprang to life.

"We should ask The Fates for guidance and for assistance with removing that book from the earth," Roza commented.

I ran my hand over the cover of the book, before I placed it into the flames. I looked to the sky and asked for help with the one good deed I could do on this earth—the one good thing I would be able to do for a long time, perhaps. I hoped it would not be the last.

When the Countess' diary finally caught fire, the smell of the burning leather was sickening and did not help my unsettled stomach. I took Roza's hand and we watched it burn together, the silence surrounding us as if it were a living being, another person standing with us. We waited while the fire steadily burned it down to a pile of smouldering ashes.

"Take the rest, dear friend. Now it belongs to you, and is only a memory to the world," I intoned, as the wind picked up and blew the ashes away.

The breeze felt like it took something else away, a subtle part of me that was still lingering around the edges. What was left of the girl of sixteen summers who had never left her village or been without her parents, also caught in the breeze and went with the wind.

I felt different, ready to face my fate, as I never had before.

"Are you ready to go now, Katrine?" Roza asked.

"Yes," I said proudly. "I am ready now more than ever. I feel we have accomplished something important today, Roza. Momentous, actually."

"I hope so," she nodded tiredly, "for I fear I am not equipped to run from place to place."

As we walked together back towards the village, all I could hear was the sound of our feet crunching in the fresh snow.

I rolled onto my side, my eyes fluttering open as I focused on a figure standing beside the bed.

"You sleep so heavily I was starting to wonder if you were dead," my mother said angrily. "Now hurry up and get ready. We are leaving this accursed place."

"I cannot go until tomorrow," I said, sitting up in bed.

She laughed. "You can sleep in the carriage, you lazy girl! I thought I taught you—"

"I cannot leave until I go back to the castle," I snapped. "Now get some sleep! You look like the walking dead."

"How dare you...wait, did you say go back to the castle? When were you there?" she demanded. Her eyes were as wide as dinner plates, the whites the colour of fresh snow.

"After the executions I went to the castle to speak to the Countess. She asked me to do—"

"To do what?"

"Let me finish, Momma! She asked me to retrieve and destroy her diary, and I have to go and tell her I did so, before we leave."

"Someone stole her diary?"

I was unsure of what to tell her. Explaining all the details seemed pointless.

"Yes. And I will not leave until I speak to her," I simply replied.

Mother's eyes began to fill with tears, a smile brightening her entire face.

"I should prepare myself," she started to fret, "—clean myself up so I look presentable, I mean, this is quite an event! Meeting my...my mother. What is she like, Katrine?"

I smiled. "Everything you would ever hope a woman to be. Beautiful, poised, gracious, true royalty."

"Do you think she will take to me?" Mother asked hopefully.

Taking her hand, I confidently declared, "I know she will."

I sat up quickly in bed, startling Roza from her place in front of the fire.

"What happened?" I asked.

"You fell asleep after dinner," Roza replied. "A very unhappy sleep, I might add. What were you dreaming about?"

I sighed. "My mother."

"Are you alright?" Roza kept her eyes focused on the fire.

"I'm not sure. What did we eat? My stomach is upset."

"You do not remember eating? Heavens, what is going on with you, girl?" Roza cried.

I sighed again. The events of the day seemed so far in the past by now.

"I am not entirely sure, Roza. But I cannot go back to the castle until morning and, right now, that is the only thing I can think about."

XII.

Redemption

I TOOK MORE TIME DRESSING AND PREPARING FOR MY second visit to the castle than I had the first. I was nervous, more so than before, perhaps because this time, I was expected.

"What shall we do now that we have seen the Countess?" I asked Roza as she plaited my hair.

"I am not sure I understand."

"Shall we live here, in Csejthe, or move on to somewhere else? What are we going to do now that there is no court for us to join?"

She finished the plait then began to smooth the hair on the top of my head.

"I had not really thought about that, my dear," she murmured. "Perhaps you should ask Her Ladyship for advice."

"Of course."

"What did you tell her about your mother?"

I stood up and smoothed the front of my most special crimson dress, one of the few times I had worn it. The colour was as vibrant as I had remembered when that woman first pulled it from the chest.

"I told her she could not be there. Was that alright?"

"Perfectly," Roza nodded, "since saying she was dead would not do any good." She took a good look at me and seemed satisfied. "In any event, the Countess would probably not believe the truth."

"But I will still ask for her guidance. So many things have been guided by the idea of her, that it only makes sense," I said.

Roza handed me the herb bag I used for the spells.

"I put in extra, should you need," she nudged me, pointing to the bag.

I tried to breathe calmly. "Do I look alright? Are you sure the red isn't too much?"

"You look lovely. Now, go, the day has just started. If it gets any later, there will be crowds in the square."

I pulled on my cloak. "Wish me luck!"

I moved quickly through the town, the bright morning sun still not a factor. While it seemed as though my issues with the sun had finally passed, I still did not want to test it if I did not have somewhere important to be.

I passed the hangman's post that was erected outside the castle. It remained a dark, ugly spot on the otherwise perfect white landscape. I wondered if the Countess could see it from her window, a monument to her suffering and torment.

Inside the castle, it seemed even emptier than before, more furniture and tapestries having been removed in the time since I had last been here. It was as if the Lady of the House had died and her things were being divided—as if the Lady herself was not still sitting in her room upstairs.

I crept up the stone staircase, preparing myself to cast the sleep spell and continue on to her chamber. There were people above me, perhaps more now than the other day, so I sat on a step with my back to the cold wall and waited, listening. I had not thought of what to do if the Countess had other visitors.

I could hear only men, however. I understood very little of what they said, the language a mix of words so foreign to me that I was surprised.

Either these were new guards, or I had not been paying close enough attention during my last encounter here.

Nevertheless, I pulled the herbs and cast the spell, the smoke drifting out into the open air like snowflakes. I waited until I could sense a calmness pass over, the feeling that all close by were sleeping, then slowly continued up the stairs. Sure enough, the men were toppled over on the floor, fast asleep.

Unlocking the Countess' chambers, I found her back turned when I stepped into the doorway. She looked bewildered when she saw me; I dropped into a low bow.

"Katrine?" she said, her voice soft with surprise.

"Yes, Madam," I replied, pulling the key out from my sleeve. "I have done what you asked. The diary has been destroyed by fire. Here is the key to your cabinet."

"You have done...," the Countess began, walking closer to me, "how did you get past the guards again?"

"A mixture of herbs, that when combined—"

She laughed, waving for me to stop. "So, my granddaughter knows some magic? Please rise, my dear. Do not be afraid. I will not judge you."

"Thank you, my—," she raised her hand at me in correction. "I am sorry, Grandmother. You no longer have to worry about the diary."

She stared at the key I handed her as if it was some bizarre foreign object. A flicker of joy, relief and excitement, all combined, passed through her gaze, and I was overjoyed.

"How?" she said, leaving the key in my hand. "Never mind, I do not need to know the details. I trust your word. Thank you." Her voice was calm, but I could see some confusion in her eyes and felt a sense of sadness and defeat surrounding her.

"Katrine, where is your mother?"

I was afraid to answer her. I did not want to upset her, but her dark eyes expressed awareness that something terrible had happened.

"I...I don't know," I stuttered, my vision now blurring. "She...she... turned during the ritual and I—" Suddenly the horror of that night came rushing back. My arm began to ache and my tears overwhelmed me.

"What on earth are you talking about, Katrine, what ritual?" the Countess demanded.

Her question surprised me. "The ritual your women performed," I sobbed. "The women…the witches that you sent to retrieve her, they began casting some sort of spell on All Hallows Eve and she—" I cried out as the pain in my arm raged through my body.

"Katrine! Katrine! Get a hold of yourself!" She grabbed me by the shoulders and shook me. "Who are these women? Where are they now?"

"Your Darvulia and the other witch, Erza are dead. Mother killed them. Only Kardoska and I survived," I said blankly. "Grandmother, why did you send for her? Why would you allow this to happen?"

"I can assure you that I had no knowledge of this, Katrine," she vowed. "I did not send for her or even know the whereabouts of your mother until your arrival."

"What? But Darvulia said she was bringing her here to claim her birthright. What did she mean by that? Grandmother, please tell me what is going on, why has this happened to you?"

Her face became stern and the whites of her eyes flashed. "This is happening because these vile men are trying to take my land!" she declared, walking over to a table. I saw now that it was a writing desk piled high with papers.

"The King and Palatine want what I have, my dear. I must say, I am not entirely surprised. His Majesty owes a large sum of money to my family. Although my husband fought victoriously for him, the King feels no need to pay the debt to his widow," she said angrily, her black eyes flashing with fury. "And then my son-in-law, the rogue who married my sweet daughter, Kata, is trying to steal her inheritance! She could have married into any noble family in Hungary, but I chose him! Disrespectful little toad!"

I did not respond, for I could tell she was not finished.

"You are not too young to understand that the world we live in has no place for powerful women. They frighten too many people. That's why a woman can be burned with no proof," she continued, making a fist now. "You should be careful with your magic, Katrine. A woman cannot exist without a husband, regardless of her station in life… even a Báthory. But how soon they forget that my name is, in fact, greater than my husband's!"

In her wild angry state, she still looked tired. Her dark hair was pulled up and away from her face, showing the lines of age in her angry expression.

"I am sorry my dear, but I have nothing tangible to leave for you or your mother," the Countess said, turning away and walking to the window. There were small things that she did, movements and expressions that reminded me exactly of my mother and I hoped it would be something that I, too, would inherit.

"How did you get to Csejthe, Katrine?"

I approached her, pulling up my sleeve to show her my scar. "Roza brought me here, in your carriage. After Mother turned into a beast and killed the witches, she left me and Roza for dead in the forest. We've been traveling ever since."

The Countess' eyes widened as she touched her finger to my scar which was now reddened and raised. "I do not believe she's left you, my dear," she whispered.

"Grandmother," I continued, "the birthright they spoke of does not have anything to do with land or money, does it?" I pressed. "Please, do you know what happened to mother?"

She suddenly shifted back to the measured calm I had seen the day before. All the hate and anger drained from her face, the lines disappearing with them. Her stunning beauty stared back at me, the memory of my mother's face hurting my heart.

"I am certain that your mother is safe," she assured. "She is strong and possesses great power. All of the Báthory women do. Perhaps one day I will be able to share with you the story of our heritage. I am sorry that I cannot say more at this time. I will not involve you in this mess."

"Grandmother, please…I swear I will keep this between us," I urged, "I must know what happened to her, for I fear that it may be happening to me."

"Katrine, do not be afraid. The blood that runs through your veins is very powerful, and it will keep you safe." She turned her head to the left, and I noticed strange writing on the wall, four lines all in different languages. I tried not to stare, but wondered why and what she had written.

"I am hopeful my family will come to my aid. My cousin Gabor is Crown Prince of Transylvania. I can reassure you that my fate is not these four walls."

"What should I do now, Grandmother?" I asked wearily.

"Whatever do you mean?" she said heavily, her eyes staring at something out the window. She had become distant again, caught in some other world that lay in the rays of sunlight that reflected through the window.

"I have...I am...I wish to stay in Csejthe, to be close to you," I said. "I fear I have nothing else. No place else to go."

"Has anyone seen you or inquired about who you are?" she asked sternly.

"No. No one has asked any questions, we've kept to our room at the inn most of time," I feigned, not wanting to upset her further. I could not bear to tell her of the horror of the executions, let alone the stares and grumblings we received from the townspeople.

"I cannot disrupt your life because of my circumstances, my dear. You do not need to stay here."

"But I only wish to be with you. Where would I possibly go?" I cried out, heartbroken by the idea that she did not want me to stay.

She grew concerned. "I am sorry, my dear, but I received news from the village that the priest's body was found in the crypt. While I am truly in your debt for the act you committed on my behalf, I must insist that you leave Csejthe immediately and never return."

My chest started to hurt, my eyes burning with sudden tears. "But I am alone. I have no...."

"Katrine, look at me," the Countess said as she came over to me, taking my hand. "I need you to go and live in whatever way God intended for you to do so. Live for the people who were hurt by this tragedy. You are young and unmarried, Katrine. You could do anything you have ever dreamed."

She walked back to the writing desk and took something from the drawer. "My mother gave me this ring when I was sent to marry Ferenc Nádasdy. She said it had been her mother's, and it held the strength of all the Báthory that had come before me. Whenever I was afraid and needed to remember that I am a Báthory," she folded the ring into my empty palm, "I clung to this. I want you to take it now, along with that strength. And don't ever forget that you are a Báthory."

"I won't," I said proudly. "I will live every day with the grace and dignity you have shown me. I will prove that I am worthy of being called your granddaughter."

She squeezed my hand tightly. "I know you will."

She pulled me into her arms, hugging me tight to her body. Her chest heaved with a stifled sob. I could not think, I could not breathe. The very idea of not being with her was burning a hole inside me that I thought would never stop hurting.

"Thank you, my angel. You are truly a gift," she spoke softly into my hair. Her breath was warm and soothing.

"I love you, Grandmother," I whispered. I tried to hold in my tears and stay brave. I was a Báthory now. She would not regret giving me her name; I made a vow to myself that I would take this honour and become the woman she thought I was destined to be—Erzsébet Báthory's granddaughter—from my hair down to the tips of my toes.

"And I you," she said, pushing me away. Our eyes met for a final time. I tried to take in all of her, and she seemed to do the same. I would remember her at every possible moment and live in her image as much as I could.

"I swear, I will make you proud," I proclaimed to her.

"I will never forget you," she nodded. A tear rolled down her cheek, and I bowed to her one last time.

When I returned to the inn, Roza was in our room gathering our things in a frenzy.

"Katrine, we—"

"I know. We have to go," I said calmly. I slid the ring the Countess had given me onto my middle finger, her inner calm taking over me and filling my body with fierce determination.

"How?"

"Her Ladyship told me the priest's body had been found, and then ordered me to leave. But where shall we go?"

"The only place I can think where we might find work." Roza seemed to have a plan in mind. "Hopefully, I will not have trouble finding our boy to drive the carriage."

"You never said where we shall go," I insisted as she began to pile our belongings into my arms.

"Vienna, Katrine. We are going to Vienna."

XIII.

Vienna

WE RODE INTO THE CITY LIKE A GREAT STORM, RIDING on the edge of the wind. The ground seemed more solid under my feet in Vienna. It was a different sort of ground; less of the dirt and earth and more solid stones, the foundation of a great city.

I had never seen such a place, even in my grandest dreams.

In what seemed the blink of an eye, Roza had secured us employment with a baker in a part of the city where the Countess' manor house had been. We slept in a small room in the baker's basement until we could afford something else, if we ever could afford something else. It was harder work then I had ever done, and I was so exhausted by the day's end I could only think of sleep.

One morning, after we had been there for some weeks, the baker came down as we were preparing for the day.

"I need you to deliver something before you begin your regular duties," he said to me. "I know you do not know your way around the city yet, so I drew you a map."

He took me upstairs to the front of the shop. He handed me a cloth with some lines drawn on it, pointing to where a line started at one end.

"This is where we are now. If you follow the lines to the very end, you will reach Marmet's dress shop. Take this cake," he said, handing me a blue box tied with a white ribbon, "and be careful how you carry it."

I took the box and lay the map on top, the starting line facing my chest.

"Now, God forbid you should get lost, do not forget you are going to Marmet's dress shop. Got that, Katrine?" he asked.

"Yes, sir. I shall be back soon," I replied, and he held the front door open for me as I set out.

A dull ache spread through me as the morning sun beat down on my head. I had not bothered pulling up my hood as the sun's slight irritation had an odd way of keeping me warm. Winter in the city was very different from winter in the country, and it was nowhere close to as cold as it would have been if I were home.

I followed the map easily, the people of Vienna too busy starting their day to notice a baker's young delivery girl. It was nice to blend in with common people again and feel like part of the day-to-day world. I was also happy to walk. The baker usually sent our carriage boy to make deliveries, and I did not get out of the kitchen much. The boy used the carriage to perform his duties, and I wondered if that was part of the reason why the baker had taken on the three of us, even with a board nailed over the crest on the door.

I was actually enjoying our new life. It was simple and common, but it was more than I imagined I would ever have as someone's wife.

The door to Marmet's dress shop was painted bright red, and a large window gave passers by a clear view of the goings on inside. There was a shopkeeper showing a grand looking woman a piece of stunning green fabric that reminded me of pine trees in springtime.

I heard the chime of a bell, and someone stepped out of the shop.

"Lovely day, isn't it?" a heavily accented male voice said.

I turned to see a man in a very fine suit, who was not speaking to me but to the woman with whom he had stepped out of the shop. He glanced at me before taking her arm; he had the most striking light green eyes. His gaze turned back to me again, as if something about my face had caught his attention.

The woman's voice was soft and breathy. "Yes, my dear. The best we've seen since arriving in Vienna."

I could not help but stare at her; she was exquisitely beautiful yet in a much different way than the Countess.

Where the Countess had been dark and stunning, this woman was very light. Her pale blue dress matched her eyes perfectly, setting off her creamy white skin with a shape so structured she appeared to be fluid curves. Her golden hair peaked out of her matching flowered hat in small soft curls.

I tried to stop staring and headed for the door. The smell of lavender hit me as soon as I stepped in the doorway. I had little time to think, when a woman came rushing towards me. I snatched the map off the top of the box before she took it from me.

"I have your delivery from the bakery, Madam," I said as she took the box from my hands.

"Next time come to the back door," she snapped, moving away from me as I was rushed out of the shop.

I started walking back to the bakery, feeling a bit ashamed. I had not known there was another entrance. I merely followed the baker's instructions, and I had done my task. I wondered if it was something known amongst the common people, if deliveries and servants always had their own door at shops. In any case, I would have to ask. If this was part of common employment, I wanted to do my absolute best.

I walked for some time before realising I had no clue where I was. I pulled the map from my pocket, but it was no good. I tried to go back the way I came, start again from the shop, but nothing looked familiar.

My chest started to hurt. I had never been alone in such a way, in a strange city with no sense of direction, and it made me very frightened.

"Are you lost, child?"

The man with the green eyes from the shop suddenly appeared beside me. He looked at me as if examining an animal, trying to identify its species.

"I think so," I replied. "I had a map, but I seem to have gotten turned around...."

"May I see this map? Perhaps I could be of some assistance," he offered.

I held up the map for him, and he tilted his head to examine it.

"Ah! I see where the problem is," he said, pointing a gloved finger at the lines. "If you follow me, I can point you in the proper direction."

I looked at him for a moment, studying his dark hair and sharply angled face. I wondered if I should trust him. I tried to use my senses and could smell something oddly familiar about him. I followed him in the direction in which he gestured; he walked at my side as if we were equals.

"I am Signor Vincenzo Amori," he said. "What is your name?"

"Katrine," I replied.

"Do you work with your parents?"

"No, sir."

"Are you an orphan?" he asked.

"Not exactly. My parents are gone, but I have a woman I travel with," I replied.

"I have a woman I travel with also, but I am sure yours is more agreeable," he smiled.

I chuckled. "I wouldn't be so sure of that, sir."

He stopped walking, and Signor Amori said triumphantly, "I believe, my dear Katrine, that we are here."

Sure enough, we were standing in front of the bakery.

"Thank you, sir. I have no way to repay your kindness."

"Please, my dear, I am always happy to help a woman in need. *Arrivederci,* I am sure we will meet again."

I bowed to him, watching as he walked away.

I quickly went inside to get to my day's work. Though it seemed odd that he had reappeared at such a time, I found myself pleased to have made Signor Amori's acquaintance.

Several weeks passed after that, and I fell back into a routine.

I spent most of my day baking with Roza, trying to learn what I could from her. Her baking was a true art form. Later, I would go out to the front of the shop and clear the snow, while Roza was happy to stay inside, back in her element.

I soon started to see that green-eyed man in my dreams, his name having left me completely by now. He was always in the background, watching me, studying me, but never saying a word. It was as if he was trying to learn more about me.

I began to wonder if he somehow had the power to put himself in my mind, or, if the events of the past few months had finally pushed me to the brink of insanity.

***

"Hello again," a very distinct male voice said from behind me.

I stopped pushing the broom I used to clear the snow, and turned to find myself looking at the man with the green eyes, the man I was all too familiar with from my dreams..

"Hello, sir," I replied, bowing slightly.

"Katrine, I want you to meet my companion," he said, as the beautiful blonde woman I remembered seeing with him some weeks before appeared from behind him. "This is Mademoiselle Grisela Delphine."

I smiled and bowed to her, as well. "I am pleased to make your acquaintance."

"I must be honest, child, my Italian friend rarely takes interest in women such as yourself, so I had to come and see what all the fuss is about," she said, moving closer to me. She lifted her skirt and I could only focus on her exquisite shoes.

"Begging your pardon, but while I am quite flattered by your interest in me, I don't quite understand why. I am nothing special."

Signor Amori smiled slyly at his friend. "You see? She really has no idea. Perhaps she is from the country." He turned back to me. "Katrine, were you born in Vienna?"

"No, you were correct in saying I am from the country," I answered.

"I grew up in—"

"You said she was special, Vincenzo," Mlle. Delphine cut me off sharply. "I do not understand why you would bring me back here for a country girl."

"Is it quite impossible for you to trust my instincts?" Signor Amori answered patiently. "She is no common country girl, I can assure you. There is more to her, I also believe she has no idea. And, if you actually try, you can smell it."

Mlle. Delphine rolled her eyes at him, sniffing the air. Suddenly, a flash of recognition passed through her gaze as she looked at me, leaning in closer. Signor Amori nodded knowingly, and Mlle. Delphine leaned towards me, whispering in a low tone, "I sense we are of similar circumstances, Katrine, women whose lives have been altered by the actions of others."

"I do not understand," I murmured. She laughed a soft and tinkling sound, much like wind chimes.

"You crave something forbidden to this world, *oui?*" she prodded, her voice soft and lilting. I looked deep into her pale blue eyes, and something inside me reacted.

I could smell this woman: flowers, cosmetics, the sweat of men, and a deep, underlying scent of something else…fresh blood.

"I also crave such things," she continued. "We mean you no harm. My Italian friend and I have come to Vienna to collect a girl of similar circumstances. We wish to bring her to a place where she can live freely, and I would like to offer you that same opportunity, as well. You could come to my home in Paris to live and work."

I stared at her, my mouth frozen and trying to form the words. I was not quite sure how to react. I looked helplessly at the green-eyed man.

"We want to take you to a place where others like us live freely," he explained patiently. "A home for the homeless, if you will. I knew the first moment that I saw you that you were special, and I could not leave you behind here. We wish to teach you about all the things you do not yet understand. If you would care to come to our suites, I can explain more clearly."

"I...I...I must speak with my companion," I stuttered.

"Of course," he said. He pulled a small card from his jacket and handed it to me.

"Thank you, Signor Amori," I said, suddenly remembering his name.

The two linked arms and walked away; Mlle. Delphine looked just as pretty from the back as she did the front. She had the most delicate pink ribbon tied in the back of her hair.

At that moment, a voice startled me.

"Who were you talking to?" Roza asked. She was standing behind in the doorway watching me.

"Signor Amori and Mademoiselle Delphine," I muttered, still in disbelief.

"What did they want with you?"

"It was the strangest thing."

Snapping out of my reverie, I declared excitedly, "I'll explain in a moment. Let me finish here, and I'll meet you downstairs!"

"No, I don't...I do not—"

Roza paced around the basement. "Oh, Katrine! This is all too much!"

Sitting on our straw bed, I had just finished telling her everything.

"Perhaps we should just go and hear what they have to say. We don't have to go with them," I implored.

"Do you not find this strange? That there are more...more—"

I smiled. "More like me? I'm actually rather relieved. I was sure that I was not the only person in the world handed this terrible fate."

"But how did they know about you?"

"When you have been around many others you just know, I suppose," I said. "It sounded, and looked, as if they could identify me by smell. Signor Amori said I was special, and once he met me he knew he could not leave me behind. It's quite noble of him. I think we should at least pay him the courtesy to hear what he has to say."

"Alright," she finally conceded. "When we finish tomorrow, we shall go and see. Now, if we make ready tonight, things shall go quickly tomorrow."

After we had finished working the next day, I prepared to put the red dress on again. I had not worn that dress since we left Csejthe earlier this year, and it was now almost Easter. It felt strange but proper somehow. I scrubbed my face as clean as I could get it while Roza fixed my hair. Father's cross on my neck and the Countess' ring on my finger made me feel protected.

"I told the baker we were going to church, so make sure that dress is well hidden under your cloak," Roza said sharply.

"Yes, yes, of course," I replied, handing her the card Signor Amori had given me. "Do you know where this place is?"

"You can't read it?"

"No, I cannot," I snapped. "Or did you forget you had broken your promise to teach me?"

She watched me for a moment before taking the card, looking suddenly guilty, waiting for me to react.

"It's not far," she finally said.

"Good. I heard there was going to be a furious storm, and I don't want us to get caught in a blizzard."

XIV.

Unusual Acquaintances

WE HEADED IN THE SAME DIRECTION AS THE DRESS shop, I being quite careful to keep my cloak closed until we were a good distance from the bakery.

The streets were dark and deserted. Roza kept a tight grip on my wrist as we moved along. We had come to a part of the city unknown to me, where the ground was full of holes and uneven stones that made it hard to walk.

"What is wrong with the ground?" I asked as I stumbled for the third time.

"We are taking a back road. It's faster," Roza answered. "Now stop crying, we're almost there. You'd think you never walked a day in your life."

I stumbled on for a few more minutes until Roza stopped in front of a door, one in a row of houses all connected together.

Oddly, I did not think about being nervous, let alone what sort of situation we were getting into as I knocked sharply on the door, then stepped back and waited. Meanwhile, Roza stood so closely behind me, I could feel her heartbeat against my back.

The door flung open and a bright light blinded us. I saw the outline of a figure but could not tell if it was a man or woman.

"May I help you?" the figure asked, and it was most definitely a man.

"We are here to see Signor Amori," I said confidently. "My name is Katrine."

"Bring them in, Tolone," Signor Amori's voice called out from inside the house.

The figure moved out of the doorway and motioned us inside.

I had never seen a house so grand: curtains made out of such luxurious fabric I thought only fit for gowns of queens, beautiful furniture with red plush upholstery, candles longer than my arm, a silver tea service that shone like the brightest star in the sky and, hanging on the wall, the most stunning embroidered tapestry I had ever seen. I could not stop staring at it. Without invitation, I boldly walked across the room to examine it. I did not even hear Roza whisper my name sharply, trying to stop me.

"Beautiful, isn't it?" Mlle. Delphine startled me out of my trance. I began to bow to her and she waved me out of it.

"I don't think we need to bother with such formalities, *non*?" she smiled, gliding into the room.

"Mademoiselle Delphine, this is my companion, Mrs. Kardoska," I said. She turned to Roza who bowed to her.

"Interesting name, Kardoska. Where are you from?" Mlle. Delphine asked.

"Hungary, Madam," Roza replied.

"Really? Lovely place, but too cold for my French blood," she waved. "Signor Amori will be with us soon. Please come in and sit."

Roza and I sat down on the couch, while Mlle. Delphine gracefully took a seat in a beautifully embroidered chair.

"Is Signor Amori your husband?" I asked.

Mlle. Delphine let out a slight laugh. "Heavens no. He is only my travelling companion. I would have come to Vienna alone, but my employer insisted it was inappropriate. Nevertheless, you have come to hear our proposal. Let me begin."

I watched as she adjusted her position in the chair, a pose that appeared practiced for making her look as attractive as possible.

"There is a home in Paris where Vincenzo and I, and many others who are in a similar situation as you, live. We stay together to protect each other, and we seek out others of similar circumstances to try to help them survive undetected," she began. "We even have a theatre where we perform. As entertainers, it allows us a certain degree of freedom to live more freely—without so much of society's scrutiny and judgment."

"Are there many more like us?" I asked.

"Yes, there are more like us. There are also some who have more natural abilities involving magic, and even some who can alter their shape entirely."

"—Do you mean into beasts?"

"Yes, yes, of course," she nodded. "It is a horribly painful process, in fact." Her eyes widened slightly now with interest. "You have witnessed this phenomenon?"

I looked at Roza, then back at Mlle. Delphine.

"Have you altered shape yourself, Katrine?" she pressed.

"No, no," I answered quickly. "I only saw it once."

She leaned back, satisfied by that.

"So you see, my dear, our interest in you is quite innocent, and I would be happy if you would both return to Paris and join us. I would not expect you to leave your companion behind," she said, motioning to Roza.

At that moment, Signor Amori appeared in the doorway.

"Would you bring our guests some tea, Tolone?" he called towards the hallway and to the man who had let us in.

"Good evening, ladies." He bowed to me. "Miss Katrine."

Then he turned to Roza. "I am Signor Vincenzo Amori." He gently took her hand in his so that he could kiss her knuckles. "You must be Katrine's companion—"

"Kardoska," Mlle. Delphine introduced him before Roza could reply.

"Ah! From Hungary, yes?" he asked, and Roza nodded in agreement. "Lovely place. They make an incredible dish, a stew of sorts that I just adore! But Madam, I sense you are nervous. Let me assure you, you are both perfectly safe. I am sure that Mlle. Delphine has explained our mission to you. If you choose to come with us, I give you my word that your current employer will be paid handsomely for his trouble, so that if you choose to return, there will be no bad blood. You will be secure with us and be able to live your lives out of harm's way."

"It sounds like a dream, sir," Roza said hesitantly.

"And you are unsure of its truth?"

"Of course," she nodded. "We have had a tough time, the girl and I, and I'm sure you can understand that after everything we've seen, I'm rather suspicious when something comes along too easy."

"But you are unconcerned in regards to our 'circumstances', as my companion states it?"

Roza hesitated, and then said quite boldly, "I have complete confidence that the girl can take care of us, and enough sense to know danger when it presents itself."

"And the two of you are not related in any way?"

"No."

Signor Amori took a seat across from us.

"So how did you come to know each other?"

"I was once employed by her grandmother," Roza answered.

"And who would this grandmother be?" he queried.

"The Lady Widow Nádasdy," I spoke up proudly, "or as she is also known—"

"Countess Báthory," Mlle. Delphine finished my sentence. "But are you not a bit old to be her granddaughter? Her own daughters are barely older than you."

"My mother, her daughter, was born out of wedlock before the Countess' marriage," I explained, and the room immediately fell silent. "Countess Báthory was only about fourteen years when she gave birth to my mother."

They both stared at me, Signor Amori's eyes examining both Roza and me, while Mlle. Delphine watched only me.

"I know your grandmother," she finally broke the awkward silence. "Socially, from court life. She was extremely beautiful. I see the family resemblance in you."

"Thank you, that means a lot to me," I replied. "I hope I can be more like her as I grow."

"So, where is your mother now?" Signor Amori gently inquired.

"She...she was the person whose shape altered," I murmured. "Roza and I were the only survivors when it happened."

"The change killed her?"

"No, but it seems that she never changed back. She ran into the forest in Wallachia and I haven't see her since," I answered quietly. "I would not be here if it wasn't for Roza."

Signor Amori and Mlle. Delphine looked at each for a moment, and then the Signor spoke: "My dear, I insist you come with us. From what I know of the Countess, she would have wanted you to have the best life."

Mlle. Delphine nodded. "And we can give that to you, if you will allow us. I would be honoured, for that matter."

I looked at Roza, who appeared to have relaxed slightly. I did not want our life to be hard, and I did not want to be a burden to her. After we left Csejthe, she could have left me but she did not. The guarantee of a good life had been lost when the Countess was imprisoned, and yet she still took me with her, loyal throughout.

Finally, we both nodded.

"Then, it's settled," Signor Amori proclaimed. "I shall come to the bakery tomorrow to collect you, then we will acquire our other charge and be on our way."

Just then, Tolone came in with a tea service and began to serve us.

"How did you know we would agree to come?" I asked them now, taking the cup handed to me.

Signor Amori let out a laugh, a very heavy and masculine sound.

"If you did not intend on coming, Katrine," he said knowingly, "You would not be sitting here."

XV.

Social Graces

KLARA VON DORES WAS THE DAUGHTER OF A VIENNESE
baron and courtier who, according to him, was causing too much trouble.
She had been born a 'blood drinker', as Mademoiselle Delphine referred
to it, and was not handling herself appropriately. This was attracting
unwanted attention to her family's well-kept secret. Her father had
contacted Lord Westwick, Mlle. Delphine's employer and the man who
started their secret group. The two were old friends, and the baron had
brokered a deal with Westwick for his daughter's acceptance into the
secret group; of course, whether or not young Klara was happy about it
seemed completely irrelevant.

Since it was common for long-standing members of the group to
go and collect newcomers, Mademoiselle Delphine had been specifically
chosen and sent to Vienna because of her familiarity with court life.

We had been living with Mademoiselle Delphine and Signor Amori
for about a week, when I was asked to attend a court function where we
would meet Klara. I would accompany Mademoiselle Delphine on this
trip.

"It would be good for you to see the world your grandmother the

Countess once frequented," she told me. "And you are similar in age to young Klara, which may help soften the blow for her when she learns that she is essentially being banished from her home."

Meanwhile, our own transition had been smooth: as promised, Signor Amori paid the baker well, and he invited Roza and me to return to his service at any time. We had emptied the carriage and bestowed it upon the boy. Even though his life had been turned upside down by us, our carriage boy was extremely grateful for such a gift: especially the horses, something he could never afford on his own.

Roza had begun to try her hand at running the household staff at Signor Amori's encouragement, which left me more time to myself then I was used to, so, I began to observe Mademoiselle Delphine more closely. I sat on a small chair in front of her mirror and the table that held her cosmetics, something she referred to in French as her *toile*.

"You shall have your own someday," she startled me as she and her attendant walked into the room, gathering around me. "For now, we shall start you in the direction of a true beauty regime. Good habits are the building blocks of all things, *ma petite*. First, you need a proper bath."

She went to the door, her robe tied firmly around her small waist, and told the maidservants to pour me a bath exactly as they would do for her.

"And you will wear something of mine. What you have will not do," Mlle. Delphine continued. "What will you call yourself? It is certainly not common knowledge that your grandmother is the Countess—which would cause quite the scandal."

"It wouldn't be wise to mention the Countess at all," I muttered, "since she is currently imprisoned in her own castle for murder."

Mlle. Delphine had obviously not heard the news. She stopped suddenly and turned to me.

"And who on earth did she kill?"

"She was accused of torturing and murdering her servant girls, although I am unsure of how many," I replied quietly.

"And were you ever planning on sharing this information with Signor Amori and me?"

"Of course," I gestured with some embarrassment, "but it is a difficult

136

topic to mention immediately in polite conversation."

She sighed. "You are right, Katrine. I am indeed sorry for your loss. The Countess was a remarkable woman."

"She is very much alive, and I can assure you that the charges are false," I insisted. "It is, simply put, a way for the Crown to avoid repaying her a substantial debt—and to confiscate her land holdings—or attempt to, at least. Her children are fighting the King for her land."

"And are these your words or hers?" she prodded knowingly.

She pulled a dark green dress from one of her open trunks and began examining it while I fumbled for the words.

"Hers," I finally answered. "Actually, I was unaware of her until several months ago when the witches came to collect my mother and me."

Mlle. Delphine raised an eye.

"Witches? Quite fascinating, I must admit. I hope you can someday bring yourself to discuss what all transpired. Perhaps Kardoska also remembers details you were not privy to."

She picked up the green dress and brought it over to me now. Pulling the fabric up to my face, she stared at me intently.

"Yes, yes, the green will be perfect," Mlle. Delphine said. "And I must ask that you do not wear your cross. The ring can stay, but I need to have your lovely neck and chest exposed."

I fiddled with the ring that I now wore on the third finger of my right hand; I had taken to wearing both pieces since we had stopped working at the bakery. The silver ring was still shiny, the dark purple stone set in the middle of a flower design surrounded by a circle that resembled a rope.

A very distinctive ring, Signor Amori had said, but only people who had seen it before would recognise it.

The maidservant reappeared at the door. "Bath is ready, Mademoiselle."

"Perfect," she exclaimed, putting the dress down on the bed. "Come, dear, before the water gets cold."

Mademoiselle directed me to another room where the tub was located. The maid and another attendant took me inside, stripped me down to nothing and helped me into the large copper tub. This was a new and strange experience for me; back at home, we had always bathed in a small river at the very back of the farm's property.

The water was scented with rose and lavender, and when I sat in the tub, the maids began to furiously scrub my skin pink with small brushes. They then combed out and washed my hair, rubbing my scalp to the point I thought my hair would surely fall out. I was in a strange sort of pain, but I felt cleaner than I ever had in my entire life.

When they were finished, they wrapped me in sheets of cotton and brought me back to Mlle. Delphine's room, my jewellery in hand. They took my clothes; it was strange not to have to think of such things anymore.

Meanwhile, Mademoiselle was being laced into her corset, the tightness accentuating her curves to perfection. The process looked quite barbaric, but my mother had explained its purpose to me long ago. I had thought I would like to work as a seamstress, and Mother had taken me into town once to observe the work; I had planned to embroider a stomacher of one of my mother's dresses for Christmas. However, I had never before seen one actually put on a woman.

"Don't look so frightened," Mademoiselle smiled when the girl had finally finished tying up the laces. "You are too young to wear one of these just yet. The stomacher will be more than enough."

The corset hoisted her breasts up, presenting them as full, round, half mounds at the top of the lace edge of the corset, her skin pure and creamy like fresh milk.

"I haven't had time to instruct you on court behaviour," she began as the maids unwrapped me. "Do you think you will be alright? Can you do exactly as I do?"

"I think I will manage. What is your station at court?"

She smiled again, her blue eyes sparkling in the candlelight. "I am a courtesan, Katrine. I shall tell you of my life one day, but what you need to know is that people will stare at you tonight because you are in my company and they do not know you. Many of these women are jealous of women like me because their husbands seek my company before their own."

"Why?" I asked. In truth, I did not know exactly what a courtesan was.

"Because the noble women believe I am a common whore. The truth is that I am better educated than most of them! I can speak, read and write in three languages and I am polishing up my Italian. I have perfected the art of conversation. I can sing. I can dance. I can even play musical instruments."

One of her maids began to pull on her pale blue dress and lace up her stomacher, which was embroidered with flowers and had tiny pieces of pink silk on the skirt that looked like roses falling across her as she walked.

"Mademoiselle may I—"

"Please Katrine, call me Grisela."

"Of course...Grisela." My mind was racing now. "Do you think when we arrive in Paris and I have settled that you could teach me how to read?"

She paused and watched me as they pulled the green dress down over my head. "In what language, my dear?"

"Any language. I do not know how to read in any way. I cannot write either."

"*Mon dieu*! That will not do at all. I shall teach you everything I know, if you would like," she affirmed.

She sat down in front of her *toile* and began to open the small jars set in front of the mirror on the table.

"I would like that very much," I said, and I could feel my face flush. I was still in awe that this remarkable woman had found me and was so willing to accept me.

She began applying the contents of the jars to her face, and I watched her intently. One application made her pale skin seem to glow like perfect white stone; another made her lips and cheeks seem red and perfectly pinched.

"Mademoiselle, how should I dress the young madam's hair?" asked one of the maidservants, and I suddenly realised I was fully dressed.

The beauty and luxury of the dress, soft green silk embroidered with multi-coloured leaves on the stomacher, overwhelmed me. I cared not about what was done with my hair. I was happy to feel like a grand lady without entirely looking like one. I slipped my ring back on my right hand and tucked my cross into my sleeve.

Grisela sighed, standing and circling me again. Her own blonde hair fell in loose curls around her shoulders; I was overwhelmed at how pretty she was even if only half-ready for the evening.

"Brush it out with a part down the middle, then plait it back and wrap it into a knot," she directed, pointing to the back of her neck. "La nuque du cou."

They sat me down and began their work, while Grisela returned to her spot and another woman went to work on her hair. In a matter of moments, she appeared to be wearing a halo of curls with a single tendril just grazing the left side of her neck.

"You have very good hair," one of the maids said to me as she pulled a comb through the ends. "Like black silk."

"Thank you. You're very kind," I replied.

"Katrine," Mlle. Delphine spoke up, "we are also travelling *sans* escort this evening which, unfortunately, can cause some unnecessary looks. Be prepared for that. Of course," she waved petulantly, "I cannot understand why female independence is *so inquiétant.*"

"What is Signor Amori doing this evening?" I asked, turning to her.

"He has actually taken quite a liking to your Kardoska, so he's training her to share responsibility with Tolone and take charge of the female staff. She is quite phenomenal, I hear."

"I am pleased she has found a place," I nodded. "I must admit that I was concerned for a while."

The women finished their work and backed away from me. I went over to the mirror to see for myself. A woman looked back out at me, her eyes more steady and determined than they had once been. It had been some time since I had seen my own reflection and, with Grisela's polish, I finally looked like a regal lady—how the granddaughter of a Countess should look.

"You are a vision!" Grisela exclaimed. "Your grandmother would be proud!"

She eyed me up and down, and said almost to herself, "The resemblance is quite amazing."

I smiled happily, pushing my anxiety down deep into my body. When I walked into this *soirée* tonight, I would think only of my grandmother and how she would behave—how she would want me to behave. I was determined to be a source of pride for my family.

The carriage dropped us at the foot of a grand set of stairs leading to a large mansion.

"This is the seat of the von Dores family," Grisela whispered to me. "Please close your mouth, dear."

"I'm sorry, it's just...I have never seen a place so grand," I said. "Is this their home?"

"*Oui*, hence the term 'seat'. You are really unaware of all this?" she asked, quite amazed.

I nodded, slightly embarrassed. "More than I can possibly explain before we reach the doors."

"Well, we will worry about that another time. Lift up your skirt so you don't trip, and follow my lead," she directed, and we began our ascent.

We were escorted into a grand ballroom along with several others. I tried my best not to stare, but it was difficult. Everything seemed to sparkle, from the jewels flowing from women's necks and ears, to the massive chandelier casting a glow over the entire room that made it appear as if we were encased in diamonds.

I heard Grisela's light tinkling laugh from beside me. "I should warn you, my dear, that this evening's event is quite shabby compared to those in Paris."

She held out her arm at waist level, her forearm perfectly straight with her delicate hand casually hanging, her fingers pointed to the floor.

"Link your arm with mine, but don't grip me too hard," she instructed. "Keep your hand looking delicate and pretty always."

I did exactly what I was told, and we made our entrance together.

It took me several tries to fall perfectly in step with Grisela. Secretly, I was glad my feet were not visible under my dress, since I probably resembled a stumbling horse. Faces began to meld together as we said hello to couple after couple, the men certainly more pleased to see us than the women.

We fell into a pattern, Grisela saying, "May I introduce my young *protégée*, Katrine." I would bow slightly, never low enough to lose my arm link. We would stay a few moments; a few things would be said between Grisela and the group, something about the party, the weather or music, and then we would continue on. By this point, I had forgotten the names but tried at least to remember the faces.

"Mademoiselle Delphine!" a short, round woman exclaimed when she saw us. "I am so pleased to see you!"

The woman was dressed in a high neck gown of silver gray, her orange hair piled atop her head with silver netting to keep it all in place.

"Baroness von Dores," Grisela whispered to me sharply, and then said aloud: "The pleasure is all mine, Baroness! May I present to you my new *protégée*, Katrine."

I bowed lower this time, Roza's instructions in regards to higher nobility still part of my thoughts. Grisela also bowed but not quite as low.

"I did not know you had a *protégée*, my dear," the baroness said. She stretched out her hand to me, and I dutifully kissed her rings.

The baroness' eyes were a clear, dark blue with a sharp determination behind them. She also had a strange air about her, the smell of blood quite faint but deeply intertwined with her own scent. She was sizing me up, and I could feel her piercing stare right through me.

"Where is the baron tonight?" Grisela spoke up. She had been quick to speak at every introduction—I assumed to avoid questions about my lineage.

The baroness' attention on me immediately broke off. "Off in the salon," she sighed, "—his favourite place to be during any function."

There was a noticeable tinge of anger in her voice, but Grisela smiled gently, steering the baroness back into her confidence.

"I think we will get on just fine without him, *tu ne crois pas?*"

"Perfectly," the baroness agreed, "but I will advise him of your attendance when I introduce you both to Klara."

She then whispered something to an attendant as we followed her across the ballroom. Young people had gathered in one of the room's far corners, surrounded by puffs of smoke and the smell of sweat. I was amazed that they appeared not to notice the baroness as we approached, let alone pay her any sort of respect. Oddly enough, they all looked up and seemed noticeably interested in me.

The baroness stomped her foot to get their attention, and they finally bowed and cleared the way, revealing a table where several people were playing some sort of game with cards. A young woman sat at the end. Her eyes darted quickly to us and only stayed for a moment. She pushed a fallen strand of her orange blonde hair out of her face, pieces deciding not to stay in her disheveled up-do.

The baroness said something to the girl in the common language I often heard around Vienna but did not understand. The girl suddenly turned her gaze to Grisela and me, while the baroness continued upbraiding her. I assumed then that this was Klara von Dores.

"Do you see the men surrounding this girl?" Grisela whispered to me. They're entranced by her, a common problem for blood drinkers who are careless."

"Mademoiselle Delphine, Katrine," the baroness said sharply now, "this is our daughter, Klara."

Klara finally stood; Grisela cringed slightly when the girl's bright orange dress came into full view. We reluctantly exchanged courtesies.

"I thought it best for introductions to be made now before you to leave for France," the baroness said in her clipped tone. It was obvious that she had lost all patience with her daughter.

Klara, meanwhile, stared hard at Grisela.

"I have never travelled with a harlot before," she mused, looking Grisela up and down. "I suppose you will be quite happy if some of my male friends join us on our trip to Paris?"

"Passage to Paris with my company is arranged only for you,

Mademoiselle," Grisela replied calmly.

"And if I refuse?" she snorted.

Grisela remained firm. "You will be coming to Paris with us, Klara. Even if you have to be dragged behind a carriage." She leaned closer to the girl and said quietly, "—Which can be arranged, if necessary."

Klara rolled her eyes but said nothing. We stepped away then with the baroness, without further commentary, and returned to the ballroom.

"I believe we shall send Signor Amori to do the final collection of Klara," Grisela commented. "Women like that respond better to handsome men with foreign accents."

When the baroness left us, I declared, "I have never seen someone so rude!"

"Noble blood does not always make a noble person, *ma petite*," she nodded, maintaining her composure. She patted my linked hand gently with her free hand, although I could sense she was extremely angry.

We continued to walk the ballroom, I assumed to help Grisela's mood. It would be a very interesting ride to Paris if Klara continued on the way she had started. I would not be surprised if the girl actually did end up being dragged behind a cart at some point.

A small seating area was set up in another section of the ballroom for the elderly and women in more elaborate gowns who could not easily walk. Grisela decided we should sit there for a while. She directed that I position myself slightly to her right, within arm's reach.

"If we sit here," she explained, "people may come to us, and then you can observe. Do you know anything about dance?"

Grisela turned her head when speaking, her eyes constantly in front of us.

"No," I shook my head. "What should I do if I'm asked?"

She was silent for a moment, then said, "Tell him you are wearing inappropriate shoes."

I giggled, and several eyes turned to me. I was amazed by the amount of people who stared openly at us as they walked past. The gowns all appeared noticeably different from what Grisela and I wore. Unlike ours, which were very open and exposed from the bodice up, the only visible skin on most of the other women here was their hands and faces.

Watching these people, both women and men in their equally elaborate outfits, I wondered if they any of them saw something of the countess when they looked at me. I also wondered if she had ever been in this ballroom or danced here with her husband when he wasn't away at war. I twisted the ring around on my finger, the silver sparkling as the chandelier reflected off its surfaces. I bit back my emotions as they came rushing forward.

Grisela's voice suddenly caught my attention.

"Do you see the tall, lanky man coming this way?"

I looked up to find an older man with a long gray beard moving intently towards us.

"That is the baron," she whispered, "Klara's father. Be aware of yourself, for he knows your grandmother well."

We stood, and my body tensed as I bowed as low as I could manage.

"Mademoiselle Delphine, I am so pleased to see you," he began, not making eye contact with me as I continued to crouch in a bow. "My wife told me of Klara's disrespectful behaviour. I offer my sincerest apologies. You can see the gravity of our situation."

Grisela nodded sympathetically. When the baron's eyes suddenly fell upon me, she said quickly, "Baron, may I present my *protégée*, Katrine."

She gently poked my shoulder, and I rose. My eyes flew up, and I was amazed that the Baron looked quite old at close view.

"You must be quite a remarkable young woman for Mademoiselle Delphine to take you on as her *protégée*. I am pleased to make your acquaintance," he said, taking my hand and kissing my fingers.

"The pleasure is all mine, My Lord," I replied. He appeared not to notice my grandmother's ring; perhaps he did not recognise it.

"Signor Amori did not join you tonight?" the baron spoke up, turning his attention back to Grisela.

She sighed. "He sends his regrets but had a pressing matter to attend to before we can depart for Paris. He can be quite difficult when his mind is set in a certain direction."

This caused the baron to laugh a loud, hearty sound that seemed too big for his skinny body.

"Lord Westwick has a remarkable sense of humour, doesn't he?"

Grisela smiled. "He would be pleased to be recognised for one of his more admirable qualities. But, quite sincerely, Signor Amori and I get along quite well, and Lord Westwick is honoured that you would choose him to care for Klara."

"Good, good. I am very glad that he is amicable to our arrangement. Now, on to more pressing matters."

The baron took Grisela's arm and they began to walk away; she immediately motioned for me to fall in behind them.

"How will you be returning to Paris?" he inquired.

"By ship, along the Danube, and then by armed coach."

"And have you two been adequately nourished?"

"We are making do, My Lord."

"I can assure you that my daughter will be cleaned and readied before her departure and that her paramours will stay behind in Vienna."

"*Merci*, Baron. Your attention to detail will help make this a smoother transition," Grisela nodded gratefully.

"Now, let's see if my daughter's behaviour will change when I am present," he said, and I then realised we were returning to Klara's smoky corner.

This time the group of youths moved away quickly and out of the baron's way, without any prompting. The baron barked a command that I could not understand, but the intention was obvious by his tone. Klara's expression was quite different when she greeted her father: the impolite and disrespectful girl instantly transformed into a prim young lady, all demure smiles and softness with fluttering eyelashes.

Nevertheless, the baron grabbed Klara by the wrist and pulled her through a door hidden in the wall a few feet away from us. Grisela and I followed wordlessly behind him. When we were alone, behind this closed door, his tirade began.

"Ungrateful little wench! Do you have any idea what I had to do to secure you a place with these people?"

"But I don't want to go, Papa," Klara whined loudly.

"What you want matters not!"

Klara stomped her foot in defiance. "But I am your—"

The baron immediately cut her off. "You were given a chance to fix your behaviour and you refused. I will not allow your stupidity to get us all killed!"

Klara began to whimper now, while the baron raged, "I have spent my life trying to keep this a secret, and I will not allow you to destroy us!"

When Klara's whimpers turned into sobs, he struck her across the face.

"You are going to expose us all, and I will kill you myself before that happens. Do you understand me? You will go to Paris or you will die here!"

He hit Klara again. I was surprised at the strength in the old baron's body. Grisela and I stood on the far side of the room, our eyes lowered in silence.

"You will show Mademoiselle Delphine and her people the respect they deserve. You are lucky such a group of people even exists and that they would take such a vile brat as you into their ranks."

The baron pulled Klara forward. "Now, present yourself to these women properly!"

Klara shuffled forward awkwardly, her orange dress crumpling as she bowed so low I thought her nose would touch the floor.

"Forgive me, Mademoiselle Delphine. Please do not hold my recklessness against me or my family," she whispered. "I am pleased to meet you and your *protégée*, and humbled that I have been accepted into your group."

"*Merci*, Klara," Grisela replied patiently. "I truly hope the transition will be smooth." Her eyes met the baron's. "May we take your leave now, My Lord?"

"Of course," he said, kissing her hand. "It is always a pleasure to see you. I am pleased to have met you as well, young lady."

I bowed to him and then quickly followed Grisela out of the room.

We left without saying a word to anyone, giving orders only to the valet, moving quickly down the stairs and out to the slick street. Snow was lightly falling, making the walkways very slippery. I tried to be very careful: it would be humiliating if I fell in a borrowed dress.

Our carriage finally appeared, and we quickly sped off into the night.

Signor Amori was waiting in the front room when we returned.

"So?" he asked. "How did it go?"

Grisela sighed, saying something in rapid French as she dropped into a chair.

"But you would be very proud, Vincenzo," she added. "Katrine was an absolute gem, as if she had been coached since birth."

"Excellent!" he declared, smiling to me.

"Now, if only our Klara had as much sense," Grisela said shaking her head.

Signor Amori laughed loudly. "I have heard a rumour that she looks and sounds like a whore from a shipyard."

"You would think...and her dress this evening, Vincenzo! Ugh! She looked like some badly wrinkled fruit, like a common strumpet trying to play regal." Grisela threw up her hands. "Do you remember that play we saw in Rome where they depicted the life of the Valois? Klara von Dores looks almost identical to the actress who played *la reine mère.*"

"Oh dear," Signor Amori smirked, covering his mouth with one hand. "But I must remind you, Gigi, of your claimed Valois heritage."

He was obviously teasing her, but I stared at Grisela now in shock.

"You are of the French royalty?" I blurted out.

She turned to me now, as if amazed. When I didn't reply, she declared, "You who knows so little of the world knows the French houses of royalty?"

I couldn't tell if she was teasing me or not, so I waited for her to continue. She finally went on, "My mother told me my father was of the House of Valois. I have no proof other than her word. But, my Italian friend," she said crisply, turning now to Signor Amori, "I must state firmly to you now before our conversation progresses, that any further dealings with young Klara are your responsibility!"

He smiled. "I assumed as much, my dear." He then turned to me.

"And Katrine—"

"Yes, Signor?"

"Call me Vincenzo," he said quickly. "I am sorry I did not tell you immediately, but you look exquisite and I hope you will not become soiled, for it is time now to feed."

I had no idea what he meant.

Tolone came in at that moment, pushing a cart with a silver tea set on top. I was still confused, wondering if I had been handling things properly. Tea was served in delicate china cups, so I carefully watched Grisela to see how she drank, examining exactly how she held the cup and brought it to her mouth to drink. Before I could begin, Tolone came over to me with a silver container in his hand.

"One or two, Miss?" he asked.

I looked at Grisela for a clue as to what to do.

"When was the last time you had blood, Katrine?" she asked evenly.

"The priest...just before we came to Vienna," I replied.

This caused her to smile slightly. "A priest, you say? Then give her two, Tolone."

"Will you tell us the story of this priest?" Vincenzo asked with great interest. Before I could reply, I watched as Tolone dropped two small dark cubes into my tea and handed me a spoon.

"Stir well, Mademoiselle," he advised. I wanted to ask about Roza, but Vincenzo spoke before I could.

"My dear, how on earth did you convince a priest to let you feed from him?"

I shifted nervously in my seat while trying to stir my cup. "There was no convincing. He had something that did not belong to him. I had to retrieve it from him, and he was not pleased."

"Did he see your face?"

"Yes, but it is not a problem."

"Why?"

I stared at the swirling liquid in my cup. "Because he's dead."

The words fell heavily from my mouth, but Vincenzo did not seem to be upset by it.

"Has anyone you fed from survived?" he simply asked.

"No. I didn't know it was possible."

At this, Vincenzo and Grisela turned to each other and smiled slightly.

"Well, we have quite a little savage on our hands, don't we!" Grisela suddenly declared, almost laughing when she said it. I know that she never intended to be cruel, but it suddenly took every ounce of will power I had not to burst into tears.

Seeing my distress, Vincenzo countered, "You're vile, Gigi."

"Oh Heavens, I'm only joking!" she exclaimed. She turned to me now, quite sincere. "Katrine, you must know that. There's no way you could have done differently without proper training...*ma petite*, you did well considering the circumstances."

I tried to smile. Not wanting to appear upset, I sipped my tea to cover my face. The combination of the cubes and liquid flowed easily down my throat. The fact that these cubes were made of blood didn't set in until after I swallowed.

"A concoction invented by our dear Lord Westwick," I heard Grisela explain, my eyes never lifting from the cup. "The mixture is used to help ease the cravings and hopefully cut down on the amount of times we have to feed from live humans."

My body felt energised almost instantly, like every part of my being came alive.

"What sort of man is this Lord Westwick?" I asked.

"All in good time, my dear," Vincenzo replied patiently. "We shall have to save something for our upcoming trip to Paris."

Roza stood by the fireplace in the room we were sharing; I wondered how long she had been waiting for me to return. I closed the door behind me and turned to face her.

"My word, look who's gone and become a lady overnight," she exclaimed.

I ignored her compliment and dropped heavily onto the bed.

"How are you enjoying your new position as head of the female servants? They've taken quite a liking to you."

I took off the dress and began to undo my hair. Roza stayed silent, meanwhile, staring intently into the hearth. She seemed troubled.

"If you're unhappy here, you can always return to the baker's," I said quietly. "We shall be leaving for Paris any day."

"No, no, my dear. I am happier than I have ever been." She snapped out of it. "I am just still a bit shocked by our luck. This all seems a tiny bit too good to be true. Too easy."

I pulled back the blanket and got into bed.

"After what I saw tonight, I'm not sure if all this is going to be as easy as you think. It has been simple here, but it may not be so in Paris."

"Then I'm glad you're so sure of all this, Katrine. My mind's still not made up."

Thump. Thump. Thump. Thump.
I opened my eyes but stayed in bed.
Thump. Thump. Thump. Thump.
My mother was pacing back and forth in front of the fireplace. I hadn't seen her in some time.

"Mother?" I said, sitting up. "Mother? Where have you been?"

"You have us in quite a situation, Katrine. Who are these people? Why are we here?"

"These people are going to help us, Mother. We're going to go to Paris."

"What about the Countess?"

I began to play with my ring. "What about her?"

"She didn't accept us, then."

Thump. Thump. Thump. Thump.

"It is not so simple, Mother."

"Why?" she snapped.

"She was not in the position to accept us," I replied.

Mother became enraged: "Oh, I am sure she had her reasons. God forbid we should tarnish her reputation. Well, she will regret it, I swear it."

"Momma, why are you so quick to assume the worst? How do you know it wasn't something different entirely?"

She came over to me in three quick steps and pulled me from the bed by my shift. She brought my face close to hers; her dark eyes were wild and full of anger and hate, like a caged animal.

"What are you hiding from me, Katrine? What are you doing behind my back?" she growled in my face. "I could have left you for dead in that forest, and this is the thanks I get?"

"Mother, no...," I began.

She hit me so hard I crumbled in a heap on the floor. She crouched down and hit me again and again. Never in my life had I been beaten in such a way. I tried to scream but could only sob. It went on for so long I thought it would never stop. I tried to muster the strength to fight back, but it was as if the life was being drained from my body into the floor.

"What are we going to do now?" she yelled. "You think you can trust these people? You know nothing about them and you agreed to go to Paris with them? Have you lost your mind? Our blood will be on your hands, do you understand that, Katrine? Our blood is on your hands!"

I woke only when my body hit the floor after falling out of bed.

Roza lurched up, startled from her own sleep. "What's that? What's wrong?"

"Just me," I said. I stood up carefully; thankfully, I was not hurt.

"What are you doing on the floor?" she demanded.

I crawled back into the bed beside her. "I fell out. I was having a nightmare."

"Was it about your mother?"

I sighed. "Yes. Why?"

"Maybe you should ask Signor Amori what he thinks, if there's some sort of psychic connection between the two you because of that scratch."

"You've become very well versed and knowledgeable, I see."

She rolled over and turned her back to me.

"You would be surprised what you hear in a kitchen, Katrine. And besides, I have been having nightmares about her myself."

XVI.

New Beginnings

I DECIDED TO WAIT UNTIL WE SET OFF FOR PARIS TO speak to Vincenzo about my mother. It seemed appropriate for a long story to go with a long trip.

The next day the servants began to pack up the house for our departure. Furniture stayed behind, but anything that was personal to Grisela and Vincenzo was carefully packed for the journey. I owned very little, but they made sure those things were packed also. I put on my red dress and cloak after another long bath. When I got past my initial discomfort, I actually enjoyed it: looking and smelling nice made me feel better, almost like a complete person.

When the house was clear, Roza came to me. I was standing in the front room watching all the movement from the window.

"I'm to set out for the docks now with the other servants," she began. "I trust you can manage without me?"

I turned to look at her. This would be the first time we would be separated since my mother and I stepped into that carriage.

"I am sure I will be alright, but I will miss you dearly," I replied. I was already anxious.

"Goodness, child! I will not be far. This was going to happen eventually. You need to make your proper place in this world regardless of emotion, and I am of much lesser blood. I am in a better place because of where we are now, but I can stand beside you no longer." She smiled heavily. "Tis the way of the world, Katrine. You should know as much."

"But I don't," I said quietly as she turned and left. I watched her get into the last carriage with the servants and drive away.

"Are you ready, *ma petite*?" Grisela suddenly called out.

She floated into the room from behind me, the movement of her skirts sounding like fluttering leaves. She was dressed to travel in a dark gray outfit with matching cloak and wide-brimmed hat. Our journey would begin on a boat, traveling down the Danube.

"I have never been on a ship, or a boat of any kind, for that matter. I am a bit apprehensive," I admitted to her.

She smiled. "I can assure you we will be safe. Travelling on the Danube is much simpler and less dangerous than sea travel, or crossing the English Channel for that matter."

"Where is Vincenzo today? I saw him leave early this morning. Has he gone ahead to the ship?"

"He has gone to collect Klara. He went early anticipating some difficulty," she replied. "He will meet us at the dock."

I noticed that I had begun fingering the cross round my neck nervously; I wasn't sure for how long I had, in fact, been doing it. Grisela noticed my anxiety, however, and tried to comfort me.

"I have a feeling that once we set sail you will fall in love with the water. Now, gather your things, for we are leaving."

Vienna was indeed a beautiful city. My face stayed close to the window as we rode along the banks of the Danube, which flowed along one edge of the city. The carriage bumped as we rolled over the cobblestones, the houses seeming taller and narrower the farther we went. The people here were not bothered by the cold; Grisela and I, however, were bundled tightly in the pelts from the Countess' carriage. They were now my personal property and quite valuable in many ways. I did not intend to leave them behind.

I had grown to love Vienna, or perhaps it had grown on me, because I was feeling a bit sad to leave the city. I really had not expected to ever leave it, for I thought it would become home.

While none of the people we passed paid particular attention to our carriage, I still took them all in. From the street people to the regular everyday families of Vienna, I tried my best to remember them all in case I could never return here again. I wanted to remember this place for what it was—originally, a place of escape and then, eventually, the first stop on the road to a new life. I would always remember it as the place I met two people who would alter my existence forever, similar to the way I would never forget Csejthe. Csejthe, likewise, was connected to my grandmother; thus, it, too, would always hold a special place in my heart and mark my entire being.

"You have no idea how happy I am you had these pelts, *ma petite*," Grisela said, snuggling herself down into a pile of fur. "We will need these on the boat, as it gets dreadfully cold."

I kept staring out the window at the street.

"They came from the carriage the witches used to take us."

"You'll have to tell me all about it someday," Grisela patted my hand sympathetically. "Perhaps we could make an exchange? Sometime, I could teach you what I know about being a lady while you tell me of your life and fascinating circumstances. I have so many questions."

I turned to her eagerly. "As do I."

"Then we are agreed," she smiled.

I could smell the snow as it began to fall now, the cold washing strongly through my body and resting heavily on the city. My anxiety about the passage was coming to a head as we got closer to the river; I would have such feelings regardless, but the weather was not helpful. Grisela seemed unfazed; she was used to it, I supposed.

Meanwhile, I hoped that Roza was getting on well and tried to push missing her from my mind. She was right: in reality, she could not constantly be by my side, and I had to get used to our new circumstances.

Our carriage rolled into an area bustling with activity: unloading and loading, families hugging and crying as they said their good-byes. We rolled past all of this and pulled up beside one of the carts that had left earlier on. The carriage jolted to a stop, shifting my already uncomfortable insides. Grisela said nothing as she got out, leaving the door wide open. I sat and stared outside, as gusts of snowflakes streamed in and landed softly on Grisela's discarded fur. I tried to take it all in at once.

I finally grabbed my three pelts, draping one over my shoulder and holding the other two tightly bundled to keep them from dragging on the ground. I stumbled as I got out of the carriage; the pelts were heavier than I thought. I tried to find Grisela in the crowd but had no luck.

"I will take those to your cabin, if you wish," said the same maidservant who had helped with my bath this morning. She suddenly appeared at my side, and I handed her all three with my thanks. She wobbled off towards a gangplank leading up to a ship.

I tried to find someone I knew but was having difficulty, until I spotted a flash of bright orange hair. Klara was standing beside a cart that was unloading. She was wearing a ghastly lime-coloured travelling outfit that made her look like a bag of fruit in a dark room. Vincenzo was standing close to her, his eyes constantly searching; I assumed he was watching for any of Klara's admirers.

I decided not to search for Grisela and went instead to Vincenzo.

"Ah! Katrine! I am pleased to see you," he said happily when he saw me. "Your Roza has been amazing this morning. Indispensable would be the proper term."

"I'm glad to hear it."

"Klara, do say hello to Katrine," Vincenzo called out to the girl in a voice that I thought was louder than necessary and with a tone sounding quite like a parent.

She turned and forced a smile, her face looking like a wrinkled peach. Klara definitely stood out, but not in a good way.

"It will take time," Vincenzo said, keeping his eyes on the crowd, "but she will get better. She has no other option."

Klara seethed in silence, and I tried to hide a smile. Just then, Tolone appeared at the front of the plank and signaled Vincenzo.

"It's time, my dears," he said, linking his arms with mine and Klara's. As we walked together, he and Tolone helped both of us up the plank and onto the boat. Once inside, I was amazed how large the boat actually was. It seemed to me like a large wood-paneled manor house that happened to float upon water.

Tolone brought me up to the main deck, where I found Grisela staring out at the river ahead.

"Come, *ma petite*. This is by far the best view of Vienna."

I stood beside her next to the rail and looked out onto the city that was freshly covered in a light blanket of snow. It was a fabulous view; the houses seemed quiet compared to the bustling riverside, with the snow-topped peaks of mountains in the distant background. It reminded me of the high window of the tower at Csejthe, and I wondered if one could see Vienna from that height.

"I heard a rumour today," Grisela said quietly. "Well, it's more gossip, actually."

"Of what sort?" I asked.

"The Hapsburg King of Hungary is building a case against your grandmother."

"What for?"

"The same charges she faced before, but now he is seeking her death."

My stomach sank. "How? Why? I have to…"

"*Cherie*, there is nothing you can do."

"But it is all a web of lies! How can he do this to her?"

"He is King. He can do as he likes, *ma petite*."

"I have to go to him! I have to stop him," I cried.

Grisela immediately grabbed my arm and pulled me against her.

"Don't be a foolish girl. A priest in a small town is one thing. A king, especially the future Holy Roman Emperor, is quite another."

"But I have to do something, Grisela! I can't just let her die!"

"And what could you do?" she snapped. "You are a young girl who came from nothing, with no name."

"My name is Báthory."

"If you went to the king and told him you were her illegitimate granddaughter, you would be laughed at as they locked you in the cell next to hers," Grisela hissed into my ear.

I stared into her face, her pretty blue eyes, the concerned expression making me feel very small. I was a child compared to her, and she was willing to teach me how to be a lady. She could look at me like a mother would.

"All you can do is write to her," Grisela advised, "perhaps offer her some comfort in your letters."

I started to sob.

"What on earth is the matter?"

"I can't!"

"You can't what, Katrine?"

I tried to level my breathing so I could speak clearly. "I cannot write… I don't know how."

She held my hand tightly in hers.

"Then we shall work on a letter together and send it out as soon as we set foot in France," Grisela said with determination.

She hugged me tightly.

"Now, we are about to set sail, so I suggest you dry your tears and watch."

The ship set out into the Danube. In fact, all the others in the shipyard went in the same direction, except for one.

"That ship is going towards your homeland," Grisela said when she noticed I was watching. "If you stayed on long enough, eventually you would reach the Turks, as well."

I had no need to return to my father's home, but it was nice to know if the time arose, there was a clear path back. I watched as Vienna began to grow smaller and smaller behind us. People were frantically moving about on the decks of the other ships as the wind picked up, adding speed as the enormous sails caught and propelled them forward. I was amazed at how smooth our movements were compared to the constant jolt of a carriage.

I looked at the ship heading off in the opposite direction and my stomach jumped into my throat. Surely that boat went through Hungary. If we turned around now, I could get to her, steal her away. She could come with me to Paris. Better still, we could continue on to a place where no one knew us—start a new life, Grandmother and I.

"I must get off this boat," I cried out.

Grisela sighed. "No need to be afraid. It will be less choppy once we gain momentum."

"No, I have to get off now. I have to leave!"

When she realized what I was doing, Grisela firmly pulled me towards the door leading inside to the main cabin.

"I should not have told you. I knew it was a bad idea and that you would overreact," she shook her head, as if talking to herself.

I could no longer hold my emotions and began to cry hopelessly. Hers would be yet another unnecessary death, in which I had to sit back and watch. I did not want to accept this.

Meanwhile, Grisela pulled me into her arms, hugging me tightly to her chest. I could tell the movement was awkward and uncomfortable for her; all I could think to do was hug her back. The sound of her heartbeat calmed my nerves, reminding me of everything that was living.

"The world must go on, Katrine," she said into my hair. "You must go on. I am certain that is what she would have wanted. Now, let us go have some tea, then we can begin working on that letter."

She led me deeper inside the compartments of the ship until we came to a sitting room similar to the house we had just left. I was surprised at how warm it was in here.

We sat down together, my arms still wrapped around her.

Vincenzo came in a few moments later, his eyes blazing like green fire. He seemed not to notice my emotional state.

"Difficulties, my dear?" Grisela asked him.

He threw his hands in the air. "That girl is unbelievable!"

He then looked at me clutching Grisela, one eyebrow rising slightly.

"I told her the rumour," she said calmly. "She thinks she should try to help."

Vincenzo leaned down so his eyes met mine.

"I'm sorry, Katrine, but while your intentions are noble that is all they are. I am deeply sorry, but you can do nothing for her there except secure your own death sentence."

I could say nothing. There were no words.

"So, what has young Klara done to anger you so?" Grisela spoke up.

"She flew into a blind rage at Tolone for not unpacking her luggage as soon as we departed, then came to me and demanded he be let go as soon as we dock," he retorted.

Grisela smiled easily. "And what did your man say to her?"

Vincenzo sat down in an armchair, still in a huff.

"He told her if she expected such things she had better get used to wearing exactly the same outfit."

Grisela laughed, the sound reverberating into my body. I could not help but smile, but I was unsure what they expected from a girl who clearly knew no better. I felt the tips of Grisela's fingers as she gently stroked my hair. I wondered what Roza was doing now, how she would react to Klara if she were in the same situation.

"It won't be long, *ma petite*," Grisela assured me. "Soon we'll be in Paris, and everything will be better than you could ever imagine."

XVII.

Unladylike Behaviour

EVERY MORNING I WOKE UP, PLANNING MY ESCAPE. AS soon as we docked, in whatever city it was, I would somehow find a horse and sneak away. I would ride for Hungary, get my grandmother, and return to Paris if need be; it could be done. I had only one problem: I had to leave some kind of note for Roza, and I could not write.

However, we did not stop at all, and as we continued on to Germany, my hopes faded with each passing day.

On the fifth day of our journey, Vincenzo approached me after watching me walk about in a daze. I had taken up standing on the deck and watching the world drift past. Places I had never dreamed of faced out to the river in all their splendour, as if on display to entice all of the water travelers. It seemed that the river held the key to everything the world had to offer, and I hoped I could see more of these places someday.

"I must tell you, Katrine," Vincenzo said, standing behind me now, "that the riverfront is often the most beautiful part of some of these cities."

I kept facing forward and staring at the shore.

"That is unfortunate," I finally replied.

He put a hand on my shoulder.

"I see that you are still troubled. I am sorry I have nothing to soothe you. You will just have to have faith that we know what we are doing."

I sighed. "It is not so black and white. It's very, very gray."

"With such beautiful phrasing, I insist you explain."

"I have dreams of my mother," I told him. "She is haunting me. When I sleep, she is there, as if I exist in two different worlds at exactly the same time, and I feel so...I feel like I have to go to my grandmother. I have to try."

"Did she mark you?"

"Excuse me?"

"Your mother, I'm sorry to ask, but did she bite or scratch you? Leave a mark or scratch that never seems to heal?"

Surprised that he knew, I held out my arm to him. The wound was red as always, and I did not like to expose it, especially to the cold wind. He wrapped his thin fingers around my wrist and began to examine it. The soft touch of the white gloves he constantly wore made them feel translucent—not like fingers at all.

Tolone appeared, which I did not even notice until he said, "Signor, I am sorry to disturb you."

Vincenzo lifted his eyes, annoyed. "What has she done now?"

"It would be better if you saw for yourself," Tolone replied. Vincenzo covered my scratch, and we followed Tolone back inside the ship.

I could hear Klara yelling when we stepped into the hallway. A dish flew out of her open doorway, shattering as it hit the wall. Tolone stayed behind me as Vincenzo led us towards the door. He moved out of the way as a pair of shoes flew past.

"Klara!" Vincenzo exclaimed loudly. "This is highly inappropriate!"

"If that useless man of yours had done as he was told," Klara screamed, "I would not be in this state!"

I finally got a look around the doorway into what was left of Klara's room.

"He is not your personal servant—"

"But he is one, nonetheless! I should be treated with the respect allotted to my station!"

"Your station is irrelevant," Vincenzo said loudly. "If you were fitting of such a place, you would not be on this boat!"

A flash of orange burst passed as Klara lunged at Vincenzo. His body hit the wall with a loud crack. Without thinking, I reacted, a hot wave of anger streaming through my veins. I grabbed Klara by the hair and tossed her back through the doorway, a chorus of crashes and bangs following as her body made impact.

Klara screamed. I turned in enough time to catch her coming at me. I threw my weight into my counter attack, propelling us back into the room and hitting the outer wall hard enough for the ship to rock from side to side.

Vincenzo stood and dusted off his pants. "Thank you for that, my dear."

"What the hell are you?" she shrieked.

I kept her pinned down as her limbs flailed around in attempts to get to me. We made direct eye contact; there was no need for me to say anything. After a few moments, she lay still and I caught a tiny glimmer of fear in her eyes.

"A terror beyond your wildest dreams if you touch him again," I said quietly so only she could hear, "or Mademoiselle Delphine. I will no longer tolerate any form of disrespect from you. You are a horrible excuse for a lady."

She remained silent and stared at me with a mix of shock and horror on her face. Energy stopped flowing through me and the reality of what I had just done sunk in. I kept up the angry façade so Klara would not see or sense my concern. Ironically, in any other circumstance, what I had just done could have gotten me hanged.

I stood up and dusted myself off as if my raging temper was a common occurrence, something I had since birth.

Klara sat up, dazed, and looked around. She suddenly seemed embarrassed by the room's appearance: her costly clothes scattered around the room like dirty worthless rags; her hats, shoes, and ribbons littering the floor.

"You should feel privileged to have such beautiful things," I said to her.

Vincenzo entered the room now.

"I will ask a maidservant to help you clean up and organise your wardrobe so it will be easy for you to manage on your own," he began. "And you will have to learn this simple fact, Klara: you will not have any personal servants."

Klara looked at me, then back to him and said, "Thank you, Signor Amori. I apologise for my behaviour."

She looked at me again, too, and by this look, I knew that even though she was fearful of me I had just made an enemy in Klara von Dores.

That evening, Grisela, Vincenzo and I ate our meal in silence. Klara had decided to eat in her room; she and one of the young maids were busy fixing her mess. I was unsure if he had told Grisela what happened, as I went straight to my room after the incident. I was also worried that Klara might use her influence against me now to hurt me.

Thinking this out loud, I blurted out: "Do you think it will be a problem?"

Grisela looked up. "What, *ma petite?*"

"What happened today, with Klara, do you think it will cause me problems in the future?"

Grisela sighed. "She may try, but you have shown her enough of your strength that you should not be concerned. Also, the kind of loyalty that you showed to Vincenzo and to me goes a very long way in our world."

"Nevertheless," Vincenzo spoke up, "I must insist that when we arrive in Paris, you allow us to perform some tests."

"What sort of tests?" I asked.

"Nothing to be afraid of, my dear. I am just curious about exactly what has happened to you as a result of that scratch."

***

The growl started from under my bed.

I had slept peacefully without Roza since arriving on the ship; but now, I realized the rumbling had probably gone on for some time before it actually woke me.

At first I thought it was something from deep within the ship. Only after I lay completely still did I hear it clearly. Half asleep, I wondered for a moment if Klara had stuck something terrible under my bed.

I sat up and tried to think. I had nothing close by to use for my defence if necessary, but I could not sit and wait for whatever it was to decide it wanted to attack. I got up and out of bed and nothing happened—no movement—but the growling continued.

I finally got down on my hands and knees to try to see what this thing was. I was prepared to come face to face with some sort of rabid creature with foam pouring out from between its massive teeth.

To my surprise and dismay, I saw that it was my mother, who lay under the bed. When her face finally turned to me, her dark eyes were glowing yellow, her teeth barred like a creature on the attack.

She looked like an animal.

A very angry animal.

I scurried backwards across the room and up into a chair that was in the corner, pulling my feet up under me. It took me a moment to realise the other sound I was hearing was my own screaming. My body started to rock back and forth, and I prayed that it was really the boat moving with people coming to save me.

Mother started crawling out from under the bed, her hands twisted behind her, palms flat and her belly and face pointed toward the ceiling in a sort of demonic spider walk. Her growl was a disgusting, gurgling noise that came from within her body; she turned her head around, her blazing eyes getting brighter as they stared through me. Her mouth contorted and her jaw began to stretch and crack, her growls now a howl of agony...I could feel my heart racing and aching, my breath caught in my throat. This fear was even worse than what I felt the first time. I began to shake as she drew near me. I shut my eyes hoping that doing so would make this end....I could feel the heat of her breath on my face, the pain of a claw piercing my flesh.

I could faintly hear someone calling my name; the sound seemed to be coming from inside my own head and the shaking got more urgent, almost violent....

Within a blink of an eye, I woke to find Vincenzo standing beside my bed, shaking my body to try to wake me. His voice was calling my name; his expression was full of panic.

"I'm alright," I said to him. I heard Roza's voice but could not see her.

"What was happening?" he asked.

I swallowed hard, nearly choking, then blurted out: "My mother... nightmare...monster."

"Have all the nightmares been the same?"

"No. This was the worst."

He watched me carefully as I caught my breath and tried to regain some composure.

"I heard something, so I got up to look and she was there, she was growling, her eyes were glowing red like fireballs," I began, "and she crawled out from under my bed. I climbed up on the chair...she came out on her back like some sort of monster."

He gave me an unusual look. In one sense, he appeared to be thinking about what I was saying yet, in another, it seemed like he knew exactly what was happening and wasn't sure how to explain it to me.

"What should I do?" I sat up and pulled my knees to my chest.

Vincenzo sighed. "I don't know. I will be better equipped to help you when we get to Paris. Are you still afraid?"

"Of course I am! What is happening to me?"

"The simplest explanation I can give is that we all have a connection to those who changed us. They are our creators, if you will. It is not uncommon for a parent to turn a child into an 'other'. In Grisela's case, sometimes your parent brings you into this world when they are others themselves, so it is inherited. But it will get easier, I promise," he said reassuringly, as he pulled a few stray hairs away from my face

"Do you have similar dreams…of the one who turned you?" I asked him urgently.

His expression softened. "Not often anymore, since that was a very long time ago. The memories are not as fresh. But I did shortly after I had been turned."

Roza finally appeared, and seeing her face brought a strange feeling over me.

"I will sit with you until you are sleeping restfully," she said.

She sat down on the bed beside me, and I immediately noticed that she smelt different: like sweat and the river, and a mix of cooking smells I could not place.

"You are lucky to have such a woman as Kardoska," Vincenzo said calmly. "I would have given anything to have that comfort when I was in such a state."

"I know," I agreed. "I am very fortunate."

He left, and I curled up beside Roza. I did not have the heart to tell him, though, that I suddenly did not find her as consoling as she once was, not in the slightest bit.

XVIII.

Like Mother, Like Daughter

A WARM BATH SCENTED WITH HERBS WAS A SIGN THAT we were to dock at our final port in Germany soon, possibly in a day or two. I was relieved as I was feeling restless and anxious.

"You shall wear something of mine when we finally reach Paris, but I am unsure of exactly what," Grisela pondered. She was seated today in the corner of the room, dressed in a heavy silk robe.

"I have dresses," I offered.

She let out a small noise of frustration. "They are not suitable, *ma petite*. It shall be the first time you are seen in France! You must look the part, so every inquiring mind will want to know who this stunning young lady could possibly be."

My thoughts wandered back to the dress that Roza had made for my official entrance to meet my grandmother. I had still not given up the idea of going back for her, but I had to wait until we landed to get more news. Grisela insisted that it was only a rumour.

"We will have dresses made once you are settled," she continued.

"But I cannot afford—" I began, and she waved me off.

"Not of your concern, *ma petite*," she said. "Put your focus now upon making a strong impression and, of course, your health."

I stared at her as a maid washed my hair. There were so many things

I wanted to say. For one, this was not the world I expected to live in. I never imagined I would have to worry about the face I presented to others. As I was thinking this, Grisela pushed a perfect blonde curl from her forehead, sighing to herself.

"As a little girl, Katrine, did you not dream of life at court? Of gowns and balls and jewels?"

"I could not dream of something I knew nothing of," I answered.

"You did not know of kings and queens, princesses and princes?" she exclaimed. "You knew of the House of Valois, after all."

"I did. But I did not know of court life until recently when my father made something for one of the court chaplains," I said.

"What did he make?"

I looked down at the side of the tub; a nostalgic memory flashed in my mind, and I could suddenly smell my father's workshop.

"He made enamel by trade, as did my grandfather," I began, "and so will my brother, I suppose. He made that cross I wear sometimes."

She twirled a single curl around her finger, watching it casually as one might watch the clouds. Her blue eyes seemed distant, like she was in some far off place I couldn't see.

"Well, if you are ever going to experience court, Fontainebleau is the place to do it. There is nothing like it in this world," she asserted. She rose from the chair, unfolding herself like a graceful dancer.

"What shall we do in Paris, Grisela?" I asked now.

I stood, the maidservants wrapping me up as I stepped out of the tub. She wrinkled her nose at me as if I had missed something.

"I mean for work. Will we have employment of some sort? Or shall we only go to parties and wear nice clothes?" I continued.

"Parties are far more work than you could imagine, *ma petite*, but we will do other more gratifying things with our time. As my *protégée*, you will be learning as well as working."

"As a courtesan?"

She sighed. "Is that all you think I am, Katrine?"

"I'm sorry, but you have told me nothing else."

"As a matter of fact, I am also the principal dancer of the *Danse*

Macabre, Lord Westwick's safe haven for people in our situation," she began, "and any situation of exceptional circumstances, for that matter. It is difficult to explain, you must see for yourself."

I felt a smile begin to spread across my face. "So I shall dance?"

Grisela laughed that same light tinkling sound like soft chimes.

"Yes, *ma petite*. You shall dance."

I woke to the dark room. I felt a presence seated in the chair in the corner. Something seemed different.

"Hello, Katrine," the voice said clearly and calmly. My heart jumped into my throat. It was not my mother, but I would never forget that voice as long as I lived.

"Grandmother?" my voice was shaky as I spoke into the darkness.

"Yes, my dear," she replied.

"Why are you here? What is happening?"

The sound of rustling silk was strong as if she had stood and was pacing. "I have come to warn you… command you for that matter. I know you wish to come back to Hungary and remove me from my fate but I cannot allow you to do so."

"But the king would see you executed!"

"And I can assure you he will not succeed," she countered. "I may be imprisoned, but I still have some power left. It will take more than the axe to take down a Báthory , I promise you that! Both of my parents were Báthory blood, and it runs strong in my veins. You cannot come back, Katrine."

"No! I cannot stand by and do nothing!" I urged. "I have to try. I could go and plead on your behalf."

"While I appreciate the thought, a plea from my illegitimate granddaughter would only make my reputation worse. I am sorry, my dear, but I must be honest to protect your life."

"I am so sorry, Grandmother. I want more than anything to come and save you from this mess."

She smiled and came over to sit beside me on the bed. She caressed my cheek with her hand.

"That ring I gave you is a direct link to me. It is how you can help me, Katrine.

Live your life and wear that ring with pride, wear your name with honour. All that energy will pass through the ring between us."

I smiled to myself, spinning the ring around my finger.

"Your will and courage are stronger than any physical being," the Countess continued proudly as she took my hands into hers and raised them to her lips, gently kissing them. "You are my granddaughter, after all. I would expect nothing less from you."

I lay beside her and she began stroking my hair with the tips of her fingers.

"Sleep now, Katrine. You have quite a journey ahead. I think we would have been great companions, you and I. The things we would have experienced together...." She continued talking but I could no longer understand her as I drifted helplessly into sleep.

I woke again sometime later and she was gone. My mother was now seated in her place.

"My child, I think I shall die," she said flatly.

I sighed. "We shall all die one day, Mother."

"No, no, Katrine. I feel as if I am being consumed by this awful sickness, like my mother before me," she began. "It fills the body and eats away at the insides, starting as a small little lump. Like a pearl, gnawing at your life force until there is nothing left."

"Why do you feel this way?" I asked. "What has happened?"

"I do not feel right inside my mind, the world around me feels as if it is a different place. I do not feel right within myself, Katrine."

"And that means you shall die?"

She ran the tips of her fingers across my forehead and through my hair.

"I am sick, my child, my precious first born. Soon I shall leave you and this earth behind, and I pray the Lord takes me into his warm embrace, that the sins of my birth mother will not cause Him to frown upon me."

"But she did not do any of those things."

Mother paused, the tip of her middle finger resting on my hairline.

"What did you say?"

"I said she didn't commit the crimes that she is accused of. Your passage to heaven is clear and smooth."

"How do you know? What proof do you have?" she asked, her tone hopeful.

"How do you know the Countess didn't kill those girls?"
"I don't know many things in this world for sure, Mother, but that I do."

When I opened my eyes to a knock on the door, it was already morning. I heard Tolone's voice informing us that we would be reaching our port this evening. I didn't move or respond. I just laid there and kept staring at the ceiling. Even though we would finally disembark today, our trip was far from over; we still had to travel some distance by land to reach France. Whether it was from the voyage or the visions, I was becoming quite weak and exhausted. I began to wonder if my mother's words from the night before held some truth—was I also slowly dying?

XIX.

Fresh Blood

THE DRESS WE CHOSE WAS BLUE SATIN, WITH AN underskirt and stomacher patterned with different blue tones and shades of purple. I saw it before we left the ship in Germany and started in our caravan towards Paris, and not again until the final night of our passage, when we stopped at an inn for dinner and shelter from a storm.

"We shall make ready our dress tonight, for we will arrive at the chateau tomorrow," Grisela said as we sat down to eat. "You must look perfect when we meet the others."

Vincenzo chuckled. "I suppose you should prepare Klara, as well, my dear."

The three of us were dining in the main room of the inn; Klara had decided to stay in her room, claiming an upset stomach.

"She is not my concern," Grisela disagreed.

"I'm sure that our Katrine will do just fine," Vincenzo said happily, placing a hand over mine.

"I am a bit nervous," I admitted.

"Don't be," he replied. "You are quite likeable."

"Klara doesn't like me."

"Opinions should not be passed solely on Klara's judgment. We like you very much, which is most important," Grisela stated. I watched her as she held her knife and fork, the way she sat and ate and how she cut her food.

I was studying her now at every opportunity, determined to become as elegant and graceful as she was, even in the simplest of daily practices.

"Vincenzo, we need to feed. I cannot return to the chateau in this state, and *ma petite* needs to be at her best, as well," she spoke up.

What she meant did not fully sink into my mind for several moments.

"Tolone has said nothing to you?" Vincenzo murmured. "Well, then I shall break it to you. Our supplies are low, unfortunately. It seems young Klara's unrealistic demands were inappropriately catered to."

"So now we shall all suffer? I should tear out that girl's throat myself," Grisela exclaimed. She then nudged me, jokingly. "Or maybe you should speak to her, *ma petite.*"

"If the two of you are quite finished with your homicidal plans," Vincenzo interrupted, "one of the maids has agreed to be bled. It will also be a good opportunity for Katrine to feed without causing death."

"There will be enough for all of us? Without causing harm?" I asked, my eyes wide with surprise and anticipation.

Vincenzo smiled. "You have much to learn."

The two of them chatted on about Paris as we finished our meal. I tried very hard not to think of the idea that, after all that had happened and how far I had come, I might not be accepted into their world. I tried my best not to wonder if Vincenzo and Grisela would simply cast me aside if Lord Westwick did not approve.

Sometime later, Roza came down to collect us, looking scrubbed and clean in a new uniform, similar to what I had seen the other maidservants wearing. I almost didn't recognise her.

"Tolone sent me to come collect you three, Signor," Roza said to Vincenzo. "He said they are ready for you upstairs."

"Excellent! I swear I would be lost without his efficiency," Vincenzo exclaimed. We stood and followed him as he went upstairs, Roza and I taking up the rear.

"And you are alright with this, Katrine?" Roza whispered to me.

"What is 'this' exactly?" I asked.

"Cutting a girl and taking her blood," she said simply.

"Why Roza, it sounds as if you would prefer I leapt out a window and killed a man in the street!"

She grabbed my forearm tightly and pulled me closer. "'Tis not the act that bothers me, it is turning it into something simple and common that I am uncomfortable with."

"Then you shall have to learn to adjust, if you wish to stay. Because I suspect there are many strange practices in this world that will upset your sensibilities," I said as I turned and continued with the others upstairs.

Tolone sat the girl in a large chair on one side of Vincenzo's room where a large wooden screen had blocked off the sleeping area. She was surprisingly cheerful, considering the circumstances, and smiled brightly to us as we entered. I heard the door close behind; Roza had decided not to join us.

"Does the young lady have some tea?" Vincenzo asked Tolone, who nodded in acknowledgement.

Grisela leaned over and said to me quietly, "When she wakes, she won't remember anything. It is the only way we can do this."

"But what does she know? Tolone must have told her something," I whispered back.

"Only that she needs to be bled, for some reason or another; I am amazed that one would believe it's beneficial for health to do so," Grisela mused.

Meanwhile, the girl happily sipped her tea, and as she became drowsy, Tolone rolled up the sleeve on her other arm. A metal tip on his first finger pricked the curve of her arm at the elbow, and a thin line of blood moved down her skin.

"*Ma petite*, if you would do the honours," Grisela invited me.

I assumed they could see the panicked look on my face, because Vincenzo added, "If you feel any change in your mind, pull away. But we will watch you, so don't be afraid."

I placed my mouth on the girl's arm and the blood began to flow. My body immediately started to react, perfect energy and strength returning to me that I'd forgotten I could have.

I opened my eyes, not realising they had closed, and quickly pulled away.

"Are you alright, Katrine?" Vincenzo asked.

My eyes immediately lowered to the floor.

"Yes, I am alright," I said catching my breath and wiping my lips. "But I need a moment."

"Of course," he replied.

I walked over to the screen and sat on the floor beside it. I watched next as Vincenzo and Grisela took their turns. Grisela made the process look like a beautiful, elegant ritual as her delicate hand took the girl's wrist and her perfect lips touched the skin. She seemed too lovely to be what she was, and the fresh blood coursing through her body made her glow as if she were lit up from the inside.

"It will get easier. Soon it will be like breathing," Vincenzo promised. He was, to my surprise, sitting on the floor beside me.

"That's right!" Grisela called over. "And that reminds me, *ma petite*, we should be off to bed. Tomorrow is a very busy day...bathing, dressing, cosmetics. I am exhausted just thinking about it. I'll send for you early, so be ready and sleep well."

She then left the room in a rustle of skirts and energy.

"I shall take the girl to her room, sir," Tolone said, picking up the sleeping maid like a sack of flour.

"I would be happy to walk you to your room if you'd like, Katrine," Vincenzo offered. He held out his arm for me and linked it to mine.

We walked towards the door in silence; I desperately wanted to pour my heart out to this man, share my every hope and fear and any thought that might be worth mentioning, most especially my gratitude, but when we got to my door, I turned to him and asked instead, "Do you really think Lord Westwick will accept me?"

Vincenzo ran his thumb softly across my cheek.

"My dear, I am positive that in a short matter of time, you will be the toast of Paris society."

XX.

Bienvenue à Paris

THE CARRIAGE ROLLED ON. THE SKY WAS CLEAR AND bright, a welcome change from the gloom of the dreary gray haze and the harsh winds of the days prior. Even though it was a clear day, it was too cold to open the windows, so I did not get to see the wonders of Paris as we neared our final destination. I was afraid yet excited at the same time; slowly, the reality of a drastically different life was starting to sink in.

I was happy to have some quiet moments before being presented to Lord Westwick. Fortunately for me, Klara had demanded a private carriage; to my relief, Vincenzo would not have it, so they rode ahead together, leaving me again with Grisela.

"Now, Katrine, in life I don't believe in being deceitful," Grisela began, "but on this occasion, I am going to have to ask for you to behave as dignified and ladylike as you can muster."

"I would do so regardless, Grisela. Why is that deceitful?" I asked.

"Because it must appear you were raised and educated in such a fashion, as if you were born into a noble household," she continued. "Not that you are an ill mattered vagrant, *ma petite*, but only a certain type of girl could be my *protégée*, and you must show them why I chose you. I would be very distressed if judgment was passed on you simply because of where you were born. So in that aspect, there is some deceit."

"People should be judged on the content of their character," I countered.

She smiled. "And that is why I chose you, because that is exactly what I believe. As I said earlier, we are going to the chateau where I am sure the salon is in full swing. Klara will make her official entrance, and then you and I will follow."

She surveyed me once more. "I was concerned about your styling, but it turned out much better than I had envisioned. And you will grow accustomed to the stomacher."

Slightly uncomfortable, I shifted position. "I must admit it does force me to stand and sit up straight."

I was happy they had decided against putting my hair up. I had become accustomed to the plait hanging down my back and found it less restrictive, even oddly comforting. I also had my father's cross pushed into my sleeve. Grisela promised that once we got a proper chain for it, it would look nice hanging from my neck and that I could wear it as much as I liked.

I kept my hands folded in my lap, the purple stone in my grandmother's ring matching the tones in my dress perfectly. I could hear my grandmother's voice in my head: "Wear the ring with pride; wear your name with honour."

I was so lost in my thoughts I did not notice, at first, that the carriage had slowed.

"Ah! My heart feels whole once again!" Grisela exclaimed as the carriage stopped. "*Je T'aime Paris!*"

Before I had a chance to respond, we were out in the midafternoon sun standing on the snow-lined steps of a truly grand and lovely house. The stone walls seemed to stretch into the heavens; I could not tilt my head back far enough to see the roof. Light seemed to be shining from every window, energy flowing out as it radiated with activity.

"It is time to embrace your destiny, Katrine," Grisela said proudly as she took my arm in hers and we walked inside.

We stepped into the grand foyer; two servants came and removed our cloaks and Grisela's hat. I could hear exclamations of joy. When I also heard Klara's name declared, my heart sank. It sounded as if she was well known here and even liked in this place. I began to worry how that might affect my chances of being received.

"And where is Lord Westwick this evening?" Grisela asked the servants who took her hat.

"At the back of the large parlour, Mademoiselle. Shall I announce your arrival?"

"No, no, that's quite alright. I'm sure he already knows," she replied, turning to me. "This is it now. Come along, *ma petite.*"

I followed behind her, trying my best to appear calm and graceful. All eyes were turned on us as we walked into the room. Klara was already there and looked none too pleased as gazes were momentarily averted from her. Some bowed respectfully to Grisela as we crossed the room. She smiled and nodded as if she were queen of this place; perhaps she was to these people.

I could hear Vincenzo's voice as we went further into the room. He was talking to a man seated in a grand chair of plush red velvet with two women standing to the left and another man on his right. Vincenzo's eyes turned to us and he smiled happily. With that, the others noticed us, as well.

The man in the chair stood up, his dark, wide-set eyes scanning me before he turned his attention to Grisela. I was stunned by him; he was attractive and suave in a way I had never seen in a man before.

He smiled, and his eyes sparkled. "*Bonjour mon étoile. Bienvenue á la maison.*"

Grisela held out her hand, and he kissed it tenderly.

"*Bonjour, mon seigneur.* May I introduce to you my *protégée*, Katrine Báthory," Grisela said, and I bowed as low as I could.

"It is an honour to finally meet you, My Lord," I said, my face still directed downwards. I hoped he could hear me clearly.

"*Protégée!*" the man exclaimed. "This girl must be quite remarkable for you to take her on, Gigi. Please stand, Katrine, so I may look at you fully."

I rose and his eyes met mine. He was alarmingly handsome, and the thought made me blush.

"Katrine, this is Lord Charles Westwick," Grisela introduced us. I was lost in his hypnotic gaze and had forgotten there were other people in the room.

"The pleasure is all mine," he replied taking my hand and sniffing the inside of my wrist. He kept his eyes locked firmly with mine.

"May I present our other acquaintances," Lord Westwick then said, first motioning to the two women. "Victorie de la Reina, Mathilde de la Rivage, and this man to my right," he gestured, "is Don Tommas Giamedici."

Victorie was a slender woman with pale skin and warm brown eyes. Her brown hair was pulled up into a net covered in tiny pearls. Mathilde, on the other hand, was a buxom blonde with golden curls, her creamy skin like fresh milk. They were both dressed in different shades of green, Victorie a deep emerald with stunning lace trimming the edges, and Mathilde the colour of grass, perfectly tailored to her curvaceous body.

I bowed to them and to Don Tommas, who wore a fine, brown wool topcoat with matching leather boots. I had never seen so many attractive people in the same place; I wondered if it was that way with all the upper-class who could afford such nice clothes.

"So you are a Báthory?" Lord Westwick inquired. "May I ask of your family?"

"Countess Erzsébet Báthory, the Lady Widow Nádasdy, is my grandmother," I said proudly.

He nodded. "I had the honour of meeting her once at her late husband's family seat at Sárvár. He was a remarkable man with an incredible wife. You are lucky to have such lineage."

"My apologies, Lord Westwick, but Count Nádasdy was not my grandfather," I spoke up.

He raised an eyebrow, and the hint of a smile formed.

"Your life is quite a story, I see," Lord Westwick mused. "I would much like to hear it. Perhaps tomorrow morning, over tea? I'm hoping you'll stay awhile. It seems we have much to discuss."

"I would be honoured," I replied.

Lord Westwick clapped his hands together, and a tea service was immediately wheeled in. The maid handed me a tea cup and small spoon, while Lord Westwick watched me carefully. I could smell the blood in the tea. I sipped it politely, restraining my compulsive urges.

"Is it to your liking, Katrine?" he asked.

"Yes, very much so. Thank you."

When I raised my cup to take a second sip, Lord Westwick suddenly became startled and moved closer to me.

"Do you have some sort of mark or open wound there?" he asked me, his hushed voice low and haunting now as he surveyed my arm.

Vincenzo quickly appeared beside us. "She has a scratch given to her by the newly transformed."

"Oh? May I?" Lord Westwick asked, and he would not be denied.

The cup was quickly removed and my sleeve pulled back fully. He ran the soft tip of his finger along the edges of what was now a large scar, his touch as gentle as a cool breeze.

"Hmm, I see," he said, scanning the mark with practised precision. "Your transition was violent. I assume traumatising. While this may sound horrid of me, I look forward to hearing your story. After all, attracting the attention of my Gigi is not an easy task."

All at once, we heard a commotion behind us. Before Lord Westwick and Vincenzo turned to look, I could hear Klara cursing like a farmhand. Her angry cries were immediately followed by an equally outraged male voice.

"Where did you find this girl?!" the male voice thundered. I turned to see him storming towards us.

Vincenzo smirked. "I see young William has met the charming Klara."

The man named William had eyes of blue fire as he spied Lord Westwick and came towards us like a lightning bolt.

"How could you bring her here?" William snapped. "She is disgraceful!

How could you have such a vile excuse for a woman in our company?"

Undaunted, Lord Westwick simply smiled and said, "William of Naples, may I introduce you to Katrine Báthory, Grisela's new *protégée*."

The eyes of blue fire turned to me; I stepped back, startled by his intensity.

"Adding another harlot to our mix, Charles?" he probed bluntly.

"Sir, I can assure you, I am no harlot," I exploded, "and neither is my mentor!"

He laughed at me as if I was an ignorant child. I suppose, in his mind, I was.

"Pay no mind to William, *ma petite*," Grisela said easily, ignoring him. "He has no affection for women. And no manners, either."

He laughed at Grisela. "I do indeed have an affection for women, but only a certain type, and there seem to be none here."

I immediately disliked this brash, young man, and the words suddenly flew out of my mouth: "Then maybe you should reconsider your situation if it so disturbs you!"

At this, Lord Westwick covered a smile as William stared me down; I wondered if he was waiting for me to apologise or cower.

"And who are you again?" he demanded.

Vincenzo intervened. "She is a Báthory, a descendent of the King of Poland and many Transylvanian princes. Hungarian noble blood at its finest."

I was surprised to hear this, as I had not known any of those details about the Báthory family. I would be sure to ask Vincenzo questions about this at a later time.

"Well, whoever you are," William glared, completely unimpressed, "I hope you are better behaved than that one," gesturing towards Klara. "She is a horrible excuse for a baron's daughter!"

With that, he stormed out of the room, and I was relieved to see him go.

"What a strange man," I murmured, not realising that Lord Westwick was still close enough to hear me.

"Men of such power tend to be very moody," he remarked. "William has more power in his smallest finger then the entire French army.

Actually, more power than any army in the world, including the Turks."

"But how?" I asked.

My tea was returned to me, the smell of blood only lingering slightly now. I took a big sip, bigger than one may normally take with tea, and felt refreshed almost instantly.

"If I told you now, I may have nothing to add to our conversation tomorrow," he replied gently. "Now, if you will excuse me, I must be social in my own salon. Gigi will properly introduce you, and I shall have a room readied for you shortly."

He took my hand and kissed it, his dark eyes staring intently into mine for a moment before he walked away. I turned to Grisela, who was speaking to Victorie and Mathilde in such rapid French it no longer sounded like words.

Mathilde smiled, her face glowing. "Bonjour, *ma cherie*. Or shall we all call you *petite*?"

"Use her name, Mathilde, so as not to sound condescending," Victorie gently scolded, and it was clear that these women had been talking about me.

"Oh, and Gigi is not condescending?" Grisela chided them. "It sounds like the name of a lap dog, for heaven's sake!"

"Grisela, did you have no time to prepare the girl's hairstyle?" Mathilde cut her off. "It does not match the outfit."

Victorie disagreed. "She is still young. There is no problem with a simple plait. I braided my hair into my twenties."

Mathilde turned her head, and I saw that her curls were in fact piled atop her head in an elaborate fashion that showed their definition clearly.

"Don't overwhelm the girl with such things just yet, ladies," Vincenzo suddenly interrupted. "She's had a long journey and needs some time to rest and get her bearings."

He motioned sympathetically and directed me to the chair that Lord Westwick had vacated. I gratefully sat down, for what felt like the first time in an eternity. I suddenly thought of my grandmother who might have sat in a magnificent chair such as this, and I felt like a grand woman as I sipped my tea and looked out into the spacious room.

Meanwhile, Klara was standing at the other end receiving greetings as if this was her royal court. I wondered for a moment if she was ever frightened and intimidated after leaving the safety of Vienna and her parent's court, if she worried about making friends or being lonely in this new world.

She suddenly shot me a look of pure hatred. When we made eye contact, I realised my thoughts were entirely misplaced. The only thing I should be concerned with in regards to Klara was where she might place the knife in my back.

"When you have finished your tea, you may choose to retire for the evening," Grisela said from her seat beside me. "I believe I shall."

"But isn't it still early?" I asked.

She smiled. "Lesson one, *ma petite*: always leave the room before you leave their thoughts. That way they always wonder."

Following her lead, I handed my empty teacup to one of the many servants roving about, all of them waiting on our every move. At that moment, I wondered if my circumstances and heritage had been different, would that servant have been me.

"Come now, *petite*," Grisela suddenly said, moving in front of me. "It is time to go. You will have many more opportunities to stare."

XXI.

Revelation

THE NEXT MORNING, AFTER PUTTING ON THE BLUE
dress Roza had made for me, I went down to the main floor in search of
Lord Westwick. As soon as my feet touched down at the bottom of the
grand staircase, two maids appeared as if by magic.

"Can we help you with something, Mademoiselle?" the taller of the
two asked. They both stood at attention, eager to please.

"I have been invited to tea with Lord Westwick but am unsure where
to go. Can you take me to him?" I asked.

They nodded in unison, and I followed them as they led me through
the house, which seemed more massive with every step. They stopped at
the entrance to a room, a large room with the walls and ceiling made of
panels of glass.

"What sort of room is this?" I wondered aloud.

"The English call it a conservatory," Lord Westwick's voice came
from the far side of the room. He rose from a large wing backed chair
and came towards me. I bowed slightly and he motioned for me not to
do that.

"Stop, I insist," he said. "You are an equal here, Katrine."

I smiled. "Thank you, Lord Westwick. You are far too kind."

"And, please, unless we are in an utterly formal situation, I insist you call me Charles. In that same situation, I would address you as Mademoiselle Báthory."

I followed him back to the chair he'd been sitting in and sat in the matching one across from it.

"How did you sleep?" he inquired politely.

"Quite well, thank you."

He smiled. "Wonderful. I must confess Vincenzo told me you have some difficulty sleeping."

"Yes, unfortunately, I do," I said solemnly. "In fact, I have nightmares of my mother."

"Wait," he held up a hand. "Let us have some tea before you start speaking. Stories are much better with tea."

He motioned for a maid who brought in an elaborate tea service on a rolling cart. The set itself was white and beautiful, perhaps made of pearl.

Charles poured the tea with delicate precision, and I watched in fascination. The set shone in the sunlight, its luminosity giving it a soft glow that seemed to come from within. He carefully added drops of blood to my tea and not his own, taking it from a vial similar to the one Tolone had used in Vienna. Then he handed me the cup and saucer.

"Here you are, my dear. Now, tell me everything."

"My mother," I began slowly, "was Countess Erzsébet Báthory's illegitimate child, born before her marriage to Count Nádasdy. I know very little of the circumstances. I don't even know who her father was. I only know the baby was given to a midwife and banished from Hungary. Just before this past All Hallows Eve, three women, servants of Countess Báthory, came to my house and took my mother and me, saying they were taking my mother to meet the Countess and claim her birthright. On All Hallows Eve, they took us into the forest to perform some sort of ritual with my mother. Unfortunately, it was then that something went wrong."

"What do you mean 'wrong'?" he asked.

"I did not know until that moment that my mother had knowledge of magic. She cast a spell against what these women—these witches—

were doing…and she…her body ripped apart and she suddenly became a beast," I continued, relieved to be telling someone the whole truth. "She killed two of the witches, and I believe wanted to kill me, too, when she marked me. But somehow I survived the ordeal. I went to the Countess for help, but she had already been arrested."

"Arrested?"

"She was imprisoned…her servants were executed. They are calling her a murderess. The King of Hungary wants her head. She could not help me. So, Roza, my traveling companion, and I went to Vienna to begin a new life. That is where Vincenzo found me. He said that you could help me, that you help people like…me."

"Did the Countess believed you, that you are her granddaughter?"

"Even I did not believe it myself until I saw her face. She closely resembles my mother. When she saw me, she believed me. The truth is that I knew nothing of any of this until those women came to my father's door."

He took a sip of his tea. "Why did you leave your grandmother? Why not stay where she was imprisoned, to be close to her?"

I stared at him, hesitating. I took a sip, as well, trying to steady myself.

"I killed a priest and drank his blood," I finally admitted. "When his body was discovered, the Countess ordered me to leave."

Lord Westwick's reaction surprised me. He laughed.

"A priest, you say?"

"The priest who accused her," I asserted.

"Understandable," he said, nodding to himself.

He took another sip of tea, then continued, "So, you have nightmares of your mother because she was the one who changed you?"

"That is what Vincenzo thinks."

"And you have had no other changes in yourself since the scratch other than a sudden taste for blood?"

I thought for several moments and then said, "I have sensitivity to sunlight now, am very strong physically, and often find myself with a violent temper."

"Indeed. Vincenzo told me what happened with Klara on the boat,"

Lord Westwick smiled. When I looked to him with a worried expression, he immediately waved my concern away. "Your loyalty is admirable. Don't worry about it. However, we must be careful of you spending too much time with William."

"Why?" I asked.

"William is a sorcerer, my dear," he explained. "All we know of him is that he comes from Naples and has some of the most powerful magic I have ever seen." He held up a finger with a flourish. "And I can assure you, I've seen some great magic."

"Are there many sorcerers here?"

He nodded. "Sorcerers, witches, beasts and others like you. As well as vampires."

"Who, or what, are you?" I asked.

He watched me carefully, trying to decide on how to explain to a young and frightened girl exactly the kind of monster he was beneath the tailored grey wool topcoat and silk pantaloons.

"There are many names in many languages for what I have become, Katrine. The simplest way to explain is that, on occasion, my body changes from human to wolf and back again."

"Oh, I see. How interesting…so do you…does it…hurt?" When my fumbling questions caused him to raise an eye, I quickly changed the subject. "Charles, you never told me why I should not spend time with William."

I hoped Lord Westwick did not find me to be incredibly odd or rude. To my relief, however, he simply laughed.

"Oh my dear, because your two tempers combined would create an eruption I don't believe the world could withstand."

I smiled and sat back, the tension melting. "What shall I do now?"

"You must decide. You and your companion Roza are welcome to join our community, if you wish."

"Yes. I do wish it very much. I am glad to know that those of us who are…well…different have a safe place to take refuge. Thank you, Charles." Feeling more confident, I then mustered the courage to seek his guidance. "May I ask your advice? The King wishes to kill my grandmother, and I desperately need to communicate with her."

"I will have some ink and parchment brought to you immediately."

I blushed. "I am ashamed to admit that I need Grisela's help for that. But what I would like to know is, do you think it safe for me to write to her?"

He shrugged. "Of course. As long as you choose your words wisely, it is quite safe. But why are you ashamed to need Gigi's help?"

I lowered my eyes. "Because, My Lord, she promised to teach me to write."

He put his hand on my arm and I looked up at him, our connection deepening as our eyes met.

"There is no need to be ashamed, Katrine," he said gently. "Many high born women from the noblest families in the world cannot read or write."

His voice was soft and comforting. We stayed with our eyes locked for quite some time in silence.

"I feel oddly connected to you, as if we have met before….perhaps in another life," he finally said. "I think you are someone quite special, Katrine. Gigi would not have chosen you if you were not."

"I am nothing more than a simple girl thrown into impossible circumstances," I muttered, looking away.

"And see how you have handled those circumstances! That is just a small part of what makes you special." He brightened now and took my hand. "So, what do you know of dance?"

The question surprised me somewhat, but his enthusiasm was so great that I couldn't help but to feel better.

"Very little, I must confess. I saw some children performing a dance at home on May Day once."

"And where is home? Not in Hungary?"

"No. I was born in Wallachia."

"Really?" he exclaimed. "You have come a very long way then, haven't you. Did Grisela tell you anything about what she does here?"

"Only a little," I replied.

"Well, my dear, Grisela is the lead dancer of our company. We perform something that has been going on for many years at all the royal courts in Europe. I call it *balleto*. As a dance troupe—as entertainers—it is a way for us all to live together without causing suspicion. Of course, the more 'traditionally built' must stay out of sight in the underground of the theatre. All the others, however, stay here at the manor."

"What do you mean by 'traditionally built'?"

He sighed now, playfully shaking his head. "Did they explain nothing to you on the trip here? Some of us, who came by our circumstances by means that are more traditional, must stay underground and away from the sun. This is especially true for vampires, or those who must be confined when they change into a beast. This is to protect them and others. You, my dear, as well as Grisela and Vincenzo, are not of this case, while Don Tommas is. Do you see what I mean?"

"Yes, I think I understand. But what about you?"

"I, my dear, am of the other type. I was bitten by another beast, and my changes come at the lunar cycle. However, I have many years of practice and control. I am much older than I look, so I no longer need to be confined during my change," he explained. "Grisela's mother, on the other hand, was turned into a vampire, and Grisela herself was born with the thirst. I do not quite understand what happened to you, though, and you intrigue me."

"Why?"

"Your mother's spell turned her into an animal. She marked you and you are having dreams associated with having a mark, yet you crave blood," Charles mused. "This is most interesting and not typical. I would like to test your blood."

He took my hand, again pressing the inside of my wrist to his nose and lips. "And you smell quite fragrantly of wolf," he added with a slight smile.

I swallowed hard and said nothing, hoping he could not sense my fear. I was suddenly feeling overwhelmed and wished for Vincenzo or Grisela to be here with me. I also thought of Roza for a moment and felt a pang of guilt. In the beginning, I had relied on her so much and could not even sleep without her; but now it seemed that I did not think of her at all when I needed protection.

"Katrine? Are you alright?" Charles suddenly asked.

I set my tea cup and saucer on the rolling tray.

"Just a bit overwhelmed," I said quietly.

"That is natural," he nodded sympathetically. "But you will stay? I will have a room set up for you upstairs. There is one that is perfect, as if it has been waiting for you. Now, while that is being taken care of, we could go to the theatre. I could give you the tour there and explain things more completely. Are you up for it?"

I nodded gratefully, and he clapped his hands. A servant immediately appeared, then another shortly after to collect the tea tray.

"Ready my carriage, and inform Signor Amori and Mademoiselle Delphine that Mademoiselle Báthory and I shall be going to the theatre, if they wish to join us."

XXII.

Danse Macabre

VINCENZO WATCHED ME FROM HIS SEAT ACROSS THE carriage, his green eyes probing as if digging through my thoughts. I did not have the opportunity to talk to him before we were whisked away. The way he looked at me reminded me of when we first met in Vienna.

I was pleased he and Grisela had agreed to come on the tour, as I wasn't sure I could take all this in on my own.

"I spoke to Roza," Vincenzo said. "I have asked her to choose a personal maid for you. Your very own Tolone, if you will."

"Roza is not capable?" I asked. In a way, I was beginning to miss her.

"No," he shook his head. "You need someone younger and more capable. Besides, she is a kitchen worker, a baker. She knows nothing of dressing and a woman's toilette."

"Which reminds me, Charles," Grisela spoke up, "the girl needs proper clothes."

She placed her hand on Charles's knee. He was sitting to my right, and I couldn't help but to notice the gesture.

"All in due time, Gigi. Nevertheless, with you I wonder if you confuse the words 'proper' with 'pricey'. How much money did you spend on dresses in Vienna?"

"You know how I love that one shop, Charles," she smiled.

He laughed. "There is one of those shops in every city in Europe, my dear Gigi."

While they chatted, Vincenzo continued to watch me in silence, his eyes never leaving my face. He knew that I was still distressed by the thought of losing Roza's service. I finally made eye contact with him; we stared at each other for quite some time. I wanted to tell him that I believed Roza quite capable of learning to become my personal maid and, if I asked her, to make whatever effort was required.

But I could almost hear his reply, explaining to me that in this world there was a certain way that things were done, that young women didn't have older personal servants outside of wet nurses who raised them from infancy. In my mind, I then countered his argument: Grandmother's personal servants, Roza's friends, were not young women. They had lived a lot of life before being executed; they were most likely in the Countess's service for much of that time.

"There is a chance that your new maid could be, quite literally, your own Tolone," Vincenzo said suddenly, breaking the silence. "One of Tolone's own daughters is a possible candidate."

"It will take time for me to become accustomed to the idea," I said quietly.

He shrugged. "As it has been with most things on this journey. But the right maid will be able to help you quite considerably."

"You had no household servants?" Charles turned to me now, surprised.

"No," I admitted. I immediately looked to Grisela, hoping she would think of something to cover for my working class origins.

On cue, Grisela ran her hand over Charles' knee, arresting his attention.

"Charles, what shall our next show be? Have you been preparing while I've been away?"

He smiled. "The world does not stop when you leave Paris, my dear. And I should tell you now, so you have time to throw a fit before we arrive, that Victorie will be dancing the lead in this show."

"What on earth for?" Grisela exclaimed.

"The lead calls for someone darker. I highly doubt you will change the shade of your hair for one show."

"What about the vast array of wigs we have collected?" she snapped.

He sighed. "You know how I feel about my lead dancer wearing a wig, Gigi. Your part is equally as important, and it's not like Victorie has never danced the lead before."

Grisela made a face that appeared to be a pout, while Vincenzo laughed quietly.

Before I realised it, we had finally stopped and were out on the street, standing at the foot of a staircase that led to a grand door painted bright red. I took this moment as an opportunity to look around, and when the carriage moved away, I got my first real look at the streets of Paris. We had come to a street lined with many theatres. It was bustling with stagehands moving artificial trees and bedroom pieces, heavy looking red velvet curtains, tapestries and an assortment of other oddities, like planks of wood painted to look like water, into the various theatres through side doors.

Our theatre, on the other hand, had its things brought in directly through the front.

"In case you were wondering, the side doors to the *Danse Macabre* open only after dark," Charles explained. "It adds to the mystery. Now, are you coming," he teased me, "or shall you spend your afternoon watching the street?"

"This is my first view of Paris in the daylight," I replied.

"The sun doesn't irritate you?"

"Mildly. I can't stay out for too long, but I don't notice until it's extremely painful."

My eyes drifted again to the street, suddenly noticing a woman standing and watching us, similar to the way I was watching what was around me.

It startled me. She was almost my mirror image, except older.

My body went rigid as I stared at the woman who, I was quite sure now, was my mother. She immediately darted away. I tried to take everything in, sights and smells that could give me a clue as to exactly who she was.

The scratch on my arm began to feel hot and itchy.

I could hear Charles saying something in the background to Vincenzo. It sounded like, "can you smell that," but I wasn't entirely sure. When our eyes had locked before she moved away, the rest of the world seemed to fade.

Meanwhile, Charles grabbed my forearm and yanked hard, pulling me out of my trance. My insides felt like they were vibrating, and a desperate panic overtook me. I pulled myself out of Charles's grasp and bolted wildly for the doors.

Once in the entry way I stopped, unsure of where to go, while Vincenzo caught up with me.

"Katrine, who was that?"

"When she haunted me it was only in my sleep, I had no idea," I began babbling. "I thought she was dead. I swear I didn't know!"

"Who was dead? I don't understand."

I pointed to the street. "That was my mother!"

He stared blankly at me, just as Charles and Grisela appeared behind him.

"My sincerest apologies, Lord Westwick," I began, gasping, "but I was under the impression that my mother had not survived....I was unaware of her presence in Paris. I will understand if you'd like me to go—"

The three of them continued to stare at me, Vincenzo's expression carrying over onto their faces. Helplessly, I looked around at the grand foyer and massive stone staircase, a pillar at the foot with a beautifully carved angel standing atop, greeting attendants with her outstretched hands and perfect face.

Grisela turned to Charles now and stated bluntly, "We shall have to kill her then, Charles."

The colour drained from my face.

"She doesn't mean you, Katrine," Vincenzo clarified, then turned back to Grisela.

"Of course not," Grisela snapped. "I mean that woman. We cannot have her attacking *ma petite*."

"But that woman is my mother," I said, my voice quiet and small.

"*Was* your mother, dear," Charles corrected. "I am afraid, considering what you told me, that the change and the amount of time she spent in animal form may have made her quite batty by now."

I shook my head, confused, and Vincenzo explained: "Batty is a quaint English word meaning insane."

"But if she is dangerous and I leave, she will follow me," I objected. "Then I can protect all of you from her."

Grisela immediately protested: "And what good would that do? I will not call you my *protégée* then allow you to leave, *ma petite*! What type of woman would I be if I allowed you to walk into the arms of a monster?"

"But my mother—"

"Not mother, Katrine. Monster. She smelled more of animal than any human I've met, and I spent much of my childhood in the company of some odd folk. You must separate what we saw outside from your mother, for they are no longer one and the same."

"But she looks just like—"

Charles linked my arm in his and guided me firmly up the stairs. "That shall be your first lesson at the *Danse Macabre,* my dear. Looks can be very, very deceiving."

XXIII.

Common Ground

I GAZED AROUND AT THE THEATRE SEATS, UPHOLSTERED in a deep, lustrous gold. The ledge that bordered the balcony and the private seating area was gilded to the finest standard with flowered filigree carved into the surface. The heavy velvet curtains drawn over the stage were a shade of blue as deep as the colour of the night sky. As a whole, the room seemed quite dark.

We wasted little time beginning our tour, and Charles had no intention of allowing me to dwell on frightening thoughts concerning my mother.

"I acquired this theatre at an auction," he began, as he toured me about. "The men who originally owned it bankrupted themselves finishing it to its present state and either had to sell or be taken to prison. It was quite a twist of fate, as we needed a place with certain below-ground facilities, and I could not afford the finishings that this building had on my own."

Charles stopped me in the aisle as we approached the stage and pointed to the ceiling. A large crystal chandelier hung above our heads and was encircled by a beautifully painted mural of a light coloured female angel in battle with a dark one; they were both perfect, so lifelike it seemed they would fly down towards us at any moment.

"The previous owners said they wanted it to represent the darkness and light in all of us," Charles mused. "Some of the most beautiful depictions of the female form I have ever seen."

I nodded in agreement but said nothing, still trying to recover from my consuming fear. I was amazed I could understand him, let alone stand upright. Nevertheless, he deftly led me up a set of stairs and onto the stage.

"So what do you think?"

"It's all quite astounding," I managed. "And overwhelming."

He smiled. "Could you see yourself on this stage? It is not common to have a stage raised in such a way, but I think it is quite grand."

"Oh no, no," I shook my head.

He came over to me and locked his eyes with mine.

"Why not? You're blushing," he said quietly to me. He ran his finger down my cheek, and a wave of heat washed through me all the way to my edges.

"My Lord, I know very little of dancing, only from the festivals in my village," I insisted.

"Hardly a French *balleto*," he commented, releasing me from his gaze, "but beautiful in its own right. Now, come, there is much more to see."

After showing me more of the stage, I was amazed how enormous sets and backdrops were layered to create depth, and by the length of the floor itself which stretched, it seemed, to the very back of the building. My thoughts were quickly swimming at the very idea of it all.

"The performances are based on ones commonly seen at court. Ours are not quite as grand, but if you consider my finances and what meager access we have, I still think we do quite well," Charles said proudly.

He guided me to a door about midway from the front of the stage. It was heavy and looked to be made of metal. I suddenly wondered whether it was used to keep people in or out.

We descended into the lower levels of the *Danse Macabre* which were made up of simple rooms with stone walls, some with open doors and some not, some with no doors at all. On our way, I glanced briefly into an enormous room filled with costumes. I didn't have a chance to see much, however; it was quite cold down here, and Charles continued to move me along quickly.

"This is where some of the others live, and there is room for more," he began, motioning about.

"Will there be more?" I asked.

He took my arm again. "I always wonder. Something deep inside me says there are more like us than we could ever possibly imagine—and may ever have the chance to meet—but I think it is always good to be overly prepared. Don't you agree?"

"Yes, I do," I smiled, "but as you can see from before, unfortunately, I don't take well to surprises."

He squeezed my arm, pulling me closer to him.

"You don't have to be afraid, Katrine. You are safe with me."

This rather bold gesture startled Vincenzo who was just coming in from a door at the end of the hallway.

"Everything in order, my friend?" Charles called out to him.

"Yes," he replied. "We will finish the run tonight with the final show. In one week, we'll begin preparations for the new show with Victorie as the lead."

"Excellent!" Charles exclaimed. Then he gestured to me. "The young lady will get to watch one of our shows before she becomes involved. Hopefully, that will ease Gigi's temper."

"I believe she has come to the conclusion that Katrine's welfare and education are more important than her career in the theatre," Vincenzo called back. "Which reminds me, Grisela is ready to leave. She says there are many things to attend to before tonight."

Charles sighed and looked back at me. "It appears that your second lesson shall be to try to understand and navigate your mistress' moods."

When we arrived back at the chateau, Roza and a thin, blonde woman were standing in the entryway awaiting us.

"My Lady, I have someone I would like you to meet," Roza announced, all too formally, and I waited for Grisela to respond.

Grisela poked me.

"She's addressing you, *ma petite*."

"She can't be," I whispered back. "She would not speak so formally."

Roza rolled her eyes now, annoyed with me.

"As you can see, Hannah," she declared to the blonde woman, nudging her chin at me, "she's quite stubborn when it comes to formality, and in regards to most things for that matter."

"I see," I shot back. "Then shall I call you Kardoska from this point on?"

Roza ignored me.

"Katrine, this is Hannah, Tolone's daughter and your new maid."

She grit her teeth, whispered something to Hannah before bowing to us, and then left.

Before I could open my mouth, Grisela began instructing Hannah: "Good. Katrine shall attend her first performance tonight and needs help with her *toilette*. I have a dressmaker on the way but need you to start the bath. Can you do that, Hannah?"

"Yes, Mademoiselle," Hannah said, bowing slightly.

"Fine. I will be quite busy and unavailable, so this will be a test of your skill. But," Grisela finished, starting up the stairs, "as you are Tolone's daughter, I have complete faith in you."

With that, Hannah and I were left alone to figure out what to do next.

"If you'll come with me, Mademoiselle," Hannah finally motioned, I'll—"

"Please, I insist that in private you call me Katrine," I interrupted. "It will take me some time to get used to the idea of this, I must warn you."

Hannah smiled at me warmly now. "And I sincerely hope that when you do, we can come to rely on each other, as you once relied on Kardoska. I think you might find we have some things in common."

Hannah and I sat together on a couch in my room, chatting, as the dressmaker laid out various fabrics for dresses to be made as well as a number of readymade gowns. At that moment, as I watched the lovely silks and chiffons being arrayed, I looked around at my beautiful surroundings and was suddenly in awe. I thought back on the tiny room in my father's house, secluded partially under the eaves and very cold in the winter. At times, it was hard to believe that all of this was happening.

This finely decorated room had a large window facing out onto the back garden. In the morning, there was so much light pouring in, I felt as if I was outside. Hannah said it was called the butterfly room because the walls were covered in paper with butterflies. The bed linens and other furniture were a colour Hannah called purple, or *poupre* in French. She said Lord Westwick always told the others he was saving this room for someone special.

"I am quite pleased to even have my own room, let alone such beautiful clothes," I whispered. When Hannah looked confused, I explained, "I grew up on a farm in Wallachia. My father was an enameller. We didn't have much."

"Where on earth is Wallachia?" she whispered back.

"East of Austria and Hungary."

She sighed. "My word, you have come a very long way, haven't you?"

The dressmaker finished laying out the fabrics and smiled proudly.

"With whatever you pick, Mademoiselle, I have matching shoes in the carriage, if you wish."

I smiled and nodded. I looked at the dizzying mix of shapes, colours and patterns, and quickly turned to Hannah for help.

"I don't know what to pick," I said in a low voice.

"Just pick what you like. The dressmaker will do the rest," she whispered back.

I nodded, feigning confidence.

"Right," I began, "Of the ones you have on hand, I would like the black and white, the red, the dark blue with silver thread, and the green. I would also like some made in gray; several different styles in gray, please…and one in pale blue, yellow, pink and purple. And also something very simple in white, please."

I glanced back at Hannah, and she offered a nod of reassurance.

"Excellent choices!" the dressmaker exclaimed. "I will have the appropriate shoes sent up and shall return in two days' time to take a proper measurement, if that is acceptable to Mademoiselle. Meanwhile, these readied gowns here should do nicely for now."

"Yes, thank you," I replied, as Hannah helped gather up the sample items and show the dressmaker out. I remained seated and drifted off with my thoughts. A few ready-made gowns that appeared perfectly suited to my size remained from the dressmaker's offerings, and I marveled at the very idea of wearing gowns on a daily basis.

Meanwhile, Hannah returned with four small boxes that she placed on the floor beside the bed, where my potential dresses for this evening lay.

"You have good taste, Katrine," Hannah said as she sat back down beside me. "You made some lovely fabric and colour choices."

"I was only guessing," I confessed. "I've really never been able to choose for myself. My mother always made what I wore."

"Where is she now?"

I was about to tell her the details but then changed my mind. "I am not entirely sure where she is. Lord Westwick says she is no longer herself, anyway."

Hannah nodded, somehow understanding.

"Had she been changed for too long?"

"That's what he said...but how do you know of such things, Hannah? Doesn't it frighten you?"

She smiled at me. "Of course not. Why would I take such employment if I was. I'm very sorry about your mother, dear. I lost mine when I was your age and had to raise my younger siblings after she was gone. It's very hard to lose a mother, and the only people who really understand are the ones who've lost their own."

I smiled thankfully, feeling more comfortable with her by the moment.

"Which do you think I should wear tonight?" I asked brightly, changing the subject now. "This is the part I cannot decide on my own."

"What are you trying to achieve?" Hannah asked, tilting her head thoughtfully and studying the gowns laid out before us on the bed.

"Well, I cannot outshine Grisela, but I would like her to be proud of me. I am her *protégée*, after all."

"I have an idea," Hannah declared. "But first, let's draw you a nice warm bath!"

XXIV.

Debut

THE DARK BLUE DRESS I FINALLY CHOSE WAS
exquisitely embroidered with silver thread in a pattern of moons and
stars across the stomacher. The design swirled down the front of the
skirt into an edge around the bottom. The underskirt etched in silver
made it appear as if I were wearing a piece of the twinkling night sky.

Hannah curled my hair and wove it into a halo around my head with
a piece of silver ribbon.

"You are quite talented, Hannah," I complimented.

As nervous as I was about tonight, I couldn't help but to smile at my
reflection in the mirror of the vanity, which sat in a corner of my room.

"It is a pleasure to be involved in your presentation to the world," she
said happily as she worked.

I twisted my grandmother's ring round my finger; it was beginning to
become a nervous habit, and Hannah noticed it.

"Are you nervous, Katrine?"

I wondered how long I had been playing with the ring.

"Is it obvious?"

I stood up and smoothed my hands over the front of my skirt. She
took my chin in her hands and smiled at me in a mature, confident way.

"You will do just fine," she said encouragingly. Although we weren't very much different in age, she suddenly seemed so much older than me, so much wiser, in more than just years.

"Hannah, why aren't you married?" I asked gently.

"How do you know I'm not?" she replied with a slight smile. When I inhaled at the thought of having given offence, she admitted, "To be honest, I have not had the time or strength. Besides, it would take quite a man to please my father. If he had his way, he'd want me to marry Signor Amori, or someone just like him."

"Really?"

She laughed. "Oh yes. My father thinks he's one of the greatest men who ever lived."

"He is a great man, I must agree. But I am unsure he will ever marry."

"In any case," Hannah shrugged, "I am far below his social station, so he could never marry me."

She began looking through the boxes the dressmaker had brought, and I thought there was a slight air of sadness about her now. Nonetheless, she handed me a pair of dark blue velvet shoes with a heel higher than I'd ever seen, erasing any undue emotion from her face.

"I do not know how to walk in such grand shoes," I confided as she slid them on my feet.

"It's quite simple," she reassured me. "After you have walked a few steps you will get used to it. Here, come try."

She held my hand and walked me around the room. The shoes I wore to accompany Grisela at the baron's home in Vienna were not nearly as high in the heel. However, at every step, I became surer on my feet. Finally, my once wobbly gait smoothed and straightened.

"Keep your head up," she advised. "Perfect. You'll do wonderfully, I am sure of it."

I walked over to the table now, picked up my father's cross and handed it to Hannah, who looked slightly confused.

"Grisela told me I could not wear it," I explained, "unless I had a proper display chain for it. My father made it, and it's very important to me. I would like to have it on me this evening. Do you think you could find something proper for it?"

She smiled, putting the cross in her sleeve the same way I had been doing.

"I will do my best," she replied. "Now, let's go downstairs. I cannot wait to see their expressions when they get a look at you!"

We caught sight of Klara heading towards the staircase from the other end of the hallway. I immediately held Hannah back as Klara made her way downstairs. She was wearing an enormous dress that was not quite yellow but not quite green and decorated with pink rosettes. Thankfully, she didn't see me. I breathed a sigh of relief.

"What's wrong?" Hannah asked once Klara was out of sight.

"She's not very fond of me. I try to stay out of her way."

Hannah snorted. "If I were you, I wouldn't mind. She's vile, and she's been driving the servants mad since she got here. I was actually frightened that I would be put with her."

"No need to worry any further," I laughed. "I believe the phrase is that you are stuck with me now, so get used to it," and together we went downstairs. We parted company at the entryway to the salon.

"Good luck to you, Miss Katrine," Hannah winked.

It seemed somehow fitting that I entered the same room I had on that first day here. The sun was just setting, casting a golden glow over the beautiful salon. A few heads turned, and a few nods of admiration followed. I smiled across the room to Grisela and Charles.

Klara made her official entrance just behind me, and all eyes immediately fell upon her. Her dress caused quite the reaction, needless to say. I could see Grisela's face from her seat beside Charles; she cringed slightly when Klara approached them. I was about to point this out to Hannah when I realised she was gone and I was alone. It would take me some time to get used to the idea of being close to someone who could not participate in my social life.

I continued my way through the room towards Grisela, aware that heads were turning as I walked. I could also tell that she was pleased.

She stood and came towards me; Charles also stood when he caught sight of me.

"Well done, *ma petite!*" Grisela said proudly, kissing me on both cheeks. "You are exquisite! I wanted to see you before I left for the theatre."

"I'm so glad that you're pleased, but I must give Hannah all the credit. She was a perfect choice for me," I said as I embraced her, and this made her very happy.

Grisela was dressed simply in a dark gray dress this evening; I assumed it was because she was performing tonight. However, even dressed in simple clothes with little cosmetics, she was absolutely beautiful.

"Don't forget now, *ma petite*, you are my representative when I am not present. I do not need to tell you how to behave. I have complete faith in you, but you must be careful of gentlemanly advances," she admonished. "I'm sure your escorts Vincenzo and Charles will keep a close eye on you."

She kissed my cheek one more time before leaving, the scent of roses following behind her.

"My word, you are a vision," Charles declared, his soft hand squeezing mine.

"Thank you, My Lord," I replied. "And I am quite pleased to tell you that Hannah was the perfect choice to be my aide."

He smiled, lingering with my hand clutched in his for a few moments too long before releasing it. His eyes never left me as I looked around the salon, slightly embarrassed by his attention.

Meanwhile, Klara was glaring at me from within a small group, anger clearly written on her face. I wondered what else I might have done to incur such emotion.

"I am glad to hear that," Charles suddenly said. "Now, we're just waiting for Signor Amori to finish some business, and then we shall go."

"What sort of business?" I asked.

Charles pulled the edge of his shirt out a little further from the sleeve of his topcoat made of the darkest gray wool.

"He is heavily involved in trade, my dear. Any thing you can possibly imagine, he has traded it least once. Of course, he told me not to wait, but I insisted."

"Charles," Klara spoke up. She suddenly appeared at his other side and took hold of his arm. "Are we ready to go? I am getting so tired of waiting."

"Soon, Klara," he replied patiently.

But Klara was like a relentless child.

"Shall I be sitting next to you in your private box?" she cooed, batting her eyelashes.

"No, Klara. I already told you that my box is full tonight," he said with a slight edge in his voice. " But don't worry. You shall have a place fitting to your station."

"My own box, then?" she asked eagerly.

During this conversation, I watched in fascination at how deftly Klara hid her hatred of me from Charles. She also made very plain her romantic feelings for him.

"This time," he said coolly.

Satisfied, she blew him a kiss and then turned and walked away.

"May I ask you something, Charles?" I asked when I was sure she was out of earshot.

"Anything," he replied.

"What is so important about a box? Isn't it hard to see the performance from a confined space? You would think she'd prefer the private seating close to the stage."

He laughed, kissing my hand again. "The private seating is called a box, my sweet."

Embarrassed by my mistake, something Grisela would have called a *faux pas*, I tried to change the subject.

"Why are you not sitting with Klara? She is the daughter of a baron, she's pretty—"

He interrupted me. "She most certainly is not pretty."

"But would it not be good for you to be seen with her?" I continued. "Someone of her station...."

"I care little for such things, Katrine. Besides, the French care very little for nobility other than their own. Although they know her parents, most have never seen her before. And anyway, where would you sit, then?"

He was chiding me, and I tried to ignore it.

"What about William?"

"He will sit with us," Charles said with a sigh. "In any case, I would rather deal with him than Klara, which is why my box is full."

I did not quite understand but did not think it wise to press further.

Suddenly, at that moment, the smell of fresh blood caught my attention. It appeared to be coming from a young man who currently had Klara's arm. Before I could stay something to Charles, Vincenzo appeared.

He smiled at me, his green eyes twinkling mischievously.

"You look beautiful, Katrine."

"Thank you," I replied with a smile. "Not just for the compliment but for my own personal Tolone."

"I am very pleased," he nodded.

Charles took up my arm now before Vincenzo had the opportunity.

"Come, *mon ami*! Our evening can finally begin!"

I ascended the crowded steps of the *Danse Macabre* with Charles on the left holding my arm, and Vincenzo on my right. I only had a brief opportunity to glance around as I stepped out of the carriage. I did notice, however, that Klara had a different young man at her side now, this one looking vaguely familiar. Vincenzo noticed, too, and his brow furrowed for a minute.

Fortunately, I did not see my mother, although I had little chance to look carefully. I was being swept up the stairs through the crowds and could sense only that I was being watched. I could not determine who or from where.

We passed doorways leading out onto the balcony and into a tiny hallway which led to more doorways. Each one was draped in heavy velvet curtains in place of actual doors. When we reached the end of the hall, Vincenzo pulled back the curtain and ushered us inside.

He pointed me to a large velvet chair in the far side of the box close to the ledge. When I sat down, I realised it had the best view of the stage.

William was already inside, sitting close to the exit.

"Is it just you three tonight, My Lord?" William asked Charles. I smiled at him, but he paid no mind to me.

Charles sighed, taking his seat in front of me. "Mathilde may be up later but, if not, then it's just us tonight."

William nodded and appeared to relax.

"We couldn't handle the scandal of you lashing out in public," Vincenzo spoke up, his tone surprisingly terse. "We can't risk exposure because you refuse to keep your temper."

William immediately bristled. "Have you spoken to that girl, Vincenzo?"

"Of course I did. I had to escort her from Vienna. Or did you forget how your complaints spared you from that trip?" Vincenzo shot back.

Before William could reply, Charles spoke up, "But you brought us Katrine, so the trip was a success as far as I'm concerned. And I will not have you two ruin the young lady's evening with your quibbling."

"I apologise, Katrine," William finally said to me. "I am pleased to have your company."

"Thank you," I nodded.

I realised then that they were speaking of Klara. William obviously had no affection for that girl. Meanwhile, Vincenzo took his seat beside me now, and I felt a bit boxed in by how close he and Charles were to me.

I looked out at the seats and the crowd, the likes of which I had never dreamed of. People of all shapes and sizes, dressed from plain to flamboyant, filled the seats with such excitement that it became infectious. I had no idea what I was about to see but could not wait for it to begin.

When the curtain rose. a beautiful, lush garden scene appeared with dancing flowers and trees and a bright, radiant golden sun. At first glance, the yellow-and-gold-painted woman appeared to be Victorie. Two other dancers portrayed Beauty and Happiness, a vision of a perfect world.

A man came on scene next, followed by Grisela. They were both dressed in what looked like leaves, Grisela's golden curls falling loosely around her body. She was radiant, captivating, and I couldn't take my eyes off her.

It appeared to be the story of Adam and Eve in the Garden of Eden.

The two leads danced together, their love for each other obvious in their movements. I had never seen emotion expressed in such a way; I did not know it was even possible. The minutes flew by during the performance.

A figure in black suddenly appeared on the stage, a shiny red apple in his hand. The audience oohed and awed as he headed towards the couple. The man's attention never wavered, but the apple caught Grisela's eye. Everything on stage slowed as Grisela spun her way towards the figure and the temptation of the apple. When she stretched out her hand to take the apple, the stage went black and the curtain fell. Applause erupted like a thunderclap through the audience.

"Is it over?" I asked, panic in my voice. "That's not the end, is it?"

"No, it's just the intermission," Vincenzo said easily.

I was about to speak again when the smell of blood caught my attention. I looked out at the crowd in search of it, but nothing seemed out of place.

"Vincenzo, do you smell that?"

"Yes, and I have since we left the chateau," he nodded. "It appears we may need to be more concerned with young Klara than I had originally anticipated."

"Because of her followers? Because they are entranced by her?" When he nodded, I pressed, "Is there a way to break it?"

"I hope so."

Charles interrupted us. "So, my dear. What do you think?"

I smiled eagerly. "It's so wonderful I do not have words."

"Would you believe me if I told you that not a single person on that stage had done anything like that before they came here?"

"No! I don't believe it!" I exclaimed.

"It is true, I swear it. They may have danced with a partner, as every person has, but nothing more," he continued. "I think you would also be wonderful on stage."

"Ah! However, there is a difference. For you must believe me when I say I have never danced alone *or* with a partner," I exclaimed.

"I don't believe that!" he said, laughing. "Vincenzo, do you believe the girl has never danced a step?"

"I think we should throw a small fête in her honour at the chateau so she can learn with a partner," Vincenzo replied.

"Brilliant idea! Grisela would want a coming out party for her *protégée*," Charles said.

"What about Klara?" I asked.

"What about her?" they said simultaneously.

"I am concerned about her distaste for me," I admitted.

"Don't be," Charles waved a hand. "She is harmless."

I looked to Vincenzo, and he nodded in acknowledgement. But he had been with me on the boat—he had seen her fury.

The intermission finally over now, the curtain rose again to Grisela standing alone in the forest with the apple in her hand. She caressed it as if it were made of diamonds, performing an exquisite solo dance. Her left leg went in the air behind her as she spun on the other, balancing perfectly on the tips of her toes.

The flowers and the trees came out to dance with her, and it took several minutes for me to see the black clad figure behind the trees. I felt like screaming at Grisela to watch her back! That sinister man was coming to hurt her but she already knew. I could feel myself blushing and I looked quickly at the men to see if they noticed how involved I was becoming in the performance.

Grisela paused, standing with both feet on the stage and bit into the apple. The crunch could be heard throughout the room, like wood breaking and splitting in half. I stopped moving, stopped breathing in anticipation as to what would happen next.

The forest started to fall apart around her, leaves and petals turning brown and wilting before they hit the ground. Branches of the largest tree started to twist and turn as if caught in a storm; the smell of rain and the forest floor flowed into the room along with fire. I covered my mouth as the bile rose in my throat, the smell bringing me back to when I opened my eyes for the first time after the attack. My arm started to burn. I looked down and realised I was rubbing the part of my sleeve that covered the scratch.

Grisela's dress even changed colour, the leaves turning from dark green to brown and then the colour of her skin. Her hair glowed like spun gold.

The black clad figure came forward and suddenly stripped out of his costume. I realised then that he wasn't actually a separate individual but, instead, had taken the form of Grisela as she had been before biting into the apple. The two danced together in a kind of combat, as if she were having a fight with herself. Everything—all of the sets—all at once collapsed around her, symbolizing that she had brought this devastation upon herself. Grisela crumpled into a heap on the ground. A startling crash came from the musicians, and the stage went black.

Applause started low and then erupted into something so loud it shook my whole body. I stood and joined the house in hearty applause. The lights came up, and the entire cast came forward to take their bows. When Grisela stepped forward, the audience exploded with joy. She was clearly their darling, and they worshipped her. At that moment, I hoped someday I would be able to perform as beautifully as she did.

People came to our box to offer their greetings and congratulations, while William received them. After the patrons dispersed, Charles finally stood. The stage had cleared by now, and the curtain closed. I simply watched, fascinated by everything.

"You'll grow accustomed to all this," Vincenzo told me. "In a few minutes, we can meet up with Gigi."

"Do you think she will teach me how to do that?" I asked him hopefully.

"I believe that is her intention."

"Wasn't that magical?" I couldn't contain my enthusiasm now. "I've never been so enchanted. I have never seen anything like that before in my life!"

"I'm happy for you," he smiled.

"I would not be here if it weren't for you, Vincenzo. I have you to thank for so many things, you and Grisela are my saviours, really. It is truly amazing that the two of you could be so wonderful and generous to some strange delivery girl you met on the streets of Vienna."

He leaned forward. "You are so much more, Katrine. Anyone who looks at you can plainly see that."

At that moment, William approached us in a huff, his face red with anger. I had come to realise that the only person who could drive him to such fury was Klara.

"There is a crowd outside her box," he fumed. "She has only been here a few days and already has a cadre of enchanted men? Does she crawl out the window and stalk them at night like a common monster? *Perché lei è qui?*"

"*Non lo so*, Will. This is Charles, not me," Vincenzo replied.

William sighed. "The man has lost his mind."

Vincenzo stood now, holding out his hand to me. "Shall we?"

I took his hand and we exited our box. Charles, meanwhile, was ushering Klara's devotees out of the hallway, then turned and entered her box next to ours. An argument immediately followed: Charles's angry, muffled voice followed by the occasional biting words from Klara. Vincenzo and I headed back towards the front entry, with William close behind.

I regretted leaving Charles behind, but Vincenzo was right. He had to be the one to deal with Klara. We stood at the top of the stairs now and watched the last of the patrons exit the theatre. I looked about for my mother but, thankfully, saw no one who looked like her.

"We attract a diverse group of people," Vincenzo was saying. "I'm always surprised, and a bit impressed, when I watch the exit after a performance. Tonight's turnout was excellent, and this is one of our least controversial shows."

"What do you mean by controversial?" I asked.

"I mean the shows that leave people talking, discussing, and wondering. What some might call questionable. Those shows seem to draw the largest crowds," he explained.

"People are always fascinated by what they don't understand," I offered.

He laughed quite loudly at this. "Are you sure you are just a peasant girl, Katrine?"

Slightly embarrassed, I replied, "Maybe I'm just a girl who sees things differently."

"Well, my dear," he leaned in and whispered to me, "for what it's worth, I quite admire your perspective." A shiver ran down my back.

"Do you think we can see Grisela now? I'm eager to congratulate her."

Vincenzo nodded and took my arm, and we began down the stairs. I gripped the banister in one hand and gathered my skirt in the other, careful not to trip. We walked to the stage door and then through another entryway, down a second flight of steps and into the cold hallway which was now abuzz with people.

My excitement grew as I saw people changing out of the grand costumes I had seen on stage, the trees and flowers being dismantled to reveal the actors beneath. As I had expected, Victorie had played the part of the Sun. A maid was washing the gold paint from her skin as we passed. She smiled at me, and I wondered if my excitement was obvious. I was surprised at how many people acknowledged me as if I had known them forever. In that moment, I knew that I was one of them.

The smell of fresh roses filled the corridor as we neared the end of the hall. Grisela was seated in front of a vanity in a room full of fresh cut roses.

"Darling, the flowers are beautiful," she exclaimed, motioning towards the yellow roses.

Vincenzo kissed her on both cheeks. "You were magnificent tonight. Oh, and it seems Katrine was also quite taken with your performance."

She turned to me and smiled.

"It was the most amazing thing I have ever seen! Will you please teach me? I so want to learn!" I embraced her.

She laughed and hugged me back warmly. "Of course, you are my *protégée,* after all."

"She has never danced before, Gigi," Vincenzo warned playfully.

"Really? Not even with a partner?" she asked, and I shook my head no. "My word! I shall have to speak to Charles about having a *fête* for you...by the way, where is Charles?"

"It appears there is a problem with Klara," he murmured, and she glanced from Vincenzo to me and back again.

"And you left him alone?" she asked Vincenzo.

He shook his head. "William is with him, and I think maybe Mathilde."

She sighed. "Ah then, if she instigates something with William, Charles won't feel so guilty if it ends badly."

"He would kill her?" I asked, startled.

"He could, very, very easily, *ma petite,*" Grisela nodded. "And not be bothered in the slightest. Actually, whether he would or not seems irrelevant."

"Now, don't make William sound like such a monster, Gigi," Vincenzo chided.

"Not my intention, *mon ami,* but *ma petite* must know he is a very powerful man with a very bad temper," Grisela replied.

Suddenly, a female voice erupted loudly from the other end of the hallway in a language I didn't understand. A male voice responded in the same language, both of them extremely angry. I looked out into the hall to find a resolute Charles striding intently toward us, Klara close behind and red-faced in anger. She saw me and more words came out. Even though I didn't understand, I had a feeling it had something to do with me.

All the commotion came to an abrupt halt as soon as the others stepped out into the hallway, a freshly scrubbed Victorie ready for a fight. Along with William, Mathilde appeared behind her, still barefoot and dressed in her flower costume. Tommas stood beside Vincenzo.

Charles stopped and turned, Klara almost walking into him, yelling back in that same language. Klara resumed her squealing and arm flailing as Charles stood back to watch the girl make a fool of herself in front of everyone.

I whispered to Tommas, "What's going on?"

He sighed. "She believes she deserves his undivided attention and his affections, apparently."

"Why on earth would she think that?"

"Most girls want to be married, and I gather she thinks Charles is a suitable candidate," Tommas replied. "He is the only man in this company suitable in terms of station, from what she knows. Clearly, she is not asking the right questions."

"She also does not understand that she's been banished from Vienna by her parents," Vincenzo added. "Charles took her on as a favour and out of pity."

"Indeed. The baron owes us quite a favour for taking on that vile excuse for a woman," Tommas agreed. "Charles is really putting himself out to tolerate this girl. And, for some reason, she has quite the distaste for you, Katrine." He leaned back on his heels and smiled slightly. "Do you know why?"

"She attacked Vincenzo on the boat coming to Paris, and we got into a bit of a scuffle," I said shyly. "I'm not proud of what I did, but her behaviour was uncalled for and disrespectful. I couldn't tolerate it."

"I could have been badly hurt if not for Katrine," Vincenzo spoke up in my defence.

Tommas merely chuckled. "I shall remember that if I ever need protection."

"Enough!" Charles suddenly yelled, the echo erupting through the hallway. "I made it perfectly clear the rules you were to follow if you wished to have a place here. If you continually break them and disobey me, you shall suffer the consequences. Do you understand me, Klara?"

She was about to argue, then thought the better of it. All eyes upon her, she nodded meekly in agreement, then turned and went back upstairs. What was once a buzzing hallway, full of activity, fell silent after the argument and Klara's exit. Charles said very little, his dark eyes clouded with anger and the fury brewing inside him. We waited for Grisela to dress, then rode back to the chateau together.

The chateau was quiet and dark when we arrived, and we all went to our separate rooms after saying goodnight. I had expected Hannah to be waiting for me to help me undress but found Roza there instead.

"I'm pleased to see you," I said, closing the door behind me. "We have much to discuss."

"How is Hannah treating you?" she asked.

"She's wonderful." I started to undress myself. "But I still don't understand why you couldn't do the job."

Roza fumbled to release me from the elaborate trappings of the gown and various undergarments. "Honestly, I don't know how. I'm just a simple bread maker. She is better equipped as a maidservant, and I am old." On second thought, she sighed. "But so was Jo Ilona."

"Who?" I asked.

"One of your grandmother's personal servants. She went first to execution at Bytca."

"That was why I wanted to speak with you," I began. "Do you remember how we thought my mother had followed us from Wallachia?"

"Yes, but now I see it was silly and quite impossible."

"It's not. I saw her. Out in the daylight here in Paris."

"I'm sure you were just...."

I put my hand on her shoulder. "Lord Westwick and Signor Amori also saw her, and I'm sure Mademoiselle Delphine did, as well."

She looked at me for a moment, then turned back toward the window. I could feel her breathing and steady heartbeat through her shoulder and into my hand. An uncomfortable feeling came up from her and into my body.

"You don't believe me," I said, pulling away.

"Of course I don't," she snapped. "I watched the woman's body destroyed as the beast ripped its way out of her. She could not have survived that."

"I think where we are is proof enough that she could have survived it and that she did. I know my own mother, Roza."

Roza quickly changed the subject.

"The King wants the Countess's head for what they say she's done, do you know that?"

"Yes," I replied, trying to keep my voice steady. "Mademoiselle Delphine told me."

"And you are out parading around Paris when your grandmother could die for something she didn't do? The Holy Roman Emperor wants her dead, and unless there is some kind of miracle, he'll get his wish. Do you understand that?"

I lost my temper now. "What am I supposed to do? Go and plead for her life and reveal myself as another stain on her reputation? I'm nothing more than the child of her illegitimate daughter!" I started to pace. "Believe me, I've thought a lot about what to do. I almost turned back in Vienna.."

"Well, why didn't you?" she demanded.

"Because I would do more harm than good!" I looked Roza straight in the eye now. "The truth of the matter is that the Countess told me to leave and never return, no matter what."

Roza stepped away and went to the window. "I suppose you're right," she finally muttered. "Her children would not take the news of your existence very well. Especially the oldest, Anna."

I looked up.

"Her other daughter's name is Anna?"

"Yes. Her children are Anna, Paul, and Katalin, or Kata for short."

My rage suddenly melted. I smiled to myself at the thought of aunts and uncles and cousins. I had none in my other life, and the idea excited me.

"Anyway," Roza continued, "I came to see how things were with Hannah, and to check on your sleeping." She looked around the room resentfully. "But I can't imagine you're having problems in this grand room with your fancy new clothes and personal servant."

I sighed. "I had no idea we'd be separated after all we've been through.

You know that you can leave at any time, if you're unhappy."

"Not on your life," Roza said firmly. "I have a position in this house I'd only dreamed of. Leaving here would be foolish."

Roza put my gown away with the others, then she untied my hair and helped me into bed.

"I hope you're still not having nightmares about your mother."

"Not since we arrived in Paris," I replied, pulling up the covers. "Maybe because she's close by. Signor Amori mentioned something about having a link to her because of the scratch."

Roza sighed loudly and then sat down on the bed next to me. "Please don't get your hopes up about your mother, Katrine. Even if it is her body, it's not the same person in her mind."

We sat together in silence for a few moments, and then I grabbed her wrist as Roza went to leave.

"Please don't be sure I'm imagining things. I would hate for you to encounter her unprepared."

"What are you getting at?"

"We have always thought you saved me from her," I said slowly, "but perhaps I was the one who saved you."

XXV.

 *Protégée*

THE *DANSE MACABRE* OFTEN TOOK A FORTNIGHT TO prepare a show, so the next morning my training began. I would have a small part in this upcoming production, and Grisela was determined to have me ready in every way.

The first few mornings were spent with Hannah and the dressmaker, being measured and fitted for gowns. Then Hannah began teaching me to speak French. During the afternoon, I studied reading and writing with Grisela, along with etiquette and table manners and what she called 'proper conversation. Proper conversation involved having a wide knowledge on a variety of topics, to be able to discuss them at length and form an intelligent opinion without being overbearing.

Then, we danced. First, we danced together, because Grisela insisted I learn with a partner before she taught me anything about stage performance. In the meantime, Charles was always somewhere in the background watching me. He had fresh flowers put in my room every day and came to check in on us; it was seemingly by accident but always at the perfect time for us to break and eat with him. He also had fruit sent up for breakfast along with delightful breads called croissants. Given Hannah's expression when she brought these things in, I knew I was being favoured.

At the end of the first week, I asked Grisela if I could write a letter to my grandmother.

"A splendid idea, *ma petite*," she said. "It will be like a little project and a good way for you to practice."

"Should I be worried about her other children finding out about me?" I asked.

At this, she stopped what she was doing. We were in the main room downstairs where we had been practicing our partnered dancing. The chateau was empty except for us and the few servants on staff that day.

"Where on earth did that come from?" she demanded.

"Roza said something about them. It happened when I told her we saw my mother outside the theatre."

I sat down in the chair Charles usually occupied.

"Really? What for?"

"She doesn't believe my mother is following me," I replied.

"Did you tell her we saw her, too?"

I nodded. "I did, but it doesn't seem to matter. She insists that if the Countess children find out about my mother and me, they'll be upset. Of course, I wouldn't want them to find my letter and come to Paris."

"My dear, I'm sure with their mother's current problems, your existence is the least of their worries," Grisela said confidently. She put the matter out of her mind. "Now, we've done this for one week and you're doing beautifully, so tomorrow we shall start working on the dance for the show."

"Do you think I shall be ready in time?" I asked.

"You will have a small role which is connected to mine, so you won't be far away from me when you are on the stage."

"What will the show be about?"

She smiled at me, a glint of mischief in her eyes. "It is a dance of death, *ma petite*. We do some form of this quite often. That's actually where the theatre's name came from. I usually dance the lead, but for this particular show, Victorie is best suited."

"Why?"

"Because this particular dance is about a girl who suffers because of the sins of her kin—much like you, *petite*. Perhaps Charles was inspired by your story," she began. "Anyway, the story is about a girl who's suffering, as I said, and we shall play the part of the aspects that contribute to her destruction."

"It sounds exciting. I am so looking forward to being part of it."

She laughed, extending her hand toward me. "I am pleased at your enthusiasm, but we have many other things to do today. I will send for some nourishment, and then we will begin working on your grandmother's letter."

Later that day, after an exhausting couple of hours of reading and writing practice, as well as an awkward first draft of the letter, we finally settled into a carriage and headed off to the theatre for my first costume fitting.

The under-stage levels of the theatre were quiet, except for Mathilde's thunderous laughter which vibrated off the stone walls. She stepped out into the hallway dressed chin to ankle in a tight, shiny red dress with her arms bare and free. Her body's curves were accentuated so perfectly I couldn't help but to be jealous. Her hysterical fits of laughter continued even when she saw us approach.

"Can you believe this, Gigi?" Mathilde exclaimed. "I am supposed to be the sin of lust! Yet I can barely walk in this!"

A woman I had not met before came out of the same room with a knife in her hand. I stepped back, preparing for an attack, when the girl bent down and slit Mathilde's dress from the floor almost to her waist.

"Ah! *Merci*, Josephine. I was beginning to wonder," Mathilde exhaled gratefully. "By the way, this is Katrine. Grisela's *protégée*."

Josephine smiled and nodded to me, her brown eyes and plain face a refreshing change from the constant stream of exceptionally beautiful people I'd been meeting.

"I think we should add a wig so your hair falls to your bottom," Josephine advised Mathilde. "You'll appear like Aphrodite."

"Josephine is responsible for our incredible costuming," Grisela complemented her, and a smile stretched across my face.

"I greatly admire your work. What you did with the sun and the forest in the last production was astounding."

"*Merci*, Katrine. I heard it was your first experience at the theatre. I am pleased to hear I added to your enjoyment," Josephine said as she worked. "I cannot wait to dress you both. Grisela, I think your costume is my finest yet."

"I would love to help," I quickly offered, "if you should ever have the need. At home I spent several years doing extensive needlework."

She smiled at me. "I'll keep that in mind. Now, Grisela—"

"What shall I be?" Grisela asked excitedly.

Josephine's smile grew wider, until she sprang the surprise: "The Angel of Death, of course!"

I sat on a chair in one corner of the costume fitting room as Grisela dressed behind a screen and Josephine reinforced the top of the slit in Mathilde's dress.

"I know you are used to doing otherwise," Josephine was saying to Mathilde, "but I think we should keep your bosom covered in fabric. They're much more prominent that way. You can see their full shape instead of only the top."

Mathilde only sighed. "And I shall have to dance like this?"

"I think you may be lounging on a chaise most of the time. You don't actually have to dance. You will simply be swept up and carried around during the dance itself," Josephine replied.

Just then, Grisela emerged from behind the screen in a dress that looked as if it was made of smoke. As she walked, it shimmered darkly, like pieces of coal.

"And my *pièce de rèsistance*," Josephine exclaimed as she lifted an enormous pair of wings from the other side of the room. She carried them over and attached them to Grisela's back by means of shoulder straps.

"Astounding," I said as Grisela spun around the room, the tips of the wings just brushing the ceiling.

They were made of black feathers and what resembled spider webs. Grisela admired herself proudly in the mirror.

"*Mon dieu*, Josephine. You have truly outdone yourself."

"And now you, Katrine," Josephine turned her attention to me. "Because you resemble Victorie, you shall be representing her dark side as Vanity. Your costume shall be almost identical to Victorie's, except with some simple adjustments that show Pride and Vanity in your appearance."

Grisela chuckled. "Go easy on her, Josephine. Our young friend has never worn a corset."

"You're kidding!" Mathilde exclaimed. "How old are you?"

"Sixteen," I told her.

"Sixteen and no corset, you are a lucky girl. Most girls your age are bound tight and about to be married!" Mathilde declared.

"Thank heavens I am not," I answered, and she laughed.

"You have no wish for marriage?"

"Not unless I am in love," I replied firmly. The three women exchanged glances, all of them smiling at some humour I didn't understand.

"Well, you'll fit in quite well here," Mathilde finally said to me.

Josephine began to dig through the racks of hanging costumes while Grisela went back to posing.

"What shall be done with my hair?" Grisela wondered, playing with the curls that hung around her face.

Josephine grabbed a purple dress from the rack and brought it to me.

"Put this on," she said, motioning me towards the screen. She grabbed my wrist before I went. "Down to your chemise, then I'll help you into the corset."

I went behind the screen and took off my dress, one of the simple ones Roza and I had bought in that first village. I had taken to wearing them when I was doing my lessons, changing to one of the new, much more elaborate gowns in the evening. When I got the dress off, I stepped out of it from its pile on the floor. I folded my arms across my chest, my nipples hardening from the cold. I had never stood naked in front of others, even when the dressmaker had taken my measurements, and was feeling quite shy.

I stepped out into the room, the other women paying me no mind except Josephine, who came at me with a bizarre contraption I assumed was a corset.

"Some call them stays, I call it a corset. I won't pull it too tight your first time, but you should really get used to wearing them, whatever word you chose to call it, before you dance," Josephine said. She wrapped it around my middle and I felt its stiffness for the first time. It made me a bit nervous.

"Fasten the hooks in the front, Katrine," Josephine instructed, and I realised the corset actually separated into two pieces that were held together by a line of hooks. She pulled it tightly around my waist. The tops of my breasts bulged outwards. I felt another pull from the back as she began to tighten the laces.

"Just breathe as you normally would, *ma petite*," Grisela said gently. Concentrating on my breathing, before I knew it, she was done. Josephine next helped me pull the purple dress over my head and tied the stomacher in the back. She motioned me towards the mirror, while Grisela moved away so that I could see myself.

The image startled me.

"I look like a woman," I said, staring at my newly created curves. My figure was hugged in a light fabric, the skirt slightly sheer so the shape of my leg was visible. The lace trim of my chemise made a border around the neck of the dress.

"*Ma petite*, you have a bosom!" Grisela exclaimed. I smoothed my hands down the sleeves of the dress, pulling on the edges as I had seen Charles do so many times.

"Is it alright?" I wanted to know. "I must be lovely enough to play Victorie's Vanity. I'm concerned that I'm not glamorous enough—"

Grisela sighed, but before she could say anything, Mathilde spoke up: "Are you mad, child? Even I know your grandmother is known for her beauty, and some may mistake your modesty for a chance to feed your pride."

When Grisela looked up, Mathilde continued, "Gigi, do you get your beauty from your relatives, as well? What do you know of your Valois family?"

"All one needs to know about family is whether they are a threat or not," Grisela replied testily. "Come now, *petite*. We must go up to the stage to practice."

At this, Josephine quickly helped me change out of the gown but left the corset in place under my regular dress. It completely altered the way it fit, making the plain and simple look so feminine and beautiful.

"It was a pleasure to meet you, Josephine," I said, hurriedly following Grisela as she left the room.

"Is something wrong?"

I caught up to Grisela, still following at her heel. We went up a set of stairs I had never seen before and came out on the stage behind the curtain.

She turned to me angrily now. "Why has no one questioned you? You say you are Báthory, and even with no proof, they all believe you."

Her sudden annoyance both startled and confused me. "Maybe it's because you believe me. Your word gives me credibility. They believe me because they believe you," I offered.

"If my word is so good then why do they question my own lineage?" she yelled. Then, composing herself, she lowered her voice. "I'm sorry, *petite*. I am just frustrated."

I frowned and then said quietly, "It may count for very little, but I believe that you are a Valois."

She smiled, then laughed loudly, the sound still like tinkling bells no matter the volume.

"And what do you know of the Valois?" she asked. I watched her carefully before lying and saying I knew a little, when I really knew nothing at all.

"Valois are a dynasty of French Kings, *ma petite*, that died out some years ago. The father of our current King Louis was the first Bourbon

King, who inherited from the House of Valois."

"Your father was a king?"

"According to my mother he was a prince, and she was a courtesan at the court of Francis I. Nevertheless, my mother bore many children by different men. Only my three elder siblings we are sure of who fathered them. Things changed after she was bitten and became a blood drinker," she began. "I was born subsequently and any who came after me were not quite right. That is why I followed in her footsteps, and why none of my younger siblings have joined our ranks."

"Your elder siblings knew? And why not you?"

"My mother had a long standing affair with the Spanish ambassador, and those children were legitimised. She was turned by what she called a 'foreign monster' after their births. I know very little of the incident other than that.

"When the ambassador left France, she had a brief tryst with one of King Francis' sons," she continued. "She refused to say which; she always told me it was irrelevant. When I was born, she kept on until she realised that people might begin to notice that she did not age. After two of my younger siblings died and many years at court, she decided to pack up the youngest three and move on, leaving myself, and the closest in age after me, in the care of my three elder siblings. Fortunately, that was after she taught me everything she knew about being a courtesan, and I had already been accepted at court."

"Do you know where your family is now?" I asked.

"My mother and the younger ones, thankfully no. My elder siblings, and the next after me, all went in different directions: Constantinople, Greece, Scotland, and even to the New World."

"Do you miss them?"

She considered. "I used to, but they've been gone for so long I rarely think of them anymore. I'm sure it'll be the same for you, *ma petite*. It just takes time. Now, stand to the side and watch me and we'll see if you can follow."

Grisela danced and I tried my best to copy until my feet started to ache. It proved to be much more complex and difficult than dancing with a partner. When we finally stopped, I was convinced I would never get it.

"You did well for your first day, Katrine," she assured me as we headed towards the front doors. "You learn quickly."

"Thank you," was all I could think to say. Once we went outside and the cold air hit my face, exhaustion set in.

Suddenly, I detected in that air the scent of blood. I immediately panicked, thinking that my mother was close. I did not want to give her reason to follow our carriage or attract attention to Grisela. I was trying to look for her out of the corner of my eye, when I noticed a young man hurrying towards us.

"*Excusez-moi*, Mademoiselle!" the man called out to us.

Grisela ignored him and got into our waiting carriage, but he grabbed my arm before I could ascend.

"Pardon me, sir, but I think it's best you let go of my arm," I said angrily.

He stepped back as if startled by my annoyance. "My apologies, Mademoiselle. I was looking for the Lady Klara von Dores."

He was one of the young men from the night at the theatre, the entourage that flanked Klara. His pupils were large and eyes glossy, haunted looking. I had never looked directly in the face of one so enchanted, so completely under Klara's spell.

"She's not here," I replied coldly.

Panic washed over his face as I pulled away and got into the carriage. He continued to speak, but I closed the door and we drove away.

"Admirers already, *petite*?"

"Not mine, I assure you," I huffed, sitting back in the seat. "It appears enchantment is a hard habit to break."

Grisela said nothing, and we rode back to the chateau in silence.

"Your presence is requested downstairs," Hannah said, pulling me from my last attempt at a nap. We had come home from the theatre and

I had fallen into my bed, exhausted.

I pulled the covers up to my chin. "Can you tell them I'm ill?"

She sighed. "You know as well as I do that he'll come up here to check on you."

"Who?"

"Lord Westwick. He's asking for you, because a certain someone is starting to get annoyed."

"Who?" I asked again.

"Just Klara. She's the only one who doesn't understand his behaviour," she replied, going to my armoire to look through my dresses.

"I don't understand." I sat up and wiped the sleep from my eyes.

"She wasn't immediately the favourite and she's not taking it well. She's jealous of you."

"Maybe if she stopped causing trouble and behaved with some dignity, people would like her more," I replied angrily.

Hannah stopped what she was doing, looking a bit startled at me.

"I'm just so tired of Klara! Since we first met her, it's been one thing after another!"

"Relax, Katrine. Don't let her get the best of you. You're better than that," Hannah comforted me. "And if Lord Westwick wants to favour you over her, there is nothing wrong with that. You are smart and pretty and worth someone's favour."

She suddenly narrowed her eyes. "Katrine, did you sleep with that thing on?" Hannah gestured at the corset as I got out of bed. "Who put you in that thing?"

"Oh, the costumer at the theatre, Josephine, put it on when I tried my costume. I needed to practice dancing in it," I replied. "Don't you think it makes me look more womanly?"

"Indeed," Hannah nodded with the hint of a smile. "I can't wait to see you on that stage. Now, for this evening, I'm thinking the emerald green. I believe there's a meal involved, and the upper part of the dress is so pretty you'll look stunning, both when you sit and stand."

She pulled the newly-made gown and matching shoes from the armoire. I said nothing as Hannah helped me into the dress and tied my stomacher in the back. The corset sculpted the shape of the dress, which was ideal since the dress was simple. Made of heavy green silk with no embroidery, it had only perfectly folded pleats where the skirt connected to the bodice.

"What's on your mind?" Hannah asked as she sat me in the chair and began styling my hair.

"I am unsure of how to react to Lord Westwick's attentions."

"Has he done anything that could compromise your virtue?"

"No, nothing like that. But the night is still young," I mused.

"So, what are you afraid of? Lord Westwick is a lovely man. Perhaps he wants to marry you."

"You could be right. He's never shown me a reason to think anything other than his attentions being entirely noble. Perhaps I'm being overly concerned. It's just that Klara's reaction to this whole scenario makes me nervous."

Hannah was brushing my hair out, and it now stretched all the way to the small of my back. She continued brushing, even when I winced in pain.

"I wish it was fashionable to wear the hair loose. You have such lovely hair!" she admired. "I'm unsure of how to style it, because it looks so lovely out."

"I'm satisfied with a simple plait, Hannah. I'm already lucky enough," I replied. "Anything more is a luxury."

"Just be grateful, and do not concern yourself with other things," she admonished. Hannah deftly wrapped my hair in a twist on top of my head, securing it with pins before covering it with a net made of gold thread.

"Although I am deeply grateful for all of this, I am also afraid," I explained. "This world is indeed a strange place which I don't quite understand."

I stared at my hands which looked more polished and groomed than they ever had. My mother had always made Bodi and me clean our hands before church so we appeared presentable, but they had never looked as they did now. Never did they look so soft and delicate.

I hadn't thought of Bodi in months. I wondered how he and my father were getting on alone, if Bodi was taking care of things or they had hired a helper. I also wondered what they had told the other villagers about my mother and me, if they said we'd run off or if there were two empty graves with our names on them.

"Alright, my dear, you are finished. Be careful of your movements. I'm sure it will be fine, but I wouldn't want it to fall out," Hannah warned.

I looked at myself in the mirror. My eyes looked sad. I tried my best to shake it off, smiling wide and pinching my cheeks to add some colour.

"I think I am ready," I said, turning to face Hannah. "How do I look?"

"Like a vision," she complemented. "Now hurry downstairs before they notice the time."

Everyone was gathered in the dining room around a long table, as if waiting for something. Charles was the first to notice me as I entered the room.

"Were you waiting for me?" I whispered as he embraced me, kissing both my cheeks.

"No, my sweet. We are actually waiting for Klara. She had some visitors whom I insisted had to leave. She was a bit sore about it, so I sent her to freshen up before we eat."

He led me by the hand to my place at the table. "We were having before-dinner conversation, and she just would not stop. I am hoping she will decide to stay in her room for the rest of the evening, but I doubt it."

"I'm pleased to hear I did not delay anything."

He stood back and appraised my appearance, a half smile on his face. "If you always look as you do now, I would wait a lifetime."

"You flatter me, Charles."

My face was hot from blushing. He brought me to a seat between Grisela and Vincenzo, the three of us just to his left at the head of the table.

Suddenly, there was a flutter of commotion as Klara came back into the room like a tornado, anger radiating off her body. She was dressed in heavy red silk, the colour of blood, and resembled what I imagined the bride of Satan to look like. She shoved her way to the table as we all prepared to sit down, stealing Victorie's seat to the right of Charles.

All eyes turned to Charles, everyone awaiting his reaction.

His eyes lowered as if deep in contemplation, and then he said evenly: "Klara, that is not your seat. Please move three chairs to your right."

"My station..." she began.

"I am tired of hearing this incessant commentary about your station!" Charles yelled, slamming the flat of his hand against the table. "You have no station here! You were banished from your station! Do you understand that? You have no rank. I took pity on you by taking you in, Klara, and I'm beginning to think it was a mistake! You live in my house and you will obey my rules. I am the master of this domain, and any station you held before coming here is irrelevant!"

She was about to reply but he cut her off: "Do not argue with me, woman! You either obey my rules or stay in your room until you are ready to do so. I have no problem sending you back to Vienna in a box if necessary, do you understand?"

I noticed I had been holding my breath throughout the entire argument; my body had gone stiff as a board. Klara shoved the chair back with an unnecessary amount of force, then made a dramatic show of moving to where she was directed. I avoided her eyes at all costs now; the position of my own chair, so close to Charles, likely infuriated her.

Charles finally relaxed. The weight of the tension in the room lifted as he motioned for all of us to sit and for Victorie to return to her chair. In the weeks since arriving at the chateau, this was the first time we all sat down together for a meal, and I was quite overwhelmed by the grandness of it all. The plates of roast pork with glaze glistened in the light. Hearty mixes of cooked vegetables in rich sauce, a clear broth coating the thinnest slices of meat with potatoes and carrots, and heaps of Roza's buttered bread were all the more delectable to me, because I knew exactly what went into preparing such a meal. The time I had spent cooking with my mother and working in the bakery in Vienna were some of the greatest moments of my life. I had learned so much in such a short time.

I paid little attention to the conversations swirling around me, Grisela in rapid French on my one side with Mathilde, and Vincenzo and Charles in a debate about trade on the other. I wished I was sitting with Josephine at the opposite end of the table; I had so many questions about costuming, I thought my head would explode.

Meanwhile, Klara ate quietly, barely looking up from her plate. I imagined she was quite embarrassed. I suddenly realised I had no idea what part she would play in the dance. I also wondered why she was having so much trouble fitting in, while I was getting on fine.

I gorged myself on the rich food as I got lost in my thoughts. Was my grandmother eating well? I wondered if she had visitors, if her children were still in contact after all that had happened. Grisela and I had begun composing a letter to her, but between my insistence on perfect script and her desire for intelligent and eloquent language, it was going to be a slow process. I would wait, though, for I wanted it to be perfect.

"*Petite*, are you alright?" Grisela inquired after some time.

"Yes, quite fine. Why do you ask?" .

She took a small sip from her wine glass. "Because you seem like you are somewhere else entirely."

"I was just thinking about my family," I said quietly.

"You know, we could send a letter to your father, even if it's just to inform him you are alive," she offered.

I put down my napkin. "It doesn't matter. I'm just a burden to him without my mother."

Charles suddenly tapped his fork to a glass in an attempt to get everyone's attention.

"Everyone, everyone, if you please," he began. "I have an announcement. I gathered you all here so I could inform you that at the end of this next show's run, we shall be taking a trip. Everyone is required to attend."

"Where shall we be going, Charles?" Victorie spoke up.

"Ah! That is the exciting part, my dear. For years, I've been receiving invitations for us to perform at various courts across Europe. I've usually declined but, recently, I had a change of heart. So," he drew out this last word, "we are all going to Russia!" and clapped his hands together.

"Russia, Charles? What made you change your mind?" Grisela asked.

"Yes, does this have anything to do with those stories about the skinwalker?" Mathilde prodded. "We have no proof, Charles. You would travel all that way for nothing—"

He waved a hand. "We are going as guests of the Imperial Russian Court, nothing more. Of course, if anything else were to come up, we would deal with it at that point. Besides," he said mischievously now, "the skinwalker rumours are not the only thing I have heard."

"I heard they have a Turkish *dhampir* in their prison," Tommas piped up.

"I heard she's a princess," Victorie added.

"May I ask something?" I asked now, and all eyes turned to me. "What is a skinwalker, or a *dhampir*, for that matter?"

"One who is born from a human mother and a blood drinker father is called a *dhampir*," Vincenzo explained. "A skinwalker is one who can shift to more than one type of animal; in some instances it involves wearing the pelt of that animal."

As the various conversations began again, I turned to Grisela and asked quietly, "So does that make you a *dhampir*?"

"Yes and no. I am really something else entirely," she replied. "By the way, *dhampir*, to the best of my knowledge, is an Eastern European word. It is much like the word *strigoi* and has many meanings."

"I only know one meaning for *strigoi*, and it is not a pleasant one," I said quietly. She laughed, then whispered to me, "Maybe you should rethink that, for you are essentially *strigoi* yourself."

I bit down on my tongue to stifle my gasp. She looked quite surprised by the look on my face.

"Well, what did you think had happened to you, *ma petite*?" she asked quietly. "You are most certainly no longer human, and you exhibit several different characteristics of a *strigoi*. Now, whether you will actually shape shift or not still remains to be seen."

I could do nothing but stare back at her. She was right, of course; it was just the first time that words had been put to my condition, and it startled me.

"Regardless of what is or isn't there, we are going to Russia," Charles was saying in the meantime. "If there is a *dhampir* princess or skinwalker at court, we will deal with it as necessary."

The chatter continued, Vincenzo now extremely excited at the prospect of gathering Russian contacts. While this was going on, I continued to eat until I felt like I was going to burst. When the desserts were brought out, I had to turn them away. I noticed Grisela did also, and took note of that as part of my training. How to sit, eat, drink and speak were equally important parts of the etiquette required to become a proper woman.

I tried my best, in fact, to observe everyone, male or female, when I noticed Charles looking intently at me. I smiled slightly and nodded back to him, hoping no one else was paying attention.

XXVI.

Breathless

AFTER DINNER, WE MOVED ON TO THE SALON WHERE
people were beginning to gather for gambling, music and dancing. I kept
close to Grisela as the others dispersed through the room. Charles took
to his regular chair, and Klara submersed herself into a group of waiting
admirers.

"Are those the same young men that Charles asked to leave earlier?" I
asked Grisela, who shifted her eyes for only a moment.

"It appears so, and I believe that is also the same young man who
approached us outside the theatre," Grisela replied, surveying the group
briefly. "Not our concern, *ma petite*."

She pulled a small fan from a chain round her waist and opened it,
using it to conceal most of her face as she scanned the room. Without a
fan, I felt a bit silly and unsure where to put my eyes.

At that moment, a maid approached me with a small silver tray. "From
Lord Westwick, Mademoiselle."

At first I thought she was talking to Grisela. When I realised she
wasn't, I looked at the tray to find a fan. I picked it up and opened it. I
could see it was made from smooth dark wood; the shapes of flowers
were cut into it so some light shone through.

"Do as I do, *petite*. You look like a stunned animal," Grisela murmured, and I immediately followed her lead.

I smiled and nodded to Charles, who was watching for my reaction. He appeared pleased, while Grisela seemed tense and irritated. Meanwhile, men fluttered around Klara like moths to a flame, their eyes wide and glazed over as they stared longingly at her.

"Look how she enchants them," I muttered. "Why would one not want to be honestly admired?"

I said this to no one in particular, not realising that Mathilde had just come over to sit with us.

"Some women do not feel good enough within themselves to believe they would be," she said.

"Yet it would make those women feel better to attract men through tricks?" I pressed her for an answer.

"For some women, any way is good. They are defined by the attention they receive, whatever way it comes," Mathilde shrugged. "It is unfortunate, really, that such pathetic creatures get by in this world in such a way. Yet, they are often women with high rank and married well."

"And it appears," Victorie added, "that she is not receiving attention from the only man in the room she desires it from."

Victorie sat down with us, as well, and I followed her eyes as she watched Klara's hopeful glances towards Vincenzo and Charles. I moved the fan closer to my face, and was immediately struck by the faint smell of pine. Like the trees in my village, I thought as I closed my eyes for a single second, but how did he know?

Charles rolled his eyes, meanwhile, and said something to Vincenzo before crossing the room and asking Klara to dance.

"How courteous of him," Mathilde observed, nudging Grisela, "that he should take pity on his charity case. I hope the baron paid him handsomely."

"Perhaps that's how he's financing this little trip of his," was all Grisela replied.

"You know how he gets when someone mentions skinwalkers," Victorie smiled. "All shifters are fascinated by that fairy tale."

"Not true, Victorie," Mathilde interjected. "I, for one, could care less.

No, I am much more interested in this Turkish princess...could you imagine what our show would be like with a girl like that?"

"You make it sound like smut," Grisela sniffed.

"No, no! I just know other productions have painted the women to appear dark skinned, and now we wouldn't have to do that," Mathilde explained quickly.

"But why would she come with us?" I cut in.

Grisela turned to me. "Why did you, *petite*?"

From the other women's expressions, I knew this was not a point to debate, so I turned my attention back to Charles and Klara. Klara was talking, her face completely animated, while Charles stared blankly into the distance, not even pretending to be interested. She didn't notice and continued on, even as the song ended, keeping hold of him through the next dance.

"Katrine," Vincenzo's voice grabbed my attention. "May I have this dance?"

I looked at Grisela, who nodded her head in approval. I then took Vincenzo's hand and let him lead the way.

Everything went smoothly; I moved at a measured pace to make sure I did every step correctly. It was my first dance in public, and I was not prepared to embarrass myself or my partner. Vincenzo was graceful and elegant with a smoothness that reminded me of a cat, his green eyes twinkling with delight as I relaxed and began to allow him to lead. He was perfection in his impeccably tailored suit made of the darkest brown wool, along with white gloves of such fine fabric they seemed like a second skin.

I found myself smiling; Vincenzo's enthusiasm had become infectious. Charles appeared to become more cheerful with our presence, while Klara's inane chatter carried on. I wondered how she thought she could continue on a conversation while dancing; maybe it was something that got easier with practice.

When the song ended, I bowed out. Vincenzo led me away before Charles had the chance to ask for the next dance. I was pleased by his affections but unsure of how to react. I also wanted Klara to forget about me; there was no need to agitate her further by a dance with Charles.

"Well done," Grisela said quietly to me when I sat back down. I sighed in relief and returned to watching the room through my fan. I had somehow lost track of Vincenzo, who disappeared the moment he returned me to my seat.

"He does that sometimes," Mathilde said, reading my mind.

"Who?" I asked.

"Signor Amori," she replied knowingly. "On occasion, when you turn your back he is gone. Almost as if into thin air."

"Any idea why?"

She smiled slightly. "Not a clue. But I am convinced it's purposeful and an attempt to create mystique."

I couldn't help but giggle, which abruptly stopped when one of Klara's admirers cut in to her dancing, giving Charles a chance to escape and sending Klara into an absolute fit of rage.

"What is she going on about now?" Victorie asked as we watched the commotion. I was about to reply when I felt the strength drain from my body, like something turned off somewhere inside me.

"If you'll excuse me, I think I need to get some refreshment," I said to the women, and was about to stand when Grisela grabbed my wrist.

"Are you alright, *petite*?" she asked. "You look terribly pale."

"I suddenly feel quite…empty."

"*Comment tant?*"

"Like someone has drained me of my strength," I explained awkwardly. I saw something in her eyes that I did not quite understand. It passed almost as quickly as it came, and she motioned with her fan across the room for Hannah to appear.

"Please help Katrine get some nourishment," Grisela said to Hannah. "And let me know that she's alright."

Hannah nodded, took my arm and led me to the back of the room and through the servants' door. She sat me down on a stool in the kitchen and began to rummage about preparing some tea.

"It was just like something sucked the life right out of me," I tried to explain.

She paused, examining my face for a moment. "And it just came on, all of a sudden?"

I nodded. She pushed a nearby plate of buttered bread in my direction, which I devoured without another word. At that moment, I hoped she realised I needed a bit more than food.

"What's wrong? Is everything alright, Katrine?" Vincenzo startled me as he appeared in an open doorway. He stepped into the room and closed the door behind him.

"Were you outside?" I asked him. He looked uncomfortable and shifted about like he was hiding something.

"No, my dear. I was in the basement," he said, William coming up behind him. "But you are avoiding my question."

"The Lady had a sudden loss of strength," Hannah advised him as she made my tea. She then left the room briefly and returned with a silver canister.

"Why were you in the basement?" I asked. "Where did you go? After our dance, you sat me down then disappeared into thin air."

"Is that when you had this loss of strength?"

"Yes. And now you're avoiding my question, Signor Amori."

He and William exchanged looks and then, without a word, William left us together in an awkward silence.

"It's complicated, my dear," he finally said.

"I have time," I replied.

Roza suddenly came in from another part of the kitchen and handed him a basket of food.

"Are you going on a picnic in the dark, Signor?" I asked.

He sighed loudly. "I told you it's complicated. Tomorrow I'll explain everything. Over lunch, perhaps?"

Before I could reply, he disappeared back into the basement. Roza also left the room without saying a word. I wondered what she knew about what he was doing. Meanwhile, Hannah pushed a cup of tea towards me. I resolutely drank it in one gulp, tasting the blood and feeling my strength returning.

"Do you know what's happening down in the basement, Hannah?"

I asked. She smiled slyly at me, refilling the cup and handing it back to me.

"I wouldn't have anything to tell you at bedtime if I said it all now, would I?" she replied. "But you shall have to go back out and make an appearance once more before you retire. We cannot allow that girl to believe she has done you any kind of harm."

"You think she did that to me?" I asked, gesturing in frustration. "But how is that even possible? She has no magic powers or special abilities, does she? How could she do that?"

"It does not involve magic powers necessarily, My Lady. But that is beside the point. You need to go back out before Mademoiselle Delphine gets into a panic."

Hannah helped me up and ushered me towards the door. She took one last appraising look before pushing me back out into the crowded room.

"Good!" Grisela exclaimed when I came into her view. She seemed to be deep in conversation with two well-dressed men who looked up when I approached.

"Gentlemen, this is my *protégée*, Katrine," she said, her fan open and fluttering in front of her.

"My apologies, I was momentarily indisposed," I said. "I am pleased to make your acquaintance."

"Katrine, this is Monsieur Richleau and Monsieur Fabreaun, friends paying us a visit from the French court. I have no idea how they could tear themselves away, but I am so glad they did," Grisela smiled to the men.

"Oh, it is not as lively as it once was," Mr. Richleau began. "Mademoiselle Delphine is sorely missed."

"Indeed," his companion declared, "the two of you should come pay us a visit—if you're not too busy with this new profession of yours. I never would have imagined you, Mademoiselle, as a dancer! I'd have thought it was beneath you."

"Oh, I assure you, Monsieur, it is one of the most satisfying things I have ever done, next to becoming this young lady's mentor," Grisela replied.

"You must be quite the exceptional young lady for Mlle. Delphine to take you on as her *protégée*. I have seen her pass by many suitable candidates," Mr. Fabreaun said, looking me up and down. "I wonder why you caught her eye."

"If you'll excuse me, gentlemen," Charles appeared quite suddenly beside me, his voice commanding and forceful, "but the young lady promised me a dance."

I smiled at the men as I let Charles lead me away. I wasn't sure what to say and felt awkward around them. On the other hand, I was also relieved: the awkwardness with Charles I could manage.

"Thank you for the fan, it's beautiful," I said to him as we began our dance.

"I am glad you like it," he replied. "Are you alright? I noticed your woman came to get you."

"I am better now, just a sudden loss of strength." Trying to make conversation, I added, "I saw what happened with Klara, and I am sorry for that. She thinks she deserves your attention because of her station."

He snorted. "To be quite honest, she is lucky I like her parents."

"You are very generous, some may say to a fault."

"Maybe my generosity is better placed elsewhere," he said, smiling to me.

I felt the heat of a blush coming on.

"Perhaps."

Our eyes remained locked as we danced. I knew every part of his dark brown eyes: perfect lashes, almond shape, and that glint of something only he knew, giving them a sparkle that made warmth spread through my heart. I liked it when he smiled at me. It made me feel special, like I was the only girl in the room, in the whole world for that matter, for whom he had eyes.

But that couldn't possibly be true. After all, I was merely some girl from nowhere with nothing to offer other than love and devotion, and that couldn't possibly be enough for someone like him, could it? No. The world did not work that way.

"Are you sure you are alright, Katrine? You suddenly look very sad," Charles asked.

"It's nothing," I said, moving my gaze away from him.

"If it upsets you then surely it isn't nothing, my dear. Anything I can do to make you smile again, even if it means moving the heavens, I will do," he said quite plainly. When our eyes met again, his intensity made me miss a step and stumble. He caught me.

"I...have no words. I am humbled by your kindness."

As the song ended, he held my hand tightly in his. "Will you meet me in the dining room in a few moments? I must ask you something of the utmost importance, but it must be in private."

"Of course."

"Good! I shall go now. Wait several minutes, then follow me, but do not attract attention," he said, and then quickly left.

I moved off the dance floor to wait, watching people and preparing to make my escape. I wondered if I should tell Grisela, then decided not to bother her. Anyway, she was deep in conversation with her court friends, and it seemed silly to interrupt her. I could certainly handle myself alone with Charles. No one seemed to notice or pay any mind to me as I crossed the room and went toward the dining room.

The room was bathed in the soft glow of candlelight, with only a few tapers lit in the large candelabra near the head of the table. Charles sat in his seat, seemingly deep in thought until he saw me crossing the room towards him.

"You came," he said quietly.

"Of course. It is what you asked," I replied. "Now, what is so important that you had to tell me in private?"

He stood, moving slowly towards me until we were mere inches apart.

"You see, Katrine, I wanted quite badly to kiss you, but it would have been wildly inappropriate to ask in public," he began.

"Is that what you would like to do now?" I asked, my voice barely a whisper.

"Yes. May I kiss you, Katrine?"

He locked his eyes to mine as he slid his hand across my cheek. Then he placed his fingers under my chin and gently kissed me.

I could feel a warmth and tingle rise inside me as if a swarm of butterflies had been released inside my stomach. They were all steadily flapping their wings as our lips pressed together, my eyes closing as I drank in the moment. When he finally pulled away from me, it felt as if the whole room sighed.

"I have to go," he said. I opened my eyes and stared up into his. He ran the tip of his finger down my cheek, my face moving with his touch.

Then, without another word, he left.

XXVII.

End Of Innocence

"SIGNOR AMORI HAS PREPARED A PICNIC," HANNAH said as she helped me get dressed. I had gone straight to bed after meeting with Charles and hadn't yet spoken to her. I'd woken up late and we were getting ready for my lunch with Vincenzo.

"Should I prepare for this?" I asked. "Is he going to tell me something horrible?"

"It depends on what you see as horrible," she continued. "But I won't tell you a thing, and we'll see if it's any different."

"What?"

"What he tells you and what the servants know, silly. You seem distracted this morning."

I smiled and shrugged my shoulders. "No, just tired. And thinking about my grandmother."

"I was told the dressmaker is still working on your underskirt," Hannah went on. "With the addition of your corset, it will give you more shape."

"I have no memory of what you're talking about, Hannah, I'm sorry," I shook my head.

She sighed. "You'll see it when it gets here. Now, you insisted on wearing this. Are you sure about it?"

"Yes," I replied. She finished plaiting the hair down my back, and I examined myself in the mirror. Even my plain gray dress looked nice over the corset.

"I informed Mlle. Delphine of your lunch, so she's not expecting you today. In any case, she's staying at the chateau and not accepting visitors."

"Is she alright?"

"She says she's fine but seems irritated," Hannah answered. "Also, Klara left with a new gentleman caller about an hour ago."

"And Lord Westwick?"

"Interesting that you ask. I believe he is the reason why Mlle. Delphine is in her current state."

My heart skipped a beat. "Why would you say that?"

"They quarreled this morning, and then he went to the theatre without even taking his morning meal. Why? Do you know anything about it?"

"Of course not!" I said too quickly. "I just don't want to leave Mlle. Delphine if she's upset or needs me. Now, am I ready to leave or not?"

Tolone and Hannah loaded Vincenzo, me, and our picnic basket into a carriage. The sky had turned a dark gray, which meant a coming snowfall.

"A picnic in the snow?" I asked, as the carriage set out.

"Not exactly," Vincenzo explained. "I'm taking you to my office, and the basket is for lunch. I thought you would like to see what I do, and it will give us an opportunity to speak freely and openly."

"About the basement?"

"Yes, and about where you went last night," he countered. He stared right through me when he said it, but I refused to make eye contact.

I suddenly felt tight with anxiety. "Have I done something wrong?"

"I don't know. Have you?," he asked sharply, and I cringed like I'd been hit.

"I shouldn't have left the room to meet him without telling anyone," I blurted out. "I'm sorry, I wasn't thinking. I assumed because it was—"

"Don't ever assume anything," he snapped. "But you don't have the whole story. Because you are young and naive and new to this life, you don't know any better and are easily taken advantage of. It's not your fault, though. You don't know better and he does."

"I don't understand."

"I'll explain when we arrive."

We stopped in front of a three-storey building close to the river; Vincenzo grabbed the basket and led me up flights of narrow stairs. He took a set of keys from his pocket and brought me inside, placing the basket atop a large wooden desk that sat in front of the window.

I could not help but wander over to the window and stare out at the river, with its clear view of a dock and shipyard. I was surprised by the amount of activity: unloading and loading, ships coming and going, and people of various shapes and sizes, all of whom seemed to pay no mind to a coming storm.

"Katrine, I think it would be best if we cleared this up early," Vincenzo began as he unloaded the basket onto the desk. "While you may think differently, Lord Westwick's attention for you is not entirely noble."

"Is that why he and Grisela were arguing?"

"I am afraid so. She tried to tell him you were off limits because you were under her care, and he became angry. He seduces every new girl to come into our company, then puts them aside when they're no longer to his liking. It's why most of the women now live at the theatre," Vincenzo explained. "Grisela wanted to save you the heartbreak that she and the others have suffered at his hand. His latest, before you, was Victorie. She'd pushed him away for years, and he was caught up in a long term affair with Grisela when it began."

I did not feel the tears until they fell off my chin. How could I have been so foolish?

"Why does he not desire Klara?" I muttered, feeling dead inside.

He placed a hand on my shoulder. "She is not as pretty as you, and most certainly not innocent. And I believe he enjoys the pursuit."

"I will not let the two of you down," I said, wiping the tears on my sleeve. "You have taken a chance on me, and I will not ruin myself at the first opportunity. You are right. I am naïve, but I'm glad you told me. Thank you, Vincenzo."

"Please know that I objected to what he was doing, but he wouldn't hear me. I will do my best, though, to protect you from unsuitable suitors."

I hugged him tightly. He was startled by this at first, but then gently put his arms around me.

"Thank you," I said again into his chest.

"Think nothing of it. Now, I do have something to tell you regarding the basement, but let's eat something first."

He went back to laying out the bread and cheese and other bits of food from the basket, along with a silver canister similar to the one Hannah and Tolone had. We sat and ate a little before he began. He poured us each some wine.

"First, let me begin by saying, if you did not already know, that William and I are heavily involved in trade. That is how we make our money. One day, a ship came in from England. I'm not entirely sure what cargo it held, but William happened to see a young girl on its deck using spells to move the sails about. Of course, we were intrigued.

"We boarded. At first, this girl was angry and tried to use her magic on us, but she was no match for William. When she realised this, she finally agreed to speak with us. She explained she'd come from Scots, and left the island because they were going to burn her as a heretic. William assured her she'd be safe with us. She came quite willingly, but then became agitated and very violent, so much so that we were forced to restrain her. We brought her to the chateau. Unfortunately, to protect her and the rest of us, we had to confine her to a cell in the basement. I was tending to her when you saw me."

"But why not just let her go?" I wondered aloud.

"Because she could have become extremely dangerous to all of us and it was best we took her by force. It seemed easier to apologise later for it."

I took a bite of some bread. "And what would you like me to do?"

"I was hoping you'd be willing to try to talk to her, tell her we mean no harm and want to keep her safe. If William could teach her to control her powers it could save her life—the same as teaching you not to feed from humans will help you immensely."

I said nothing for several minutes, trying to absorb all I had learned. I wanted to believe I was ready for the responsibility of helping others like us, but after being so blind to think that Charles actually cared for me, how could I trust myself?

"I feel very foolish," I admitted. "I don't know if I can help you."

I lowered my head and started to cry. Vincenzo didn't say anything. I wasn't sure there was anything that he could say. But it would not happen again, I vowed. I wouldn't allow myself to be so blind ever again.

I wiped my face, and looked up at him. "I will help you. I can't promise it will do any good, but I will try my best, I swear."

"And that's all I can ask, my dear," Vincenzo said, his voice very soft. "I am so sorry I had to be the one to break your heart with this news, Katrine."

We finished our lunch and, as Vincenzo packed up, I went back to looking out the window, nursing my pain. The snow had not slowed the people below; a fine layer of white simply blanketed everything.

We rode back to the chateau in silence, and as soon as we stepped out of the carriage, I went looking for Grisela. Hannah and Tolone were waiting in the main hallway when we came inside.

"Where's Mlle. Delphine?" I asked as Hannah took my cloak.

"In her room," she said, and I immediately started climbing the stairs before she could stop me. "But she's not taking any visitors!"

I went down the hallway. Grisela's chamber was two doors from mine. I knocked on the door and waited.

"Grisela? Grisela, it's Katrine," I said rather loudly. I wasn't sure she could hear me, so I leaned in close.

"Your faith is not lost on me, Grisela," I began, holding back my tears. "I promise I will do you proud, and you will never regret for a second choosing me. Can you hear me?"

I knocked again, hoping I was not talking to an empty room.

"Please talk to me," I begged. "I cannot bare the idea of you being angry with me. I did not know any better, but I do now."

I waited a few more minutes, then went to my own room, dejected. I heard someone behind me, and assumed it was Hannah. I didn't bother with the door, and flopped down in a heap on my bed. I heard the door shut behind me and then Hannah's voice quietly saying, "So that explains some things."

I kept my face buried in my pillow and said nothing.

"I should have told you, but I did not think you would believe me. But now that you know, I will do what I can to protect your virtue," she said.

I turned my head to speak clearly. "I will not have them regret taking me in. I could not bear their disappointment."

"Do not fret, child. I know just what to do," she comforted me. I felt the bed sink down as she sat on the edge.

"Will he be angry? Could he send me away?" I fretted.

"He could try, but he would likely lose Mlle. Delphine and Signor Amori if he did."

"I don't want to be any trouble."

"He needs to learn he cannot have every woman he chooses," she said firmly. "If he just wants to fornicate, I am sure Mlle. von Dores is ready and quite willing."

"I cannot believe I was so foolish to think he liked me," I said, wiping my face. "I'm so embarrassed."

"You are not the first to make that mistake, and I am sure you will not be the last, Katrine. Be happy you were told before you compromised yourself."

I sighed. "By the way, did you know they're holding a girl in the basement who can cast spells? Vincenzo says it's to keep her safe. He wants me to talk to her, try to calm her."

"I've heard," Hannah nodded. "One of the maidservants said she speaks some strange foreign tongue."

"He said she's Scots. I am not sure what that means."

"I think he means that she hails from Scotland. It is part of the island of England. I understand now why the maids said that. They are quite difficult to understand. So he thinks you can calm her?"

"I suppose so. He said she was happy to come here for a while but then became very angry and hostile. When they found her, she'd left her homeland, because they were going to burn her as a heretic."

At that minute, there was a quick knock at the door. Hannah rose quickly to answer.

"Lord Westwick requests to see Mlle. Báthory in his study," I heard a woman's voice say.

"Tell him that she is resting and sends her apologies," Hannah replied.

"He told me not to leave until she agreed," the now frightened voice said, and Hannah remained firm.

"I'm sorry. The answer is still no," and I heard the door click shut.

"Thank you," I said without moving.

"Have a rest now, dear," she replied, "and I will come collect you when Mlle. Delphine becomes available."

I woke from a heavy sleep to a black and silent room. I sat up and waited for my eyes to adjust. I listened for a sign of what was going on in the rest of the house, but there was nothing, as if the world was asleep.

I headed slowly into the hallway. Grisela's door was open a crack with a soft light leaking out. I looked in and saw her sitting on a chair reading. I knocked softly on the door. She looked up and, to my relief, smiled when she saw me.

"*Bonsoir, ma petite.* Please come in," she said. I closed the door behind me and fell at her feet.

"I promise I won't let you down," I cried out to her, but she raised her hand to silence me.

"I heard you before, *petite*. I gather Vincenzo told you?" she asked.

"Yes, and I will not be so foolish again. Your faith will not be wasted on me. I will work to pay my way so I don't owe him anything—"

"What do you think he has paid for of yours?" she cut me off. "Do not be confused, my dear. I have paid for you with some help from Vincenzo. Lord Westwick may try to take credit, but it's not true. You are my *protégée*. I am responsible for your care, and you are not his plaything."

"Thank you, dear Grisela." I twisted her robe in my fingers as I started to cry. "I thought he cared for me."

"We all did," she said angrily. "I so wanted to save you from that fate."

"But what if he asks me to leave now?"

"Oh, my sweet girl, you are so naive!" she lamented. Then she held me firmly by the shoulders. "He would never do so, but you and I could return to court. We would not be lost. And if not at court, Vincenzo would make a place for us."

"Are you and Vincenzo in love?" I asked.

"Heaven's no! He is a dear friend to us both. He cares very much for your welfare. He told Lord Westwick to let you be, and he has never done such a thing before. He took a risk for us both," she said. "I am confident that between us two and your Hannah, Charles will get the point."

"And I will tell him, I am no strumpet!" I declared. I was still crying, my skirt beginning to get wet.

"No, *petite*, you will not be rude! Tell him politely that his attentions are better placed elsewhere. There is no shortage of women who would fall willingly into his bed. He does not need to be persistent with you. I think I have taught you enough that you are capable of brushing him off with grace."

She patted my hand now. "Now, stop crying! You have been given a task by Vincenzo, and I expect your best. He will fetch you after your breakfast, and then you will talk to the young lady for a few hours before we practice your writing. Then we'll go to the theatre to rehearse."

"Yes, Grisela," I nodded. I wiped my face and stood up, trying to compose myself.

"You have the evening to yourself, *petite*. Get some food and practice your dance. I will see you tomorrow."

"Thank you Grisela. I won't disappoint you."

She smiled. "I know you will not. Oh, and…my dear? I think we have come to the point in our relationship that you can call me Gigi."

XXVIII.

Daughter Of Darkness

THE STAIRS CREAKED LOUDLY AS IF THEY WOULD SNAP under my weight. I tried only to think about the light at the bottom but was quickly overwhelmed by the smell of earth and something damp as it filled my lungs. I knew there were people down here in this basement, but I could not hear anyone. It made my descent feel more and more like I was walking into a pit.

When I finally reached the bottom, I was surprised at how big this basement was, with a large main room and cells on each side. It seemed to go on forever, much like we were really in the dungeon of a castle. Vincenzo and William were sitting in front of a cell near the back wall. I felt for the girl already: I know I would be angry if they locked me in a dirt cell after telling me about the fabulous life I'd lead with them.

"Good morning, Katrine," Vincenzo spoke up. He rose from his seat and offered it to me, but I declined.

"Good morning, gentlemen," I nodded to them both. I peered into the dim cell at the girl sitting in the corner in the dirt, her pale blue eyes staring defiantly at me.

"Katrine, this is Morgana," Vincenzo introduced us, raising the flame on the lantern he held. "Morgana, this is my dear friend Katrine whom I was telling you about."

"Hello, Morgana," I said to her.

She continued to watch me. I took in her overall pale features, from her long, light hair to her translucent skin; she was one of the fairest people I had ever seen. She looked quite young, her face simple and plain.

"Morgana, you do not need to be afraid. We only want to help you," I said as I moved closer to the bars to see her better.

"Help me?" her heavily accented voice jeered. Despite her delicate features, something more ominous began to show through as her expression twisted in anger. "You think locking me in a cage will help?"

"Allowing you to attack us would not improve matters, either," I countered. "You wouldn't be locked up if you could control your temper."

She suddenly smiled, and surprisingly had very nice teeth. "Is that why they brought you down here, for you to knock me into submission?"

"No. But if I must, it wouldn't be the first time."

She laughed openly. "You've fought with a witch before, have you?"

"You are not the first witch I've had contact with, if that's what you're asking."

"And where are you from?" she demanded. "I can tell by the way you speak you are not French or Italian."

"I was born in Wallachia, but my family is from Hungary," I answered. "My mother knew some witchcraft, and I stand here before you because of circumstances involving witchcraft. Signor Amori found me in Vienna and brought me here to help me, as well."

"And what do you need help with?" she sneered. "What could possibly have happened to you?"

"I was scratched by my mother after she cast a spell that turned her into a wolf, and I've had blood cravings ever since."

"So you're a vampire?" she probed. I stared back at her in silence, unsure of how to answer such a question. She herself began to consider the circumstances now. "No, a wolf scratch should not turn you into a creature of the night," she pondered, and then she brightened considerably. "Perhaps then you already have some vampire blood in your bloodlines!"

"What are bloodlines?"

"One of your ancestors was likely a vampire," she huffed. "A scratch from a wolf should have made you a wolf, but I've heard tales of vampires who could shift form, and who could control the minds of some animals. Perhaps you should try sometime, see what happens!"

I looked at Vincenzo to see how he would respond to that, but he looked just as confused as I felt. William, on the other hand, seemed annoyed by all of this. He rolled his eyes and motioned for me to get on with it.

"So, now that you know something about me, tell me something about you," I prompted her.

"There is little to tell. My family is long gone. If I had stayed in my homeland, I would have faced the fires. Tell me, have you ever watched a person be burned alive, Katrine?" she asked coldly.

I shuddered. The memory of my grandmother's servants being thrown into the flaming execution pyre—along with that terrible smell— would always haunt me.

"You never forget that smell," she nodded, her eyes wild now. "I can still hear them screaming. I haven't slept well in many years."

"I cannot even imagine the horrors you have seen," I said, keeping my voice steady. "But you are safe here and in the company of good people who want to aid and guide you."

"There are other witches here?" she demanded.

"William is...."

"Do you mean the blue-eyed demon?" she cut me off, pointing a thin arm and finger at him.

"He's not a demon," I said gently. "He just has a quick temper. And from what I've heard of you, Morgana, you are not so different from one another."

She looked quite shocked by my boldness, and I wondered for a moment what William might have done to this girl for her to think he was a demon.

"You are frighteningly naive," she suddenly accused.

"You are not the first person who has told me that," I sighed heavily.

She raised an eye. "And that does not scare you?"

"Sometimes. Other times, I think it protects me from things that would destroy those who are more aware."

I could feel Vincenzo staring at me now, and ignored him. Morgana, meanwhile, let out a laugh. "So then, do you think that you could convince these two to let me out?"

"Not yet," I told her. "They need to know they can trust you and that you're not going to hurt anyone."

"Do they do this with all newcomers?"

"They do something for everyone. It all depends. For me, they made sure I did not kill in order to drink from a person. I had to learn how to control my urges."

She seemed interested by this. "You have killed many?"

"One is too many," I muttered.

Before I could say anything else, in the space of a blink, Morgana was off the floor and standing directly in front of me, staring me in the eye.

"A true daughter of the darkness…you are a rare find," she said in a low voice.

I tried very hard to pretend she hadn't startled me, but the way she moved so quickly was unnerving.

"Do you purposefully try to make yourself seem menacing? Do you want me to be frightened of you?" I lowered my voice. "I may not have seen some of the atrocities you have, but I have seen my fair share. It will take more than that to scare me off."

She smiled at me now. "I think you and I will get along quite well."

By this time, however, William had seen enough.

"You'll sit here until you can behave like a civilised being," he snapped at her. He was standing directly beside me now. Her pale eyes turned away, and I took that as my cue to step back.

"I am not sure I did much good, Vincenzo," I whispered to him. "I don't feel she is taking me seriously."

Vincenzo sighed. "I'm not sure she takes anything seriously, my dear. But she did not try to kill you, which is good. And you managed to get her to speak, which is even better."

"But what else can we do? It seems like she is determined to be defiant at all costs."

He thought for a moment, and then mused, "I suppose it is what has kept her alive, all this time."

"What do you mean? She looks younger than me!"

He chuckled. "Katrine, do not forget that looks can be deceiving. She is much, much older than she appears."

I looked at the girl again. She was having a quiet argument through the bars with William. I squinted, trying to find any signs that might identify her true age.

"Oh, I did the same at first," Vincenzo commented, watching me. "Don't waste your time. The only things that identify her age are her hands and her feet."

He gestured knowingly, and I was immediately shocked to see the hands and feet of a 75-year-old woman on Morgana's body; the rest of her looked no more than 15.

"Are the two of you quite finished?" Vincenzo demanded when Morgana and William finally tore their eyes away from each other. Disgusted, William turned and stormed out, slamming the door behind him.

"Perhaps only the two of you should come speak to me," Morgana hissed. "The blue-eyed demon is no longer welcome."

"Morgana," I finally asked, "why would you first agree to come here, only then to give them such a terrible fight?"

"I saw something," she mumbled, lowering her eyes from me. "Something terrible about this place. Its people. I no longer wished to come here."

"And what could you have possibly seen that would so suddenly and dramatically change your mind?"

I approached the bars again and studied her face.

"Do you believe that people can see the future, Katrine?"

"Are you saying you saw the future?" I demanded.

"Yes, and it was frightening. There is a force at work, watching you all and waiting for a time when it can destroy you," she began. "One who knows all about who and what you are. All will be revealed....I've seen it. During one of your parties, someone will be killed out in the gardens... butchered, ripped to shreds like the prey of a wild animal."

I tried to keep my face as blank as I could as she spoke, but the talk of a wild animal, a terrible beast, caused a shooting pain through my chest.

"I do not expect you to respond. He didn't either," she continued, poking a finger at Vincenzo. "He couldn't understand for the life of him why I would not want to come along, even after I told him all of that."

"But do all of your visions come to pass?" I asked.

She stared peculiarly at me now, obviously shocked that someone would question her ability.

"As far as I know, yes," she replied, amused.

"Well, not that I don't believe you, but I would rather just wait and see."

She suddenly grabbed my hand through the bars. Her pupils swelled and then both eyes turned completely black.

"You have a great power within you," she said, her voice a low growl, "but much to be afraid of. The sins of your kin will haunt you for the rest of your life, your long unnatural life. You will outlive everyone you have ever known. Everyone you will ever know."

I resisted yanking my hand away. She obviously thrived on fear, and I tried to banish all thought from my head. Nevertheless, she continued to stare at me with those eyes, examining my face for a reaction.

"Thank you for the information," I said, my voice breathy and barely there. "I will keep that in mind."

She let go, pulling slowly away as her eyes returned to normal.

"I'd like to be alone now," she said.

I did not ask questions, just turned to Vincenzo—he and I left together.

"So what do you think?" he asked after he had closed the basement door behind us. "Do you think she can really see into the future?"

"All I think is that she's more trouble than she's worth," I said plainly.

He sighed. "Maybe. It seems William and I have put ourselves in quite the position."

"I don't think she can be trusted. I think including her in our world will be much too complicated."

I didn't want to admit just how deeply her words had frightened me.

XXIX.

Impolite Advances

LORD WESTWICK REQUESTS THE PRESENCE OF MLLE. Báthory in his study," a servant said from just outside my door. I had returned to my bed after meeting with Morgana. Hannah had brought some food up for me and went to answer the door.

"The Lady is resting," Hannah said politely.

I had told no one what Morgana had said, but her prophesy haunted me. I was still trying to make sense of it and could barely form my thoughts into sentences.

"Lord Westwick insists I see the young woman myself," the voice urged.

"I told you, she is resting. Surely you are not asking me to allow you to watch my mistress sleep?" Hannah demanded.

"All you must do is step out of the doorway," the voice continued. "I swear I will not wake her. My Lord just wishes to know that he is not being manipulated."

"Fine," Hannah said between clenched teeth, and I quickly closed my eyes, pretending to be asleep.

The two women exchanged more words, and then I heard the door click shut. I sat up, bewildered.

"Do you think he will come to my door himself?" I asked Hannah.

Hannah shook her head. "Heavens no. More likely, he will intercept you in the salon, or take some other opportunity where it would appear improper for you to refuse."

"And what should I say when he does?"

"What would Mlle. Delphine have you say?"

"I am not sure of exactly the words, but I believe she would tell me to be honest but not disrespectful, to remember that I am representing her."

Hannah nodded. "Well then, there you have it." She smiled slightly now. "You know, I'm certain no woman has ever rejected him, let alone told him why they are doing so."

"And I have never had the pleasure of turning someone's advances away, so it will be a first for both of us," I smiled back.

"It will be good for you to learn, because soon you'll be beating them off with a stick," she laughed.

I giggled. "I highly doubt it, but thank you for saying so."

"Now, let us get you dressed for the evening."

I decided on one of the simple dresses in blue, the colour of the midnight sky, and asked Hannah to pull my hair off my face and into a knot at the base of my neck. I was tired and quite anxious by the time I was ready to go downstairs. I considered telling Hannah to fetch me an escort but decided against it. This was no time to be faint-hearted.

I quickly spotted Gigi as I entered the salon and headed towards her, paying no mind to what was going on around me—until I bumped into a servant who held out a silver tray to me.

"A gift for the young lady from Lord Westwick," the servant announced. Trapped, I looked at the two perfect, white handkerchiefs neatly folded on the tray, both with the letters 'K B' embroidered beautifully in silver thread on the corner, and my heart skipped a beat.

It took everything I had to say, "Send my thanks, but it is quite unnecessary."

"You won't take them?" the flabbergasted boy asked.

"No. No I will not," I stated, and continued moving forward towards Gigi.

"*Bonsoir, ma petite*," she greeted me as I approached, motioning for me to sit on the small couch beside her. "Did that boy offer you something?"

"Nothing important, I assure you," I replied. "Have I missed anything?"

"Not at all. How was your visit with Vincenzo's little project?"

I watched her expression, wondering exactly what he had told her. "Exhausting," I finally confessed to her. "If it wasn't for Hannah, I may have stayed in bed tonight."

"Well, it won't happen again for a while, because we must continue our lessons. You cannot be expected to go on stage with such little preparation, and formal rehearsals with the rest of the group start the day after tomorrow," she began. "And we have our other lessons. You are progressing quite beautifully, but there is still so much more…and then, if we are to go to Russia—"

"Do you think it shall happen?"

"I would rather be fully prepared than not," she declared. "We both have some things to learn before that time. I would like to learn the language, but I hardly think…." She suddenly stopped and looked up.

"There you are, Katrine," Charles's voice boomed in between us, and I jumped. "I was beginning to worry you had the pox."

"I am quite fine, My Lord," I replied quickly. He stood directly in front of us, and I saw others moving towards us now out of the corner of my eye. Did everyone know what was happening?

"So what reason do you have for not coming at my request?" he demanded. "I hear you've been sleeping quite a bit lately."

"I was otherwise occupied," I said, feeling breathless, "and I must say that I strongly believe your attentions are better placed elsewhere."

He laughed loudly. "Oh? And why would you feel that way? I am merely concerned for your welfare."

My body tensed, but before I could reply, Gigi declared, "It is as I told you, Charles. She is my *protégée* and should be treated as such. I will care for her welfare."

"I believe the young lady can answer for herself," Charles said rather curtly, and that made me angry.

"Then I shall answer for myself, Lord Westwick," I snapped. "First and foremost, I am Mlle. Delphine's *protégée*, and beyond that I find it quite insulting that you would assume I was a foolish child."

Gigi quickly put her hand on my arm as a signal to relax, but I couldn't help myself now: "So, My Lord, may I state that I will only accept honourable intentions regarding my welfare."

His face turned bright crimson. For just a moment, I felt a pang of guilt for embarrassing him, but then realised that allowing him to behave as he did would only harm me. If he sent me away, so be it. I would not allow him to treat either me or Gigi in such a disrespectful way.

He walked away. By the tone of the room, it appeared that only a few members of our household had heard the conversation. I was relieved.

"Well done, Katrine," Gigi whispered to me.

"That was hard for me to do," I admitted. "He also sent me two handkerchiefs with my initials embroidered in silver," I said quietly to her. "Turning those away was harder."

She laughed, her sound like tinkling bells and so absolutely genuine. We sat alone for some time observing the room, Gigi making the occasional comment, when Klara came in. She was a mess of lavender silk and lace, followed this time by only one of her admirers. Klara was the first woman I had seen other than Gigi tonight.

"Where is everyone?" I asked her, referring to our usual party.

"They are coming. Victorie will be especially pleased to hear about your dismissal of Lord Westwick."

"Was she deeply hurt by him?"

"Deeply, but never mention it to anyone," she said quietly. Gigi quickly changed the subject. "Klara is quite the assault on the eyes tonight, don't you think?"

"Very much so," I nodded. "I don't understand why she feels the need."

"Can you ask Hannah to bring us some tea and fresh blood for when the girls arrive? I think we should celebrate," she declared. I nodded and went off in search of Hannah.

I approached the servants' entry at the back of the salon, but before I could pass through, Lord Westwick grabbed my arm and pulled me through another doorway.

"My Lord, this is highly inappropriate!" I said loudly, trying to pull away, but he held my arm firmly.

"Do you really believe that, Katrine?" he hissed.

"Believe what?"

"Do you really believe I care nothing for you?"

"My Lord, you bed every woman who joins your company. Is it not logical for me to think that is exactly what you had intended to do with me?"

He stepped back, stunned, but did not release my arm.

"So, you cannot believe that I actually care for you, do you? You cannot even entertain the idea, can you?," he declared aloud.

I stood my ground and shook my head no.

"You cannot possibly think you may be different?" he implored me now. "Then it must be that she would not allow it."

"My Lord, Grisela sent me on a task. She will come looking if I do not return soon," I shot back.

"Then I will prove them all wrong," he proclaimed, releasing me. "I will show you the truth of my feelings for you!"

I hurried out of the room, refusing to look back at him.

When I found Hannah, my face was white but I said very little, asking only for what Gigi had requested. I then went back into the salon. I would not allow him to penetrate my thoughts again. I knew he wanted that. He wanted me to continue to think about him at every moment.

"Was there a problem?" Gigi asked worriedly, as I took my place next to her.

"Lord Westwick tried to assure me that his intentions were honourable, that his feelings for me were true," I said nervously.

At that, she smiled, her eyes still watching the room.

"Boys will be boys," she said, her confidence making me feel more relaxed.

Victorie and Mathilde arrived shortly. Hannah followed with the tray of tea after they were settled. I noticed the handkerchiefs also sat on the tray beside a plate of cakes sprinkled with powdered sugar.

I sighed loudly. "Hannah, please take those handkerchiefs away with you."

"He placed them there just as I was crossing the room, Miss. I am very sorry," Hannah apologised.

"Wait, let me see," Gigi spoke up, leaning over the tray to take a better look. "My word, I see your point, *ma petite*. They are quite lovely."

"It's quite alright, Hannah," I told her. "See if you can slip them into the gentleman's pocket when he isn't looking."

She giggled and took the tray away, leaving us with our cups and the plate of cakes on a small table in front of us.

"Congratulations, Katrine," Victorie whispered now. "We heard the news earlier. You are a better woman than I."

Mathilde laughed, as well. "Than all of us!"

"That's not true, my friends," I shook my head. "I'm just lucky to have all of you to protect me, along with Vincenzo to watch my back."

"I have to ask, Mathilde," Gigi interrupted, "because now I am deeply confused. Why are you dressed like a milkmaid?"

"What, you don't approve? I thought I was appearing modest," Mathilde exclaimed. I had not noticed her brown dress and white apron, or the bonnet that held in her mass of curls, until Gigi pointed it out.

"You resemble the farmer's wife whose lived next to my father," I said with a giggle.

Gigi began to laugh. "Did you hear that, Mathilde? A farmer's wife! Is that modest enough for you?"

Mathilde scrunched up her nose; I hoped she wasn't insulted by what I had said.

Meanwhile, we hadn't noticed Charles approaching. He appeared all at once, towering over me. The three women fell silent as he held out his hand.

"May I have this dance?"

All eyes were upon me, and I steeled myself.

"No thank you, Charles." He was about to say something when I added, "Perhaps another time."

'Very well," he nodded and then bowed.

As he walked away, I noticed Klara watching me from across the room.

At the end of the night, I headed upstairs alone and tired. I suddenly heard the sound of someone clapping as I entered the hallway to my room. A hulking figure loomed in the dim light: it was Klara. She started to come towards me, and I could feel the hairs on the back of my neck bristle, readying for a fight. I tried to steady myself and appear calm even though I was feeling a stomach knot.

"Congratulations, you stupid little bitch," Klara instigated. "You have succeeded beautifully."

"At what?"

"At rising up to a place where you don't belong," she accused. "You may have Lord Westwick's eye and Mlle. Delphine's ear, but it won't last long. When they realise you are nothing more than a stupid little peasant, you'll be out of this house! Tell me, did you get a look at the basement, little rat?"

I pretended to ignore her threats. "If you'll excuse me, I am going to my room."

She made a face, sticking out her bottom lip. "What, did I upset the little favourite? That's the one thing you don't understand about this life, little rat. You won't remain the favourite when you won't do as your Lord requests."

"And you are going to intervene in all of this?"

"Oh no," she leered. "You will do it all on your own. I'll just be there to watch when it all falls apart for you. It is just a matter of time now. You'll see."

Klara flared her nostrils as she smiled a twisted grin. She then pushed past me on her way to her room. I waited until I heard the door close before running to my own.

XXX.

Lessons Learnt

WRITING A LETTER WAS A MUCH MORE COMPLICATED process than I had imagined. There was so much more to it than simply having the proper words and phrasing. There was the angle that you held the quill, and the precise way the letter should mark the page. You had to keep your forearm up so as not to smudge the writing and add a series of lines to the end of important documents so nothing else could be added afterwards. There was the sand you shuffled over the pages to help dry the ink, and finally, the wax seal that pulled it together, nice and neat.

"You will use my seal until we can have one made for you," Gigi said. "But the cost is atrocious."

"I doubt I will write enough letters to need my own seal. I find this terribly exhausting," I confessed, looking up momentarily from my pages. I was seated at her beautiful wooden writing desk, copying phrases, as she would say them aloud. This was what most of my writing lessons consisted of, and after much time doing this, we would sort through the pages and pick out the perfect words to write to my Grandmother.

"You see, *ma petite*, discretion is of the utmost importance in this case. We would not want to make our beloved Countess' position any worse," Gigi reminded me each time we began. "Perhaps I should add to the letter in my own hand," she proclaimed this day. "Reassure her you are well taken care of. I hope she would remember me."

I smiled. "I do not believe someone could possibly forget you, dear Gigi. Do you remember several days ago, when Mathilde mentioned a Báthory being Prince of Transylvania? Did I already ask you this?"

"I will not know until you speak it, *ma petite.*"

"Do you know him? This prince, have you seen him?"

"Not that I remember, but I did see the late King of Poland, who was a Báthory. That was some time ago, he may have been your grandmother's uncle. Regardless, he was an oddly handsome man, very charming," she began. "Many people believe the eastern part of the continent to be quite backwards and full of savages, but it is not that way, in my experience at least."

"I am so curious about what they are like, especially the Countess' children."

Gigi stopped pacing across the room for a moment and said, "We should ask about them. That way, you'd know their names."

"Roza told me their given names."

"She probably does not know the daughters' married names. You said she had two other daughters and a son, yes?"

"As far as I know," I replied. "But I know very little, which seems more obvious every day."

"You are a remarkably fast learner, my dear. I hope that you will soon feel quite at home with your new life," Gigi said, and she returned to her walk around the room. "Write that down! *'I am adapting well and learning new things quickly'.*"

I carefully began to copy, Gigi spelling out the more difficult words, and this time seemed easier than the last. I was sure it would continue that way as it had with many other things.

"Oh! And I almost forgot! There will be a full cast rehearsal, hopefully tonight," Gigi declared. "These things are surprisingly hard to arrange."

"What about Morgana? Perhaps I could ask Vincenzo to bring her to the performance."

"Who are you talking about?" she asked, and I could feel the colour drain from my face. "Ah yes, Morgana. Vincenzo's little project." She immediately waved her hand. "No. He maintains she's too dangerous."

"Perhaps if we could all see her and be involved in her transition it would go smoother," I suggested, "if we don't treat her like a caged animal."

She laughed loudly. "Since we don't put the actual animals in cages."

I remained silent. She stopped for a moment and looked at my face.

"I had forgotten that you hadn't seen a natural change. Believe it or not it does happen. Some people's bodies need to shift forms once every full moon. Sort of like a woman getting her monthly courses, only with fur. It's a less violent version of something you've already seen," she explained.

I kept my eyes down and continued writing. It was only recently that I had stopped thinking of my mother daily, and I felt guilty. I wasn't sure if I should carry what happened to her with me for the rest of my life. It seemed a question one might normally ask a priest, but I was too frightened to even approach a church. After all, a priest, *that priest*, was involved in the imprisonment of my grandmother. I was unsure I could even trust someone who held that position.

"Gigi?" I asked without looking up.

"Yes, *petite?*"

"Have you ever heard of vampires shifting their shape?"

She did not stop walking when she replied, "Yes, but I have never met one. Why do you ask?"

"Nothing. I was just curious," I mumbled.

I had so many questions, but I wasn't sure now if Gigi was the right person to ask.

We stopped our lesson only when my hand started to ache. Grisela decided to catch up on some reading, so I went around the house looking for Vincenzo. I found him as he was about to enter the kitchen.

"Excuse me, Signor?" I called to him as I rushed through the empty salon to catch him.

"Yes, Katrine? Is everything alright?"

"Yes, I just had something on my mind that I wanted to ask you about. Do you have a moment?"

"Of course," he said, pulling me aside to one of the small seating areas.

I phrased the words carefully in my mind before asking: "What do you know of vampires that can shift their shape?"

He looked a bit stunned. "A little. Why? Has something happened?"

"No, no, it was just something that was on my mind. I was questioning why, if I was scratched by a wolf, did I become something else entirely?"

His green eyes twinkled in delight as he studied my face. I gathered he was playing out potential scenarios in his mind before he spoke.

"That, my dear," he finally said, "is a very good question. And, it seems the right question to ask in this situation. Unfortunately, I do not have an answer to give you right at this moment, but I will do some research."

He turned his eyes to the window for a moment. "The sun will be setting soon. We were to have a full rehearsal tonight, but Lord Westwick has disappeared."

"Can we not continue without him? I am sure he won't be gone long."

Vincenzo shook his head. "Unfortunately, he is needed. It is his vision to execute." He stood and prepared to leave. "I must get back to Morgana. Perhaps you should relax this evening, for when the rehearsal does happen, you will need all your strength."

With little else to say or do, I returned to my room to find Roza setting out my meal.

"What a lovely surprise," I said, quietly closing the door behind me. "I wanted to speak with you."

"And I want to speak to you," she declared. "This visit is for a specific purpose. But perhaps you should start, for I am sure my questions will be more time consuming."

I sighed, trying to hide my irritation. "Alright then. Do you know the married names of the Countess' daughters?"

She looked up sharply. "Why?"

"Curiosity, as well as for my own safety."

Apparently satisfied, Roza began: "Anna became Countess Zrinyi, and Katalin became Lady Drugeth de Homonnay. Katalin married her husband at Csejthe a little over a year ago. I thought I had mentioned it? She's not much older than you."

Meanwhile, I found a small piece of parchment on the table and tried to write out both names. Roza nudged her chin up and folded her arms.

"I see your education has progressed. I am glad for it," she said, but without a hint of excitement in her voice.

"So what did you want to speak with me about?" I asked, not looking up from my writing.

She got right to the point: "That strange-speaking demon Signor Amori has in the basement!"

I bit my tongue to stop myself from smiling. "She is not a demon, she's a girl."

"She'll kill us all, whatever the hell she may be," Roza snapped. "She is beyond the point of insanity, and her magic is too strong for someone so young. He should have left her where she was, and you should tell him to get rid of her."

"She is much older than she appears," I countered patiently.

It looked as if that was not the answer Roza wanted, and her face contorted in anger.

"Has he got you brainwashed, as well? Why does no one see this?"

"What in heaven's name did that girl say to you?"

"Does it matter?" Roza grumbled. "She's dangerous!"

"Roza, please. I see your point, but I also see his. The girl needs guidance, and she would be far more dangerous if they freed her. If she's as strong as you say, I am sure she could leave if she really wanted to."

"How could he be so—"

"Need I remind you that if he wasn't 'so,' you and I would still be living in a baker's cellar in Vienna?" I retorted.

The anger in her face eased somewhat; it was a fact she could not dispute and had apparently forgotten.

"If you are so concerned, tell him you're afraid to go down there, that you won't serve her anymore. He'll respect your wishes, I'm sure of it," I continued. "Now, will you dine with me?"

She silently stared at the tray of food she had just laid out like it was some foreign object, as if eating right now was completely out of the question.

"If you don't want to," I shrugged, "it's quite alright. I wouldn't want you to be uncomfortable."

Roza had clearly been spooked by Morgana, and likely, by one of Morgana's prophesies. I wondered what she said that Roza refused to tell me.

"My apologies, child, but I have some things I have to attend to. Another time."

Roza swept out of the room without looking at me again.

The room fell silent except for my breathing. I had not been alone in some time. I decided to take advantage of this rare opportunity to be alone with my thoughts. Hopefully, it would give me the chance to think through the things that had recently been brought to light: a prophecy, a threat, and a possible answer. I really

had to decide how to sort through all of it.

9 August 1611

To the Lady Widow Nadasdy, Countess Bathory,

I hope this letter finds you well by the Grace of Almighty God. I am writing to tell you that since we last spoke, I have found myself under the tutelage of a fine lady. She believes you were once acquainted at the Royal Court of Vienna.

Here I have learned to read and write in French and Latin and am beginning to learn Italian, as well as dance and the manners and disposition of a proper lady. I am adapting well and learning new things quickly.

A day has not passed that I have not thought of you. I am continuously concerned for your welfare, your good name, and my desire to have the chance to see you if only once more. I pray daily for your safety and protection and that the Good Lord delivers you from this situation. I have dreamt often of Mother and you. Perhaps you have seen her, as well, and might someday be able to share with me the story of our illustrious bloodlines.

I wish to reassure you that I am very well and happy and am doing my best to live by your example and become a woman as great as Your Ladyship, to pay honour to your illustrious name.

If the Good Lord wills it so, I wish to hear of you, your health, and how you are keeping. I pray I might soon receive word from you.

Your Ladyship's Humble Servant,

Katrine Bathory

XXXI.

Foreshadowing

I RECEIVED THE MESSAGE AROUND MIDDAY THAT there would be a full rehearsal and we would be leaving for the theatre at sundown. I'd spent the earlier part of the day alone, when Hannah appeared with lunch.

"Eat, then Mlle. Delphine has requested you be bathed and groomed. Your feet need to be properly prepared for shoes and dancing," Hannah ordered. Her voice was flat and commanding.

I ate and watched her clean the room with remarkable efficiency. She thumbed through my dresses and finally settled on one that was simple and blue She held it up and then laid it across the bed.

"Here."

"Is everything alright, Hannah?," I asked when I had finished my last bite of bread.

"Why did you not call on me when you were ready for sleep last night?"

"Because I wanted to be alone. I had some things I had to think about."

"Did Kardoska come and talk to you? Did she say something upsetting?"

I sighed loudly. "No, in fact she would not tell me anything. If you are so concerned, maybe you could enlighten me as to exactly what the fuss is about?"

Hannah turned, put one hand on her hip, and dropped her gaze upon me.

"She really told you nothing?"

"No, and she was in just as big of a twist as you are, so I gather it is something big. Now tell."

She sat down on the stool beside my bed, where I was eating lunch, and started twisting her skirt between her fingers.

"Signor Amori had Kardoska serving food to the girl in the basement," Hannah began. "In the beginning, everything was alright, Kardoska said nothing and continued her work as if she'd always had to go down there. When the younger girls would ask her questions she would ignore them. I am sure you understand her temperament better than anyone. Then, one evening, she came up the stairs, and her face was as white as a sheet. She started saying things about heaven and hell and the demons killing us all. My father said he heard her say something about the 'others'— the curse of what he thought was 'Darveena'—but was sure he was pronouncing it wrong."

"Darvulia? Could he have said Darvulia?" I asked immediately.

"Yes! Yes! And she said something to him about how she's going to burn, just like the others, and it was the girl in the basement's fault... though, she didn't call her a girl, ever, she called her a demon. You have seen her, is she really a demon?" Hannah pressed, her eyes growing wider as she spoke.

"I can assure you, Hannah, she is no demon," I stated emphatically. "A witch, yes, and possibly a fortune teller. If you ask my opinion. she's angry, she's in a cell, and just wants people to fear her."

"Do you know Darvulia?"

I took a deep breath in before saying, "Yes."

"Did she burn?" Hannah whispered. She seemed on the verge of panic now.

"No, other's did, but not Darvulia," I said. "My mother killed Darvulia and one other when she shifted her shape into a wolf. That was when

I got the scratch; they were performing a spell on my mother. She used her magic to try to escape and she ended up shifting. When she was done, she killed Darvulia and another woman named Erza. Roza and I somehow managed to survive."

"Then, who burned?"

"Two women and one young man, all servants of my grandmother, were executed. They—and my grandmother—were accused of torturing and murdering dozens of young girls."

"Young girls?"

"Also servants of my grandmother…young seamstresses, wash girls, and the like."

"But why would they do that?"

"It's all a lie," I said bitterly. "They're trying to steal my grandmother's property, lock her up and put her away. The charges are all false!"

"And your grandmother has not been executed?"

"Not yet. Her noble blood seems to have saved her from the ultimate betrayal by the king," I said angrily. "But her three servants were scapegoats. They were tortured and then burned."

Hannah looked away, then back at me. "The girl must have said something to Roza. But how would she know about these executions? Did you tell her?"

"No, of course not—only the details of how I got the scratch. I did not offer names or any information about my grandmother. Hannah, please, I would appreciate it if you kept those details private."

"Of course, m'lady," she nodded quickly.

We both sat silently, staring blankly at nothing for quite a while.

"So, you are afraid," I finally whispered.

"Aren't you?" she asked.

"No," I said resolutely. "Nothing that girl said has actually happened yet, so I don't feel a need to be."

Unsure of herself, Hannah smiled uneasily and began to nod. "That is a very good point, Katrine. I had not thought of that."

"Right. Not much point in getting upset if nothing has happened," I repeated. "Now, my friend, could you run that bath for me? It sounds like a time consuming process to prepare my feet."

"Yes, of course," she answered quickly. "If we do not, you may end up with difficulties and injuries that could have easily been avoided. I would be failing you if I allowed your feet to become maimed and mangled."

She smoothed out the blue dress on the bed beside me, with my simple leather shoes that held up well in the snow. I imagined I would be given dancing shoes at some point. I hoped it would be tonight.

After what seemed like an eternity of bathing, grooming, and cleaning my feet, which involved cutting the nails and scrubbing the old skin off, I was ready. My feet felt strange when I stood in my boots. They had never felt so clean.

Gigi was descending the stairs when I stepped out into the hallway, and I hurried to catch up to her.

"*Bonsoir, ma petite,*" she said when she saw me. "I wanted to warn you earlier that you will be meeting some new people today. There are some involved in the dance who do not socialise on a regular basis, but they are very nice, so don't worry."

"Are they like us?" I asked.

"Yes, in the way that they drink blood, but their lives were very different. Like Nathaniel the farm boy, who tends to our horses and the upkeep of the theatre. High society functions make him very uncomfortable, so he stays behind the scenes. Josephine often does the same," she said.

We stepped off the staircase, and the servants were already waiting with our cloaks. Hannah was not there, and the two young women here appeared quite nervous.

"I wonder what on earth is happening in the house," Gigi declared when we were settled in the coach and on the move. "The servants are practically shaking!"

"Vincenzo's little project is causing a stir," I replied. "She's scared them quite silly."

"And why haven't you told me!" Gigi exclaimed.

"I only learned of it recently. Hannah just told me while I was dressing, after I'd had an odd meeting with Roza last night. The girl said some things to Roza that frightened her and, in turn, she's frightening the staff."

When Gigi raised an eye, I explained, "The girl claims she can see the future. She's telling everyone terrible things about what will come to pass."

Gigi giggled. "A witch who can see the future? Vincenzo has really outdone himself this time."

"I say, we must wait until her predictions come true before we take her too seriously. But it seems she does have some ability, because there were some things she knew that no one told her beforehand."

"Are you sure of this? What sort of things?"

"Names only Roza and I know. Names I have never said aloud to anyone else," I replied, thinking of Darvulia.

"Well," Gigi murmured seriously now, "I hope this doesn't go on for too much longer, or we may have an issue."

"I'm sorry to be the bearer of bad news, Gigi, but we might already have an issue. Every time the girl opens her mouth...did I tell you she calls William 'the blue-eyed demon'?"

To my surprise, she laughed so hard that tears came to her eyes; it took several moments for her to regain her composure.

"Oh, my dear," Gigi finally said with a wink, "I must be honest. I feel comforted by that, because the blue-eyed demon will keep a close eye on her. He's much more dangerous than she could ever be."

I sat up straighter now. "Everyone says how dangerous and powerful he is. I am quite fascinated by that fact, since he does not appear that way to me. Is it simply because I have never seen him truly angry?"

She patted my knee lightly. "Indeed, and I pray that you never do."

The front doors of our theatre were closed but, nearby the building, the street was humming with activity. The neighborhood was crowded with people and their carriages as they arrived for shows going on at the other theatres. The occasional side glance towards the *Danse Macabre* indicated we were missed, and that people were curious about the closure. I wondered if they were buzzing yet about what our new show might be or when we would open again.

We ascended the stairs and Gigi knocked a certain rhythmic pattern on the door: it quickly opened, and we were rushed inside. I did not realise how cold it was outside until the doors closed behind us, shutting out the weather behind us and enveloping us in heat from the inside. I could hear a heavy, rhythmic thumping from somewhere inside now, much like a drum beat.

"It sounds as if they have started without us," Gigi said with a sigh before taking me by the arm and walking with me into the main gallery of the theatre.

The stage was filled with people. Charles stood off to one side thumping a cane on the ground as the players moved in time to the beat. They danced in a circular motion around Victorie, who, at that moment, was watching Charles impatiently. No one noticed Gigi and me as we quietly took up seats in the front row to watch.

There were several new people present tonight: a tall, slender woman with flaming red hair; a muscular, light-haired man with the weathered skin of one who works outside; and another very pretty man with golden hair. I also noticed two dark-haired people who stayed close to the back: a woman with a head of big curls, and a man with long, straight hair. There was also a very handsome man with close-cropped blonde curls who remained close to Victorie. Victorie's dark eyes suddenly shone with happiness and warmth when they turned to that particular man with the blonde curls.

After some time, I looked at Gigi.

"Will we just be watching tonight?"

"Keep your eyes on the stage, *ma petite*. See if you can pick out where we fit from what I've taught you thus far."

Charles changed the tempo of his beat into what was now clearly a song pattern, and the company fell into time quite smoothly.

"See if you can keep up, picture yourself there," she continued, her eyes never leaving the stage. "Do you remember all the things I said? I explained this all to you. Every step. Every person. Every place. You know it all, darling."

"It's still rather intimidating," I admitted.

"But it should not be. That is what I am trying to say. If I am an effective teacher, it should be quite simple for you."

I watched the people on stage carefully now and tried my best to focus. Even though I did not know all of them, I definitely knew the parts being played and exactly how I was to fit in. The longer I watched, the clearer I could see myself, hovering in my place behind Victorie but in clear view of all the others. I was to mimic her in an exaggerated way, representing her Vanity. I had to appear full of pride and joy over my own appearance. I could see myself as if I had left my own body now, the anxiety in my stomach beginning to lessen into something that felt more like excitement.

Charles suddenly struck his cane especially hard, causing me to jump.

"Ah! Glad you finally decided to join us, Gigi. I was starting to wonder if you were coming at all!"

She made a hand gesture at him that I gathered was obscene by the others' expressions and Mathilde's laughter. Then we both made our way onto the stage.

She directed me with her eyes, and we silently took our places. I saw some of the other women grab their skirts, just a bit to help them dance, and Gigi shot me a look of menace, reminding me to never consider lifting my skirt for any reason.

"A lady only lifts her skirt when on the stairs or to avoid dirtying the bottom," Gigi had always said from the beginning—actually one of her first lessons regarding clothing.

"Shall I begin with a simple beat?" Charles teased us.

"*Non. Petite est plus que capable*," Gigi snapped. "The song, Charles."

He shrugged then commenced; we all waited through the first beats of the opening, then began.

My position mirrored Victorie like her shadow, slightly behind and to the left of her as if I, her Vanity, loomed in the back of her mind. I mimicked her movements exactly. I was impressed how Gigi knew so well what to teach me beforehand. I tried my best to exaggerate, flaunt my looks as if I were a goddess, while I danced. Playing such a character was liberating.

When it was time for a man to pass by me, I fluttered at his attentions. The man with the close-cropped blonde hair circled both Victorie and me, her shadow. I smiled and bat my eyelashes as his eyes connected with mine. I pushed out my chest and primped my hair as he made his circle, only deviating when he returned to Victorie's eye line. They danced together for a moment, and then I returned to my part as her shadow. All along, I felt Gigi's presence as she floated around us, moving with elegance even under the weight of her skirts. She was beautiful.

"*Bon!*" Charles exclaimed. "Katrine, you are *magnifique!* A natural!"

I couldn't help but to show my extreme joy and overwhelming sense of relief. But this was only the rehearsal.

"Charles, I need a break," Victorie called out after some time. I was glad. My feet were beginning to ache, and I was quite exhausted. This would take some time to get used to, as I was rather unaccustomed to such exercise.

Without a second thought, I went back to the seats we had left and relaxed. Gigi followed, along with several others.

"Well done, Katrine!" Mathilde said, taking the seat to my right as Gigi took to my left. "You did better than anyone would have expected. I am impressed! Grisela is a much better teacher than I'd expected."

Gigi's nostrils flared slightly, and I turned to Mathilde. "Why would you say that?"

"Dancing can be quite complex when you are first learning," she prattled lightly, "and a good teacher makes it all the simpler. It takes real talent to teach. I was unaware our Gigi had such talents."

Before Gigi or I could respond, Charles suddenly appeared.

"My dear girl," he declared, kissing my hand, "you were transcendent. Perhaps I should compose a dance exclusively for you?"

"Perhaps you should wait until she has danced a show before you make plans," Gigi snapped, repeating exactly what I was thinking.

"Can I not pay the girl a compliment?"

"It is no compliment, My Lord. Only an added burden," Gigi shot back.

"Regardless, you did well, Katrine. You should be very proud."

He tapped his cane on the ground to catch the performers' attention.

"That's enough for today, everyone. We shall begin again tomorrow at the same time. Please speak with Signora Sarcozi about your fittings, and perhaps we can have full dress tomorrow."

"Who is Signora Sarcozi?" I whispered to Gigi.

"Josephine," she replied, rolling her eyes. "She somehow gets a formal address from him. I am unsure how. I should ask. I would prefer he not call me Gigi in public."

"Shall we go for a fitting?"

"I am sure she has a schedule and will tell us exactly when to come." Gigi rose from her seat now. "If not tonight, then we will return to the chateau to read."

Gigi had been correct, as always: Josephine would see us in two days' time, so we returned to the chateau to read. Our current book was the Bible in Latin. I was slowly beginning to read, write and speak the language with a slight understanding that I hoped would improve over time. I assumed that once I was proficient in one thing, we would not have to practice constantly and the entire learning process would be much less exhausting.

I finally got to bed just as the sun was rising. Hannah helped me undress and pulled the curtains tightly closed, as I immediately fell into a deep sleep.

I heard the floor creaking, as if someone was trying to walk across my room very quietly. I sat up immediately.

"Who's there?"

I looked around the room.

"Momma?"

"Yes, my darling?"

Her voice was calm and clear in the darkness.

"Why didn't you wake me?"

"I wanted to watch you sleep, like I did when you were a baby," she said. "Babies often die in their sleep, and a mother must remain attentive."

"I remember you did that with Bodi. I must admit I was jealous of all the attention he got."

She sighed. "It was not easy for you being the first born."

"Do you think they miss us?"

There was silence, long enough for me to think that she had gone, and then she said, "Not yet. I don't think they realise we are never coming back. It will bother your brother the most when he has to do all the chores and cook. If Nikoli is relied upon to cook, then they will starve, I guarantee it."

I giggled to myself, remembering my father's failed attempts at cooking.

"He is a talented man in many other ways. Perhaps he will finally allot some money to hire some help. There are plenty of poor women in the village who could use the work. If your grandmother was still alive, she would have a new wife waiting in the wings for her precious son," she said, groaning loudly. "She never liked me."

"Why did she allow you to marry him?" I asked.

"Because I had money," she laughed. "Money the Báthorys gave the midwife to disappear, I suppose. I wonder what she would have thought of that. Maybe the bastard of nobility would have suited her better than the daughter of a rich widow."

"I don't think of you as a bastard. What if you were conceived out of love between two people who could never be together?"

"What, did the Countess tell you something?"

"No, I just don't think the situation was so bad as you make it sound."

"A child born out of wedlock is a bastard regardless of love, Katrine," she

replied testily.

"I suppose. But what shall we do now, Momma? What shall we do with our life?"

"You shall sleep, and I will watch you do so. We will make some decisions another time. But there is one last thing that must be settled before we can do anything else."

"What's that?" I asked as I lay back down.

"Don't worry about that, my dear. I shall take care of it. It's nothing you need to concern yourself with. Now, get your sleep."

I arose midday to a quiet house, easily slipping into the basement without seeing anyone. As I hurried down the steps, I tried to sense if anyone else was there besides Morgana. I wanted to have a private conversation with her now.

I took up the chair Vincenzo had been sitting on during my last visit. I pulled it over so that I was seated about a foot away from the iron bars. Morgana was sleeping quietly on a bed of straw; at least, I believed she was asleep. She looked much smaller and more childlike than the last time I'd seen her, her pale hair in stark contrast to the yellow straw. She looked peaceful.

Suddenly, she spoke.

"I was wondering when I would see you again," she said, not moving from her bed. "You are the first I've seen in a while. They're afraid of me. They've begun leaving food while I sleep."

"Morgana, you said something to one of the servants, an older woman named Kardoska. What did you tell her?"

"You mean the old witch?"

"She is not a witch."

Morgana laughed, taunting me. "You are incredibly naive. You were there when the old witch's friends were burned."

"What I saw is not important. Why did you say those things to her if you know what she faced?"

"Because that is her truth, Katrine. The things she has done, the people whose paths she connected with; all of those things will catch up with her. Her connections will bring about her own death."

Startled, I couldn't help but to ask: "Then what about me? She is connected to me."

Morgana sighed, and said quietly, "The witches will all pay for what they did to you and your mother."

"They already have," I said angrily. "They are all gone except her and me, and I will not allow anyone to take her from me, do you understand?"

"There will be several attacks coming, Katrine, and there is little you can do about it, other than to prepare. You believe the old witch to be your saviour, or perhaps the Italian or the pretty French woman. So many, but your true saviour has yet to show his face."

"Who are you talking about?" I demanded.

"The blue-eyed demon is your true saviour."

"What? William?" I became angry now. "Why are you doing this? You are frightening people with your words. Do you always want to be alone? Do you want to push the whole world away?"

Morgana considered.

"I apologise if I frightened anyone, but the old witch needed to hear the truth."

She suddenly stood up, and I was immediately flung out of my seat onto the ground.

"But maybe they should be afraid," she continued calmly, walking slowly towards me.

I gathered myself up and stared angrily at her, emitting a low growl that seethed from deep within me. Morgana seemed genuinely surprised by this, as she stumbled backwards.

"You say you know the truth? You can see what I've seen? Then you should know you are not even remotely the scariest thing I have faced," I hissed.

She composed herself and then laughed at me. "My dear, there will be many more, but none quite like Darvulia. Evil like that doesn't come along very often."

"You spoke of her curse..."

"Yes, I wonder if that is what has really happened to you and your mother. But you will be seeing your family very soon," she said mockingly.

I moved closer to the bars. If I put my hands through, I could grab her neck—

She smiled. "Angry, are we?"

"This will stop, do you understand?" I cried out. "For one who believes she can see the future so clearly, can you not see that if you don't stop all this, that they will kill you? And if you continue with these comments about me, perhaps I shall be the one to do it! Do you understand?"

I stared her down until she finally acquiesced, nodding in agreement.

"You are more powerful than you could possibly imagine," she said quietly, "but will see things differently when you realise I speak the truth."

"*If* I see it," I seethed. "They may kill you before I have the chance. If you don't think the 'old witch' would do it given the chance, then you are as naive as I am. Don't say another word about my past!"

I did not give her the chance to reply, heading back up the steps and away from her as quickly as possible. She would spend much time alone if she kept this up, I thought in a rage. We couldn't possibly take her to Russia if she continued this way.

When I reached the top of the stairs, the house had already awakened for the day, the kitchen staff busy with their duties. Emerging from the basement, I headed back to my room.

"Where in the world have you been? I've been looking everywhere," Hannah said, catching me in the hallway.

"That's not important. I have to be fitted for my costume today. I must get ready to go to the theatre," I said and started up the stairs before she could say anything more.

I certainly did not want to tell her that I had been to the basement or that I had been bothered by what Morgana said to me. Meanwhile, my mother was still out there somewhere: that fact frightened me more than anything else.

"Father and I will be coming to your performance," Hannah told me as she was dressing my hair. "Signor Amori assured me that our tickets are for very good seats."

"Do you not come to all the shows?" I asked.

"Heavens no! I had to pester him for days to ask Signor Amori."

"Why did you not tell me? I could have gotten you tickets."

"No, no dear. Protocol states that Father has to ask his employer for permission. It took some time, but he finally did and we're coming!"

"Well, then we shall have to get you a gown...or perhaps you can wear one of mine?"

"Oh no, no, I could not. I have something of my own, I'm sure of it."

"You will not allow me...?"

"No. It is not my way," she said sharply, brushing out my hair.

"Well, I'm pleased that you and Tolone are coming. It's nice to know there will be at least two familiar faces in the audience," I replied.

"Are you nervous? I heard you are quite the natural born dancer."

I blushed. "Is that is what they're saying? It was only a rehearsal. We shall see what happens during the actual performance. Grisela is just a very good teacher, that's all."

"Modesty is very important in this world. It's a trait you should never forget."

I smiled at her in the mirror. "I am sure you will not allow it."

She stepped back from me to admire her handiwork.

"Your hair is getting quite long and is rather straight, Katrine. Should we cut some of it, or will you let it grow? Perhaps you should ask Mlle. Delphine for her opinion. Her hair is a good length. Maybe we should cut it like hers. I could use the excess to make hair decorations." She ran her fingers absently through my hair. "There is quite a lot here."

"I'll be sure to ask," I said, rising from my seat and smoothing the front of my skirt with my hands.

Hannah studied me. "You seem unsettled."

"Just anxious about the show, that's all. Now, I must hurry."

I went to open the door and was suddenly startled to find a man in my doorway. His eyes were glazed and he smelled of blood.

"I am looking for Lady Klara von Dores."

Hannah immediately rushed to my side.

"How did you get up here?" she demanded. "You are not supposed to be in this part of the house!"

She shoved him back into the hallway, yelling loudly and alerting the other servants as she continued with him towards the stairs. He kept his eyes on me for some time, his anger towards me glowing through his glazed and enchanted look.

I stared back, trying to let this man know that he didn't scare me: I had done nothing to deserve such behaviour from a stranger, and especially one of Klara's obsessed suitors. I made my way downstairs to find Hannah arguing with Klara. The suitor stood watching me as two male servants guarded him. Gigi had come out and was off to the side looking quite frustrated. Another man stood beside her holding a box.

I waited for my cloak, not sure what to do amidst this chaos.

"For you, Mademoiselle, from Lord Westwick."

The man with the box suddenly came towards me, and everyone fell silent.

Flabbergasted, I exclaimed: "Please give him my sincerest thanks, but I cannot accept. Take it back, sir." Turning to the male servants guarding Klara's suitor, I added, "And would someone please show that gentleman out!"

Gigi and I left. I did not bother to see Klara's expression.

Josephine's costumes were hanging along the walls as we walked through the underground to her studio. She was standing amidst bolts of fabric, ribbons, lace, and bits and pieces of costumes scattered around the room, one hand on her hip and the other on her head.

"*Bonjour*, Josephine!," Gigi called out to her. She then turned and whispered to me, "She gets in quite a panic just before a performance. Speak nicely to her. She is quite a fright when she's angry."

I smiled my best. "Good day, Josephine."

"It will be a good day when I am given an assistant, Katrine," she quipped. "But I'm pleased the two of you are here on time. It seems no one else is capable of such a feat today, even though they live within mere footsteps."

"It may sound silly," Gigi tried to joke, "but for some court functions, arriving late it is an accepted practice."

Josephine sighed. "You can understand why I would avoid court at all costs. Hopefully, the Russians are not as particular as the French, and our visit will be smooth and comfortable."

"I am planning to learn as much as I can of their customs and protocol before we depart, so I will keep you informed, " Gigi smiled. "God forbid, we should get stuck there for some time. We need to understand what we are stepping into, *non?*"

"Indeed. Now have a seat while I get organised," Josephine said.

We perched ourselves on two stools as she moved around the room and began to collect things, placing them in two separate piles.

"Perhaps now is a good time to ask about cutting my hair," I spoke up.

"You wish to cut your hair?" Gigi asked, startled.

"Well, Hannah mentioned it. It's getting quite long and will soon become complicated to style."

Gigi examined the braid down my back.

"Perhaps so. Tell her to cut it at the shoulder blades. She will understand my meaning," Gigi advised.

"You are wearing your corset, Katrine?" Josephine called up.

"Yes, of course," I nodded.

She motioned me behind the screen and handed me the purple dress.

As I changed out of my own clothes, I wondered about the contraption women wore under their skirts to give them a full, round shape. One was supposed to have been made for me, but I wasn't sure what happened to it. I stepped back into the room and Josephine started pinning and tucking the dress on me, stepping back to admire her work and examine the fit.

"Grisela, if you please," she said, motioning towards the screen. "I fit Victorie this morning, so Katrine will be quick."

Gigi nodded then called out to me.

"So, *petite*," she began, "since you have a small part, you will perform your role, then come down here to assist Josephine. There will be too much time spent standing around, so you could make yourself useful that way."

"That would be wonderful!" I exclaimed, turning to Josephine.

"It would be lovely," she replied tiredly.

Meanwhile, Gigi stepped out from behind the screen in her stunning black and gray costume, which looked like smoke and spider webs.

"*Bon!*" Josephine exclaimed. "You are flawless, Gigi, the perfect Angel of Death. I have no adjustments to make to that dress. I know your physique like my own hands."

Gigi laughed. She seemed happier when she was with Josephine, perhaps because it was easier than constantly being on display as she was with the other women.

"I am finished with you both," Josephine declared now as she unbuttoned my dress from the back. "And because you were on time, you have allowed me a break before my next fitting. Thank you."

We both changed quickly, while Josephine exhaled forcefully as she sat down on a stool.

"I shall see you both at the show," she waved as we said our good-byes. I reassured her I would be there to help as soon as my part was finished. I was extremely excited by the prospect.

"*Ma petite*, there is something I must show you," Gigi said as we got into the carriage. "I should have done so sooner but the time was not right."

"Should I be worried?" I asked hesitantly. The last time I was in this sort of situation, they told me about Morgana.

"*Non.* It is important, but not a problem of any kind," she assured me as we sped off deeper into Paris.

The carriage came to a stop and the door opened. She took my hand and we stepped out into the early evening. We stood in front of a great stone building. Three doorways were framed by large archways, with two main towers that stretched up to the heavens. They were connected by gorgeous, detailed stonework and a round glass window above the center archway, with a row of statues in between.

"What manner of place is this?" I asked as I stared up in astonishment.

"This is Notre Dame Cathedral, the greatest in all of Europe," she declared. "While I am not enormously keen on religion, this particular house of worship is quite different. There are creatures atop the building, do you see them? They are all made of stone. They keep watch until they are really needed."

I looked up and squinted. The stone creatures looked something like dragons or wyverns. Some had wings, while others had beaks or the heads of men.

"They are called gargoyles, Katrine. They guard the city and a few who are truly pure. If you are ever in trouble, come here for safety. This place will protect you."

"Even though I am not—"

"Specifically because you are not," she conveyed. "A real house of the Lord does not judge you as you have been led to believe. You are safe here. We all are. Do not forget that. Promise me, Katrine."

"I promise," I said, overwhelmed, trying to take in the grandeur of this cathedral.

She grabbed me tightly by the upper arm now, digging her nails into my flesh. I looked at her, and there was a fury in her eyes I had never seen.

"Promise me!" she said angrily. I tried to understand the emotion, the intensity, in her face.

"Grisela, I promise," I said quickly, still not understanding.

She said something when she released me, then got back into the carriage. I took one last look at this great house of refuge then followed. I realised it would be best for me to save my questions for another day.

XXXII.

Onslaught

I AWOKE THE MORNING OF THE PERFORMANCE IN high spirits. After several more rehearsals, my confidence had greatly improved, and I felt as if I could do anything. Hannah was in the process of laying out a breakfast of bread, cheeses, salted meats and fruit, with a pitcher of water so fresh and clean I could smell its crispness.

"Mlle. Delphine insisted you have a widely varied meal to help give you strength," Hannah began. "Blood will come later. Now, eat. Then you will bathe, and we will work on your feet so that you are fully prepared. When it is time to go to the theatre, you are out of my hands."

I sat in bed and ate, watching her flutter around the room straightening and tidying things.

"Eat with me, Hannah," I urged. "Your movements are making me nervous."

"Oh, I cannot!" she exclaimed. "I must go attend to your bath and other preparations. I barely have time to think!"

"Then why are you fussing with my room?"

She stopped, realising what she was doing and turned to me. "Thanks for that. I will go start your bath. Don't think you have to eat all that food in one sitting. You can nibble while you're getting ready."

"Am I supposed to see anyone before I leave today?," I asked, setting the napkin down.

"No, Mlle. Delphine said no visitors, it takes too much time," Hannah quickly replied, and she left to tend to her duties.

I went and sat in the seat by the window, watching the gardeners work as I ate and waited for the bath. Some minutes later, Hannah motioned when she was ready. Before I realised, Hannah approached with a pair of scissors in hand and cut my braid at the shoulder blades before undoing it to wash it. I suddenly felt lighter without it, as if it had been causing more strain on my head and neck than I had realised.

Next, my skin was scrubbed until it was pink and smelled like roses, then my hair washed several times until a comb ran through its length without snagging. Hannah left it loose for the time being. After drying off, I was dressed.

I spent the hours after that rehearsing in my room, practicing my movements, my facial exaggerations, over and over, reviewing each of the steps in my mind. Eventually, I was sent out to the front of the chateau to wait for my escort to the theatre. The sun was getting low in the sky by now and darkness was not far away.

"My word. The Lord must be missing an angel," Charles's voice boomed from behind me.

I flinched.

"I apologise. Did I startle you?" he smiled.

"Yes, but it is quite alright," I replied. "I'm rather distracted, anyway."

"You are an absolute vision," he said, taking my hand and kissing it.

I could not help but laugh. "You, sir, may need your sight checked."

"You are far too modest, my dear. One might begin to think you are prudish."

I smiled coyly. "Far better for one to believe I am a prude than a harlot, My Lord."

As Charles laughed, I suddenly noticed someone watching us from the stairs, trying very hard to remain concealed behind a wall—which was quite comical, since that person was wearing a gown the colour of lemons.

"I look forward to seeing you perform tonight," Charles was saying.

"I had a gift but—"

"The only gift I need is to see the joy on your face while watching me dance," I replied, sweeping into a low bow as a servant appeared with my cloak.

"Well, until tonight, then," Charles nodded, bowing to me as I put on my cloak and swept out to the carriage.

The theatre was like a beehive buzzing with activity: sets being put into place and musicians tuning their instruments while, behind stage, dancers were warming up, and costumes donned, with Josephine overseeing. I sat next to Victorie as we were groomed together. By the time we were finished, I was her perfect reflection: I had never felt so beautiful.

Time flew quickly and, before I knew, it was my cue to take the stage.

Those who went on first took up their places behind the curtain, and the rest of us who would follow lined up along the sides behind the wall in order of appearance. The very last to go on, I was positioned at the back near one of the doors to the underground.

Drums erupted like thunder, and the curtain rose. I watched in awe as it all unfolded and tried my best to ignore any stage fright.

I heard the underground door open behind me but paid no mind; my turn was soon to come, and I could not ruin my debut. All at once, my shoulder was nearly ripped out of the socket when someone grabbed my arm and pulled me into the stairwell.

"What is the meaning of this?" I shrieked before coming face to face with my attacker. One of Klara's crazed suitors—the same man who had stopped me outside the theatre looking for her—loomed over me, his eyes wild as he pinned me to the wall. He went to reach for something.

I heard the knife clatter to the floor as I grabbed him by his arm and bent it until it snapped. He doubled over in pain, then tried to use his good arm to grab my throat. I grabbed both his ears and twisted his head as hard as I could until I heard another snap. His body fell limply to the floor.

I stepped out of the stairwell and ran from him, not sure if he was dead or alive. Not knowing what else to do, I hurriedly fell into step with the others back on stage.

I danced as if my life depended on it. Trying to separate my mind from what just happened, I focused only on what I was doing now: I was part of something that was beyond any dream I had ever had for myself, and Klara von Dores would not take that from me. I moved smoothly and full of grace. When my part concluded, I left the stage, triumphant that I had done it well.

I immediately rushed to find someone I knew, heading underground in search of Josephine. But no one was here now, and her studio was empty.

"Hello?" I called out as I ran back and forth through the hall. "Is anyone here? Hello!"

"It is just us, little rat," a voice called out from the opposite end of the hallway. I stopped where I was and turned slowly; Klara stood waiting, casually smoothing the front of her lemon gown.

"Klara, look," I called out, exasperated, "Have I offended you somehow?"

"The fact that you breathe offends me," she snorted. "But I intend to change that."

"If you hurt me, you will be forced to leave," I threatened her, wondering if I kept her talking long enough someone would find me.

She shrugged nonchalantly. "I'm sure I will manage."

"Mademoiselle Delphine will not let you get away with it."

"Are you serious?" she exclaimed. "The great courtesan, Grisela Delphine, get her hands dirty for some little peasant girl? You think too highly of yourself. You'll be dumped in the Seine like all the others. In fact, I can always make it look like you ran away."

"I will not go without a fight."

She shrugged again then came at me with such force we must have fallen back a few feet. My body hit the stone wall with a thunk: she wrapped her hands around my throat and began to squeeze.

As I stared up at her, her face started to look fuzzy. Little flashes of light lit up around her as it became harder for me to breathe. Something in my body suddenly awoke, a wave of energy that surged through me as I flipped her onto her back, using my legs to push her over my head and myself on top of her.

But I was not fast enough and she was able to shove me hard, causing me to fly back and smack into the wall a few feet away from us. My body began to feel weak and I knew my head split open. Her fangs suddenly came out and I tried not to recoil in fear.

She laughed. "Afraid of what you really are? Too bad. You'll never learn that we are all the same in the end, little rat. We need blood, and yours smells divine."

"I am nothing like you," I screamed, trying to pull myself up from the floor. She laughed again, pouncing on me like a wild animal and smacking my body back against the wall with such force I felt the warm liquid of blood begin to drip down the back of my neck.

I tried to fight, but all my strength was flowing out from the wound in the back of my head. I could not take anymore. I heard her angry, birdlike laugh ringing in my ears. I screamed as loud as I could. I screamed and screamed until she slapped me across the face to try to silence me. She grabbed tight enough on my throat that I thought she was going to tear it out with her fingers. She hit me hard again, and I was sure my body had left an imprint in the stone. I heard a knife slide out of its sheath.

I silently apologised to my grandmother for not being strong enough to fight. I was no longer worthy of her name.

"Where are all your dear friends now, little rat?" Klara taunted me. "Do you think they even realise you are gone?"

She brought the knife down on my cheek, splitting open the skin.

"Lord Westwick will never look at your pretty face again," she sneered, rage welling up in her eyes.

"You can have him," I choked out, my voice just louder than a whisper.

"I already would if you weren't here!" she screeched at me. "My life would be perfect if YOU WEREN'T HERE!"

She pushed me farther up the wall and I caught a glimpse of the blood- stained knife. It came into my line of vision for only a moment, and we stared into each other's eyes as she put the blade to my throat.

"*Au revoir*, little rat," she said quietly, and I braced myself.

But it never came. The air around us began to move like we were caught in a storm. Confused, Klara squeezed tighter on my throat, and my vision started going black around the edges. I felt the tug gently at first, then as if someone had tied a rope around her waist, Klara was pulled off me, screaming as she flew down the hallway at an incredible speed. She smashed into the wall, her body falling limp to the floor.

I sank slowly to the ground, sobbing as I tried to breathe. I suddenly became very afraid and tried to stand and run.

"She might get back up," I babbled, stumbling under my own weight.

A pair of strong arms pulled me up.

"I have to...she could get back up...we have to run," I continued between sobs, trying to pull away so I could run.

"She won't get back up for a while," a male voice said, and I turned to see eyes of blue flame. "If she does, I will protect you, Katrine. You are safe."

It was at that moment I collapsed into William of Naples' arms.

***

"I will not stand for this, Charles!" Gigi cried out. "You must deal with this accordingly!"

"Gigi, please—"

"Either you reprimand Klara, or we are taking Katrine and leaving," Vincenzo agreed.

They were standing around me. I was lying down with my eyes closed, and someone was stroking my hair. He hadn't spoken, but I knew it was

William.

"She is the daughter of one of the most important families in Vienna," Charles was imploring them.

"—Who handed her over to you with a large sum of money! She was discarded, Charles," Gigi exclaimed. "The baron may also have disinherited her, for God's sake. If I must take matters into my own hands, so help me...!"

"And did you forget Katrine is a Báthory, Charles? That name carries more weight than von Dores," Vincenzo added sternly.

"Rubbish! The King of Hungary wants to execute her grandmother," Charles argued, "and she has no claim to the family inheritance."

"She has the bloodline," Vincenzo snapped, "And her cousin currently sits on the throne of Transylvania."

"I don't care if he's the future King of Egypt she is my *protégée* and I will not stand for this!" Gigi yelled.

William finally spoke. "Lower your voices, all of you. You'll wake her. She's badly hurt!"

"*Badly hurt, Charles*," Gigi snapped. "If you do not fix this you will never see either of us again, I swear it. If you had only stopped your constant flirtations—."

"Enough!" Charles declared. "She will be put in one of the cages down here until further notice."

William stayed with me while the others left, likely to deal with Klara.

I had no idea how much time had passed. I opened my eyes and looked up at William.

"Welcome back," he said, a smile slowly stretching across his face.

I had never seen him smile. He was quite handsome when he did.

"Where am I? How long have I been asleep?"

I tried to sit up but he encouraged me to stay down.

"You are still at the theatre. Stay down, you are quite safe," he reassured me. "You have been out for a while. You will be alright, but you need your rest."

Many things passed through my mind as I looked at his face. He had saved my life. And Morgana had been right. That fact would not leave my thoughts.

"Thank you, William. Thank you for saving me," I whispered.

His face turned scarlet, his eyes only leaving mine for a moment.

"My pleasure, Katrine," he said.

He did not leave my side as I closed my eyes and fell into a dreamless sleep.

***

XXXIII.

A Gift

Two years later – October 1613.

"I AM HOPING WITH THE RIGHT COMBINATION OF herbs I can change the colour of your scar," Morgana said. We were in the garden. She bent over, rubbing her fingers on leaves and smelling them before pulling up handfuls and adding them to her basket. I ran my fingertip along the thin white line on my cheek.

"It would be better to try to correct the colour than plaster your face with that horrible white makeup the bloody French love so much," she continued, and I smiled at her.

In the two years since the attack, Morgana and I had become quite close. She now lived happily among us. When we learned her prophecies to be true, Charles and Vincenzo concluded that she would no longer be a danger but, rather, a powerful ally. They gradually allowed her more freedom and self-sufficiency. This newfound trust pleased and calmed Morgana a great deal, and she accepted us more readily. She and I felt comfortable with one another; perhaps it was because we seemed so close in age, or perhaps because we did share more in common than previously thought. Once I had recovered, we spent as much time out in the gardens together as we possibly could.

While I was attending to my studies with Gigi, Morgana was either outside with one of the servants, learning the French name of every living thing, or in the library reading books on the subject. I had been genuinely shocked that Morgana could also read and write quite fluently in Latin. She said her parents thought it important.

Meanwhile, I had adapted well to my new life, taking great pride in my achievements. Under Gigi's tutelage, I made considerable strides in both my education and etiquette training. Even though Klara's attack had been brutal, other than my scar, I looked remarkably well. I was a projection of both my mother and grandmother and looked very much at home at Grisela Delphine's side.

"Do you think it would help?" I asked. "Do you think it can really hide the scar?"

"No harm in trying," she shrugged, as we continued down the center path leading away from the chateau. "I'm surprised the blue-eyed demon has not made an attempt to heal your face."

I smiled at the mention of William. "He has not mentioned it."

"That is quite alright. If I can do it, then I can tease him about it later," she smiled happily.

William had saved my life and overseen much of my care since then, although bickering constantly with Gigi along the way. It was not an angry fight fortunately; in fact, she was quite shocked that William could even care for another human being. I worried, at first, that my feelings towards him were directly related to the incident. As the years passed, however, my heart attached more to him, and now I could not imagine life without him.

Despite all of that, Lord Westwick's constant pursuit of me had not lessened, although a recent business trip took him away and brought some peace to the house. Actually, both he and Vincenzo had gone to Germany on a trade mission. They were only supposed to be gone for a fortnight, but it was now over a month since they left.

"Do you think Vincenzo and Lord Westwick will return soon?" I asked Morgana, as she was picking her lot of lavender.

I had received a letter from Vincenzo once, inquiring about my health and asking me to remind William to keep Klara securely locked up, but nothing more.

Morgana smiled a toothy grin. "He will be back soon."

"Why do you look at me like that? What did you see?" I tried to grab her shoulder, but she slipped past, laughing as she hurried ahead.

"You wouldn't believe me if I told you," she called back as she ran down the path.

Meanwhile, Gigi was standing on the back porch, waiting for us as we approached the chateau. It reminded me of a mother looking for her children out in the field.

"*Bonjour*, Mademoiselle," I greeted her as we walked up the back stairs.

"Lord Westwick has returned," Gigi announced. "He would like us all to gather in the parlour at sunset. He says he has a gift to present to you, *petite.*"

I rolled my eyes, and Morgana chuckled. "I wonder where he keeps all the 'gifts' you have refused," she teased me. "There must be a roomful somewhere in this house."

"Say," I said to Gigi, "Morgana thinks she may be able to change the colour of my scar."

"*Bon.* That is lovely news," Gigi said, but her tone was dismissive.

'What's the matter?"

She folder her arms. "I would prefer he not make such pomp over his gifts," she continued curtly. "He continues to embarrass himself—as well as you—and it is pathetic!"

I agreed with her; it was getting quite silly. Charles was not in the least dissuaded, despite my obvious affection for William. I looked at Morgana who gave me a wickedly evil grin that made my stomach flip. I wondered if she knew what was going to happen.

Gigi sat on a small stool in front of me, applying the white plaster to my face with the expertise and precision of a seasoned painter, as Hannah dressed my hair. She had insisted the second the wound healed, it had to be covered. She also didn't think very much of Morgana's natural remedies.

"I don't like the way this feels on my skin," I said to her.

She ignored my complaint. "The scar I'm covering is what keeps that little heathen in prison."

"What happens when Klara's parents pass? She stands to inherit a title, doesn't she?"

"I am unconcerned with her or her future," Gigi sniffed, keeping her eyes on her work. "She is Charles's problem."

"I thought we were going to Russia," I muttered finally. "Why haven't we gone yet?"

"To the best of my knowledge, we are still going to Russia, but the longer we wait, the better. That way, we can learn more, and I hope by then, Russia will be more settled. They have had some troubles in recent years."

I sighed, thinking now about Charles' return and the gift he had for me. "I hope Charles isn't planning something too preposterous."

Hannah said nothing as she plaited my hair and wrapped it at the back of my head, securing it with a golden net. I wished I could see her face in the mirror.

"Hannah," I said, and she jumped at the sound of her name. "Do you know something?"

"Madam, all I know is that whatever Lord Westwick is planning had Kardoska blubbering like an infant," she replied.

"I'm not sure if that is favourable or not. Perhaps I should ask her… no, never mind; it matters little since whatever it is, I will refuse it," I said.

"What if you cannot?" Gigi implied.

"What do you mean?"

"What if he gives you something you cannot refuse?"

This surprised me. "What could that possibly be?"

She shrugged, pulling back to examine her work. "You never know with him. But whatever it is, we are soon to find out."

When Gigi and I entered the salon, the room fell quiet. We continued to our usual seating area where the other women were already gathered. Morgana sat amongst the group tonight, wearing a simple gray dress, waiting patiently for the two of us to arrive. She and Gigi had warmed to each other over time, but the other women were still unsure of her. I secretly hoped that Morgana might be able to work with Josephine someday, but that would take a while.

I briefly made eye contact with William who was standing against the wall behind them, and he smiled warmly at me. I smiled back. I wished he would sit with us but knew better than to ask. He was not interested in socialising with anyone but me and, occasionally, Morgana.

Before we had a chance to speak to anyone, Vincenzo and Charles came into the salon, escorting a man I did not know. The man had medium-length dark golden hair, pushed back from his face as a gentleman would, with deep brown eyes and a gaze that looked oddly familiar. The angles of his face reminded me of someone, but I could not quite place whom. The way his mouth moved when he spoke and the way his eyes shifted suddenly caused my heart to flutter. I felt a sudden pain in my chest as they approached.

"My dear, you are stunning as always," Charles declared, appraising my green dress as he took my hand. "Katrine, this is someone whom I would like you to meet."

He brought this gentleman over to me so that we were standing face to face. I looked to Vincenzo who appeared quite panicked now. I suddenly heard a loud wail from the other side of the room. Roza hurried in through the salon, tears streaming down her face. She said something to the stranger in another language, then smacked my arm.

"Bow before your prince, you twit!" she snapped.

"My...my...what?" I asked, turning back to the man, just as Roza fell to the floor in a dramatic curtsey.

"Katrine Báthory, may I introduce you to His Royal Highness, Prince of Transylvania, Gabor Báthory, your grandmother's cousin," Charles announced proudly.

Vincenzo blanched, and I stood there, stricken. The gentleman appeared puzzled.

"Grandmother?" he asked, looking at me intently now. "Who is your kin, child?"

"My...my...mother's name is Anastasia. Countess Erzsébet Báthory is my grandmother."

The puzzled look on Gabor Báthory's face turned to one of surprise, and then deepened in anger.

"Erzsébet Báthory has no child named Anastasia," he said bluntly.

I fumbled, "She was born before her marriage to Ferenc Nádasdy—"

"My Lord," Vincenzo hastily interrupted, "We can explain this—"

But Gabor's face had turned red by now. "So you lie and defile her good name! I should beat you!," he exclaimed as he raised his hand.

Instinctively, I put my arm up to guard my face. He then stopped midway with a stunned look, and demanded: "Where did you get that? Did you steal it?"

"What...I'm sorry...what...?"

He grabbed my hand and pulled it toward him, examining my ring. "You wear the Somlyo ring of my family. I asked you, where did you get that?"

"My grandmother gave it to me when I left her in Csejthe," I cried out, and his once red face went blank. "She said it was her mother's, and she said it would protect me."

His handsome face blanched as his eyes met mine. He stared at me for some time before saying, "My God. Is it possible? Where is your mother?"

"I don't know. She had an...it's very complicated," I stuttered. "But I assure you, I am who I say I am. I have no reason to lie, considering the gravity of my grandmother's current situation."

"I wanted to help her but I could not," he began, his voice quiet but not quite a whisper. "They got to me before I could....we should speak in private of such matters," he said, examining my face. "You do look so much like her, I cannot believe it."

"Thank you, My Lord. You pay me the greatest compliment."

"Please, child! I insist you call me Cousin."

He looked down at Roza now, still suspended in a bow, then back at me. "You had no idea who I was, did you?"

"I am quite sorry, but I did not. I knew a Báthory sat on the throne of Poland, and heard of one who sits as Prince of Transylvania. I know a little of The Black Bey, but nothing of the Countess's children, or my mother's real father."

Gabor laughed loudly, a sound like thunder. "I, my dear girl, am the one who most recently sat as Prince of Transylvania...but sadly, no longer."

"What happened?"

He smiled. "If I tell you now, my dear girl, we'll have nothing to discuss tomorrow."

XXXIV.

Family Ties

WE SAT ALONE IN THE CONSERVATORY JUST AFTER sunset. Gabor was now one of the traditionally turned who could not come out in the daylight. Hannah had brought us some tea with a canister of blood, and I asked her to leave it with us when she left. I had no idea what had happened to him, so I thought it would be helpful.

"What happened to her?" I implored him now.

I was thrilled to finally speak with someone who had knowledge of my grandmother's situation. Unfortunately, Gabor was in no mood to speak of that yet.

"I'll get to it," he said, waving me off. "I had an army raised, I was going to battle against the king, and I was planning on rescuing her. Had I been able to get her out of the country, she would have been in exile, but at least she would have been free.

"One night, a man came to me, clad in a dark robe with a long beard. He resembled a priest of the old faith. He told me I was going to be assassinated, but that he could offer me eternal life if I let people think that Gabor Báthory, Prince of Transylvania, was dead. I do not know how he managed it, but he turned me into a vampire and sold me into slavery."

When my eyes widened, he nodded.

"The man gave me the new name of Gabriel. I was lucky, I suppose. After all, who wants to go through all that trouble only to be killed in the end? You could say," he cleared his throat, "that I was traveling for a short time before your Lord Westwick found me. I am unsure what my fate would have been if he hadn't."

He sat back and poured himself a cup of blood. I thought I saw a slight smirk of satisfaction sneak from his lips as he sipped and perused his new surroundings.

I certainly was not amused. If this was his attempt to lighten the moment or lessen the gravity of the situation, it was not working. I was also quite appalled by the idea that Charles had only saved him as a way to impress me, likely intending to tell him as much at the first available opportunity. My disgust began to overwhelm my disappointment. An underlying feeling of confusion washed over me as I sat silently, watching Gabor Báthory.

"The Palatine of Hungary, a man called Thurzo, fought hard to exile Erzsébet to some convent. He thought if he got her out of Hungary, it would please the King, but His Highness was quite in debt to your grandmother. She was very wealthy, you see, and he borrowed a lot of money from her. Now, if he had her head—if he could arrest her from some crime—then the king would be able to take away her lands, and his debt to her would be cancelled."

When I looked confused, he nodded. "Yes, it would all be forfeit. But he knew, as we all did, as long as she lived, she would fight for what was rightfully hers. She tricked him in the end."

When I learned forward, eager to hear more, he declared, "Oh yes, she's very intelligent. She knew the king was conspiring against her. So before he sent his men after her, she made out her Will and gave all of her property to her three children. That way, the king couldn't take anything from her—or from them. But—" he held up his hand with a flourish—"in the end, Thurzo had to do something to please his King, so he had Erzsébet walled into her chamber at her beloved Castle Csejthe."

My breath caught in my throat. "I do not understand. What do you mean by walled in?"

"He had the windows and doors to her private rooms completely filled in with bricks, with her inside. Only small slits for air and spaces large enough to pass food through were left." Gabor hung his head now. "When he pronounced sentence, he said she would never see the sunlight again."

I felt like someone had suddenly kicked me with a pointed shoe very hard in the chest. I tried my best to breathe but could only do so, shallow and slow. Everything in my head started to spin.

"We must go back!" I said with as much force as I could muster.

He immediately placed his large hand over mine, and from it, more power than I had ever imagined emanated.

"I am so sorry, Katrine. We cannot. The Báthory family is not what it once was. Right now, in Austria and Hungary, the king has made it illegal to speak the name of Erzsébet Báthory in polite society."

I was stricken.

"But how can you stand by now? How can you be so accepting of this? What about her children? Is this really our fate?"

He sighed. "Her imprisonment, and the execution of her servants, spared her children. But her children are also not true Báthory. You must not forget, they are their father's children. They are Nádasdy."

"But you are a Prince! You could raise an army—"

"I told you, I tried," he groaned. "She sent me money and I raised an army but, as fate would have it, I could not reach her! Believe me, child, if there was anything I could have done, I would have done it. We simply have to accept what God has given us."

"God?" I cried out. "He gave up on me a long time ago. I can tell you quite confidently that all He has ever given me is pain and heartache."

"Well, no more of that, my dear," Gabor said, patting my hand now, "because we have each other now, and we're family. From now on, we will take care of each other as family would."

He placed his hand on my shoulder.

"Family... yes," I nodded back, half-heartedly.

Even though I now realised he might be the only connection I had left to my grandmother, I was somehow still unsure of Gabor. Of course, despite my doubts, I did wish to try to form some sort of relationship with him. I dreaded the thought, though, that it could lead to further hurt or disappointment.

At that moment, I heard a throat clear from the other side of the room. I turned to see Gigi standing in the doorway.

"Cousin, I would like to formally introduce you to my mentor," I said, greeting her as she entered the room to join us. "Mademoiselle Grisela Delphine, may I introduce Gabor Báthory, my grandmother's cousin."

"It is quite a pleasure," Gigi smiled, and Gabor kissed the top of her gloved hand.

"The pleasure is all mine, I assure you. And please, call me Gabriel," he said. "Won't you join us? We have much to discuss."

"Gigi is quite taken with him," I told Vincenzo.

"To be honest, my dear, all the women are," Vincenzo rolled his eyes, "and have been since we met him in Germany. He appears to have that effect, much to the dismay of our other local womaniser."

The mere thought of Charles immediately made me angry.

"I'm quite upset by this whole thing."

"I could not imagine you being any other way. I hope Gabriel never learns that he was saved only as a means to please you."

"I suppose I should be flattered," I muttered, "but it only makes me worry that Charles is not quite right in his mind."

"Well, I suppose that you have actual family now, my company will no longer be needed," Vincenzo said, and I could hear genuine sadness in his voice. He looked away from me and down the garden path. We had been walking quite slowly just outside of the chateau.

I immediately took his hand. "Heavens, no! Now I wonder if *you* are not quite right in the head, my friend. I do not believe I could exist in this life without you. You have shown me so many wonders, so many things I'd never even dreamed of. *You* found me in Vienna. I would have nothing, be nothing without you! If I can say, I believe you are my very *best* friend."

I squeezed our linked arms closer to my body. The idea that Vincenzo would leave me brought tears to my eyes.

"Thank you, Katrine," he smiled affectionately. "That is nice to know. Now," he cleared his throat, "on to more pressing matters. I need to talk to you about Klara."

I sighed loudly as he continued, "You cannot avoid this discussion forever."

"I was under the impression that matters were being handled well."

"Not everything is going well," he said gravely. "We received word that Baron von Dores is dying. As far as we know, Klara is his only heir, but we cannot send her back to Vienna—not in her current state, at least. We are in contact with the baroness, trying to decide on a solution. Of course, she sent her deepest apologies for her daughter's horrid behaviour and offered compensation, but she has no interest in allowing Klara to return. So, I suspect we will be paid to keep Klara imprisoned."

"The baron is dying? But how? I thought vampires were immortal," I asked in disbelief.

"They are, unless they do not take care of their health. Believe me when I say that the baron is one of the unhealthiest men I have ever met. Luckily, the baroness is not in such a state. We are hoping the baron will change his Will to make his wife his heir. If Klara is left out of the Will entirely, we will have no further problems: William would kill her if we allowed, and so would Morgana, for that matter."

"I would not have blood on either of their hands at my expense," I murmured, "but I do appreciate the thought."

"William would move the planets for you, I am sure you know that," Vincenzo assured. "Don't ask him to, though, for I am sure he could if he tried. Of course, that would most likely lead to an unpleasant result for all of us." Vincenzo cracked a wide smile, and I couldn't help but to smile, too.

"But, honestly, I am quite confused by the fact that Charles does not see it."

Vincenzo chuckled. "Oh he sees it, but he cares not. He doesn't think it will last. You see, he believes William's volatile nature will tear you apart and, in your grief, you will run right into his arms."

"Then he's a fool," I said flatly.

"Ah. But you have said nothing about Gabriel's appearance. How does that make you feel?"

"Morgana said I would see my family soon," I replied thoughtfully, "but I wished she would have said more, prepared me for the shock of it!"

He smiled to himself. Vincenzo and Morgana had finally begun to get along. He had to admit that she spoke the truth, although he still had trouble accepting it.

"What makes you so angry about it, Katrine?"

"Charles should have thought it through more clearly," I stammered. "He introduced me and Gabor without telling either of us anything. Gabor—Gabriel—could have killed me if he did not believe me! Charles should not have gambled with my life that way."

"But you are who you say you are."

"Of course I am, but Gabriel could have chosen not to believe it. He could have also insisted that I stole my ring and done to me what he liked. My claim does shame my grandmother's name. He could have taken it much worse."

"I must confess that I was quite nervous myself," Vincenzo admitted, "but he didn't. He knew and believed you, just by looking at you, as anyone who has seen the Countess would. Charles felt very convinced of that. And now you have a cousin!"

I smiled to myself, pondering that thought. I did like the idea.

"Well, at least Charles did one good thing: I'm relieved that Gabriel is no longer a slave. I hope it was not much trouble to secure his release, or very expensive."

"I can assure you it was neither. However, one day when we have some time, I will tell you of the market in Germany where we purchased him. Perhaps you, William, and I can do something together soon. I would like to tell him also," Vincenzo said, thinking out loud.

We turned around as we reached the end of the path and began to walk back toward the chateau. The sun was reaching its midday height now.

"I should be available when Gabriel rises," I spoke up. "I believe he should be formally introduced to the group by me. What do you think?"

Vincenzo nodded in agreement. "There has been some talk of having a *fête* in your honour. I think Charles intends to host it on All Hallow's Eve. You could do it then, perhaps."

The thought of All Hallow's Eve suddenly gave me a chill. It had been three years since my life was destroyed on that night, since my mother had disappeared. The idea of hosting a *fête* for me on that day seemed very strange.

We stopped just before entering the back door. Vincenzo kissed my hand, and his lips were cold even through my gloves.

"Until tonight, my dear," he said, opening the door for me.

"Until tonight."

I passed through the conservatory and, as I made my way to the stairs, I thought about how I had not seen Gabriel since having tea with him. His need to stay out of the sun compelled him to some very strange hours. When I had gone to bed, he apparently socialised with some of the others, making quite an impression. I began to wonder what would become of him, where he would live, and if he would eventually stay at the theatre with the others of his same persuasion.

XXXV.

Formal Introductions

GABOR BÁTHORY, PRINCE OF TRANSYLVANIA, WHOM we were now referring to as Gabriel, was residing in a cell in the basement at the opposite end from where they had once kept Morgana. The idea that they were keeping this once grand man in a dungeon weighed heavily on me. As I went down the basement stairs, the thought caused me to pause. I tried to convince myself that it was only for his safety. Also, even though we were related, he was still a stranger whom they had to be certain could be trusted. Nevertheless, despite my misgivings, I still had to approach him confidently. For me, this place was home, these people were my family, and I was going to try my best to help Gabriel become a part of it all.

Gabriel was no prisoner here, however. The cell door was not locked. A bed fit for royalty had been made up for him and a tray of food lay on the floor beside it. I could smell blood nearby.

"Not bad for a pit, eh?" Gabriel called out, stepping into the dim lantern light so I could see him.

"I am sure Lord Westwick could have a proper room set up for you in the underground at the theatre, if you prefer," I replied.

He smiled at me, standing in his chemise and hose, the upper part of his muscular chest exposed. He stared at my blue dress, then my hair which was pulled up in a silver net that matched the trim on my dress and white gloves.

"My goodness, child. Every time I see you, I see something else in your face that reminds me of Erzsébet," he said with eyes full of intensity. "I am sorry that I ever doubted you, even if only for a moment."

I felt the colour rush to my face. "You flatter me. Now, I have come to see how you are faring. Dinner shall be served soon, and I came to see if you wanted some water to wash with, or if there was anything else you might need."

"Since when do you serve me?" he teased. "That lovely Transylvanian woman has seen to my every need." He locked his hands behind his head. "In fact, all I need to do is dress. Did she accompany you when you arrived here?"

"Yes, she did," I replied quickly. "If you don't require anything, then I will come back later to collect you."

"No, no," he held up a hand. "I won't be a moment. Please stay. Ah, she even pressed my clothes, splendid! I suppose I will need to have some made. The Italian gave me the ones I have."

I stepped out of the cell and turned my back to him. "Signor Amori found me in Vienna. He is a good friend."

"Then he shall be mine as well," Gabor exclaimed. "And I suppose I should meet that boy who's been making eyes at you from the other side of the room—and I do not mean Lord Westwick."

"Lord Westwick is a notorious womaniser," I said flatly.

"Then we shall get along swimmingly," he laughed as he emerged from the cell, taking my hand. "Now, my dear, tell me: is your Mademoiselle Delphine going to be there?"

The dining room fell silent as we entered, all eyes turning to us. I decided not to wait until Charles' party to introduce Gabor. I would do it now.

"Ladies and Gentlemen, I am pleased to introduce to you to my

cousin, His Royal Highness, the Prince of Transylvania, Gabor Báthory."
I heard a few gasps of admiration, and immediately added, "But he is
part of our family now, and today he goes only by the name of Gabriel,"
I said with feigned confidence. "Some of you have already met him, and
I hope all of you will show him the same kindness you have given to
me."

Mathilde immediately stepped forward and extended her hand to
him. "It is an honour to meet you, My Lord. My name is Mathilde de la
Rivage."

Before I could say another word, Gabriel was shaking hands with
everyone. The women's eyes sparkled as he kissed their hands, the formal
introduction seeming to put them all aflutter.

"So, you are pleased with my gift?," Charles whispered in my ear. He
was standing so close behind me, I could feel his breath.

Smiling to the crowd, I hissed between my teeth, "I am disgusted
that you would think purchasing a man like him would win my heart.
If only you had brought him here as an act of kindness, I would have
been honoured. But you best pray now he never finds out why you really
brought him here."

I did not give Charles the opportunity to reply and immediately
crossed the room to join William.

"Charles is trying to gloat?" William asked quietly as I slid in beside
him.

"He's not very smart."

"He's not used to rejection. He doesn't quite know how to deal with
it."

I sighed. "You would think it obvious that I only have eyes for you."
He pinched my elbow affectionately.

"William, he wants to meet you formally," I whispered.

"Who?"

"Gabor...I mean Gabriel," I replied. "He seems excited by the idea of
being my cousin."

I could hear William stifle a laugh.

"Did you not want a family?"

"Not that way. Charles crossed the line, but I won't fault Gabriel for it. He is my grandmother's cousin."

"Does he know how she is faring? I know you were concerned."

"She has been walled into a chamber in her castle," I said, but before he could reply, Gabriel came towards us.

"Gabriel, this is William of Naples. William, this is Gabriel."

"A pleasure, sir," William said, bowing.

"The pleasure is all mine," Gabriel replied. "I look forward to getting to know each of you."

"As I do you," William replied.

After a few moments of idle talk, when Gabriel finally moved on to another group, William leaned in and whispered to me, "Katrine, I adore you, but I am not good at conversation. Or being friendly."

I smiled. "I know, dear, but am sure you will try your best."

Charles tapped his fork on the side of his wine glass, quieting the group. I could hear Morgana sigh from across the table; she appeared quite frustrated and impatient. I wondered if she knew what he was going to say.

"I wanted to let you all know that plans are still in the works for our trip to Russia," he began. "I know there have been troubles in the country recently, but I am quite confident that these matters are being settled. Since we will not travel until the snow has cleared, I am sure the situation will improve by then. Also, if you have not heard, I am planning a *fête* for All Hallow's Eve, in Katrine's honour."

"Are you sure that is wise, Charles?" Mathilde spoke up now with concern. "That night is known to bring on the change."

"Indeed, and why in my honour? What have I done to deserve a party?" I asked.

Charles's eyes dropped when he turned his gaze to me. His voice lowered, but everyone was still able to hear it: "Katrine, I thought you would appreciate the support. Indeed, having a *fête* in your honour would show our continued stance that we made the right decision to keep you here and will continue to support you in any way we can."

It was a veiled threat, but it rippled easily from Charles' sugar-coated tongue.

Meanwhile, Gabriel lifted his glass. "What has my cousin done to garnish such esteem?," he beamed innocently.

"Unprovoked, one of our former members viciously attacked Katrine, nearly killing her. I just wanted Katrine to be aware of our continued support for her," Charles replied, much too proudly.

Gabriel, unfortunately, had already had a bit too much to drink.

"Who did that to her?," he demanded. "No one attacks a Báthory and lives to speak of it!"

"It happened years ago," I spoke up. "There is no need for concern."

"The girl is Klara von Dores," William ignored me, "daughter and heir of Baron von Dores."

I scowled at him from across the table.

Gabriel immediately let out a sound that was something between a howl and a laugh. "That horrible girl was here? What on earth for?"

"She is still here," Charles corrected, "although she has been in confinement since. She was born a vampire. Both Baron and Baroness von Dores are vampires, and Klara had become too reckless with the family secret. We took her in a few years ago as a favour to her parents. She will remain imprisoned here until we can decide what to do with her."

"He means until he finds out how much her parents are willing to pay to keep her alive," Victorie called out, and she winked at Charles. "You would finally have enough money to buy that home in Ibiza you always wanted, Charles!"

He glared at Victorie, and the chatter immediately began again. I went back to eating my dinner. No one asked my opinion, and I had little to say on the subject. As long as I never saw Klara again, I did not care what happened to her.

The evening went on without further incident. We moved on to the salon afterwards and the world continued on as it always had, but something inside me felt different now.

"It will take some time for your life to be settled," Morgana consoled me.

"If it happens at all," I grumbled.

"What I originally told you has not entirely played out yet," she warned.

I turned to her. "Then should I trust Gabriel's intentions?"

Gabriel was off dancing quite close to Mathilde, meanwhile, for what I thought was the third time now.

"Yes," Morgana nodded. "Believe it or not, he is telling you the truth. He actually cared for your grandmother very deeply. I sense they were close. He hopes that taking care of you might somehow redeem him for not being able to save her."

"Did he say this to you?"

She smiled a toothy grin. "No, not a word. Why do you ask?"

"I knew you could see the future, but I didn't know you could read people's thoughts."

She shrugged innocently. "I am a woman of many talents."

"Are there any other things you have conveniently forgotten to tell me?" I demanded.

Her smile began to fade. "Grisela cannot kill Klara. And—"

I stared at her, my one eyebrow raised slightly.

"—Perhaps we shall be meeting her family soon, as well."

XXXVI.

All Hallow's Eve – 1613.

Another Fateful Night

I STARED OUT MY WINDOW INTO THE DISTANCE, THE colours of the gardens changing, the sky a shade of gray that often signals the threat of snow. However, the crisp, fall air coming in through the window cleansed my palette of the fear and anxiety that was bubbling up in my throat.

The sun was getting low, which meant I would soon have to begin my preparations. Frankly, I wanted to take to my bed: I was feeling sick with grief and even concerned that the meal from earlier in the day would fly back out if I opened my mouth. It had been three years now since that terrible day on All Hallow's Eve, and this was the first time I had ever been physically sick because of it.

I really did not want to be part of this evening's festivities. I imagined that some of the others probably had difficulties of their own on the anniversary of their change. Perhaps after enough time passed, one would learn and grow from it.

However, something about today felt different. Hannah quietly came into the room then.

"It's time to start getting ready, Katrine. I have run your bath with rose water and lavender, as you requested," she said. "Morgana and I prepared the rose water ourselves, and she is working on a poultice for your scar as we speak."

The old wound on my arm began to itch at this. I knew Hannah meant my face, but I wondered if she could make something for my arm, as well

"Katrine? Are you alright?"

I turned and tried my best to smile.

"Have you finally decided on something to wear?" she asked as she examined the piles of gowns on my bed. "It looks like you have been at this for hours."

"It was on my mind," I admitted. "I'm concerned about dressing appropriately."

"You always do, child."

"But today is different. It's the anniversary of my change, and I want to respect my mother's memory."

Hannah's eyes widened. "I am so sorry, Katrine. Of course you need to be respectful."

I rose and went over to the bed. "I chose the black and white. I haven't worn it before, and it seems appropriate. I can't wear black entirely, since I'm not sure if she's dead."

Hannah nodded thoughtfully and began to gather the things I needed to dress. Tonight, I would wear the full regalia of a woman. In addition to my corset, I now possessed a farthingale, a contraption worn under my skirt to give it a fuller, rounder shape. I had practiced with it, and while it felt awkward, especially with the corset, I was sure I could handle myself in both. With time, I supposed they would become more comfortable.

Hannah smiled at me and took my arm. "I shall put the other items away while you bathe. Please try to relax. I am sure it will be a lovely evening. Besides, with Gabriel here now, your life will get better and better."

The bath soothed my nerves, even though I'd been scrubbed until I was raw and my scalp massaged until it ached. Morgana came to my room while Hannah was lacing me into my dress. I could smell whatever was in the stone bowl she carried as soon as she stepped through the doorway. It was pungent and made me nervous.

"Morgana, will that smell stick to me? It's quite strong."

Hannah draped a cloth around me as I sat down on the stool in front of my mirror.

"No, girl. You will leave it on as Hannah prepares your hair, then we'll wipe it off with warm water and a cloth. The smell will come off with it, I promise," Morgana said flatly.

"Is something troubling you, Morgana?" I asked, casting a sidelong glance at her.

"Nothing of note. Just another Samhain," she replied.

"What's that?"

"A festival—a time when some believe that the border between here and the underworld becomes thin. When creatures from that world can come into this one."

She began applying a slim line of the poultice to my face. It actually felt quite cool and soothing.

"Do you believe that?" I asked.

She shrugged her shoulders. "Why not."

Hannah brushed my hair out, putting it into a plait and twisting it around itself, finally securing it at the back of my head.

"And what of you, Katrine? Are you troubled?" Morgana baited me now.

I paused, then told her, "Tonight is the anniversary of my change, and I'm feeling a bit fearful. I'm sure I'll be fine, though."

Morgana tried to smile, but I could see the strain in her face as she dampened a cloth and removed the poultice.

"I am sure you will."

When dressing and styling were finally complete, I rose carefully in my elaborate gown.

"How do I look?"

I stepped out into the room so that Hannah and Morgana could get a good look. I turned around slowly for them to see.

"Lovely," Hannah said, smiling proudly. "It's a lovely gown—quite appropriate to mark the occasion."

Morgana came closer to inspect and then stepped back again.

"The scar is invisible unless one is extremely close," she declared, satisfied, "and after some time, that will fade also."

"Wonderful," I nodded. "Now I won't need to wear that awful white plaster on my face. Thank you, Morgana. I am most grateful."

"I'm pleased I could help. Now, are you ready to go downstairs?" she demanded.

I took a deep breath.

"Yes."

We locked arms and headed down to the salon.

I was stunned by the amount of people who had already gathered when we entered the room. Applause broke out, and Morgana quickly stepped away, leaving me alone to face my guests. The colour rose to my cheeks making them feel like they were burning. All eyes were on me. Everyone stood waiting for me to say something, but the words would not come out. I stood there helpless, feeling panicked.

Gigi suddenly appeared amidst a flurry of lace and smiles.

"Oh, my dear *petite*, you are so modest!" she declared, taking hold of my arm. Her fingernails bit into my flesh. "Thank them," she hissed into my ear.

I looked around at the spinning room: "Thank you all so much for coming," I croaked, "and I—we—appreciate your continued support."

The crowd applauded again, politely, but this time not as vigorously. Gigi linked arms with me and quickly ushered me into the room, whispering along the way, "What have I been teaching you, that you would make such a fool of yourself and of me. How could you think of nothing to say, to have had nothing prepared for your entrance?"

Tears began to well in my eyes, as she went on, "It would have been wonderful if you could have said something. We would not want them to think you are arrogant, would we?"

"I had no idea there would be so many people here waiting for me," I mumbled quietly.

"The *fête* is in your honour. I assumed that would be obvious. All of these people have come to pay you respect," Gigi snapped under her breath.

"I'm sorry, Gigi," I mumbled again.

"You still have so much more to learn…take note, my dear, a lady must always be prepared!"

She composed herself, then waved a hand dismissively. "No matter now, the moment has passed. As you can see, many people have come out tonight. I certainly hope it shows Charles what must be done…."

"You cannot do it!" I declared. A few people looked over toward me, and I immediately dropped both my eyes and voice. ""You cannot be the one who kills her, Gigi. Morgana said—"

"Be serious, Katrine," Gigi immediately interrupted me. "Do you really think I would do such a thing? Let me reassure you, I would never carry out such a thing—but not for lack of ability, my darling."

Her intensity was frightening me now.

"Just promise me you will not."

"Fine, I promise. Are you well, *ma petite?*"

"Yes, yes." I lied. "Can we please sit down?"

We took our regular seats, while the other women gathered around us, all smiles. I had been in the room for mere moments and was already exhausted. I paid little attention to the gossip that immediately swirled around me.

Gabriel came in a short time later. Mathilde rose and quickly crossed the room to greet him.

Gigi noticed this as well, and casually remarked, "I have to discuss with him the problems of courting women who live and socialise together. Perhaps he could learn from Charles' mistakes."

William appeared then, floating into the room as if riding on a breeze. As I watched him, everything around us seemed to fade away, the world falling into quiet as he skillfully maneuvered his way around the room, avoiding as many people as possible. He greeted only Gabriel, said something to Vincenzo, and then turned his eyes to me. Relief flooded through me.

He smiled, and I knew it was a look reserved only for me.

William finally crossed the room after what seemed like an eternity. He bowed before Gigi and me, then extended his hand, asking me to dance. Grateful to get away, he was all I could see as he led me around the room. During our dance, I put all my effort into my movements, matching his carefully, finally flowing into a perfect rhythm with him in hopes of showing him just how I felt. I hoped he could see how I enjoyed every moment spent with him.

Three years ago, my world fell apart, but now with William in my life, I knew it could be built back up again.

I was so caught up—we were so caught up in the moment—that we did not notice at first when the music stopped and the other dancers stood motionless, listening. Charles and Mathilde turned in the direction of the back door. I saw Gigi stand and cross the dance floor to reach Vincenzo.

"What's happening?" I asked William.

He took my hand and we approached Vincenzo.

"It seems we have a surprise guest wandering in the garden," Vincenzo explained.

Charles came over to us, worried. "Is everyone present and accounted for?"

"I believe so," Vincenzo replied.

"Everyone," Charles announced, "We are going outside to see what manner of beast has decided to pay us a visit."

We all followed him to the back door.

Screams erupted from within the garden, and I could smell fresh blood as we stepped out onto the back porch. My body went stiff, as if about to go on attack. I was suddenly overcome by another smell, a familiar one. I could not yet tell if it was the blood or something else.

"Someone is being attacked!" I suddenly realised, pulling William along behind me.

"Are any of the servants missing?" Charles demanded, and I heard some commotion.

I did not bother turning back to ask; the familiar smell caused me to panic. I tried to pull William with me when I started to run, but he struggled, so I pulled away from him and took off on my own.

"Who's out there? Show yourself!" I called out as I walked up the path alone.

The smell of blood grew stronger. My vision sharpened, and I knew the others had lit torches and were following from behind. My arm suddenly started to itch and burn, as if someone was trying to peel the skin off.

"What is it?" Vincenzo ran up beside me, as I clutched my arm in pain.

"My arm…there's something wrong…." I desperately tried to pull up my sleeve.

Suddenly, out of the corner of my eye, I saw a bloody hand lying discarded on the ground. In my memory, I was running out of the forest with Roza, and instinctively grabbed onto Vincenzo.

"Oh, God. Do you think it could be—"

I turned and started running, and Vincenzo came after me.

"This…this same thing…when it happened…oh, God!"

I began looking frantically for any body part that could connect to that hand. I found an arm, and then a leg with a well-worn leather shoe still attached to the foot. I knew that foot. The torso was in the herb garden near the back of the property, the head connected and lying face down in the dirt. Gray hair splayed around it like clumps of wet hay.

I started gasping for air, the world rushing around me. I knelt down beside the body and rolled it over. Roza's face stared back up at me. Her black eyes were opened wide in death, as if she had seen her attacker.

I heard a number of people coming up behind me now.

"My mother is loose in the gardens!" I cried out. "Please protect yourselves!"

"How do you know this?" Vincenzo demanded, trying to help me up.

"I can smell her," I warned, starting to cry. "And she had to finish it—she had to kill them all—the ones who did this to us. She had to make them pay for what they did!"

"I thought she already killed the ones who performed the ritual."

"She did," I said, sobbing now, "but Kardoska was there with me. My mother tried to kill her that night, but I was in the way."

My body heaved as the bile rose up in my throat. I screamed as loud as I could.

"Momma, why not take me? You left me alone in this world, but she saved me! She is the reason I survived! Why did you take her from me?!"

I screamed this at the sky. I tried to sense if she was still there, if she could see us...my new friends and family. I knew then that the beast was still lurking somewhere in the garden.

"You all have to go back to the house," I warned now, grabbing Vincenzo. "Right now, quickly, you must go!"

They stared at me, and I desperately reached out for Gigi.

"Please, please go back to the house. She'll come back for the rest of you!" I cried out.

"*Petite*," Gigi pleaded with me, "You are not thinking clearly."

I continued to sob. "Please, just go inside. Please, everyone, I am begging you. Just go!"

Gigi said patiently, "*Petite*, are you forgetting who and what we all are? I do not mean to be condescending, but this is not the first time we have encountered a violent beast. I assure you we can defend ourselves."

"Please," I shook my head, "I could not bear it if something happened to any of you. You don't know what she's like!"

In the meantime, Tolone came from the back of the house with two large muskets. It took me only a moment to realise what that meant.

I stood and watched in fright as he handed one gun to Charles and the other to Vincenzo. A cold hand suddenly touched my cheek, and I turned to meet Gabriel's eyes.

"I am so sorry, child," he said. "I will take you back to the house, if you wish."

I tried to inhale through a muffled sob. "I cannot leave Roza out here alone. She would be ashamed of me if I did something like that."

"We will stay until she can be moved respectfully," Gabriel assured me, then turned to the others. "I will stay with her while you hunt for the beast."

"We will both stay with you, *petite*," Gigi added.

I noticed that Mathilde and Victorie had just joined us, along with Tommas and Josephine standing a few feet away. Charles and Vincenzo somberly loaded the guns.

"We will find her before she can hurt anyone else," William promised. He had been standing alone nearby.

"Where is your weapon?" I cried out.

He only smiled at me, then wiggled the fingers of his left hand until a ball of spinning white light appeared just above his palm. He passed it back and forth between his hands, then extinguished it by closing one hand around it into a fist.

"I can assure you, my love, I am well protected," he said.

At this, Vincenzo and William went off in one direction, Charles and Tommas in another.

"Where is Morgana?" I suddenly cried out.

"She went back to the house," Victorie spoke up.

"And Hannah?" I asked Tolone.

"Inside, Mademoiselle. I asked her to stay behind," he replied.

Gigi handed me a handkerchief now to wipe my face, then turned to Tolone and told him in rapid French that we needed to remove Roza's body and clean up the mess. He replied just as quickly that the servants were afraid to come outside and that there was still danger.

"We'll have to wait until it's safe," I said, wiping my cheeks with the kerchief.

"I'm sorry they're hunting your mother," Gabriel murmured.

"She is my mother no longer," I declared. "Black Magic turned her into a beast. I can't imagine there is much left of the woman I knew."

I turned away from them then and went back to kneel beside what was left of Kardoska… my Roza. I could not imagine my world without her. She took care of me and protected me when she could have left me alone in the forest. Without her, I would have been lost. I would never have gotten to Csejthe, let alone Vienna.

I brushed the hair away from Roza's cheeks, and could not help but wonder if she was finally with her friends in heaven; those poor women, and that sad strange man, who had been executed. I wondered if they had welcomed her with open arms. Her life had been so hard; she finally found a good place here in Paris, where she was respected. I hoped that now she finally got the peace she also deserved.

"All she spoke of was you getting your birthright, your proper place in this world," Tolone's voice brought me back from my thoughts. "She loved your grandmother so much. She thought by helping you, it would be the greatest tribute she could make to her. She was a good woman."

I smiled at him through my tears. "Thank you, Tolone, you are so kind. I hope she knew how much she was appreciated."

Suddenly, a shot rang out. That first shot fired startled me so much, it felt as if I'd jumped out of my own skin. Then something began to rise within me, making my spine tingle and skin crawl. I closed my eyes and tried only to think of Roza. My insides tightened as my body went stiff. I wanted to scream again, but this time, it was not coming from me. It was coming from somewhere—someone—else.

"Can you sense her, Katrine?" Tolone demanded.

"Her scent has overpowered all my senses."

"I can smell her," Gabriel interjected, and when Gigi looked at him with curiosity, he explained: "The Báthory have a distinct smell."

"If she is still here, they will find her, Katrine," Gigi consoled me. "You have no need to worry any further. Just be with your Kardoska."

But I could hear the anxiety rising in her tone.

When the second shot rang out, I did not jump, but the others did.

Gigi covered her mouth with a kerchief.

"Perhaps if I ask the servants, they will come," I said to Tolone in the best French I could manage.

I suddenly heard someone running. William came out of the darkness, his expression rather panicked.

"What's wrong?" I asked.

"Run! All of you! Now!" he yelled. Without thinking, he tried to herd all of us back towards the house.

"What's happening?" Gigi cried out.

"They've got her trapped...circling back this way...go now!" William exclaimed.

At this, I turned back to retrieve Kardoska's body.

"No time," William objected. "Go now!"

"I am not going to leave her here to be further mangled, William!" I argued.

I heard running in the distance. Except for Tolone, the others had gone on ahead. Tolone gestured hurriedly towards Roza.

"Mademoiselle, if you would allow me—"

"No!" I cried. "She's my responsibility. Go, Tolone! William will protect me."

Tolone nodded to me then started running.

"You have absolutely lost your mind, Katrine," William said angrily. "You could get us all killed!"

I got down on the ground and tried to pull Kardoska's limbless body into my arms. "I will not leave her here like this, William. I cannot!"

I pulled the torso into my arms and stood, wobbly at first, under the weight, dragging her and stumbling back towards the chateau. I could barely see through my tears.

"Stop!" William called out. "Give her to me. Your dress will be ruined."

"Your dress will be ruined," William said.

"And?" I replied.

"And....I really like that dress."

"I am not going to put her down, William. Not till we get to the doors."

"Its a shame to ruin such a beautiful dress."

"I will have a new one made especially for you."

William suddenly pulled me towards him. "Then you better hold onto that body very tight, *mi amour*, because they're coming," he whispered in my ear.

I suddenly caught the scent of my mother not far away from us. I heard the sound of paws sneaking through the brush before I saw her at the other end of the path. She snarled at me, her upper lip curled back to show what were once large, white fangs now stained with Roza's blood and flesh; pieces still clung to the side of her jaws. Her red eyes stared intently at me. I saw her clearly now: she was a large, dark wolf with monstrous paws the size of plates and a massive head that weighed more than I did.

"Did you come back for me, Mother?" I called out to her. "You should have left me. The mark you gave me that night—it turned me into something I cannot explain."

I heard the others come up from behind to surround us. I waited for her to react but she did not move.

"I am happy here, Momma. I have friends, a new life...I have a chance, Momma. Can you see that? Please...get out of here! If you come closer, my friends will kill you. You must go and never come back!"

She didn't move but rather stood her ground and continued to growl. I could still somehow see a semblance of her inside the beast's body, as if she were trapped in that vicious shell.

"Mother if you want to die, then that's your choice!" I screamed, "But we will not aid you in any way. These men will not shoot purely for the sake of it!"

At this, she suddenly lunged towards us. I clutched Kardoska and held her tightly to me.

A shot rang out, leaving a vibration in my ears that caused the world to spin. I heard the beast yelp in pain before I saw the blood spray. She let off her attack, the injury too great. Taking one last look at me, she leapt away in the opposite direction, leaving a trail of blood behind her.

We all stood still for several moments until complete silence followed.

I sniffed the air one last time, then said heavily, "She's gone."

Vincenzo approached me, He effortlessly took Kardoska's lifeless body from me and carried her back in his arms like a child.

My emotions snapped free and poured out like a broken river dam. I started sobbing again as I turned and began to stumble towards the chateau, past the rows of plants and herbs that Morgana had once picked to fix my scar. I would have nothing to mark this occasion with except my memories, the smell of Roza's blood stifling even as Vincenzo walked farther away with her body. The gardens would no longer be a place of refuge for me.

"Katrine," William's voice was soft and quiet behind me.

How I wanted to turn to him and fall into his arms, but I could not bring myself to stop. I drifted aimlessly into the house, past the group of crying servants, past my friends, and upstairs to my room. Before I could get into bed, Hannah appeared. She said nothing as she removed the soiled gown, right down to my chemise. She wiped my face and hands with a wet cloth then helped me into bed, holding me like Roza did, as I cried myself to sleep

XXXVII.

Dust

KARDOSKA'S BODY WAS LAID TO REST ON THE SACRED grounds of Notre Dame Cathedral. No questions were asked when Charles provided a large donation of money.

We stood outside, listening to the funeral prayers, as they shoveled the dirt over her, returning her to the earth. On the one hand, I hoped that God would take good care of her; on the other, I knew she would be happiest to return to the earth, the one place she believed everything came from.

"What are you thinking, *petite*?" Gigi asked gently.

"It seems appropriate for this to end with my mother," I said quietly, "since it all began with her."

"Do you think it is over? —That this marks the end of your troubles and the start of something more?"

I turned to her, admiring the blue eyes as soft as the blonde curls that framed her beautiful face.

"I'm not sure," I told her, "but I hope with time, I might have but a fraction of your poise and grace." When she smiled warmly, I added, "You have been my greatest teacher and the woman I admire most."

I prayed silently now for Roza's peace and hope for my own future.

Deep in the fibre of my being, I knew that even if I never saw my mother again, her blood ran through my veins: Báthory blood, proud and strong. And I was determined to do the name proud regardless of what lay ahead. I was Erzsébet Báthory's granddaughter, and that meant more than anything I could ever imagine. For all those reasons, I knew that this was far from over. It was only just the beginning.

"Goodbye, Roza," I whispered. "Thank you for everything."

Gigi extended her hand to me now, and I took it. We walked wordlessly back to the carriage. Just before getting in, I happened to look up and notice the winged gargoyles flanking the rooftop of the cathedral. At that moment, I realised that they would protect her, that they would keep Roza safe—that they would keep all of us safe.

EPILOGUE

AS SOON AS THE WOMAN PRICKED HER FINGER, THE smell of fresh blood spread quickly throughout the small cottage. Young Anastasia was in her bedroom when the scent first touched her, like a soft hand. The deep metallic aroma was gentle and seemed like nothing of consequence. She'd smelt blood before and she knew it well. It always stirred something deep inside her, but this time it was different. Her body immediately reacted. She could not control herself as she left her room and went to the hearth where her mother, and her mother's three friends, were gathered.

Anastasia watched as her mother's friend took a finger and squeezed the tip of it. Drops of blood fell into one of the great pots her mother kept by the fire. The women paid her no mind as she came further into the room.

Something about the blood drew her forward. Anastasia had the sudden and very forceful compulsion to taste that blood, her body aching for it with hunger now. Anastasia's mother, Kristina, watched in horror as the girl suddenly grabbed and bit down on the newly nicked finger.

Kristina struck her daughter, knocking over the stacks of herbs and the powders they had been making.

"What's wrong with you?" she cried out angrily at the girl.

"I smelt it from the other room," Anastasia replied innocently. "I could not help myself. I'm just so hungry, I want more."

Magda, the woman whom she had bit, gasped. "*Mój Boh*! What is this girl?"

"She is just a child, Magda!" Kristina growled.

"No, she wants blood, Kristina," Darvulia, the elder of the group, warily admonished.

"Perhaps she has some kind of sickness," Paola, the youngest and newest member, chimed in. Her young face was eager and excited, while the others seemed quite frightened.

Anastasia only giggled. She sounded like a child, although she was on the verge of becoming a woman. She had her monthly courses for more than a year now, her fifteenth birthday quickly approaching.

"Please, Mother. May I have some more?" Anastasia begged, her voice lilting like a girl half her age.

"You are ill, my dear. We shall make you something to feel better," Kristina said softly, smoothing the girl's hair.

Magda snorted. "Even you may not have that kind of magic, Kristina."

"And what do you suggest we do?" Kristina snapped.

"We shall find something to help the girl, Kristina. Do not fret," Darvulia said. "And perhaps, Magda, you should stop eating so many cakes. Then your blood wouldn't taste so good."

"So good...," Anastasia mumbled to herself.

Kristina sighed. "Between the four of us, there must be something we can do."

Paola began rummaging through the small jars Kristina stacked on a shelf. They contained various herbs, oils, and mixtures the women had prepared for other ailments. On occasion, the four of them would make a healing concoction for someone in the village; herbal cures were their specialty.

Their work was often kept quiet, however. The preparation of healing herbs was sometimes used as a way to accuse unpopular women of witchcraft. Fortunately, Kristina's reputation was solid enough that no one would dare accuse her, even though, ironically enough, it was the truth. Paola, however, was confident that she and the others were free from suspicion because of that association alone.

Paola immediately pulled some jars and began working on a mixture for the girl, while Kristina fretted, "What could make her want blood?"

"You don't know all of the girl's bloodlines," Darvulia whispered. She left the table and began working on her own mixture. "Magda, either do something to help or go home. You are useless just standing around," Darvulia suddenly quipped before Kristina had the chance.

The women combined their various mixtures, along with a touch of pine oil, and then began brewing. The potion was originally meant to be a tea but ended up as more of a broth. First, they cast a protection spell over Anastasia before handing the girl the potion, hoping that if it did not work, the spell at least would keep it from killing her.

"It smells terrible," Anastasia complained to her mother as she took the bowl in her hands. She wrinkled her nose in disgust.

"I don't care if it smells and tastes like horse dung, you will shut your mouth and drink it before I force it down your throat," Kristina said between gritted teeth.

"But...," Anastasia began.

"Do you know how they kill *strigoi*, child?" Darvulia spoke up. "No? Well, if someone catches you doing what you did, sucking blood like that, you will not have a chance to explain yourself. They will immediately cut out your heart and chop off your head without a second thought!"

Anastasia drank two bowls of the potion without another word. Almost immediately, she went back to her room.

When the girl was out of hearing range, the women began to fret again.

"That girl has bad blood, Kristina," Paola whispered. "What sort of man was her father?"

Kristina glanced briefly at Darvulia, who was the only person who knew the truth about the girl's parentage. The older woman's eyes widened, as if signaling Kristina not to say anything.

"That is irrelevant," Kristina said angrily.

Paola rolled her eyes, and Darvulia nodded in approval.

"Thank you for your help," Kristina finally said to them. "I greatly appreciate it."

She crossed the room and began helping Darvulia fill small, clay bottles. There was enough potion to last for several days.

"She will be fine, Kristina," Darvulia assured her, and she put a hand on Kristina's shoulder.

Kristina sighed loudly. "I hope so. Perhaps God will be on our side, for once."

Meanwhile, Anastasia sat crouched behind the door to her room, listening intently. Her eyes had turned red, like the colour of blood. The girl's hand began to move compulsively across the dirt floor now, thumping and scratching, over and over.

Four long marks cut deeply across the dirt: they were the claw marks of a wolf.

WHAT HAPPENS TO ANASTASIA AFTER SHE RAN?

WHAT HAPPENS TO KATRINE WHEN THEY GO TO RUSSIA?

WHAT HAPPENS TO KLARA ONCE HER FATE IS DECIDED?

FIND OUT IN THE NEXT INSTALLMENT OF THE AFFLICTED

IKON

AVAILABLE WHERE BOOKS ARE SOLD

AUTHOR'S NOTE:

This is a work of fiction, developed in my own mind. While some of the characters were living people, any interpretations and liberties are my own, and how I felt this person would behave within the context of my story.

There is speculation of the existence of Countess Báthory's illegitimate child, but it has yet to be proven. But the very idea of such a child's existence fascinated me, one could only imagine what it would be like to learn you were the offspring of such an infamous lady.

There are many lovely books about Countess Báthory and the time period, a very tumultuous time within Europe. It was an era of great women, many named Elizabeth.

For my recommended reading, further reading, and resources for book clubs, please visit my website,
WWW.AUTHORRAVINTMAURICE.WEEBLY.COM

ACKNOWLEDGMENTS

A lot has changed since the previous release of this book. I've lost and gained a lot, and learned more then I had ever expected.

I have to start by thanking all the people who stuck by me through this process, especially the readers who have found me various places and offered me words of encouragement.

I have to send a special shout out to a Goodreads member named Alicia, who not only wrote an awesome review but has been offering words of encouragement through the whole process. You have no idea how much your support means to me, it's because of people like you that I am able to continue. Thank you.

Thank you RM Gilmore and RMGraphX for my amazing covers, and for being a great friend. Love you, boochie.

I have to thank my Mother, my greatest influence and teacher and my best friend. I am so happy that she got to see my words in print and her daughter's dream come true. I miss her every day, and I hope that she has found some peace. I hope I have made her proud.

I lost my Mother on April 29, 2012. It has changed me in so many ways, and has been the hardest time of my life. I've been lucky to have people rally around me and help me along. Knowing that she would have expected me to continue on has helped pull me along. Anyone who has lost a parent knows how fleeting words can be in such a situation.

Thank you to Sheila for being one of my greatest supporters, and for standing by me when I needed a motherly hand. Thank you to Marjorina and Londale, for their constant and unwavering support. Thank you to Thyrza and Keliyah for being there in times where I didn't even know I needed someone. Thank you to Melanie and Dorothy, and the members of the Al Green Sculpture Studio School for so many things I can't even name them.

Thank you, again, to the amazing Maureen Jennings, for being a constant source of inspiration and support.

I have to thank my fiance, Michael, for supporting me through everything. I never thought I would be lucky enough to find someone who could balance me out, and I am shocked every day by how lucky I am. Thank you for giving me the space to do what I need to do, and for encouraging me to keep going. I love you.

I dedicate the paperback edition of this book to my Mother and my daughter Khaleesi. I have a legacy to pass on and I hope I can do it justice.

www.ingramcontent.com/pod-product-compliance
Lightning Source LLC
Chambersburg PA
CBHW071750110726
47908CB00006B/1757